THE ROSEY VIEW OF THE WORLD

The

ROSEY

VIEW OF THE WORLD

One Woman's Journey Through the 20th Century

———◆———

ANDREW SCOTT BASSETT

LUMINARE PRESS

WWW.LUMINAREPRESS.COM

Luminare Press
442 Charnelton St.
Eugene, OR 97401
www.luminarepress.com

LCCN: 2022918929
ISBN: 979-8-88679-103-7

I dedicate this work of love and passion to my family because this story is inspired by the rich traditions and memories we have of those who came before, especially my mother Rosetta, the real-life Rosey. She laughed, she danced, she loved, and we all miss her in so many ways each and every day.

To my sister Lorraine, we remember so much of this story by heart, and your memories helped fuel my fire to write this book. I hope this book brings a piece of mom back to life for you, as it did for me.

To Glenn, my big brother, a part of our life was just you, me, and mom, and I will always treasure that time when it was us against the world, and you kept me safe.

To Dianne, my wife, thank you for loving my stories and telling me how great a writer I am. I know if you like my work and you are proud of it, it has to be good.

To my children, I hope that when I am gone, there are stories about me you would want to write, at least I think I hope that.

And finally, for my family and relatives across the pond in England, where half of this story was written, this book is dedicated to you as well, especially my cousins David, Tracey, and Michelle. Your parents, Aunt Sheila and Uncle Trevor played an important part in our family's story, and will always have a place in my heart and memories.

PROLOGUE

As she told her soldier husband, the man who broke her heart, "the point is, husband of mine, I never cheated on you, even though you and the Army left me alone for all those years. I spent more than half of our marriage being more married to an idea, than a man. I think you should say to me, thank you for your service, isn't that what some people say to you who respect what you went through in Vietnam? Well, I went through a lot here at home, and I think I deserve the same consideration.

CHAPTER 1

The annoying cell phone alarm goes off next to Danny's head as he lies in bed. He's hoping the world will just leave him alone. The morning sun sneaks through his bedroom drapes. It reinforces the phone's message to him: that it's time to fight his way out of bed. He can't resist anymore as he staggers first to his kitchen to make himself a cup of coffee and then to his shower to let the cascading hot water bring him back to life. It's not nearly enough, he realizes, when his cell phone resting on his bathroom sink begins to play *"Let It Be"*, the Beatles song he chose as his ringtone. Blinded by shampoo and dripping water everywhere, he steps out of the shower to pick up the call.

"Yep," he says in a defiant tone, which reflects his current mood oh so well.

"Hey," the voice on the other side replies.

The voice belongs to Julia Krofcheck. She's Danny's girlfriend, maybe, neither one's quite sure what the official status is right now. Julia informs him that she will be picking up the rest of her stuff today from what was their apartment. Instead of trying valiantly to talk her out of her plans, he instead reminds her that he has an incredibly important lunchtime meeting with his literary agent. Julia reminds him right back that she still has a key to the place, so she doesn't need him to be there. In fact, she would prefer it if he wasn't around.

"You really have to do this today? Today, when I am under so much pressure and still haven't come up with the first two chapters of anything resembling a coherent manuscript. So, really, this is the day you pick to pull this on me?"

"Enough with the book!" she complains. "That's all you exist for right now is your new book! You don't consider me or anything else. It's only the new book that matters. It's like you blame me for your writer's block."

Danny can't believe she's bringing up this crap right now. He can't believe she can be so self-obsessed and not even see how important this new book is to his career. "I've spent over ten years of my life trying to get a publisher behind me, trying to make it as an author, and finally I get backed by a huge publishing house. Now, to everyone's surprise, including my own, my first book with them becomes a bestseller. Why are you pulling this?"

Julia answers with silence to the last thing he said. She's sick of fighting with him and after about fifteen seconds of dead air, she tells him as much. Calmly, with measured words, Julia states what she's already said before. "This second book, or maybe the pressures that go with it, have changed you, Danny. You seem angry at the world. You are like a lost child who doesn't know what to do next. I tried to help you, but you wouldn't let me."

Danny attempts in vain to disprove her words, but Julia is done listening. She reminds him again she'll be by to pick up the rest of her things, and then she ends the call forcefully. Danny is fuming. He wants to keep debating her. He can't believe she doesn't understand all he's going through right now.

"My career is possibly on the line!" he hollers as he slams his fist down on the sink.

He gets back into the shower and makes the water colder. Danny hopes to shock himself back into the living, or something like that.

———— • • ————

"So, I don't have to tell you how important this is going to be for your career," Danny's literary agent, Kimberly West, casually tosses into what had up to this point been a light and breezy little lunch get-together.

Danny says, "Uh-huh," back, as fast as he can. He says nothing more, so Kimberly continues. "The second book that follows a bestseller by a new author is a crucial work. It's where an author proves that they truly belong in the industry. It answers the question."

The question, Danny ponders to himself. Should he even ask her what she means and take the risk of looking like a noob. After she rambles on for a couple of more minutes, with Danny still wondering what the question is, he takes the gamble and asks her directly.

Kimberly looks at him as he feared she might. She stares at him with astonishment that he doesn't understand everything she is talking about. She asks him if he is joking with her. Reluctantly he tells her he's not. "Well…" she utters back. "The question, Danny, is, is this writer who no one had ever heard about before a fluke, or possibly someone who just got lucky and captured lightning in a bottle the one time? The question is, do you really have what it takes to be a serious, professional author?"

Danny leans back into his chair. He knows he should say hell yes or make up some boastful statement about how great his second book is going to be. However, since he has only a few good ideas, and every outline he comes up with reads like a pile of steaming rubbish, as his British mother likes to say, Danny is unable to muster up the necessary enthusiasm to defend a second written offering that is soon due. Not getting what she wants from Danny makes Kimberly press him for details about this new manuscript. He has kept it so mysteriously secret from her, his agent, this entire time.

He assures her in an unconvincing manner that she will be pleased with this second book, and so will the publishing company.

Kimberly gulps down her glass of wine as if trying to douse her ever-growing fears that this second manuscript isn't going to be anywhere near as good, as Danny's first one. Her experience with past writers in her stable is that when they are reluctant to give many details, it's for good reason, usually, the reason is their new work sucks, or maybe it doesn't even reach the level of sucking. Maybe it's much worse than that. Kimberly reaffirms to Danny again the deadline for the first few chapters to be ready. She squeezes his hand and tries to encourage him that everything is going to work out great. Regrettably, for them both, Kimberly's encouragement is about as convincing as Danny's defense for his upcoming second book.

AFTER THE MEETING, DANNY CAN'T WAIT TO GET BACK to his apartment. He wants to push everything else in the world out of his mind, including Julia, and finish those first few chapters by blasting a giant hole through his writer's block. Unbeknownst to him, fate has other plans for his life.

As he jiggles his keys to enter his apartment, his cell phone begins to blow up. Once inside, he answers a call coming from his older sister, Lori. She is spitting out words at a speedy clip, which makes her difficult to comprehend. Danny can tell that something is wrong as he patiently waits for her to spell it out. When she keeps on saying lots of nothing, frustrated, he finally cuts her off and demands to know what it is she's ranting about.

"It's Mom…"

Danny believes he knows what's coming next, but he acts like he doesn't. "What?"

"She's gone…she's died," comes the reply from his sister, now fighting to force out words between the sobs and the gasps for air she's finding difficult to contain.

Danny is more shocked than he thought he would be. He's been scared of receiving this call for some time. You do when your mother is in her late eighties. Still, his mother, Rosey, has enjoyed great health for many years. For Danny, there was nothing to suggest her imminent passing, other than her age. He falls into his easy chair as he attempts to digest all his sister is trying to share with him.

"She just passed in her sleep. I guess that's a good thing," Lori rationalizes. "We're assuming it was natural causes, you know, because of her age."

"Of course," Danny manages to muster.

"But I need you here. I need your help with all this. I need your help with the funeral, Danny. The funeral parlor nearby has an opening for a week from Saturday. Mom's minister has said he's available to take care of directing the proceedings."

Danny hears the pleas in his sister's voice, and he knows it's the civil and expected thing to do, but…his book.

Lori begs him again as if he didn't hear her the first time. She waits anxiously for his response.

He deflects by asking about their brother, Greg. Greg is the most successful one in the family, with numerous business interests in Southern California.

"Greg is tied up with his businesses, but he'll make the funeral and he's wiring me ten thousand dollars to help pay for most of it. He told me that you and I can pay for the rest of it, what's left," Lori explains.

"But he can't get to Phoenix early and help with the funeral planning, that's what you are saying?" Danny infers from his sister's words.

"No, that's why I need your help. I can't go through this alone, Danny. I need you to come home and help me with all this! I'm out of my mind and I don't think I can handle all this on my own!"

He believes her. Lori is not one who should be responsible for such a task as burying their mother by herself. But his book deadline is playing in the back of his brain like African tribal drums. The beat of those imaginary drums reminds him that time is running out for him, and maybe for his career as an author. He tries to explain this to his sister, but Lori doesn't hear it. She's so distraught at the moment that only her brother telling her that he's on his way back home will she understand. Seeing that he is getting nowhere, and with Lori beginning to break down with more sobbing and gasping, Danny promises he'll fly back as soon as he can.

"Oh! Thank God!" she exclaims with relief and gratitude. "I knew I could count on my little brother," Lori states, as she regains her composure. When she pushes him a bit further to find out when he will be home, he offers her only, that it will be as soon as possible. Lori finally accepts that as good enough. She'll be waiting for Danny at the Phoenix airport when he arrives.

With the conversation over, he puts down his phone. In the silence of his apartment, he tries to wrap his head around the idea that his mother, or mum, as she liked to be called, is no longer part of his life. No matter how prepared you are for such an event, you never really are. His reflections on the subject are soon interrupted by another set of keys, fumbling with his front door lock. Julia, as she promised, has come by to get her stuff. At first, they barely acknowledge each other, as she scans the place for anything belonging to her. Then, after a few minutes of grabbing things and boxing them up, and with Danny still slumped in his chair, she breaks the ice. "I guess I can assume that your meeting didn't go really well."

Danny doesn't answer. He just stares out into space as if he didn't hear her.

"You could at least be civil. This is hard for me too, you know," Julia says bristling with frustration.

Eventually, Danny listens long enough to respond. He asks her what she is talking about. This makes her even more upset that he didn't hear a word she just said to him. "What is your problem? I try to be nice and concerned with what's going on with you, and I get this in return?"

Danny turns to make actual eye contact with Julia for the first time since she entered the apartment. "I just found out that my mother has died."

Julia is sidetracked at the news. She now feels like shit for scolding him as she just did a moment ago when she thought he was just being his moody, jerk-like self. She asks the questions that people always ask when confronted with such news. He does his best to answer them.

"I'm truly sorry, Danny. I know your mother meant a lot to you."

He thanks Julia for her sentiments and acknowledges that she is correct. "Without my mother's support and pushing, I guess you could say I would never have been able to hold on as long as I did, as a struggling writer."

Julia then inquires about the arrangements for his mother's funeral. He shares with her about his leaving right away to help his sister with all of it.

"What about your book deadline?"

"I'll take my laptop with me and just get it finished at my sister's home, that's all," he answers stoically.

Julia wants with all her heart to comfort him, regardless of what they are going through in their relationship right now. Without too much consideration, she does just that. Her actions take Danny by surprise as she kneels by his chair and wraps him in her arms. He can't help but return her kindness with his own, as he pulls her closer to himself.

"Do you want me to fly with you to Arizona?" she asks him while still in his embrace.

"You mean to my sister's home?" he replies softly.

"Yes, of course, what do you think I mean?" Julia counters.

She waits for him to speak again, but it takes several awkward moments for him to do so. When he does, what he says makes Julia pull herself from his arms with one powerful tug. "So, you don't want me to go with you?!"

Danny attempts to make her understand his reasons for saying no. With their relationship in such flux these days, maybe going together to Arizona isn't the best idea. He tries to make her see his point of view, but Julia only feels foolish for offering to go with him in the first place. She wonders how she could expose herself to his hurtful ways so easily again.

"What about coming out for the funeral itself, you know the day before the funeral or something?" He throws out as a compromise, hoping Julia will be pleased with the idea.

She is not. She mocks him with it. "Yeah, we will see," she says with contempt as she gathers up her boxes from the apartment and makes her way toward the front door. Before she leaves, Danny calls out to her. It halts her progress for a second, as she waits for his next words.

"I need time to work through everything," he tells her. "But I do want you with me at the funeral, although I will certainly understand if you don't make it with the cost of flying and all."

Julia turns to him to say, "I don't know what we're doing here, Danny. You and I aren't kids anymore. For God's sake, we're in our early forties now, but you're acting like we're just out of college. Tell me if I am moving too fast and putting too much pressure on you. I'm sorry about your mother, I truly am. I'll keep some good thoughts and throw out some prayers for you."

He watches her exit his apartment. He wonders if it's for the last time. Life is so unfair he decides. The book deadline is coming at him like a tidal wave about to wipe away all he's worked for. Then there's Julia leaving him because he's not ready to make the big commitment that she so desperately now wants. And now, on top of all of that, having to deal with the death of his mother, his rock, the one person who always had his back. No, life is certainly not fair, not fair at all.

◆

DANNY CAN SEE HIS SISTER WAVING IN HIS DIRECTION as he enters the Phoenix airport. With Lori by his side, he gets his luggage and follows her out to her waiting car. Not unexpectedly, it is a yellow Volkswagen Beetle that fits her hippie, earth-child persona to a tee. The two of them have had little in common for as long as Danny can remember. However, their mother, Rosey, was an expert at keeping all the children together and in touch with each other. Rosey was the common thread that kept all the relationships from unraveling, and now she was gone.

Lori is non-stop chattering all the way back to her house from the airport. She's sharing all the things that are already in place for their mother's funeral arrangements and all the things yet to be done. It's the latter group that she needs her brother's help with so badly. Danny appeases her concerns and lets her know that everything is going to be alright. He promises that they will get through this together. His comforting words alone bring Lori greater peace.

"How's Bobby doing?" Danny then interjects, trying to take her mind off of the funeral and the loss of their mother for a second.

"Bobby?" she stutters back as if she's never heard of the person before.

"Yeah, Bobby, you know your boyfriend for many years now," he adds, perplexed by her reaction.

"Oh, that Bobby," she answers as if the lightbulb above her head has just switched on.

Lori confesses to her kid brother that they broke up a couple of months ago and that even though he has been trying to re-hook up with her, she has been resistant to such an idea.

"Why? You two were always a good match for each other, personality speaking," Danny responds.

"There was a lot of electricity between us, I won't deny it. But that electricity can burn you just as easily, and I got tired of the ups and downs of it all," she offers in her defense for the breakup. "Besides, Mom would put me through hell over him so much."

Danny is quick to point out that won't be a problem anymore. It's a glib and probably completely inappropriate thing to utter when their mother's body isn't even cold yet, but he and his sister still share a much-needed laugh over his choice of words.

"I am going to stop by Mom's house first. There are some things in boxes there that she wanted you to have," Lori explains to her brother.

"Like what?" he questions.

She racks her brains for a moment, but really there are too many things to remember, so she tells him he will find out when he gets them.

"All right then," Danny replies as they head to Mom's home in Glendale.

———◆———

WHEN THEY ARRIVE IN FRONT OF THEIR MOTHER'S HOME, a strange feeling comes over Danny. The grim realization sets in for the first time that his mom will not be greeting him from the other side of the front door. As he walks toward the house with his sister, it almost seems like they are in slow motion, like everything around them has stopped moving but them.

Maria, their mother's caretaker for the last several years, is home to greet them both. Danny barely knows her, but that doesn't keep her from swiftly giving him a huge hug, as she offers her condolences to him. He awkwardly thanks the young woman while Lori asks her where the boxes for her brother are. Maria leads them into a spare bedroom and points to three cardboard boxes lying in the corner of the room. Lori grabs one box, Danny grabs another, and Maria the last one. Without looking inside them, at Lori's direction, they take all three out to her car and place them in the backseat. Danny asks Maria what she thinks is in them.

"I don't know, Senor. Your mother didn't say to me about these things. I didn't look inside either. It's not my place to do so," Maria explains, her Latino accent making her words sound more exotic than they are.

Lori cuts in right at that moment and thanks Maria for caring for their mother as she has the last few years.

"I loved your mother very much. She was a kind and sweet lady. I know she loved you both, and you're Brother Gregory, very much," Maria says warmly.

Danny also offers his thanks. Both he and Lori are wondering if Maria will be okay, job-wise. Maria discloses that the company she works for already has other clients lined up for her. He and Lori are relieved to hear that.

"You know there are many elderly people with money living in this area, so I'll be just fine," Maria assures them.

After Maria goes back into the house, Lori and Danny begin to discuss the future of their mother's home.

"Greg told me to get an agent and get it on the market as fast as I can. He said the market around here is red hot. Any proceeds from the sale we'll split three ways. It's what Mom would have wanted, you know," Lori calculates.

Danny agrees as they get back into the yellow bug and begin to drive to Lori's house.

———◆———

DANNY CAN FEEL THE STRESS SLOWLY EBBING AWAY FROM his being as he indulges in the rum and Coke that his sister offers him at her place. It was a favorite drink of their mothers. He stretches his legs across the plush bright pink loveseat in her den. She sits across from him enjoying her own libations as she peppers him with questions about his next book, his girlfriend, and living in New York. Danny gives back little information since he's in no mood to talk about how all three of her areas of conversation aren't going too well at the present. He guides their discussion to the reasons he's here in the first place, namely their mother's death. "It still seems impossible, you know?"

Lori guesses that he is talking about their mother's passing, and she is right.

"The fact that I can't just call her up and speak to her anytime I want, it's hard to fathom that, you know."

Lori does and gets up from her chair and sits next to her brother. She pushes his long legs out of her way in the process. She snuggles up next to him from the side and gives him a peck on his cheek. "You know your success with your book made Mom so proud. She told everybody she came into contact with about her son, the famous author."

Danny figured as much, but it was still good to hear. He thanks his sister for her nice words and wishes he could say more, but the emotions of the moment begin to take hold, and he gets choked up. Lori, seeing this happening, begins to feel the same way. "Just what would Mom say if she saw us now, huh," Lori remarks. "She always told us we had to be strong, strong enough that when life knocked us down, we knew how to get back up."

Danny chuckles as he remembers. She had so many little sayings, he recalls as he rubs his sister's shoulder before announcing that he is turning in for the night. Lori shows him which bedroom he is staying in and mentions she already put the boxes that their mother intended for him in the room. Danny in a quick gulp finishes off his rum and Coke and says goodnight.

Once in the guest bedroom, he tries his best to get some shut-eye, but it's not happening. Thoughts about his mother, Julia, and the pending deadline for his next book, refuse to let Danny get any peace at all. He flips on the small stained-glass lamp next to his bed on the nightstand. He adjusts his pillows to the right position to sit up, why he doesn't know. He tries but fails to rub the tiredness out of his eyes with his fingers. Then, not knowing what comes next, he scans his room and spots the boxes from his mother. He climbs out of bed and goes over to have a look-see. The boxes are taped up as if no one ever intended to open them up. His mother, Rosey, was well known for going overboard when it came to wrapping anything. This box before him is pretty much taped up like everything else she ever taped up. In other words, it might take a chainsaw to open. Danny finds some scissors in a small desk drawer in the room. "This will have to do," he mumbles to himself.

After another five minutes, he finally manages to cut through the tape and open up the boxes. There's nothing big inside them, just lots of small stuff. Piles of photos, schoolwork Danny did as a kid, awards he won, that sort of thing, fills up the boxes. While scrounging through, he comes across a large plastic bag with a zipper enclosure. He opens it up and finds a huge stack of handwritten pages with a note on top. He looks at the pages to see what they are. He skims through them and reads a bit here and there. As a writer, it doesn't take him long to realize what this is. His mother has left him stories about her life, and lots of them. There might even be a complete auto-bio here, possibly, he thinks. Next, he reads the note. His mother's voice echoes from the pages so strong that Danny almost believes he can hear it, as he reads her words. "Danny, my wonderful boy, and my brilliant writer of a son. I have left you this, my life story. I know you're a very busy man with your books and everything else going on in your life, but if anyone would appreciate a good story, I know it would be you. I hope I hang around long enough to see you again, to pass this on to you. I would really love to hear your thoughts about my scribblings, my darling, love your mum."

It's great that his mother trusted him with such a task, he considers. Sadly, the honor bestowed by his mother's words is clouded this second by the guilt that he feels. The guilt comes from not taking the time and making the trek out here when she was still alive so she could have shared her story with him, personally.

Wide awake, with thoughts racing, Danny decides that there is no better time than the present. He gets back into bed and props his pillows up again. The large stack of his mother's papers are at his side. He grabs the first page and begins to read. He's not sure what to expect. Mom was never one to write much, and although Danny knows the larger aspects of her life, her moving to America and leaving England in the 1950s, she spoke very little about all the details that fill out a person's life. Maybe these pages his mother left for him will answer any questions he has. Of course, with his book deadline bearing down on him, he can't let his mother's story get in the way of working on his manuscript. Before starting to read, he vows to himself it won't. He decides that he will just peruse it, get the main details and points of the story, and then get back to his book. His mother Rosey strangely didn't number her pages, so he will have to be careful not to jumble them up. Because of the lack of numbers on the pages, he can't be sure exactly how many pages there are, but certainly, there are a lot.

He grabs the first page and begins to read. The voice of his thoughts is erased by his mother's own voice and words. It's as if he's a small child again sitting on his mom's lap as she begins to tell him a story. It's a warm and cozy feeling that he remembers so well.

CHAPTER 2

Rosey's story begins: I was nine years old and scared to death, just like everyone else at that time. Hitler was threatening to attack England, actually all of Europe for that matter. Sheila Saunders was my best mate at the time. She shouldn't be confused with my little sister of the same first name. One day we were playing rounders at school. I was quite good at the game. Rounders is very much like American baseball. You see in those days, the boys in English schools played cricket, while the girls played rounders. I was waiting for my turn at bat while Sheila was taking hers. The other girls we were playing were mean cows, all the bloody lot of them. Sheila wasn't very good, and they were teasing her dreadfully, they always did. The bowler or pitcher, as they usually call them in American baseball, was especially vicious. She was chanting awful, vile things at Sheila. Poor Sheila didn't know who her true father was. Her mother had remarried, and in those days when I was growing up, that was a scarlet letter that a child would carry with them. Being a bastard baby brought shame, even though it was so unfair since no person could control something like that. I can't remember the bowler's name, but many of us hated her. Our teacher, Miss Woreford, had wandered off or something and was on another field chin-wagging with another teacher, paying no attention to us at all.

"Sheila Saunders' real father did nothing but wander and wander away shortly after she was born!" the bowler repeated, again, and again.

The bowler's teammates followed after her and began to chant the same thing between every pitch. I could see that Sheila was unraveling. She was so upset that she was trembling and having a hard time holding on to her bat. She was being bloody humiliated, and I couldn't stand it for one more second. I had seen enough. My pappy preached at me to never start a scuffle unless you were defending another person's honor. He always wanted me to behave as a young lady should, but he would say there are times in this life when you can't. Pappy said a fight is one of those times when you get on with it, forget about being a lady. He told me to do what you have to do. He would always finish with, "This isn't bloody Buckingham Palace, and we aren't the Windsors." I had, had enough, and I charged toward the bowler. Not to be shown up, she ran toward me, not wanting to look cowardly to her mates. As she got closer, she screamed at me to sit back down if I knew what was good for me. I didn't listen, not in the least. All of our teammates began to move toward us so they could see any fighting, that would be taking place. Sheila watched me, frozen with panic, still trembling, the poor bird. Next thing you know, I am standing toe to toe and eye to eye with the barmy cow of a bowler. I could see she was scared to death, I honestly could. She was one of those big talkers, but not much for backing up her words. With all her mates watching she had to put on a tough face, but it was only put on and we both knew it. I told her to shut her mouth about Sheila. I didn't raise my voice, but it had an authority coursing through its tone, nonetheless. She called me a name I won't repeat here, and then the gloves were off. As my pappy had taught me, I put one leg in front of hers, grabbed her, and then tossed her to the ground. I then proceeded to sit on the daft cow's chest. I pinned her arms down with my legs, as my mates and other teammates made sure that no one interrupted our little lesson in 'good manners'. It took a few minutes, but no more for "'big mouth'" to go from talking rubbish, to crying and begging for mercy. I got her to promise to leave Sheila and any of my other mates alone, or else. When she was completely disgraced in front of everyone, crying like a little baby, I finally got off of her and let her go. I didn't even have to lay a hand on her. My old pap would have been proud, I thought to myself.

• • •

SHEILA'S HOME WAS ON THE WAY TO OUR FAMILY'S LITTLE plot of land. We grew vegetables and fruits of all sorts there, and flowers of rare beauty. My pappy could usually be found on our land anytime he wasn't working at the shoe factory in town or knocking back a few brown ales at the pub. Mum would holler at him for spending too much time on the land instead of being at home. Pap would then retaliate by giving mum umpteen reasons why it was so important for him to work the family land. Mum would do her best to argue with him, but since the Depression was still going on in all its glory, Pappy's bringing in so much food for our family from his garden, was plenty difficult to disagree with.

I waved to Sheila as she split up from me and headed to her family's home. She couldn't thank me enough for sticking up for her at school. She told me I was the greatest friend anyone could wish to have in the whole world. I of course feeling obligated, yelled to her the same thing. We then went in our separate directions. When I arrived at our land, I entered the front gate. I was greeted by Beauty, our gorgeous cocker spaniel. Oh, how I loved that dog, sometimes more than anything else. With Beauty by my side, I found Pappy. He was, as usual, on his knees in the garden digging or planting something, I can't remember what, all these years later. He asked me how my day at school went, and I considered not mentioning my fight, not that any punches were thrown. But I couldn't help myself. I just knew he would be so proud of me for standing up to a bully the way that I did. So, I did tell him, I told him everything. He didn't say a word for a bit, which didn't worry me since my father was a man of great thought and consideration. He would drop us off for Sunday school. He and my mother didn't actually attend services themselves. Pap and Mum went to church when they were young and felt it was most important for children to go, to build the right foundation for life. The good book he would tell us, would say that words were often more powerful than actions. And he would follow that up by saying, that harsh hurtful words, would stay with a person long after broken bones and bruises had healed. I was now waiting patiently for Pappy to say something. I began to waiver in my ideas of him being proud of me. But finally, he stood up from his knees, dusted his pant legs off, and turned to give me one of his smiles, the kind that I spent the early part of my life always looking for but never getting enough of.

"You know, ducky, you know what I am most proud of?"

When my pappy started to say something he's proud about, my ears would prick up fast.

This was about the best question I had ever been asked in my life, and I couldn't wait to hear his answer.

"I'm so proud of you because you showed this other girl, who was being a bugger, what's what, not with your fists but with your force of will. The power of a determined will is a great thing, my little Rosey. I only hope that our esteemed Prime Minister Neville Chamberlain realizes as much when meeting with Hitler," my pap then added.

He summoned me into his arms. He held me and told me again he was proud of me. Beauty climbed onto my back as if she wanted in on all of this.

Walking back home with pappy I asked him since he had brought it up, why Hitler and Germany would want to attack us? Again, he stopped to consider his response. "Rosey," he said, "some people are never satisfied. If they have a lot, they want more. If these same people have most of everything, they want it all. Hitler is one of those types, never satisfied until he has it all."

"All of what, Pap?" I remember I asked him.

"Everything," he said, sporting a most serious look on his face. "They want all of everything, ducky."

I mentioned to him that the scuttlebutt going on at school was that Hitler wanted to conquer England and take all the British girls back to Germany to be wed off to German soldiers. Pappy stopped me in my tracks, and with that determination of will thing he had spoken about, he told me he would never let that happen. Being nine years old and not knowing yet that there were things even your father, even a great man like mine couldn't control, I believed him, I always did.

———◆———

It was only a few months later, almost to that day in the garden, that my little sister, my parents, and myself were all awoken by sirens out somewhere in the distance. We didn't know exactly what was happening to our beloved home as we scrambled out of our beds and made our way downstairs, but we knew it wasn't good. Hitler had followed through on his threats and the "'Battle of Britain'" had begun. Being that Northampton where we lived was only a few hours or so from London, we were certainly not safe from Germany's onslaught. My pappy herded all of us up and led us to our basement where he said we would be most safe. My mother sang Sunday school songs and tried with great difficulty to get my sister, Sheila, and I to sing along with her. Neither one of us could focus our thoughts well enough to even follow mum's words. Pappy told us he would be right back as he went upstairs and then out to the middle of the street to get a better look. After too much time had passed, his right-back guarantee wasn't coming to fruition. Mum fought back tears and pretended for our benefit that we had nothing at all to be worried about, but both Sheila and I knew that wasn't true. Mum then continued her singing, while I thought about my pappy's promise that he would never let Hitler or the Germans hurt us. I now believed that even my great father at this moment, couldn't keep such a promise. So, I prayed to God with all my might. There seemed nowhere else to turn.

"Our Father who art in heaven," I started with, as I took the Lord's Prayer I had learned from years of Sunday school and adjusted it to the situation. It might not have been theologically correct, but as I continued to pray, I had God, Jesus, and the Holy Ghost taking a sword of gold and cutting Hitler in two. Right prayer or wrong, it somehow made me feel better. When Pappy came back to the basement, he whispered things to mum that we couldn't quite make out. But I knew what was happening tonight was a very dreadful thing. Mum and my old pap would smile at my sister and me and then look at each other with grim expressions covering their faces. This was the beginning of hard days for all of England. We just didn't know how hard at the time.

———◆———

What followed next was surreal and heartbreaking, as every able-bodied British male was pulled from his family and his home and set off to fight the Germans. My Uncle George, my father's younger brother, stopped by before he left to join the Army and the war effort against the Germans in North Africa. He was my favorite relative from my pappy's side of the family. Uncle George had Errol Flynn's looks and Clark Gable's charisma. Girls would swoon when he walked by on the street. I loved going to the pictures as a child. I loved all the old stars of the time, Gable, Flynn, Gary Cooper, Cary Grant, Tyrone Power, so many. In the pictures of the day, the good-looking stars always made it home. The movie would end when they walked through the door or got off the bus or train and swept the woman they loved off her feet. That final kiss with their love announced they were home safe and had triumphed in battle. My Uncle George, I remember like it was yesterday, lifted me up in the air, off my feet, and kissed me on both cheeks. He told me and my little sister he would bring us wonderful gifts back home after the war. Of course, I believed him. To me, he was Errol Flynn. We all said our goodbyes, and Uncle George headed to the Army base and then to North Africa. He never returned home, and no one ever saw him again.

Only a week later, after the bombings in London started, the English military came for my pappy. Pap had a problem with his feet we were told after an examination by their medics and was told he could not serve in the military because of it. My father was devastated as he felt it was his duty to join his younger brother George in the Army and fight for England. And though he felt that way, my mother and I were secretly thrilled with the official's decision, but then they tricked us. They instead recruited my pappy to help fight fires in London with the city's fire brigade. He still wanted to be in the military and fight the Germans, but he settled for the fire brigade because he knew it was something, and very important in its own right.

Mum and I thought we had dodged a bullet with Pappy not having to go to war, but we were equally petrified by the thought of him fighting fires in London as the damn Nazis dropped bombs from above. Just like Uncle George, a few days earlier, we stood at our doorway on Franklin Street and said our goodbyes. Mum tried to be strong for him and show a brave front for Sheila and I as well, but she couldn't hold back the tears. Her crying got me and Sheila to do the same. I remember clinging to him for as long as I could. I never wanted to say goodbye. Unlike my Uncle George, this time I had a bad feeling that I would never see my old pap again.

———◆———

DANNY WAKES THE NEXT MORNING WITH HIS MOTHER'S hand-written pages still piled up next to him in bed. As he begins to get up, he is careful not to mess up the order of pages he's read so far and even makes a nice crease in the corner of the last page he looked at. As he leaves his room, the smell of coffee leads him to where his sister is cooking up breakfast for both of them. "Hungry, sleepyhead?" Lori asks him as he pulls up a chair at her kitchen table.

"It does smell good," he has to admit.

"Good," she responds. "I've made a whole gourmet breakfast for you just like Mom used to make. I've even got the stewed tomatoes that I know you used to love so much."

"Did you cut up my toast into little soldiers the way Mom used to?" Danny quips sarcastically.

Lori assures her kid brother that she can if he wants her to. "Today's a busy day. We've got a lot going on."

He asks what is on today's agenda. Lori is more than happy to share their itinerary.

It all revolves around the funeral, from meeting with their mother's minister to setting up final arrangements at the funeral parlor. Not to mention they're going to pick out the coffin to bury their mother in.

"No cremation, huh?" Danny questions.

"Oh no," Lori is quick to reply. "Mom made it very clear to me in the last few years that she did not want to be cremated. She was scared to death of fire, Danny. She told me it had something to do with World War II when she was a small child and she would see all these men come back from war or whatever, severely burned."

"Probably from the bombings in London by the Germans," Danny figures.

"What's that?" Lori replies, acting like she's never heard of such things before.

Danny then considers to himself that as bad a student as Lori was as a kid, maybe she hadn't heard of it. He realizes after what he read in his mother's story last night that it is no wonder she had a fear of fire.

"What time are you doing all this?" He asks.

She informs him lunchtime with the minister and then the funeral parlor after that. Danny is happy to hear he has at least a few hours to work on his manuscript.

"You don't want to keep me company as I go shopping for groceries this morning?"

"I really have to get on my book, Sis. The deadline is coming fast, and my agent is breathing down my neck."

"Of course," Lori answers. She's disappointed but understands at the same time. "I'll just come back and get you before we meet with the minister."

Danny tells her that would be great as he digs into his sister's breakfast bounty.

After she leaves in an hour and with breakfast finished and the dishes put away, He starts on his manuscript on his laptop. He squeezes out a page and a little more, and then the well runs dry as it has often lately. A few more minutes of lowering the bucket into the well brings nothing better. A frustrated Danny closes his laptop and heads back to the bedroom and his mother's story.

It wasn't long before the war with Germany caused shortages of everything you could think of, including, of course, food. My mother would send me to stand in the long queues downtown for food handouts. She said she had to stay home and take care of my little sister. So, with Pappy still fighting fires in London, it was up to me to go to the marketplace. Only nine years old, it was a very scary thing to stand there with all those grown-ups. Many of them would give me strange looks, wondering where my parents were, wondering why a child so young, would be out here all alone. After queuing up for over an hour in line, I would finally make it to the front of the queue. After getting the bread and eggs and other things, I would have the arduous task of carrying the bags all the way home without dropping them. I vividly remember one day when I was only a few blocks from my home, out of seemingly nowhere, a small group of girls much older than I was, stood directly in my path. I pretended to not take notice of them as if they weren't even there. Maybe if I acted like I didn't see them they would do the same for me, I hoped, of course, it didn't work in the least. They blocked my path and then encircled me. They mucked about with me because of the flowered dress I was wearing, and then told me how a girl of my tender age shouldn't be walking around the city, that it was too dangerous. I pleaded for them to just let me pass, that I had food to get home to my family. They said their families could use some food as well. I knew what that meant but was unable to do anything to stop them. I ran home empty-handed that day, crying all the way up the stairs to where my mum and sister were. I told my mother what happened, and she cuddled me in her arms. "It's a very sad day indeed when the English turn against each other," Mum remarked, as she held me close.

She wiped away my tears and measured me up with her eyes. "You know what Rosey dear?" she started with.

"What, Mum?" I asked.

"I believe you are more than old enough now to keep an eye on your little sister while I fetch the groceries downtown. What do you think of that, ducky?"

I thought it was a brilliant idea and a very practical one as well. From then on as long as the shortages for food and other items continued, Mum would go and stand in line, and I would keep an eye on Sheila. All the time, all I could think about was how much I missed my pappy, and I prayed he would come home soon.

ONE NIGHT I WILL NEVER FORGET. I WAS FAST ASLEEP with my sister lying next to me. Our home only had two bedrooms, so we shared a bedroom and a bed. Both Sheila and I were startled out of our sleep by the sound of sirens going off, like before. The sirens were placed in each city in England to warn the citizens that an enemy air raid was on the horizon. Before Sheila or I could scream in fear, Mum came scrambling into our bedroom. She scooped up Sheila and firmly ordered me to follow her. We again hid in our basement until the sirens stopped. Since our house still stood, we assumed that the danger was over, and we were safe. Early the next morning, I woke up to voices from the outside. These voices, and there were many, were coming from the street. I went to the window and looked out to see what all the hubbub was about. Right in front of our house, there was a large crowd of people gathered in the street. My mother was one of them, so I threw on the first dress I could find and sped downstairs and out the front door. I ran to her, and she immediately stopped me in my tracks and kept me behind her. Whenever she did that, it meant she was protecting me from something, and this time was no different. To my amazement and terror, the reason for the crowd gathering in front of our house, our neighbors, and many more people I didn't recognize was just a few feet away lying in the middle of the street. It was a bomb, the unexploded kind. It must have landed on our street last night during the time the sirens were sounding. No one dared to get too close for fear of setting it off. Everyone just thanked their lucky stars that nothing had happened and that the bomb, as of yet, hadn't gone off. The men from the neighborhood waited for the local bobbies to show up. When they finally did arrive, they ordered everyone to go back into their homes and to hide down in their basements with pillows and blankets wrapped around them. A few of the men, mostly the old men from the neighborhood, stayed out on the street. If they would have been younger, they would have been fighting in the war or with my pappy helping with the fires in London and other parts of England. These older gentlemen helped the bobbies to slowly and as carefully as possible, lift the bomb from the street and into the back of a cart that belonged to the local police. Then the bobbies took the bomb away and everyone uttered a sigh of relief. My mum swore that the good Lord had saved us that day, and I for one couldn't argue against her explanation.

———— • ————

Now getting a tour of the funeral parlor by one of the employees who work there, Lori at the same time, is making casual conversation with her brother. Danny reasons the constant talking helps to get Lori's mind off what they are doing here. The lady who is putting together the funeral for their mother takes them into the showroom where the different models of caskets are displayed. Both Danny and his sister are surprised by the price differences between the different models. "I didn't realize there were so many different kinds," Danny admits.

"Oh yes, there are many models depending on what you are looking for," the lady answers.

Lori asks Danny if there are any that stand out to him. He is a bit bemused by the question. "Not to sound flippant, but it's just a box to put Mom in so we can bury her underground, isn't it?"

"You don't think she would have wanted a nice one?" Lori fires back.

Danny shrugs. He tries not to laugh at the conversation they're having. "I don't know, but one thing I do know, she doesn't care now. If we can save a thousand dollars on this coffin compared to that one, why not?"

Lori doesn't appreciate his attitude, acting as if money should matter at a time like this. She feels like a bestselling writer like Danny shouldn't be worried about money. She bluntly expresses these thoughts to her brother.

"Look, it's not the money, it's the principle of being taken advantage of because you're mourning the loss of someone and the fact that these coffin companies want to make you feel guilty enough, to gouge you," He attempts to explain.

"I don't know why a little extra money would matter to you?" Lori tosses out there, not looking her brother in the eyes when she says it.

"It doesn't. It's the principle of being screwed over, that's all," Danny argues. "Besides, I live in New York. Do you know how expensive it is to live in New York? Let me answer that for you. No, you don't."

Lori reminds him again that he is a big-time writer. This just pisses him off even more. "I have written one successful book that earned me good money in return. I spent ten years living in New York before that, just trying to survive with one rejection letter after another from every literary agent I could find. I did every odd job, every crappy job I could get to stay alive over those ten years. I did all that, Sis, just to get to the point where I had one successful book that actually made me some money."

"So, if it was so bad, why didn't you reach out to Mom? She would have helped you," Lori has to ask.

Danny hesitates as he reaches inside himself for the answer. "I couldn't do that."

Lori asks him why. She doesn't understand but wants to.

"Because I lied to her. I lied to her for years," he confesses.

Lori still doesn't get it, so Danny continues.

"I made Mom believe I was a big success. I never let her know how much of a failure I was. I never let her know how much I was struggling. After years of doing that, I was too embarrassed to admit anything different."

The lady giving them the guided tour at the funeral parlor excuses herself and offers Danny and Lori a few minutes alone to discuss which model of coffin they want. The lady can see that the two of them first need to get through whatever it is they are trying to get through, so she scampers back to her office until they are ready.

Lori thanks her and tells her it will be just a minute before they make up their mind on the coffin. Lori now points her attention back onto her kid brother. She can see that something is festering inside him, something he wants to get out, but is having a hard time doing so. "Well, Danny, all I know is that Mom shared with me that you were doing great. You've got a second book coming out soon that will be bigger and better than the first one. You're engaged to a beautiful woman."

Danny stares at his shoes the whole time Lori is speaking. He can't look his sister in the face, but he still has to set her straight. With their mother gone, and her expectations, or at least Danny's perception of his mother's expectations no longer relevant, he knows being truthful with Lori is the right thing to do. "Lies, all lies, my second book is a crap storm so far. I'm about four chapters into it, and it's complete shit. I've got a deadline coming up in a few weeks and then my agent and my publisher will find out too. And as far as my engagement, well…she moved out of our apartment, she left me. She said I was too obsessed with my writing and this second book. She said there was no time for her in my little world."

"Was she right?" Lori asks bluntly.

"Maybe, I don't know," he confesses. "But if she is, I'm obsessed with shit because that is what my writing has become. You know, I'm like one of those one-hit-wonder bands that you read about. They come up with one great song and that's it. Maybe that's all I've got in me, just one great book, and that's it."

Lori tries to console her brother. "Mom would tell you to be strong, pull those bootstraps up, right."

"Yeah right," he mumbles. "That's why I couldn't tell her."

"Well, I'm glad you told me. We have to take care of each other now," she reminds him.

Danny thanks her for that, as he asks Lori for one more thing. "You might want to keep that spare bedroom of yours available for a while. I might need a place to hang, real soon," he utters with a cynical snicker.

Lori touches his face in a comforting way, the way a mother would. "Whatever you need, Danny, I'm here for you. Now we better pick out a coffin before the lady here kicks us out of this place," she remarks with a laugh.

Waiting for Danny and Lori when they get back to her place, is her ex, Bobby. He's sitting in his black Camaro, parked in the street when they drive up. Lori still angry with him snubs him as she heads straight into her house and slams the front door behind her. Her actions let

Andrew Scott Bassett

Bobby know just how she feels about him being here. He then walks up to Danny who awkwardly says hello. He's embarrassed by his sister's actions.

"Danny boy, how the hell are you, man!" Bobby greets Danny with as if he didn't notice Lori's snub. "Hey, I'm so sorry about your mother. She was a real kick-in-the-ass kind of lady. She wasn't exactly crazy about me, but I thought she was a hoot with that great accent and all."

Danny thanks him for that and then asks him what he's up to.

"Oh, I'm pretty busy, you know. I own three Subway restaurants around Phoenix. They can be a pain in the ass, but it's a living. You know what I mean?" he says with a laugh.

Danny quickly clarifies that he wasn't asking him about that, but about what he's doing here at his sister's place.

"Oh, well, you know, I wanted to see how she's doing with everything. I wanted to see if there is anything I can do for her. I mean, we were together for a lot of years, man, you know," Bobby remarks.

Danny tells him he appreciates all that and his coming over and everything, but maybe it would be better for Bobby to wait until after the funeral and after things have settled down. That might be a better time to reach out to Lori.

Bobby shrugs and says alright. He asks Danny to tell his sister that he is thinking about her right now and that if she needs anything to give him a call. "I plan on going to the funeral, but let Lori know I'll sit in the back, so as not to bring attention to myself or sow discomfort for her in any way, you know."

Danny again offers appreciation to Bobby as he says his goodbyes to him. Bobby stops him in his tracks as Danny's about to head into the house. "Hey, Danny boy, I almost forgot."

"What?" Danny cracks back, now getting a bit irritated at Bobby.

"No biggie really, I just bought your first book when it came out and I told myself that the next time I saw you I would make sure I got it signed by you," Bobby says with a chuckle. "I haven't seen you in years, pal, so what do you say?"

How can Danny say no? Anyone buying his book is a good thing, even Bobby.

"Yeah, of course," Danny tells him. "Thanks for buying it," Danny offers as he puts down a few personalized words, and then autographs Bobby's copy.

"Much appreciated, pal, and again if Lori needs anything, no matter how pissed she is at me right now, let her know I'm there for her, okay?" Bobby asserts.

"Sure," Danny says, as he shakes Bobby's hand and then watches him drive away in his muscle car, roaring all the way down the street.

Lori is waiting inside the house to interrogate Danny on everything Bobby said to him as soon as he walks in. Danny does his best to relay Bobby's words and then adds how annoying he can be but at the same time quite endearing. Lori agrees, calling it, "Bobby's yin-yang of attraction. One minute," she says, "you want to kill him, and the next minute he has you missing him, especially his laugh."

After hearing his sister say that Danny shares that he believes she is still hung up on him.

"He cheated on me," she argues in defense of her words. "And more than once, Danny."

"Yeah, no comment on that. I'm just telling you what I see. I better get back to my book. It's not going to write itself," Danny exclaims, as he grabs a beer from the fridge and heads to the guest bedroom to get some work done.

Andrew Scott Bassett

He spends about an hour trying to squeeze every ounce of creativity he has inside him into his laptop. The process is excruciating and only reminds him how disappointing this second written effort of his is going. He needs a break. He needs to get his mind off his book, even if only for a few peaceful moments. He sees his mother's pages still lying on his bed and walks over and sits down next to them. He begins to start reading right where he left off.

CHAPTER 3

Everyone in our neighborhood was celebrating. Germany had stopped their air attacks after almost nearly four months of fighting in the skies of England. The war was certainly not over, yet there was now hope in the air for the first time in quite some time, and it was bloody refreshing. We all believed it was only a matter of time before America would come to England's aid and then Hitler would get his. The street was covered in balloons and paper streamers. The streamers were made of simple toilet tissue that usually one wouldn't waste during a time of war, yet, with newfound confidence in the future, all our neighbors did just a tad. We shared food as well on tables that were set up in the middle of the street. Now mind you, this was early November, and it was cold outside. The rainclouds were threatening, but no one cared in the least. There was just too much to celebrate. My mum made her famous shepherd's pie. Oh, how I loved her cooking. She could perform miracles in a kitchen. Music was blaring from houses all around the street. Old men and their wives, young girls and young boys, everyone was dancing and laughing. But for me, there was little joy because I missed my pappy. We still had no word from him. Mum hadn't received a letter or any correspondence in over a month. She continued to make me and Sheila pray for his safe return every night. With the bombings now over and all the fires in London and elsewhere put out, my greatest fear was more real every moment.

"Anybody home in there?" my mother asked me, as she tried to break me out of the trance I had fallen into.

"Yes, Mum?" I responded.

"Why such a gloomy puss, my dear?" she asked.

I didn't want to answer her. She was having a lovely time right now, and I didn't want to ruin it for her. She needed this more than anyone, and I knew that. So, I put on the best fake smile I could muster up, and I denied everything. I grabbed my sister, Sheila, and dragged her out into the middle of the street. People were dancing to music everywhere, and so I forced my little sister to dance with me. This action had my desired effect. My mum started smiling from ear to ear, laughing loudly, and even clapping her hands in rhythm. The sight of her being happy made me feel much better. It was like someone had turned a torch on inside of me. All of a sudden, I was all lit up with joy.

"Screech!!!!" The sound the brakes on the car made as it stopped at the top of the street. The automobile was completely unable to go any further with all the people blocking traffic as they continued to enjoy the festivities all around.

"Ann!" A voice echoed in the distance.

"Ann!" We heard a second time.

I looked in the direction it came from, and my heart leaped in my chest. It was my pappy, and he was sprinting toward us from the blocked-off car. He didn't take notice of me or Sheila in the street, but he saw Mum standing in front of our neighbor's home and ran straight toward her. All our neighbors began to cheer and clap at the sight of Pappy's return. He lifted Mum way up off the ground and gave her one of the greatest kisses I had ever seen. It was the kind of snog that would have made a Clark Gable or a Tyrone Power jealous. After they finished their smooch, he set her back down on her feet and began to search for us. Mum pointed us out in the street. I don't know why I hadn't already run toward him. I'm not really sure. I guess I was too busy enjoying the spectacle of his greeting Mum the way he did. No matter, now Pappy was running toward Sheila and me. Being the baby in the family he grabbed Sheila first and held her up in the air as if studying her for a minute. It was as if he was taking in every inch of her for the first time. He smothered little Sheila with kisses, too many to keep up with. Finally, it was my turn.

"My Rosey," he said as he finally acknowledged me. "I missed you so much, ducky."

I wanted to tell him the same thing, but my barmy weeping got in the way, and I couldn't spit out a word, not a single word. So, I hugged him with all my might and tried to hold back the tears streaming down my face.

"You alright then?" he asked.

I nodded and just squeezed him even tighter. Up to that point, that was the best day of my life.

"Shall we dance then?" he said with a grin, as he grabbed Sheila in one arm and me in the other and led us around swaying and swinging to the music that filled the neighborhood.

I move forward with my story now. Three years had passed since that wonderful day full of lovely memories. So much had changed in the world since then. The end of World War II seemed in view. When America finally joined the fight after Pearl Harbor, we all knew everything had changed. The war with Germany was still raging on, but most in England believed that Hitler's days were numbered.

One night at supper, we were sitting around the dinner table listening to our family's radio. Pappy looked at me as if he had something important to tell me. Mum seemed to know what it was and whispered to him, asking if now was the right time to discuss such things. Pappy argued quietly with her, but I could still hear him. He said that it was as good a time as any. Then, for all of us to hear, he proclaimed that I was now a teenager and needed to start thinking about such things, especially since I was very tall for my young age of thirteen. I had only turned thirteen a month ago, but Pappy was right. I appeared much older than my actual age.

"What is it, Pappy?" I inquired.

I could see he was having a difficult time broaching the subject with me, so I tried to make it as easy as possible by guessing what the subject might be. None of my guesses seemed to be on target, so I became quiet and just let him fumble his way through whatever it was. Finally, he made some headway. "Rosey dear."

"Yes, Pap," I answered.

"Well," he stammered, seeming nervous. "It's just that, darling, you are a teenager now and quite mature looking for your age, you know."

I nodded.

"Well, my darling, there are, I think, certain realities in life you need to be aware of."

At that moment I glanced toward my mum. She was staring at her lap, seemingly unable to look up and make any eye contact with me, whatsoever. My first thought was, oh god, this isn't about sex. Please tell me my pappy isn't going to discuss sex with me at our dinner table. Why wouldn't my mother be the one to talk with me about this, in private, for god's sake? I actually could feel my cheeks blushing.

"You see, Rosey dear, as your father I have certain responsibilities, and well this is one of them." He continued.

"First and foremost, I have to protect you and your sister and keep you both safe, do you understand?"

"I think so," I recall uttering back, still not sure what he was on about.

"Well, this is one of those things that you are now old enough to start thinking about, and it has to do with the war," he stated.

Oh, it's not about sex I thought, it's about the war. That was a huge relief, and so I listened more intently.

"Well, your mother and I feel it's important for you to know that after the war is over or even near its end, which we happily believe is coming soon, things here in England will be, well, changing."

"Changing how, Pappy?" I asked curiously.

Mum still wasn't looking at me. Her uncomfortableness about the subject matter was easy for anyone to see. My father continued, "Yes well, how will it change I believe is what you asked, well, right then. Let me get to the brass tacks of it all if I may. You see, Rosey, there will be soldiers coming to England from all over the world. What I'm saying is, as this war of ours, England's I mean, begins to reach its conclusion."

"Oh," I said. I hadn't really thought about soldiers from other countries coming to England. Why would I?

My pappy obviously had as he got to his main point. "And with that, dear, many of these young men, soldiers, will be lonely and a long way from home, and well, they will be looking for… shall we say, a splendid time."

Oh my, I reconsidered. This is a sex talk after all.

Pappy then went on to ask me if I knew what a splendid time meant. I couldn't say the word sex in front of my parents. I would have been mortified if I did, so I only nodded that I understood. My pappy and mum both seemed relieved that they didn't have to explain it to me in greater detail. Pappy then gave me instructions to follow to avoid leading a soldier on. It was quite simple. No flirting with one, no off-color talk if I came in contact with one, and most important of all, never, ever allow myself to be alone with one. Pappy stressed that point several times. Mum chimed in about modest clothing, finally glancing up from her lap. She also told me to avoid going to places where the soldiers congregated. She meant like pubs and dancehalls. I was really too young for that yet, so I didn't really understand why that was brought up.

At the conclusion of his talk, Pappy asked me if I understood everything we had just spoken about. I nodded again. Expressions of relief came over both Pappy and Mum's faces at that point. I think the relief was as much to do with having survived such a conversation as anything else. After that, we finished our dinner with very little discussion. I guess they were both chatted out.

A FEW MORE YEARS PASSED AND OUR LONG NATIONAL nightmare finally came to an end. My best friend, Sheila Saunders, and some other mates of ours all headed downtown to celebrate VE day. Hallelujah, the war was finally over. It was such a strange feeling to be living in a country, not at war. I had spent half my conscious life living under the storm clouds of war.

When we got downtown on foot, we were greeted with crowds of people overflowing the city park and square. The music was loud, and people of both military and civilian persuasions were dancing with anyone they could grab hold of. It was nighttime, but between the streetlamps and bonfires all around, the whole area was lit up like the Las Vegas strip that I would get to experience many, many, years later. The booze was flowing as the celebration continued. Much of it made its way into the people, but just as much spilled onto the ground. A young, handsome British soldier who I had never met before, came over and asked me if I would like to dance. My girlfriends all giggled, taken aback by his good looks. I told him yes, of course. Why wouldn't I? I loved to dance as much as anything in the whole world. Thanks to my being taller and maturing physically earlier than most girls, I still looked older than my age of fifteen and a half. I would sneak into pubs and dancehalls every chance I got to boogie-woogie to Glenn Miller or the Dorsey Brothers. Pappy and Mum would have killed me if they knew, but I couldn't see how they could possibly ever have found out.

"There goes our Rosey, nothing is going to stop her!" Sheila Saunders shouted for all to hear, as I took the soldier's hand and allowed him to lead me to the area where everyone was dancing.

Before long, all the girls, Sheila Saunders included, had also been asked. We whooped and hollered the night away, having the time of our very young lives. I'll never forget it. After it was over, the young man asked me if he could walk me home. But still remembering that talk from my pappy from years before, I politely told him no thank you. When he pushed for a reason, I told him the simple truth. My pappy would never forgive me and most likely kill you if I did let you walk me home. He said for just a walk home, and I said yes, for just a walk home. Sheila then came to my aid and the two of us alone, walked home together. It was early morning, but Pappy and Mum knew I would be late because of the party. VE Day would be one of the few exceptions for coming home late that they would tolerate. Of course, I had to be escorted by Sheila Saunders. Pap and Mum both loved and trusted Sheila very much.

"So, what are you going to do, Rosey, after you graduate, I mean?" Sheila asked me as we walked along.

"Well, the university I suppose. I guess that's the correct response, aye?" I answered.

"Are you going to work at the factory too, with your mum and dad?" Sheila then asked.

I told her that was my plan. My hometown of Northampton was one of the biggest factory towns in England and our product of choice was shoes. The numerous factories employed about a quarter of the poor sods living in the city. My pappy and mum had worked in the shoe factories for years and had already set up a job for me when I graduated from school. I could go to the university as well, but at least I would have some money coming in while I went.

"How about you, Sheila?" I asked her, wondering what her plans might be.

"University I suppose too," she chirped back. "But you know what I would really like to do, someday?"

"No," I responded, but I was very curious.

A daft smile suddenly embraced Sheila's face. She looked like she was embarrassed to tell me. But then she did. "What I would really like to do Rosey, is move to America. What I've seen in the magazines and in the pictures, that would be my dream. Maybe marry a Yank, you never know."

I scoffed at the idea of being so far away from family and merry old England, the land that I loved. How little did I know then what the future held for me.

As I mentioned, I loved to dance. A little more than a year after VE Day, and with the war behind us, the great big party in England continued. I was now going to the university part-time and working at the shoe factory full time. Still, I couldn't wait to hit the clubs at night after all that studying and working to have some fun with my mates. My pappy and mum would have been quite upset if they could have seen how we carried on at night. My old pap would ask me when I got home if I was all right. Invariably, never better would be my response. Pappy was no fool, however. He could see I was burning the candle not only from both ends but both sides as well. He would stop me at the stairs as I was heading for my bedroom in the wee hours of the morning and remind me to be careful with whatever I was doing. "You're young and free and having fun, ducky, but be watchful, dear. This is the time to enjoy yourself, but don't overdo it."

I would promise him I would be careful and that I wouldn't allow anyone to take advantage of me. He would then remind me how a few moments of fun could bring a lifetime of work and responsibility to my doorstep. Without saying anymore, we both knew what he was speaking of. I didn't find out until years later that he and Mum were forced to get married because he got her pregnant with me. Pappy didn't want my life to be dictated by the same events. I would end our chats by giving him a peck on the cheek and saying goodnight. After pushing my sister, Sheila, to her side of the bed, I would collapse into my side. I had found out already at an early age how much work it was to be young and free.

ME AND MY MATES, INCLUDING SHEILA SAUNDERS, WERE having drinks and dancing at one of the clubs after work one night. Between all of the requests to dance from the different men in the club, I took notice of one man in particular. He had blondish brown hair and the most handsome face I had seen since my Uncle George. What stood out even more about him was that he wasn't getting up and asking any of the ladies in the place to dance. With his looks and chiseled physique, he could have danced with anyone he chose to. The other thing about him that caught my eye from the rest of his mates was that he was the only one wearing a regular suit. The three men sitting with him were all in uniform, British soldiers to be exact. For the next few minutes, I tried desperately to ignore him while I chatted with the girls and sipped my brandy. Although I was now barely sixteen, as always, I looked older and no one in the clubs seemed to care to check my age or my friends' ages for that matter. I nudged Sheila Saunders in the side and pointed him out to her. She agreed that he was quite mysterious and deliciously handsome. One of my other gal pals, who spent more time in this particular club than I did, said she'd seen him in here before. She said, in fact, several times, and always surrounded by British soldiers. "That is very curious, isn't it?" I remarked.

"Maybe he's a prisoner of war or such," Sheila theorized.

"No!" I said. "They wouldn't let him into an English dance club if he was a prisoner of war."

"Well, we will never find out if he's not going to ask any of the girls in here to dance." One of the other girls spouted off.

"Maybe you can go over and ask him to dance?" Sheila said to me with a giggle.

"Maybe I should," I quickly answered.

Sheila then changed her mind and said she was only having a little fun with me. "A woman doesn't ask a man to dance, Rosey. It's unheard of."

Now, I was never one to be dared to do something lightly. She threw down the gauntlet, and I was quite happy to pick it up. "Well, really, why not?"

Sheila and the others tried desperately to talk me out of the notion. They said it was unseemly, and again just not a thing a lady should do.

"Are we still in the Victorian age then?" I argued. "Is it only men who get to decide what the rules are? I think it's about time for women to tell men to bloody well bugger off and let us ladies have a chance to write some rules up ourselves!"

Sheila grabbed at my arm when I stood up from my chair. It was a last-ditch attempt to get me to not go over there, but it was too late. I was already riled up. I pulled my arm away from her and marched right over to the conclave of men. "Can we help you, love?" one of the soldiers asked.

I said yes. I asked if the gentleman sitting there would like to dance. He didn't respond with words to my request. He just smiled broadly. The British soldiers however did. "What did you say then?" one of them asked me, not believing his ears.

So, I asked again.

"Since when does a lady ask a man to dance?" another soldier chimed in.

"She's got a lot of pluck, this one," the same soldier who seemed to be in charge, added.

The other soldiers began to grumble about how it was not done and especially in this case, but the commanding officer seemed to like me, or my pluck. He decided it was okay if it was agreeable with Maximillian. When the other soldiers complained, he cut them off and reminded them how compliant a chap Max was. "He's not trying to escape, lads. It's only dancing."

At that moment I realized that the man I had come over to dance with was, as Sheila had speculated, indeed a prisoner. It certainly took me by surprise and since his name was what it was, I could only conclude a German one at that. "So, he's a prisoner then?" I said, although I already knew the answer.

The commanding officer nodded. "He's a German prisoner of war. But Max here is one of our favorites. He's a good soul this one. He's no Nazi. He was just following orders like the rest of us when he got captured. Do you still want to have that dance, miss?"

I looked over at the man, the German man. He seemed to be studying my face, waiting to see what I would say next. "Yes," I answered. "If he does, that is."

The commanding officer then looked at his prisoner and waited for his answer.

"Yes, I would like that very much," he responded with his German accent, almost as appealing as his eyes.

With the prompting of the British soldiers and some pats on the back, Maximillian got up and gracefully and with great care, took my hand and escorted me out onto the dancefloor. We danced for hours as Sheila and the other girls watched with their mouths gaping wide open. The soldiers in charge of Maximillian hoisted drinks and cheered. When it was finally time to call it a night, Max, as he asked me to call him, shook my hand and thanked me for the evening. He said he had almost forgotten how much fun it was to dance and thanked me for reminding him. I told him he was a wonderful dancer. He seemed to blush from the praise. Then the commanding officer announced they had to get back to the camp. I said my goodbyes to Max, expecting to never lay eyes on him again. He left with the soldiers, but the commanding officer quickly circled back into the club to speak with me.

"Yes, what is it?" I asked him.

He started in by thanking me for helping Max have such a wonderful evening. He then shared a bit about his prisoner. The commander said that Max got much more freedom than most prisoners of war because he was such a nice chap and a model citizen. He also told me that the British military was working on getting him sent back to his home in Germany as soon as possible. In the meantime, the commanding officer and the other soldiers were allowed to let Max have a little more fun and leeway than most prisoners. Taking Max to a club or pub in town was one of the things he got to do. The soldier then left me with one other tidbit of information, if it made any difference. He told me that they would be back here at the club in two nights if I wanted to dance some more with their prisoner. I didn't answer but thanked him for everything. He then left, and Sheila and I and the other girls followed suit.

Sheila Saunders and I walked home together from the club that night and were out in front of her family's home when she noticed a glimmer in my eye and had to mention it. We had been talking about Max, the German soldier, for most of the walk. Sheila, of course, knew me better than anyone. "You're not thinking of seeing him again, are you, Rosey?"

"Well…I don't know, it's just dancing," I replied.

"Yes, but he's a German soldier. He's a bleeding prisoner of war!" Sheila said, raising her voice enough that we thought she was going to wake up the neighborhood.

"Yes, I do know that, Sheila," I countered.

"But what if someone you know sees you, and what if they tell your mum and dad," she continued.

I thanked her for her concern. As a best friend, it was her job to worry and fret about me, and she was very good at her job. I told her it was simple. If my pappy or mum found out about me dancing with a German soldier or doing anything with one, for that matter, they would probably disown me, at least for a time. Then they would forgive and allow me back into the family. "They would miss my charm, you see," I boasted to Sheila.

That made her laugh, but I more or less was telling the truth. My mum and pap would forgive me after the initial shock wore off.

"So, you are going back to the club in a couple of nights then?" Sheila asked me point-blank.

"I think I am," I told her. "I have always been interested in learning about the world outside of England, and Germany is outside of England."

"You're inscrutable Rosey, you truly are," Sheila said to me.

I just smiled and offered no defense. I was, and very proud of it.

———— • ♦ • ————

I MADE SURE I WAS AT THE CLUB TWO NIGHTS LATER. Maximillian and I started right up where we left off. We danced the night away. I got to know the British soldiers who were in charge of Max, in short order. They were all lovely chaps who had grown quite fond of Max after all the time they had spent guarding him. Douglas was the commanding officer of the group, a wonderful young man. Bernard was another. He was quite the cheeky sod. He was always ready with a quip or a well-timed barb. They saw in Max themselves had the war gone the other way. They knew that they could have possibly ended up a prisoner themselves in Germany, and if they had, they would have wanted to be treated the way they were treating Max.

What started out as just dancing in clubs together grew to much more in the next ten months. The lads, that's what I began to call the British soldiers, would bring Max out so we could go to lunch, shopping, sometimes just picnics in the park. It was wonderful, my first true romantic relationship. Now obviously, there was the danger of my mum and dad finding out, but I think that almost made it more special somehow. On a couple of occasions, I spotted my pappy in town when I was with Max, and we had to duck inside a store or once into a phone booth to hide. I was embarrassed to tell Max the reason for hiding, but he quickly figured that it must be a friend or relative of mine that we were hiding from. I thought he would be angry, but instead, he told me he understood. Max was such a caring and sweet man, very even-keeled, and certainly a romantic at heart. We were never, of course, alone, even if we wanted to be. The lads were always nearby, so there was no danger in anything going further than a stolen kiss or a long embrace. Then one day at the park, I noticed a difference in Max. He was distant, not engaged in conversation as he usually was. I asked if there was anything bothering him. He looked at me and touched my hand, sweeping across it in a tender manner. I could see in his eyes he had something to tell me, and I felt I knew what it was.

Andrew Scott Bassett

"I am being released," he announced, but not in a joyous way as one would expect. "I am being sent back to Germany."

I didn't know what to say, or how to even respond to the news. Part of me was happy for him. I knew how much he missed his family and his homeland. But another part of me felt like something had just died inside me because of his news. I could tell he saw that too, but I still put up a brave face and congratulated him. "Your family will be so happy to see you, Max," I told him, carefully hiding my own feelings.

"I know you are correct," he agreed. "But what about you?"

As usual, he could see right through me. He seemed to know my every feeling. I had never met anyone who had understood me so well before.

"Can you choose to stay in England and just visit your family and then come back?" I hoped and wished.

"No," he said. "As a prisoner of war, I have to go back to Germany and at least for the time being, stay out of England."

I know that was probably the fair and just thing for England to demand from an enemy soldier, but that didn't lessen the pain I was feeling. I struggled at that moment with demanding to know when I would see him again, but at the same time not wanting to burden him with guilt and have that as his last memory of me. After all, he had been through, he didn't deserve that. So, I took the high road, the difficult path, and told him how much I enjoyed the last ten months, getting to know him. How he was such a cherished friend to me. I thanked him for always being a gentleman to me. I did my best to leave him with only good thoughts of our wonderful time together, a time that I would never forget. He smiled knowingly. As I said, he knew me so well.

He thanked me for making our parting as easy as I did. Then he leaned in and kissed me. It was to that point, the softest and most tender kiss of my life. It embodied everything I would always remember about him, his sweetness, his gentleness. My heart stopped for a moment. There was so much I wanted to say to him, but I couldn't.

"I will find you again, one day we will be together when all this madness in the world is over," he whispered softly to me.

I smiled and stroked his beautiful hair. We toasted each other's future happiness and promised each other we would meet again. Before I knew it, he was ready to be on his way. The lads came and got him. They were almost as sad as we were at the parting of the two of us. Douglas came over and asked me if I needed an escort home. I told him no. At this moment, I would rather be alone. I watched as Bernard guided Max back to their vehicle. Max turned one last time and waved to me, and then he was gone. I could barely get out of bed for the university the next two days. I had to make up an excuse to my parents for why I was acting the way I was. I was sick, I told them, and in a way, I truly was. I was heartsick.

Andrew Scott Bassett

CHAPTER 4

The next six years were a busy, fun, yet somehow unmemorable bore to me. As I said, I had fun, lots of it as a matter of fact. I graduated from the university but still kept my same job at the shoe factory in town. I was working full-time by day and dancing and drinking almost every night. I knew all the clubs in the city and most of the men who went to them.

My friend Sheila Saunders was engaged, actually, most of my friends were married or engaged to be married. I, however, was still adrift in a sea of relationship disappointments. Even as flirty as I could be in mixed company, I still had kept myself pure, primed, and ready for that one great love of my life to appear. It wasn't easy to forgo earthly pleasure for so many years. There were many chaps that I could have easily given in to. But most of the dates with English men quickly devolved into wrestling matches on the way home. For my part, I always managed to win such contests. I was undefeated, undaunted, and perfectly miserable.

I kept waiting for Max to come back to England and sweep me off my feet. Sadly, year after year went by, and still no Max. I grimly came to the realization that he had forgotten me. He probably had a lovely German wife by now and three kids I assumed. I would toss back another drink after having such thoughts, trying to deaden the feelings as much as I could. I still lived at home. My pappy and mum liked having me home, and I saved a lot of pounds by living there. You know drinking and dancing almost every night isn't inexpensive, not in the least. Here I was only in my early twenties, but I already felt like an old maid. My pappy and mum were beginning to question themselves. They wondered if I would be single forever. Pappy took things into his own hands and surprised me one night. I got home from work and for once didn't feel the desire to go to the pub or the dancehalls. Pappy was waiting for me when I walked through the front door. My father had no poker face to speak of, which was quite fine since he didn't believe in playing cards and banned them from our home. I could tell he was dying to tell me something. Mum was in the kitchen cooking dinner but eavesdropping on the whole affair.

"What is it, Pap?" I asked.

He was having an extremely difficult time finding the right words to share what he so desperately wanted to tell me. He hem-hawed around for a long time before finally speaking his mind. "Mum and I just have noticed lately, ducky, well that you seem in a bit of a malaise."

Malaise, I thought to myself, that certainly wasn't a word I had heard my father say before.

"Well, anyway, I have some news for you and it's exciting ducky!" he offered me, his voice rising with anticipation.

I'm bloody game, I thought. So, I made it easy on him and asked him, "What is the wonderful news?"

"Freddy Truvail!" Pappy hollered happily.

"The cricket player?" I responded.

"Cricket player?!" Pappy answered. "He's not just a cricket player, ducky, he's England's greatest cricket player."

I answered okay, and then asked, "What about him?"

Pappy, almost unable to hide his excitement, told me his "'big news.'" "He's coming here tomorrow night to pick you up for a night on the town!"

"A date?" I spit out. "A date with Freddie Truvail?"

Mum then wandered into the living room, followed by my kid sister, Sheila. They both seemed as excited by the prospect of me going on a blind date with Freddie Truvail as Pappy did.

"But I've never even met him, Pap," I said, still digesting the news.

"It's Freddie Truvail, dear! Rosey, any girl in England would jump at the chance to go out with him," my mum without warning, interjected into the conversation.

Even little Sheila seemed thrilled for me.

"Alright then," I spoke up. "Alright, Pappy, I'll go out with Freddie Truvail tomorrow night. Who knows maybe I'll have a bit of fun?"

Pappy and Mum were beyond thrilled that I agreed. Pappy picked me up and twirled me in the air like when I was a child. Everyone seemed more excited about me having a date with Freddie Truvail than, well, me.

Hours later as I sat in bed with Sheila asleep at my side, I finally started to consider the possibilities. I mean Freddie was very handsome and fabulously rich. He was a household name in England, around the world.

If all went well, I could be married to one of the biggest sports stars in the country. I would be a celebrity wife. We would have a big, beautiful mansion for a home. Not the size the Royals have, mind you, but still very nice indeed. And our children would undoubtedly be lovely in looks and features. I was beginning to warm up to the idea of Freddie Truvail. So much so, that I had forgotten to even ask Pappy how he managed all this in the first place. Suddenly, I just had to know why England's most famous cricket player was going out with little old me. I ran downstairs and found Pappy sipping a cup of tea in his favorite easy chair. Mum was already in bed.

"How, Pap, how did you get Freddie Truvail to agree to this?"

Pappy just looked up at me from his teacup and said it was easy. Freddie's favorite uncle worked at the shoe factory in the same department as Pap. "Freddie came by for a visit the other day to see his uncle while he was in town. I showed him your picture that I carry in my wallet and told Freddie how wonderful a dancer you are. It seems that Freddie loves to dance, and I think he was quite smitten by your picture."

"Really?" I said, as I now was beginning to get more excited by the possibilities of this date.

"And he's in town tomorrow," Pappy followed with. I nodded and let out a small chuckle under my breath. Then I ran back upstairs and crawled back into bed. I dreamt all night about how our home would look, how our children would look, and, of course, how I would spend all that money.

———◆———

THE DOORBELL RANG, AND MY FATHER LIKE A GIDDY schoolgirl ran to answer it. I could hear Pappy speaking but not exactly what he was saying as I was upstairs making the final preparations to my appearance. Pappy's voice rang out loudly throughout the house as it often did when he got excited. My sister, Sheila, prodded me to hurry up and get downstairs. She acted like Freddie was going to leave or something if I didn't get down there in the next few seconds.

Andrew Scott Bassett

I have to admit the butterflies were dancing in my tummy as I checked my look in the mirror one more time and then made my way down to our living room.

It was all a bit surreal, seeing a famous face like Freddie Truvail sitting there on our sofa, chatting away with my old pap. The man whose face I had seen many times in the sports pages of national newspapers quickly hopped to his feet and made my acquaintance when I entered the room. My pappy's face lit up. His smile carried itself from one ear to the other. My mum held Pap's hand; she was sporting a bit of a grin herself.

"Lovely to meet you, Rosey," he started with as he took my hand and kissed it as a proper gentleman of the day often did. It was a promising start.

"Likewise, I'm sure," I replied.

"Wonderful then, would you like to get going? I know I'm somewhat famished. How about you, Rosey?" Freddie asked me directly.

"Of course, shall we," I responded.

Freddie then made the rounds with my family, telling my dad and mum how much he enjoyed meeting them and not to worry, he would take good care of me for them.

At that moment, I felt more like a piece of property being exchanged by two blokes in the street than a young woman going out on a first date. Freddie even made my little sister swoon when he also reached for her hand and gave it a quick peck. Finally, with Dad and Mum cheering us on, we made our exit and Freddie escorted me to his gorgeous sportscar. I had no idea the make or model, but it was red and shiny and completely befitting a sports star of his stature. All dressed up, I felt like a princess as he opened the door for me and helped me get in.

"May I know where we are going?" I asked him as we drove through town.

He answered that it was one of the city's finest restaurants, four stars, and all that malarky. When we got there, it seemed that everyone knew him, which of course makes sense being who he was. I loathed both playing and watching cricket. In school, being female, we were allowed to play rounders instead. Rounders was, as I said earlier, very similar to American baseball, which at the time I knew nothing about. Cricket, however, was for men, and Freddie Truvail was England's best player, so of course everybody knew him. Freddie seemed to relish all the attention, too much it occurred to me. We were soon shown to our table. It was in the middle of the restaurant, and I felt like we were public entertainment for everyone else there. It was dimly lit, thank goodness, but with candles flickering and bouncing light off the walls and the furniture, we were still too much on show for my liking.

"Lovely place, isn't it?" Freddie started our first conversation with.

Naturally, I said yes. Don't get me wrong, it was lovely and elegant and a place far too expensive for my pap and mum to dine at. It was fancy no doubt, and like Freddie I was beginning to notice, full of itself.

"You come here often then?" I asked him, doing my best to break the ice.

"When I make it to town here, I usually do. I come by to see my uncle, ever so often," he explained.

"That's nice that you stay in touch with him," I added.

"Well, it isn't easy of course with all the demands on me, but you know, Rosey, I think it is very important no matter how successful and famous a person gets that they never forget where they come from, don't you agree?"

I did of course, although it seemed quite pompous the way that Freddie had just stated it.

"How about you dear?" he then asked.

I had no idea what he was talking about, so I wished for him to clarify. When he did, I was about knocked off my chair.

"You know, what did you think when your dad told you, you were going out with Freddie Truvail," he actually said.

It was at that moment that I knew this might not be the dream night I had hoped for. I couldn't believe he wanted me to share how deliriously happy I must have been to have been told that I would get to go out with the famous Freddie Truvail. I politely offered that I had been looking forward to meeting him.

"Well, of course," he answered, with his nose up high. "But knowing you were going to go out and be seen with someone famous like myself must have been very exciting for you. Did you tell all your girlfriends?"

I smiled at his words. I didn't dare say what I wanted to really say to him. I wondered if he would make me curtsy before him when we stood up to leave the restaurant. Later as the evening dragged on, and Freddie bored me with more and more of his cricket exploits, places he'd been, and celebrities he'd met, her Majesty twice, I began to devise my excuse I would need for my old pap.

The last thing I would ever want to do is crush my father's spirits, but I had no interest whatsoever in this arrogant, conceited, full-of-himself specimen, sitting across from me. I took a peek at my wristwatch at one point and realized that he had been talking about himself solely for over thirty minutes straight. That's not easy for one to do, even if that's what they're trying to do.

After dinner was over, I thought about faking illness but ran out of the courage to do so. So instead, Freddie escorted me to a dancehall in town that I had been to a time or two. Everyone cheered when we entered the place. Many of the patrons shouted his name and wanted his autograph, which he was happy of course to oblige. In only a matter of minutes, a crowd began to form around him and ask him questions of all sorts. They asked him about cricket matches he had played in, meeting the new queen, and other things of little note or importance. Freddie, by now, had forgotten I even existed. He was in his own little world being worshipped, and he loved it. I slithered over to a table in the corner of the room as the spectacle continued. I watched with fascination at the scene before me, when a voice from nearby broke my daydream. "Can I buy you a drink, miss?"

I looked to see where it came from. The voice came from a soldier sitting at the next table. He was no ordinary soldier however, he was an American soldier. He was a Yank as my pappy would say. My dear old dad always warned me to stay away from them. Pappy would say that they only had one thing on their minds and that was to get a pretty British girl to drop her knickers for them. He said other than helping save England from Hitler, he had no use for them at all.

"What would you like?" he asked.

"To go home," I said sarcastically.

He didn't understand my meaning, until I pointed to Freddie, still surrounded by adoring fans. It's then that I shared with the American that Freddie was my date for the evening.

"Who is he? He sure seems popular," the soldier commented.

I told the soldier about Freddie, who he was, and the rest.

"Oh, I don't really know anything about cricket. It's something like baseball, I suppose," the Yank responded.

"Sherry," I said without explanation.

"Oh, is that your name?" he asked.

"No. No," I said. "You wanted to buy me a drink. I think I am in the mood for a glass of sherry."

The soldier laughed at his confusion. I giggled a bit myself. Then he got the attention of the bartender and placed his order for both of us. Next, without hesitation, he asked me what my real name was. I told him, and we shared a couple of drinks and lots of laughs, mostly at Freddie's expense. The young soldier next asked me if I would like to dance, with a caveat. "Unless you think your date over there would mind."

"Right now," I said, "I believe my date doesn't remember I'm alive, so why not."

That was all it took. The Yank and I headed to the dancefloor where we cut the rug. He was a good dancer, even better than Max. I was finally having a lovely time when Freddie happened to spot us and somehow extricate himself from his adoring fans long enough to make it over to where we were.

"Hey, mate! What do you think you're up to then, making time with my lady?!" Freddie bellowed at the soldier.

The American soldier I was dancing with unexpectedly didn't stand his ground as I had hoped. He did the opposite of what most Englishmen would do. Instead of defending my honor, he apologized for stepping on Freddie's toes. He started to walk away when I stopped him and then turned my wrath toward Freddie. "Wait a bloody moment!" I spit out at the top of my lungs. "I am not your lady, Freddie! And since we came to the club, I haven't even been your date!"

"What are you going on about?" Freddie said, he actually seemed to have no idea how he had been ignoring me since we got there.

I had, had enough, I just told him to bugger off and go back to his fan club. I was done for the evening. I was leaving.

Instead of doing the gentlemanly thing and offering to at least drive me home, Freddie told me to bugger off back. "If that's the way you are then good riddance to you. Just remember, missy, that you missed out on being with Freddie Truvail, being Freddie's girl!"

I yelled back that I would never forget how close I came to that and how I dodged the biggest bleeding bullet of my life. With that snarky reply, I walked away and left the club.

"Wait a second!" the Yank yelled in my direction.

I stopped in the middle of the street that I was crossing and looked back to see what he wanted.

"Let me walk you home," he suggested.

"Why should I?" I barked back, still smarting from what he didn't do back in the club.

He didn't seem to understand my ire with him.

"You didn't even stand up for me in there!" I told him.

"I didn't want to get between you and your date. I was just being respectful, you know. I'm sorry."

I looked at him and his pathetic countenance. It started to rain out of nowhere, which it often does in England. I hadn't planned for such a thing and didn't even bother to bring an umbrella with me that night.

"They've got free umbrellas back in the club for just such occasions," he shared with me.

"What are you on about, free umbrellas? Are you talking about the ones that people take in with them and hang next to their coats?" I responded with a chuckle.

With a sly grin, he answered, "Oh, they won't miss one, now will they?"

I started to laugh at his brazenness. "I guess not," I replied.

The rain really began to come down hard. We were both suddenly getting soaking wet.

———◆ ·———

"Do me the honor and let me walk you home?" he asked me.

I was tired so I offered little resistance to his idea. He certainly had a different kind of charm about him, and I was getting drenched.

I let him walk me under that stolen umbrella to the top of my street and no farther. The last thing I wanted tonight was my pappy seeing me come home with a Yank. Having to break the news that things didn't go well with Freddie would be difficult enough. I thanked my escort for all he did and praised his dancing abilities. He thanked me for a wonderful time and praised me as well. He wondered if he could see me again, possibly.

"If we meet at one of the clubs, I will dance with you." That's all I would promise.

He then asked me if I would be going out tomorrow. I told him probably to a pub for a drink after work, that's about it. He said boldly he would see me tomorrow night.

"How will you know which pub? I didn't tell you which one."

And then with a twinkle in his eyes, he proclaimed, "It doesn't matter. I'll search them all till I find the right one."

He started to walk away. I shouted out to him. "I don't even know your name!"

"It's Albert, Albert Adams," he answered. "And I'll see you tomorrow."

Then he disappeared into the night. Now I had to gather myself to face my old pap. I knew that pappy and mum would be waiting for me when I got home. And I knew that I had just shattered all their hopes and dreams by not becoming the future Mrs. Freddie Truvail. I feverishly devised a story as I put the house key into the lock of the front door and prepared to face the music. It was going to be a long, long, night.

Andrew Scott Bassett

CHAPTER 5

Just as he promised, Albert did indeed find me, two nights later. I have to admit, I was hoping he would. For the next four months, we spent every free moment together, and I was having a wonderful time. He was a gentleman in every way, and a kind, introspective person. We would often hold hands while sitting in the park for hours, talking about whatever came to our minds. While I'm not sure I had the same passionate feelings for Albert that I once held for Max, we did have more fun. Albert had a dry sense of humor and a quick wit. He was educating me about life in America, and I was teaching him the ways of the English. Both countries may have spoken the same language, more or less, but there were still many differences between the two.

Albert was also a romantic, and that too was good for me. I was always too pragmatic and too much of a realist. I protected myself by having a hard-boiled edge to my personality. Albert was different. He showed me his vulnerable side and let me know he wasn't embarrassed as most men were at the time when they displayed their feelings. He began to bring out a softer side of me, and I needed that. One night we were alone, which was rare considering he was living on base outside of the city, while I still lived at home with my mum and dad. Sheila Saunders and her brand-new husband Eddie asked if I could house sit for them while they were away for the weekend. I didn't hesitate to say yes. Any chance to get out of Pappy and Mum's for the weekend was a welcomed treat. Albert came by to see me. I hadn't given much thought to the fact that we would be alone and with a bed nearby. After he got there, we both began to consider the tempting opportunity that had befallen us. A quick peck on the cheek by Albert while we sat on the sofa in the living room, quickly became much more, and soon we were both wanting and desiring the same thing. Breathing heavily, and with both our hearts racing, Albert pulled his mouth off of mine long enough to ask me "'the question.'" "What do you think?"

His eyes glanced for a moment toward the bedroom, only a few feet away from us. I have to admit at that moment, I was ready, more than ready to make the short journey back there. But then my pappy's words began ringing in my mind. And I knew if something happened and I got pregnant by a Yank of all things, my parents might never forgive me. With that, I grabbed Albert's hands in mine and put on the brakes to what both of us were feeling at that moment. "I want to, I really do. But I just can't," I told him, hoping he wouldn't suddenly hate me.

"Why not, Rosey, is it something I've done wrong?"

"No, of course not," I whispered back. "I just can't. My father would kill me if…you know."

Albert considered what I just said and then realized what I was trying to tell him.

"Let's get married then," he threw out there into the air, without hesitation.

I didn't know what to say. I was stunned that he'd made such a statement. No one had ever wanted to marry me before. I was thrilled beyond measure and at the same time scared as hell at the prospect of being a wife.

"You want me to marry you?" I asked, making sure I heard him right the first time.

"Yes, I do," he answered with force and determination.

Out of nowhere, the idea popped into my head that maybe this was just Albert's way of getting me to go to bed with him. He was a Yank after all, and Pappy had always said to me that they only had one thing on their minds. I quickly assured him that if this was a trick to get me to sleep with him, it wasn't going to work. But Albert insisted it wasn't, not in the least, and then he really threw me for a loop.

"No, I won't do that to you, Rosey. Your morals are one of the things that I love about you. Besides, the best things in life are worth waiting for."

That garnered him a slow, passionate kiss. That showed me he really did care about me, possibly even loved me. Mind you, there was however one other problem, and this problem was a big one. He was still a Yank, and my parents were still my parents. Of course, I had never introduced him to my dad and mum. I never dreamed that this relationship with Albert would become what it has. But now there was no way around it. If we were to be married, Albert would have to meet Pappy and Mum. I was a prisoner to my deep thoughts while considering all this. I guess in all this soul searching, I began to ignore Albert. He suddenly interrupted my daydreaming. "You know you haven't really answered me yet."

That's right, I hadn't. In all the hoopla I had forgotten to do that, at least officially. Once again, I asked him if he was sure about all this. We had only known each other for four months so....

He cut me off and promised me he was. "When it's the right person, it doesn't take long to know if you want to be with them for the rest of your life."

I rewarded him with another snog, for such a good answer. Then Albert once again demanded my reply to his important question.

"Yes…I do want to marry you, but…"

"But what?" Albert challenged. He was surprised and quick to cover his feelings of disappointment.

At that point, I took his hands in mine a second time and explained my hesitation.

"Then it's about time you introduce me to your folks," Albert responded defiantly.

I told him that it wasn't that simple. I shared with him about their distrust of Americans, especially Americans in the military.

"You set the date and time, and I will come to your house and meet them. Everything is going to be fine, Rosey. By the end of the evening, your father will love me and your mother too," he declared to me, exuding quite the confidence in himself.

To help his cause, Albert inquired about what kinds of things my father and mother enjoyed. He thought maybe candies, flowers, things of that sort. I shared with him my pappy's love for sports of almost any kind but particularly boxing. We went on to talk for hours that night, and mostly about my pap and mum. I didn't even think to bring up the massively huge elephant in the room, you know, where we would live after we got married. Of course, that would only be something to fret about, if…Albert could convince my mum and dad that he was worthy of my hand in marriage. It was a large "'if'" indeed, and we would soon find out if Albert was as much of a charmer as he fancied himself to be. I still wanted, and I suppose even needed, my pappy and mum's blessing before I could plan a future with Albert.

He promised me he would get it. I hoped and prayed he was right.

———◆·———

A FORTNIGHT LATER, AND AFTER MUCH BEGGING AND pleading, Pap and Mum gave in and agreed to meet Albert. The afternoon he came over I was a nervous wreck. My mum put her best foot forward and made her famous roast beef and Yorkshire pudding. I took this as a sign that she at least was attempting to meet me halfway. Mum especially wasn't thrilled when it came to the thought of her daughter dating an American. Pappy hadn't really said much about it to me. He was unusually quiet and serious. He seemed to be dreading the decision to have Albert over for dinner. Then it was time. A knock on the front door had me running down the stairs to greet Albert. He quickly took his hat off when he entered our home. He wisely resisted the urge to greet me with a kiss. I had already warned him about any shows of affection in front of my parents. Pappy and Mum stayed in the back of the house, toward the kitchen. They didn't immediately come forward to make Albert's acquaintance. So, Albert boldly walked toward them. He reached his hand out to my pap. Pappy flashed an uncomfortable smile at him at first but then did indeed shake Albert's hand. Albert next smiled warmly at Mum and without hesitation, moved closer to give her a quick hug. Mum blushed a bit at Albert's actions. Albert mentioned how delectable the aroma coming from the kitchen was. Mum told him it was the roast beef and Yorkshire pudding. He charmingly shared with Mum how he had always wanted to try the dish. Mum couldn't believe her ears that someone could possibly have never had roast beef and Yorkshire pudding before in their life. Albert also made sure to dote on my little sister, Sheila, enough to win her approval. Sheila now a teenager lapped up all the compliments that the handsome Albert sent her way. She especially liked the one about her looking much older than her age. It was a promising start to the meet and greet, which only got better once everyone sat down for the meal. Albert, having done his homework about my father and his love of sports, especially boxing, thrilled Pappy with stories of the many fights he had seen firsthand in New York City. My pap quickly began to warm up to Albert's company and enjoyed his knowledge of boxers and the like. I could tell Mum was enjoying his company as well. Sheila thought he was cute and acted mesmerized by him. She sat at the dinner table with her head cocked on her fist, glued to every word that Albert uttered.

After supper, Pappy and Albert shared some glasses of brandy in the living room while old Pap started up a fire. The boxing discussions continued. By now Pappy was enjoying himself so much that I think he had completely forgotten about Albert being a Yank. Albert was just another bloke who shared pappy's love for sports. Mum cornered me in the kitchen as we were cleaning up the dinner mess. "I must say, Rosey," she started with. "He's quite the personable young man."

"Not bad for a Yank," I remarked, taking a small jab at her and Pappy's bigotry.

She smiled in a hollow way. I don't think she really understood the meaning behind my words. She told me how nice it was for Pappy to have someone to talk to like this. "Your Pap is having such a jolly good time with him."

I agreed. Pap looked lit up inside. He was enjoying himself so much.

Pappy later patted Albert on the shoulder as they were saying their goodbyes. Albert promised to purchase tickets at the local sports club for some boxing matches that were to be held there in a few weeks. Pap insisted that he didn't need to do such a thing, but Albert insisted just as much that he wanted to. In the end, Pap happily relented and agreed to go with him. Albert made sure to hug Mum one more time, and even Sheila on his way out. Afterward, I walked him to the corner of the street. Out of earshot of Pappy and Mum, I told Albert how incredible he had been tonight.

"I told you, Rosey, I would win them over, didn't I?"

"You certainly did, Mr. Adams, and you certainly didn't lie about that. You had my pap and mum eating out of your hand by the end of the night," I confessed.

"Well, I was just happy to keep your father talking about sports and the fights. I figured as long as we're talking about that, we're not talking about if I'm going to be taking their daughter away from them," Albert said, only half-seriously.

In the last few weeks since he basically proposed to me, I had not once, as hard as it is to believe, really considered where we would live. Albert and I had not discussed it as of yet. And now this was the first time Albert had shown his hand on the subject. His words clearly told me he was planning on taking me away from England and back to his country, America. It dawned on me with the weight of an anvil landing on my head that this was something we had to discuss and come to an agreement on very soon. I wouldn't be able to marry Albert without having a clear understanding of this subject first. I thought about broaching the topic right then and there, but I knew that both of us, and especially Albert, were quite exhausted from the events of the evening. Instead,

I gave him a tender smooch and thanked him again for such a delightful night.

When I went back inside, Pappy and Mum were sitting, listening to the radio in the living room. Mum was knitting, and Pap was still working on his glass of brandy. "Rosey dear, he's a real nice chap, for a Yank." My old pap uttered between sips.

I agreed and was glad that he and Albert had gotten along so well. I then excused myself to go upstairs and turn in early. I was tired from the whole day and the pressures that came with it. When I got into the bedroom and closed the door, I could still hear Mum and Pap discussing the night. Mum echoed Pappy's thoughts about Albert. But then I heard my pap say something I'll never forget. He said after what I think was another sip of brandy and a long pause, "I think we just lost our daughter to America, Ann."

Albert did indeed take my pappy to the fights. They actually went several times over the next few weeks. Pap even began to forget about Albert being a Yank. Instead, he thought of him as just a proper young man who knew how to treat his girlfriend's parents with the kind of respect that you seldom saw displayed anymore. It warmed the cockles of my heart to see the two of them getting along so fabulously. Mum had taken to Albert as well. She would tell me sometimes when we were alone how much she wished she could find real character flaws in him, so as to talk me into not carrying on with him anymore. Mum would say that he was going to take me away to America with him and then they would hardly ever see me again. And because of that, she wished Albert wasn't such a thoroughly delightful young chap. I, of course, would assure my mother that no matter what happens, they would never be rid of me. I would see her and Pap every chance I got. Nothing would ever keep me from my family in England, not even America itself. That would bring some comfort to Mum, right before she would say something to the effect that things change over time, ducky. "What you are saying now, my dear Rosey is all good and well, but no one knows what the future holds, except God almighty."

———————◆———————

ALBERT PROPOSED TO ME ON THE GRASS OF ONE OF Northampton's most beautiful flower gardens located in Abington Park. He sweetly and gently placed an engagement ring with a small diamond onto my finger. Now that it was official, all we had to do was have our serious talk about where we would reside. Albert shared at that moment, why it was so important he proposed now. "I got the news from my c.o., Rosey, I'm being sent back to the States next month. I'll be getting stationed somewhere in the U.S. after I get back home."

I congratulated him and silly me, for a second, I thought his popping the question was his way of keeping me from marrying someone else while he was back in America. I soon found out that wasn't Albert's plan at all. "I want to marry you before I leave. I want to take you back to the States with me, as my wife."

Albert, I think, expected me to jump into his arms and kiss him with delight. But I was taken aback by the whole idea. I would have to leave my family, my pappy, all of them, even my mates.

"You're not excited, Rosey?" he questioned, seeing my reaction.

Still debating in my mind so many things, I cleared my thoughts like fog in the morning to embrace his question so as to not hurt his feelings. "Yes, of course, Albert!"

"Are you sure? You don't seem, very excited, to me." he came back with.

I again told him I truly was. I said it was one of the most wonderful moments of my life to be asked by him to be his wife. Still, I honestly told him that the idea of leaving my family and traveling so far from home would be very hard for me indeed.

"Well, it's not that far, Rosey, but I understand your concern. Maybe I was just thinking of myself too much. Maybe, darling, we should wait on the engagement and the wedding until later."

Wait on the engagement! Wait on the wedding! These statements were ringing in my ears. I knew what they both meant. I knew if Albert went back to America, just as Max had left for Germany, I would likely never see him again. He would meet some young American girl and forget all about me. If that happened to me, it would be like all this with him never existed. No, that wouldn't do. That wouldn't do at all. I took Albert's hands and held them against my heart. I looked into his big brown eyes that sparkled like the stars in the sky at night and told him, "I want to be your wife, and I want to go to America with you. I love you, Albert."

He smiled. It was as sincere a smile as I had seen in my young life. He took me in his arms and squeezed me tight. After we pulled away from each other, I told him we didn't have much time. He asked what I meant.

"Well, silly," I said. "We have to break the news to Pappy and Mum, get their blessing, which I now know they will give, and then plan a quick wedding, an extremely quick wedding."

"Yes, we do, I guess," he replied.

We began to walk back to my home, hand in hand. All the way home my mind was flooded with so many thoughts.

I couldn't believe I would soon be Mrs. Albert Adams and that I would be an American housewife.

It was cold and windy on the day of our wedding. Albert and I decided since we didn't have the time to plan a large wedding, and with all his family in the States, that we would have a quick and simple ceremony at the courthouse in front of a judge. Pappy and Mum were undoubtedly disappointed but understood the time pressures we were under. They were still trying to come to grips with their oldest daughter leaving for America, just as they had feared. With only my pap and mum, and sister, Sheila, and a few other relatives looking on, the judge pronounced us man and wife. There were no sounds of thunder or flashes of electricity; it was all very anti-climactic to be truthful.

Once outside the courthouse, we posed for a photograph that one of my cousins took. The wind was whistling and trying to rip the flowers my mum had given me to hold right from my hands. Pap and Mum, even Sheila, smothered me with love and affection. Albert attempted to shake my father's hand, but old Pap would have none of that. He gave Albert a great big bear hug, right on the steps, outside the courthouse for all to see. With all the hugs and kisses out of the way, Pappy and Mum wished us their best as we departed for our short honeymoon jaunt to Brighton Beach. The weather would not accommodate romantic strolls on the beach, but that was fine with us. After saving myself for the man I loved, and knowing how much Albert was anticipating the consummation of our love, neither of us planned on spending much time outside of our cottage room. The room was in earshot of the ocean. We could hear the waves beating down on the sandy beach. At night, I listened to the tide coming and going as I lay in bed next to my husband, for the first time. How strange it was to say that word and realize that it was now a word I would say often, and probably for the rest of my life.

Hours later, after we had already made love a couple of times, I lay wide awake in bed while Albert sleeps. I was deep in thought considering how much importance had been put on this act I had just completed. Somehow, I thought, it didn't really live up to its hype. Don't get me wrong, I enjoyed it completely, especially the second time when it was more comfortable for me and I knew better what to expect, but still…

Then, with the bedroom dark and only the moon offering bits and bobs of light as it slipped through the blinds on our French doors, and with Albert lying next to me, he reached out and intertwined his fingers in mine. In a hushed tone of voice, he asked me if I was okay. I whispered back, yes.

He then propped himself up on one of his elbows. "Well… what do you think?"

"The dinner was fine," I answered like a cheeky sod, knowing exactly what he was really asking.

He pinched my arm in response. "You know what I mean," he said.

Of course, I did. I told him what I had to, that he was wonderful and that it was all I thought it would be. That brought a large, satisfied grin to his face. I wasn't about to tell him the truth, that the build-up for a lifetime of this event made it a tad disappointing. But then I rationalized this was our first few attempts, so likely it would probably get better in time, as so many things do. Of course, that's if

Andrew Scott Bassett

Albert is proficient in these areas, which I assumed he was. I presently had no real barometer to measure him by, which made it difficult to know for sure. Then again, maybe it was me after all, maybe I was no help to the cause. I had no idea what I was doing and that probably made Albert's job much more difficult than it should have been. Albert once again pulled me toward himself and wrapped his limbs around me. "Let's get some sleep, shall we," he said softly in my ear.

"Whatever you say, Mr. Adams, my husband," I replied, as I squeezed even closer against him.

"Goodnight, Mrs. Adams, my beautiful wife, sleep tight," he whispered back.

We then fell asleep in each other's arms. The warmth of his body next to me almost seemed soothing in a way. I always wondered what it would be like to sleep with a man, and I'm not speaking of sex. I mean to lie next to a man, in his arms, his breath tickling the back of your neck. Now I knew. It would be one of many things in life I was about to become educated on, like it or not.

———◆•◆———

BLIMEY! FINALLY, THE DREADFUL PLANE RIDE WAS almost over as we were now landing in New York City. I could see the Statue of Liberty from our seat's window, although I made sure to be sitting on the middle seat, not the window seat for the flight. I had never flown before this and wasn't anxious to do it again. The U.S. Army was nice enough to let Albert fly home with me on a regular commercial flight, and I was very thankful for that. I don't think I could have made the long flight from London to New York on the white knuckle express, without Albert's hand to squeeze ridiculously hard the entire way.

Once we embarked, we had to wait very little time as Albert's father, Kenneth, was waiting for us near the airport gates.

"Is this the little British Rose you've been speaking of?" he said to me as we met.

I reached out my hand to make his acquaintance, but he instead decided to give me a welcome kiss on my cheek, which took me by surprise. Then he helped us with our bags and began to lead us out of the airport and to the parking area where his truck was. To my surprise, it was an older truck, whose paint had seen better times. I was expecting something with a bit more room to stretch out in, as we were now going to journey up to Albert's family farm, located in Vermont. Albert, for his part, however, seemed completely unsurprised by his father's choice in escorting us. Kenneth threw all our luggage in the back of the truck, which forced me to ask, "What if it rains on the way to Vermont?"

Albert and his father both laughed off my inquiry as if it made no logical sense at all, but to me, it was a very sensible question.

"I have a tarp lying back there. If it starts to rain, Rosey dear, we'll just cover everything up and tie it down," Kenneth promised me, still chuckling at my expense.

Albert then added, "Don't worry, honey, my father has everything under control. This isn't his first trip to the big city."

With that, I just smiled and nodded. Albert directed me into the middle of the truck's seat, squished between his father and him. This was going to be a long trip to the family farm I thought to myself, and in this truck, it would feel long no matter what. Welcome to America, Rosey, I told myself, so far I have to say, it was a bit underwhelming.

CHAPTER 6

Much like the pick-up truck driven by Albert's father, the family farm was not what I expected. I guess I believed it would look like some of the beautiful Southern estates I had seen in American cinema. But this wasn't the home of Scarlet O'Hara. No, this Adam's family farm was an old run-down farmhouse that looked more like something from the *Grapes of Wrath* than *Gone with the W*ind.

"Here she is, the old homestead," Albert exclaimed with pride.

A long dirt road led us up to almost the front door. A large front deck wrapped around the front of the home. Albert's step-mum, Gwyneth, and his own younger sister Geraldine were there waiting to welcome us. The two women quickly gave me a tour of the place. It had an upstairs where all the bedrooms were and the creaky kind of old wooden staircase you see in scary picture shows. While I took the guided tour, Albert and his father put our bags away. In the kitchen area was a large old-fashioned stove. This Gwyneth woman told me she would show me how to use it properly in the coming days. Then to my astonishment, she disclosed that there was no indoor plumbing of any sort. They would get big pots of water from outside and then heat them on the stove. We hadn't made our way to the upstairs and the bedrooms yet, but I couldn't help but ask a stupid question. "So, no toilets then?"

Gwyneth laughed, "No! No! We have a toilet, dear."

"Oh blimey, what a relief then," I said with a snicker.

"It's just outside in the back," Geraldine, Albert's little sister chimed in, to my shock.

"Outside loo?"

"Yes, if you mean bathroom, it's an outhouse," Gwyneth responded. "You will get used to it, dear."

When Albert and his father ventured into the room a few seconds later, I grabbed Albert's arm and asked if it would be possible to have a quick word with him.

"What is it?" he asked me from the living room, with his family still in the kitchen.

I tried my best to help him understand my concerns. "I'm not one to complain, Albert, and I truly love your family to this point, but how long, may I ask, are we going to be staying here?"

"A few weeks, Rosey, maybe a month until I'm stationed at the new base, why?"

As gently as possible, I tried to explain without looking like an ingrate or acting like I'm some muckety-muck. "No indoor plumbing, the toilets outside, this just is a bit much for me, Albert."

"Oh, I know, it's a little different than what you are used to. But you'll get used to it, believe me," Albert promised confidently.

"I'm not quite positive I want to get used to it," I assured him, just as much.

Albert burst out in laughter and swore that it would only be for a short time. "I'll get my orders very soon, Rosey, and then we'll be gone. I swear, okay."

I told him fine. I'd do my best to keep my chin up and learn to pee outside.

"I can't ask for more than that," Albert replied as we both shared a laugh before he pulled me into his arms for a comforting embrace.

———•———

"That is very nice of you to make up a bath for me, Mr. Adams," I said, with some seduction hiding in my voice.

It was a lot of work since he had to boil large pots of water and then drag them upstairs and pour them into the turn-of-the-century bathtub. He was working very hard to make sure I could have an enjoyable bathing experience. There was, of course, more to it than that. The tub was big enough for two. I knew what he had in mind. But alas, nature was making a house call to me at the same time. "I'm sorry, dear, but I really need to use the lavatory first."

Albert was understanding. He smiled as I took off my bathrobe and began to dress for the trip outside. It was a cold night in Vermont, so I made sure to dress appropriately. I wore so many layers that my thighs didn't recognize each other as I made my way down the stairs and out the backdoor of the house. I just had to navigate the steps off of the back porch and victory was mine. I managed that, and then the next thing I knew I was standing at the door of the outhouse. It was not too bad really, as far as lavatories made up of splintering wood, spider webs, and big dark holes to do your business in go. The worst part really was that it was such a bother to have to tromp all the way out there, each and every time the need would arise.

Nevertheless, after finishing my business I began my journey back. There was no light on that back porch and the clouds had covered up the moon sufficiently so that my visibility was poor at best. I grabbed for the railing to help manage the first step up, but when I put my foot down, the step suddenly moved. Some small creature of the night that I couldn't make out was perched on the step. I didn't see the bleeding thing until it was too late. The next thing I knew I had fallen to the ground, hard. The little sod that caused me my grief then scurried away after doing the deed. Not wanting to be a bother to Albert or his family, a very British trait, I tried on my own to rise to my feet, but instead fell back down in excruciating pain. I had damaged something in my leg, and I couldn't stand. I had no choice now but to scream out for help. It didn't take long for everyone to come to my aid. Albert was the first. He sprinted out the backdoor and to my side. When he heard my screams, he thought that possibly a wild animal had attacked me, and it scared him to death. His father, his step-mum, and sister all followed suit, as they rushed to see what all the hubbub was about. I immediately told Albert what happened.

"That's the last time I'm going to let you go out to the outhouse at night, alone," he declared to me in an upset way.

I started to say that wouldn't be necessary, but Albert would hear nothing of that. He put his foot down before apologizing to me for allowing me to get hurt. I told him it wasn't his fault, but he still felt responsible.

"Son, let's get her into the house and see what's wrong," Albert's father suggested.

Albert listened, and the next thing I knew, they both picked me right up and carried me up the steps and into the house. Carefully, he and his father placed me on the family sofa. Albert's gentleness with me certainly was stirring me up inside. His father pushed him aside for a moment to examine where I was injured. "Does this hurt, Rosey?" Kenneth said as he squeezed my right ankle.

I squealed in pain.

"Looks like a sprained ankle to me," Kenneth remarked. "You'll probably need to stay off of that for about a week."

"A week!" I responded. "But I was going to town tomorrow with Albert!"

"Not now, Rosey," Albert's father insisted. "You'll just have to stay home with us and rest that ankle."

———◆··———

ALBERT INTERRUPTED AND SAID THAT HIS FATHER WAS right. "I'll do all the things I have to do and anything you want me to do, honey. I can pick up whatever you need from the store in town, just let me know what you want."

I reluctantly agreed. I knew they were right. My ankle already felt like it was beginning to swell up. I couldn't believe after a life of playing field hockey and other risky pursuits and never once getting hurt that a small animal on a step in the dark could cause me such sorrow.

"Don't you worry, Son. We'll all take good care of little Rosey for you until you get home," Albert's dad promised. "Now, why don't you help her get upstairs and into bed. Oh, umm… I would hold off on any marital hi-jinks until that ankle heals if I was you."

Albert and I shared embarrassing glances. Americans, I would soon find, were much more open about talking about such matters than Brits. What Albert's father had just said in jest, my dad and mum would never have said in a million years.

Nonetheless, Albert did as his father wished, and he carried me up to our bedroom. There he gently laid me on our bed. For the rest of the night, he held me in his arms as if protecting me from all the dangers of this new world I had just landed in. I never felt safer in my whole life.

THE NEXT MORNING, WITH ALBERT ALREADY OUT OF THE house and meeting with his Army superiors somewhere in Burlington, I managed with the help of some old rickety wood crutches to get myself downstairs. Awaiting me in the kitchen was Albert's father. He apologized for not having hot tea available for my enjoyment. He said that no one in the house really drank it. "We're a black coffee bunch around here," he explained.

He then invited me to sit down with him at the large farmhouse-style kitchen table that dominated the room. He poured me my coffee and then was nice enough to bring me milk and sugar to put in it. "I don't know how you can drink it that way. It's like drinking a milkshake or something with all that in it," he said with a hearty laugh.

I shared with him that, that's just the way of the English. We like our tea and coffee sweet and our steering wheels on the opposite side of our cars. That brought an even heartier laugh from him.

"Yes, the British are a lot different from us, I suppose," he added. "I guess your people probably look at us Americans and wonder what the hell we're up to over here."

I didn't quite know how to respond to that. Instead of adding my two cents, I just sipped some of the strongest coffee I had ever tasted. Honestly, I don't think I ever gave it much thought. That is what Americans are all about. Mostly, the English just assume things are like what they see in the cinema. "We do love our American cowboy pictures," I shared.

"John Wayne's popular over there?" Kenneth assumed.

"Yes, of course," I answered. "But the singing cowboys

Andrew Scott Bassett

like Roy Rogers and Gene Autry have always been very popular with my family."

He then offered me some toast with butter and jam. I gladly accepted it. I asked where Gwyneth and Geraldine were, and he told me that his wife went to town to do whatever it is that she does, while Geraldine was attending her high school.

"She seems like a lovely girl," I remarked. I said nothing about his wife who I had an instant dislike for.

"She is," he responded. "And she has already taken a shine to you."

"Well, isn't that sweet," I replied. I was pleasantly surprised to hear that in such a short time of knowing her that Albert's younger sister was fond of me.

"Albert tells me that you and your family had a very difficult go of it during the war."

"Yes, I suppose, most Brits did," I said.

"Did you lose any family?"

"Yes, my favorite uncle, George. He went missing in North Africa," I shared, still choking up a bit from the mere thought of his loss.

"Terrible thing that war," Albert's father then stated. "It's a funny thing, though. I always thought Hitler had some right ideas, you know."

Right ideas... I thought to myself. Right ideas, what bloody ideas of Adolph Hitler could have ever been right.

He served me my toast as he continued his point. "You know, as pertaining to the colored's and the Jews."

I could hardly believe my ears. I was flabbergasted by what he just said and had no words.

"Not that I condone the Jew camps, and all that of course."

Of course, I thought to myself, how could you or anyone do that.

"I just think that Hitler understood the danger to his country that too much power and money in the hands of the Jews, and even the colored's, could mean, I'm sure you've seen the same in England," he said shockingly.

"I can't say I have," was all that I could muster.

He went on in great detail how in America that the Jews run many of the financial institutions and control Hollywood. "Where there's money, there's usually Jews," he stated with a disturbing chuckle.

I smiled respectfully and felt ashamed of that. I wanted to argue with him but was still in a state of shock from his words. I couldn't believe a man so warm and seemingly kind-hearted, could be so full of hatred and bigotry.

"And the coloreds… they are really starting to get uppity everywhere. The Southern states have done the best job so far of keeping them in check, but still, they're forgetting their place," Kenneth went on to say to my dismay.

Finally, I came up with some kind of response. "I thought the Civil War was over."

Kenneth looked at me with a strange expression on his face. He seemed to be trying to comprehend what I meant.

"I guess it is over, Rosey. At least the part where whites fight whites, and states fight against other states, that part is surely over."

At that moment, I told him I didn't understand, and I didn't.

He went on to clarify. "Now the battle in the country is between the whites and the coloreds directly. They want to take over everything."

"I always thought they just wanted to live as anyone else would and be free to do that," I said, speaking up.

Kenneth smiled. It was at that part of the discussion that he knew that I didn't share his abhorrent ideas. "Well, anyways, Rosey, if you and Albert get stationed in the South, you'll see better what I mean."

I didn't answer that. I smiled and kept what I really wanted to say to myself. Kenneth suddenly announced that he had to get outside and feed some of his animals. He had many.

After he left, I sat there still in shock from the entire conversation. My pappy and mum had always taught me not to judge anyone from the outside. The racist and anti-Semitic words from Albert's father were unique to me. I had come across in my life in England people who didn't care for both Jewish people and black people, but not to this extent. I had always been raised to stand up for the ones that are being picked on and bullied. Being they're the minority in England, I had always been especially kind to the blacks I would come across. I had known several, to my shame not closely, but well enough to enjoy their company. Now, as I sat there finishing my toast and coffee, I only hoped that my Albert hadn't inherited from his father some of his hate-filled beliefs.

<hr />

I TRIED MY BEST TO PUT MY CONVERSATION WITH Albert's father out of my mind as much as I could. I thought about bringing up the subject with Albert, but for some reason, I didn't. I guess maybe I was afraid of what I might find. The next few weeks flew by as Albert and I waited to find out his next assignment. He was about to be promoted to staff sergeant. He said it would bring more pay and more responsibility, and he was ready for both. I, for one, took the two weeks to get used to living on the Adam's farm. I even somehow adjusted to outdoor plumbing, as best as one could. The outhouse trips in the middle of the night still were a bloody pain in the bum. Albert would always accompany me back and forth as he promised. My ankle was just getting back to normal, and he didn't want any more risks to my life and limb to take place just because I needed to take a bleeding pee.

I also took advantage of my downtime to write letters to Pap and Mum, my little sister, and even my good friend Sheila Saunders. Sheila was still infatuated with everything American. She had the silly idea that America was just like it seemed in the picture shows. She adored the pomp and glamorous lives that so many Yanks seemed to live. I shared with her how little of that I had seen in my first few weeks here, but maybe I would, I told her, when we got to Albert's new assignment. I hoped for some Army base in California, close to Hollywood. I, of course, had no idea how big America was. Compared to the United States, England is just a blip on the map. I didn't realize that at the time. To my old pap and mum, I wrote wonderful, uplifting letters about how marvelous everything was going with Albert and with my time in the States. I exaggerated much of it, but certainly didn't want Pap and Mum worried about me for a second. I knew it was already hard enough for them to be without me and to have me so far away from them. I made sure my letters home would bring them much-needed comfort.

———— ◆ ————

ONE NIGHT AS WE ALL SAT AT THE DINNER TABLE, ALBERT cut off whatever his father was rambling on about and announced that he had big news.

Andrew Scott Bassett

"Well, what is it, son?" his father asked him.

I hoped it was news of his next assignment.

Albert looked directly at me. He knew how important this was for both of us. I have to admit it was exciting as I waited with bated breath. Please let it be California or at least someplace near the ocean. As a Brit, born and raised on an island, if I didn't get to visit the beach ever so often, I would begin to feel like my skin had broken out and I would develop a sort of closed-in feeling about things. All of that is a bit of an exaggeration, of course, but I did miss the sea. The sea was in my blood, as my old pap would say.

Albert raised his water glass in the air as if toasting something. No one else at the table followed suit, but we did politely wait for his big announcement. "I got my orders today!"

"Well then, tell us!" his father demanded. "Where are you and Rosey going to be stationed?"

Albert paused for dramatic effect and grinned at me. I shook my head at his actions and asked him to end the suspense. With that, he relented. "I'm going to be stationed, well Rosey, we're going to be stationed at Fort Benning, in Georgia."

"Going to be living in the South, are you?" Albert's dad observed as he glanced in my direction.

"So, what do you think, honey?" Albert turned and asked me.

I told him I didn't know much about the South, except from what I'd seen in movies like 'Gone with the Wind'. Albert and his family poked fun at my comment. "I'm sure it's probably much different from that now," Albert stated in a cheeky manner.

Kenneth then promoted the idea that I was about to see firsthand what he and I had talked about the other day at the kitchen table. When Albert asked him what that was, Kenneth said it was nothing important, just some differences between the States and England.

I kept quiet and said nothing. Now was not the time or place for such discussions. I just told Albert I was very happy, very happy indeed.

Albert's dad officially made a toast of his own, wishing us all the best. Gwyneth and Geraldine joined in and raised their glasses in unison. I smiled at Albert and held his hand under the table. I didn't know much about Georgia, but I did know I was ready to be alone with my husband, just the two of us. I was confident that wherever that would happen, it would be wonderful. My life with Albert was now about to really begin.

———————◆··———————

Lori knocks softly on Danny's bedroom door. He mumbles something that sounds like it's okay for her to enter. He's reading from his mother's pages when she interrupts him with some news. "The funeral is all set pretty much except for a few details. So Saturday is a go, Danny."

He hardly responds, just keeps on reading.

"How's your book coming? You've been like barricaded in this room for the last few days," she comments.

Her truth succeeds in getting him to stop what he's doing and properly acknowledge his sister. "Oh yeah, it's coming along okay."

"Good, to me it seems like you've been spending more time reading Mom's stuff than working on your book," Lori remarks, slightly sarcastically.

"Don't worry about it," Danny answers.

Lori shrugs her shoulders at his attitude.

Danny quickly changes the subject not to hide anything, but because of how enthralled he has become by his mother's writing. "Did you know Mom witnessed a lot of racism when she first got here?"

"I remember her saying a little bit about that," Lori recalls.

"Yeah, it's kind of crazy how it was back then," Danny observes.

Lori wonders what he thinks of their mother's story, disclosing that she has never read any of it.

Danny reveals first and foremost that he is surprised by how good a writer their mother was.

"Maybe that's where you get it from," his sister tosses into the air for his consideration.

"Maybe so," he replies.

"Any more revelations from Mom's life that I should know about?" She asks.

"I don't know. There are probably going to be a few more. I'll let you know. But, I will tell you one thing, so far her story has been pretty darn interesting," he admits.

Danny's cell phone goes off. He looks to see who it is and then declines to answer it.

"Nobody important?" Lori assumes.

"Not so much, anymore," Danny tells her.

He watches as Julia's name, lights up his cell phone. Lori sees it too. She can't help but comment. "Are you sure you don't want to take that call?"

He shakes his head. "I don't know, alright?"

This time it's Lori's turn to shake her head but not without an accompanying comment. "I hope you know what you are doing, Danny, because as I'm finding out loneliness is all it's cracked up to be."

Danny watches as Lori closes his bedroom door and leaves him to get back to his writing, reading, or whatever the case may be.

CHAPTER 7

In no time at all, we were getting settled in at Fort Benning. I was now what they called a base wife, doing my best to keep up an adequate, two-bedroom home. Our place sat in a row of houses that all looked identical. I hadn't yet had a chance to get out and see the city of Columbus the nearest city from Fort Benning. Nor had I had the pleasure of meeting any other base wives to this point. I was looking forward to my first shopping trip in the city, so far it had just been quick trips to the base PX. Albert had little time for me since we got here. He was busy getting his feet wet, training the new recruits who came flooding into the base on a regular interval. That morning, as I was finishing up washing some dishes from last night's supper, Albert darted past me in a hurry to get to work.

"Haven't you forgotten something then?" I hollered at him in a cheeky way, as he was making his way out the door.

He looked at me with no idea at all what I was speaking of.

"You know, we haven't been married long enough for you to already be taking me for granted," I said in a forward manner to get his attention.

"What, Rosey, I'm sorry," he stopped to say, still having no idea what I was going on about.

I pointed to my lips. He still was confused. "You have to pay the toll, dear, before I will let you leave."

Then he suddenly realized what I was getting at. He finally gave me a kiss. Not his best effort, mind you, but for a man in a great hurry, it would do.

"I'm sorry, Rosey, I'm almost late. You have fun if you make it to town today. There's a large river near here where we could do some boating. We'll rent a boat. Let's plan on that on my next day off," Albert told me as he ran out the door.

I was finding that the life of a base wife, at least so far, was a lonely one.

After taking a splendid bubble bath, I was now deciding on my outfit for my shopping endeavor in Columbus. I had narrowed it down to two possibilities when a knock at my front door stole my attention. I threw on my bathrobe to answer the door. It was officially my first visitor, and I was anxious to see who it was. When I opened it, I was greeted by three well-dressed, smiling, young women. One of them reached out her hand to me. "You must be Rosey. We have heard so much about you," she said to me.

She told me that her name was Vivian and that with her were Dolores and Margaret. They were all base wives and had taken it upon themselves to welcome the newbies, as they called them. The nickname was given to the newest base wives, the ones who had just arrived. Vivian told me they were particularly excited to meet me. I was flattered but not completely sure why the interest. But, realizing I was being quite rude, not to mention that I was also excited to make their acquaintance, I invited them in. I told them to please make themselves comfortable in the living room, as I rushed to my bedroom to get dressed. When I came out, the ladies' friendly expressions were there to greet me. I couldn't help but notice how lovely looking they all were and how impeccable their clothes looked on them. "Would any of you like some coffee or perhaps tea?" I asked.

Vivian who seemed the leader of the trio laughed at my gracious offer.

"What is so humorous?" I inquired.

Vivian still giggling, explained. "It's just wonderful that a person like yourself would offer us coffee or tea."

I still didn't comprehend the humor of the situation.

Vivian, seeing my confusion, explained it for my benefit. "No, we just know how important tea is to someone of your heritage, darling. I think that it is delightful that you would offer us coffee as well, so very American of you and all."

I said thank you. I wasn't quite sure what else to say.

"Being that you're from England made us even more excited to meet you, darling. You're the only British wife on the base, that we know of," Vivian continued. "We want you to feel especially welcome, so how about lunch in town, in Columbus?"

"It is important to get away from the base sometimes," Dolores interrupted.

"Especially if one wishes to keep their sanity, it certainly is," Margaret declared, causing the other two women to break out into a hearty case of tee-hees.

I went along with them best as I could. I smiled and nodded as they laughed.

"So, what do you say, dear? Why don't you finish getting your face on and we'll make a morning of it in Columbus, and then have lunch at this delightful restaurant that caters to military wives like ourselves," Vivian proposed.

I accepted, and though I wasn't quite sure about these three, I could certainly use a good time with the girls. It had been quite a while since I had done anything with anyone except Albert. "Give me a moment then?" I asked as I went to put on my face, which sadly I already thought I had on when I answered the door.

I could hear the girls chatting and giggling through the bathroom door as I attempted to better my appearance for their sake. I only hoped their humor wasn't at my expense.

THE LADIES SHOWED ME THE SIGHTS AROUND COLUMBUS. It was nice to get away from the base and experience a change of scenery. We strolled through much of the downtown area that was filled to the brim with dress shops, shoe stores, and cafés. Many businesses had signs in their windows that said "'no coloreds allowed.'" I shook my head at such a sight but said nothing to the other girls. They didn't seem to even take notice of the signs. I guess they were all too common a sight down here.

We ultimately arrived at the restaurant I had heard so much about. This was the place that the girls had spoken so highly of. The base wives were catered to here, like no other eating establishment in Columbus, I was told. After getting to our table, we shared drinks while waiting for our meals to be prepared. The place was packed with mostly ladies, and as Vivian shared with me, mostly base wives.

"So how are you finding the United States so far?" Vivian out of the blue asked me.

"Big and quite different from England," I answered, as it was the first thing to come to my mind.

Margaret then chimed in about England being so small that it would fit into the state of California three times. I told her I hadn't heard that, but it wouldn't surprise me.

"It must be very difficult to be so far from home," Vivian remarked.

"Yes, it is," I replied.

Dolores finally broke into the conversation and asked me how the men in England compared to American men. She commented that the American men must hold up well since I chose to marry one. I chuckled at her words for a moment before giving some thought to them. I hadn't really considered the differences between Albert and other men from England, or even Max from Germany, till that point. "Men are men, I suppose, all the world around."

Vivian chipped in that she most certainly agreed with me.

"What about under the covers, Rosey?" Dolores then asked.

I first blushed at such a question from a person I had just made acquaintance with only a few hours earlier. Vivian scolded her friend for asking me such a thing. Margaret however defended Dolores, offering that it was only normal that they, not having carnal knowledge of anything but American men would have a natural curiosity about such things. Now, I found myself with all the ladies' eyes fixed on me, waiting for my feelings on the topic. "I wish I could speak on the matter, but I can't."

"What do you mean?" Dolores countered.

"Albert is my only one," I explained to their disappointment.

"Really?" Vivian let out with surprise. "So, you stayed a good girl until marriage?"

"I did," I said.

The other ladies looked at me like they had just swallowed something sour. Margaret and Dolores to make me feel accepted, shared that they too waited for their wedding day. Vivian said no comment when asked the same thing.

I had a distaste for the whole subject and began to listen less and less as the other ladies went on to discuss different things. Somewhat bored, I began to take stock of the large dining room where we were seated. I couldn't help but notice the very back corner area. Back in that area of the dining room was a small table with several black ladies sitting at it. They were all dressed well. I asked Vivian if they too were wives from the base. She turned to study them for a moment before saying they were. A solemn look took over her face, as I caught the other ladies at our table passing knowing glances among themselves.

"Do they always put them back in the corner like that?" I questioned.

"Well, they have to put them somewhere, I suppose," Vivian replied sarcastically. "The big-wigs at Fort Benning have told them as much."

I didn't understand what she meant, so I asked Vivian to explain.

"Well, dear, many places here in Columbus cater to base wives, and like it or not they are base wives and Fort Benning doesn't want them singled out, so to speak."

"So, what you are implying is that places like this let them in but herd them into a corner," I observed with a drop of disdain, sprinkled on my words.

"Well, I guess it's the decent thing to do so everyone can be happy," Vivian fired back.

Containing my disgust best as I could, I asked the ladies about the signs we saw downtown, the ones that said "'no coloreds allowed.'" They wondered what I was on about. So, I clarified. "How do those businesses get away with such signs when black soldiers and their wives may wish to frequent their businesses?"

Margaret and Dolores looked at each other with clue-lessness. Neither had an answer to my inquiry.

Vivian, however, did offer a dirty look in my direction. She seemed to not be happy with where I was going with all this. "I don't know for sure, Rosey," she started with, "but I would hasten to guess that such businesses would likely allow coloreds who are self-confident enough to enter and are also members of the military or spouses of those who are. The signs in the windows are probably more intended for those coloreds who are not members of the military."

"Is it me then, or does that seem a bit unfair?" I couldn't help but say in response to Vivian.

A silence suddenly gripped the table at that moment. Vivian and the girls continued to pass aghast looks back and forth among themselves. After a few minutes of this, Margaret broke the ice by saying, "They really were a big help in the Korean conflict, so I've been told."

Dolores and even Vivian nodded in agreement. I saw this as an attempt to pacify my ideas on the subject. By now, I needed a break from the "'lovely'" chit-chat at my table. I asked the ladies where the toilets were located. They pointed to the back of the restaurant near where the black ladies were sitting. I got up and walked that way but stopped as I approached the table with the black base wives. Their con-versation halted when I approached. They seemed almost afraid of what I was about to say.

"Hello, ladies," I started with. "You're from Fort Benning?"

The three of them smiled politely at me and then nodded. I noticed that they looked around at the other patrons in the restaurant. It was as if I had broken a sacred rule, to even talk to them in public. And because of that, these poor women were scared to death of the ramifications of my actions. Nonetheless, I slogged on. "My name is Rosey Adams. My husband just got stationed here at Fort Benning."

They kept smiling at me, not uttering a word back. Nor was there a word being said in the rest of the dining room. I looked back behind me. I could see all the eyes of the people sitting at tables, and even the waiters and waitresses themselves, glaring in my direction. It was as if all those eyes were trying to poke a hole right through me. Even Vivian and the other girls were studying my every action and intention as I conversed openly with the black ladies.

"Well, it's very nice to make your acquaintance," I declared as I reached out my hand in a gesture of respect.

The ladies at the table looked at each other as if trying to decide who if anyone, would shake my outstretched hand. Finally, the lady in the middle of the small table honored my request and shook it. She told me it was nice to make my acquaintance as well. I nodded thankfully and then without looking around, I walked into the back of the restaurant where the toilets were. As I looked for the ladies' loo, I came first to the men's lavatory. Eventually, I did find the ladies' room, and then there was oddly, one more bathroom down the hall. My curiosity got the best of me, and I searched it out. On the door, painted with red paint in a haphazard manner, it said: "for coloreds". The door for this lavatory was slightly open, so I knew it was vacant. I dared to take a peek inside. I was flabbergasted by what I saw. The place was a bloody mess. It looked as if it hadn't been cleaned in a long juncture. The toilet seat was barely still attached to the commode. I wouldn't have let my dog use such a room to relieve itself, yet this establishment believed that these facilities were somehow suitable for human beings. I closed the door in disgust. I found the ladies' room for people of my skin pigmentation to be elegant and spotless in comparison. This discovery of unfairness was utterly disgusting to me.

———•———

THAT NIGHT, AS I AND ALBERT WERE EATING DINNER, I decided to find out for the first time what his ideas on the subject of race, truly were. Part of me was afraid to find out the answer, afraid that I might not like what he has to say. However, my curiosity was greater than my fear, so I began to share the day's events with him. Albert showed no reaction when I spoke of the no-colored signs in windows, or the table in the corner of the restaurant where the black base wives were separated so as to not infect or bother the white-skinned base wives as they enjoyed their meal. No, he just said uh-huh or grunted between swallows, which was supposed to declare to me he was listening. It was quite obvious that my little experiment with Albert wasn't working, so I took more drastic measures. "Albert dear, I am wishing to ask you something to see what you might think."

I finally got his attention as he looked up from his plate.

"I took the opportunity to introduce myself to the three black base wives in the restaurant, and I found them to be quite nice," I began with.

He let out another "uh-huh".

Then I dropped the grenade, so to speak, into the conversation. "I thought I would ask the ladies over for dinner one night this week."

I could see the gray matter mashing behind his eyes. Albert had a grim look come over his face as he addressed my proposal.

"I'm not sure, Rosey, that's such a good idea," he said in almost a whisper as if he didn't want to say the words at all.

When I asked him for his reasons for such a statement, he struggled, even more, to come up with the right words to explain his argument. "It's just that some people…"

I cut him straight off at that and demanded to know what people he was referring to.

"Other soldiers here at the base, soldiers I work with," he fessed up.

"You mean white soldiers." I couldn't help myself now.

"I suppose…okay," he blathered back.

I was finally getting the results of my experiment; unfortunately, they were not the results I was hoping for. They were, nevertheless, what I deep down suspected after my encounter with Albert's father back in Vermont.

"I thought Northerners were supportive of blacks and their right to freedom," I challenged Albert with.

He squirmed in his chair at such a comment aimed directly at him. He demanded what I meant by what I just said. I didn't hold back. I told him exactly what I meant. "I think you're showing some unbecoming things to me right this moment."

"And what is that Rosey, I'd really like to know?" Albert shot back.

So, I told him. "I think you have bias toward, possibly racist views toward black people. I think your father might be the cause of such thoughts."

Albert didn't like it when I pulled his father into the conversation. He told me I didn't know what I was talking about.

"Well, you can easily prove to me I'm wrong by being a splendid host for the ladies and their husbands when they come for dinner this week," I said boldly.

"Their husbands?!" he answered, his voice getting louder and more frustrated.

"Yes, of course, do you think I am going to just invite them over on their own?" I responded sarcastically.

"Rosey, it's not a good idea!" He yelled.

This was probably only the second time I had seen him speak angrily toward me. "You just don't understand how things work, that's all!"

Sadly, I told him, I do. Then in no uncertain terms, I told him to prepare himself for the ladies and their soldier husbands to be coming over this week for dinner.

"I won't be here then!" he assured me.

"Then shame on you!" I said to him, with much zeal.

"You're supposed to care about me! If my colleagues, my friends here at the base see me inviting coloreds over for dinner, at my home… they won't understand!"

I paused to consider his words best as I could, but I found the ideas behind them to not be worthy of any consideration. I responded the only way I felt that I could. "Then shame on you, Albert Adams!"

He shook his head as he went to the closet and grabbed his jacket. "I'm going to the base club. Don't bother waiting up for me," he proclaimed, as he stormed out the front door.

After that, I sat quietly in our living room for the next hour and did nothing but think. I wish that I had seen this side of Albert before we were married. A woman being courted has much power over the man who is in pursuit. But now I was married, for better or for worse. This was certainly the worst so far. I wondered how a man so wonderful in so many ways could also be so bigoted and have such ugly thoughts. I also considered the consequences of disobeying my husband's wishes and going forward with this little dinner of mine. I went back and forth for a bit but then decided that I could never look myself in the mirror if I didn't go through with it.

Maybe, as his father surely wasn't, I could be a good example for Albert. Like it or not, I was going to have this dinner, and Albert was not going to stop me. My pappy always told me when I was growing up that any husband of mine would soon come to the realization that he would have to share the pants in the family with me. Pappy would tell me that I was cut from a different kind of cloth. He would compare me to a wild unbroken horse, not the most flattering comparison I remember thinking at the time. He would further say I was like a horse that a rider was trying to saddle for the first time but quickly realized that they couldn't break enough to do so. Pappy would then say the rider in my case would just have to learn how to enjoy the ride, saddle free. He would say to me that some things aren't meant to be tamed completely, that if they are, they lose too much of their spirit. Pap would kiss me on the forehead and express to me that I was one of those things. I hoped that Albert would see me the same way as my old pap did in time.

Late afternoon the next day, I stormed into the same restaurant as the girls had taken me to the day before. I pushed through the front door of the establishment like the troops at Normandy when they landed. I was single-minded and full of piss and vinegar. I had already staked out the place for more than an hour by sitting on a bench nearby, and then waited for ladies of color to appear, and enter the restaurant. I ignored the maître de' and his request to seat me and instead went straight toward the table in the back corner. There were only two women at the table today and they seemed startled as I approached. As I had the day before, I quickly introduced myself. Then I asked them directly if they were base wives from Fort Benning. After they politely answered yes to my inquiry, I told them that I too was a soldier's wife from the base. Quietly they said it was nice to make my acquaintance. The two women could, as I could, feel the rest of the eyes in that dining room, watching and listening to our every word and action. I asked them what their names were, and they both introduced themselves in as quiet a voice as possible. They were Mabel and Esther, they whispered. I got to my point as quickly as I could as the atmosphere around us became more and more uncomfortable.

"Ladies, I'm sure you're wondering why this strange lady with this equally strange accent is beckoning your table and disturbing your meal."

Both of the women giggled a tad at my opening volley of a statement.

"Well, you see, I am new to the base, my husband and I, and I am looking forward to making the acquaintance of other base wives like yourselves."

The giggling stopped immediately and was soon replaced by a look of bewilderment. I believe they both truly thought I was bonkers at that moment.

"So, I would like to invite you to dinner at my home on base one night this week," I finally got out of my mouth.

The one lady named Mabel wondered if I really wanted to invite them. I assured her that I did. They smiled and nodded, still wearing that bewildered look.

"Is Friday night good for your two? Say about six o'clock, shall we."

They smiled and nodded respectfully, and with that, I handed them a note of paper with the house number for our home on base. I made sure to tell them to bring their husbands. They grinned again. As I was leaving, Mabel spoke up, and not this time in a whisper. "Thank you very much for your kind offer, we really do appreciate it," she said.

I thanked her back, vigorously. "See you Friday then, and cheerio."

The eyes of the room followed me like I wore a spotlight attached to my dress. As I exited the dining establishment, the rest of the patrons in attendance sat there with their mouths hanging wide open from the shock of the spectacle they had just witnessed. It was not every day that a white woman invited two black women over for dinner. This was Georgia in the 1950s, and what I had just done was rarely ever heard of. How I thought Albert and his father would have felt so at home with that room full of bleeding gawkers.

⸻ ◆ ⸻

MY MASCARA WAS RUINED BY MY TEARS. ALBERT AND I had barely spoken for the last two days. He told me, well growled at me, how I had no right to set up this dinner without his permission. When I refused to relent and cancel the entire affair, he boldly announced he would not be home when the two couples came over for dinner. I pleaded with him not to act this way. I went on and on, with tears rolling down my cheeks about the humiliation he would bring me if he chose not to be here. But it was all to no avail, as he now was locked up in our bathroom readying himself to leave for the evening and spend the night, or much of it, at the base's pub with his Army mates.

I re-did my face one last time. I knew that our dinner

guests would be arriving at any moment. "If you're going to leave then, you better bugger off soon," I told him angrily through the bathroom door.

As if timing it perfectly, Albert came out of the bathroom at that instant, and without saying a word, started searching for his car keys. When he finally spotted them, he snatched them up and began to leave. A knock at our front door stopped him in his tracks. I quickly pushed Albert aside and greeted our visitors. Albert tried to make it out through the backdoor by the kitchen and nearly did until Mabel saw him and then spoke to him as she entered the living room with Esther right beside her. "Oh, at least one of our husbands is a man of courage," she uttered toward Albert.

Albert froze at her remarks and did an about-face. "What do you mean?" He replied.

"Oh, it's just that neither of our husbands was brave enough to come tonight, but it is so uplifting to see a man like yourself not afraid to do the right thing," Mabel proclaimed.

I watched with interest to see Albert's next move. He had just been complimented for not being a coward as he was cowardly sneaking out the back door. Suddenly, he raised his chin up, a small smirk now sat on his face. I could see that he enjoyed the flattery he had just received, even if it was undeserved.

"You don't say. What is wrong with those guys?" Albert spoke up and said to our houseguests. "Why don't you two ladies have a seat with my wife, Rosey, here, and I'll whip up a few drinks for us all."

"Oh, that would be so lovely, thank you Sir," Esther replied to his idea.

"It's nothing really." Albert offered back.

The ladies did sit down and so did Albert, to my surprise, after he brought over drinks for us all.

When I had to get up and go into the kitchen to check on our dinner, Albert stayed and continued to chit-chat with Mabel and Esther. He seemed to relish their admiration for him.

During dinner itself, we all sat around the table as Albert questioned the ladies on why their husbands were so afraid to have a simple meal with us. His hypocrisy was nauseating, but I was relieved that the evening was turning out to be so much better than I could have ever imagined.

Eventually, Mabel and Esther both confessed how their husbands were afraid of reprisals from white soldiers at the base, that is, if they came here tonight. Albert listened to their concerns respectfully and thoughtfully. He made me sick.

"I suppose that is still a problem in the Army, even today, all these many years after what Truman did. But I can tell you that I will certainly speak against anything I see untoward soldiers of color at this base," Albert promised to our two dinner guests.

"Thank you so much," Mabel responded as she reached out her hand without thinking and cupped his.

My eyes probably became the size of saucers as I waited for Albert's reaction. He studied that dark-skinned hand holding his tightly. It was probably the first time in his life that he'd felt the touch of a black person. I wasn't sure if he would recoil in horror or learn something new. I was pleasantly and truly surprised, by what followed.

"You're welcome," he stuttered back.

After dinner, I brewed up my special English tea and served it with homemade shortbread cookies that I had baked earlier. Albert in a now, jovial mood, insisted on playing cards if the ladies enjoyed such endeavors. We spent the next two hours playing hearts. We all enjoyed ourselves immensely and had a smashing good time, even Albert.

Mabel and Esther were so thankful for the evening and especially appreciated Albert. They thanked us both the entire time they were saying their goodnights. I shared with them that we must do this again very soon, and this time with their husbands joining them. They were in complete agreement as they offered us one last goodnight.

After they left, I could not contain my thankfulness to Albert for the way he had behaved the entire evening. He had brought me unexpected joy, and I was very indebted to him.

He smiled as he received my compliments with that humble, almost shy, boyish charm of his that was so attractive to me.

"Now, that wasn't so hard, was it?" I asked him.

He looked at me and shrugged his shoulders. He acted like he had no clue what I was on about.

"What I mean is, people are the same, Albert. One's skin tone doesn't affect who they are inside, I don't believe. Everyone's blood is red."

Albert didn't argue. But he did share that he would likely still receive much grief from other white soldiers, and possibly commanding officers at the base for the events of tonight.

I was about to scoff at such talk, but I could see he was completely serious on the matter.

"Don't expect a warm welcome from other base wives either, Rosey," he told me.

"The white ones you mean?" I replied.

"Yeah, when the news gets out about our little dinner, we won't be the most popular people or likely asked to go to many social events, other than the ones we are having," Albert stated, matter-of-factly.

I didn't want to believe him. I didn't want to accept that such mean-spirited ideas still had such a foothold, but I knew sadly that he was right. I couldn't help but wonder why he had made such an abrupt about-face in such a short time. I challenged him to explain himself. He thought about it intently for a moment and then did his best to answer. "I just looked at the two of them when they first came in," Albert responded, referring to Mabel and Esther. "They looked so scared in the eyes; you know. It reminded me of some of the animals back at the family farm right before we had to put them down. They would look at you like they knew what you were about to do with them. You could see the terror in their eyes. I always hated that, I hated it so much." I didn't know how to answer that.

He continued. "Then they came in, Mabel and Esther, and they were so nice you know. They were nice and scared at the same time. They were nice to us and scared of us at the same time. I didn't want them to feel that way."

I suddenly felt a closeness to him I hadn't felt lately. I invaded his space and wrapped my arms around his waist. "We're doing the right thing, love."

He nodded and pulled me closer. We spent the rest of the night in each other's arms, making love and being in love. I felt like nothing could ever separate us again.

CHAPTER 8

The next few weeks were pure bliss. Albert and I were absolutely giddy in love again. It was like our honeymoon all over. Mabel and Esther came over for dinner a couple more times and even coaxed their husbands to join them. You could see how reluctant the two guys were when they first entered our home, but I was so proud of Albert for making them feel comfortable. He had shared with me how he was being ridiculed and worse by other white soldiers at the base after the word of our 'dinners', came out. But to his credit, Albert kept a stiff upper lip and told the other soldiers that the times were changing and everyone had to change with them. He was growing so much as a person right before my eyes. In one exchange with another white soldier on base, Albert fought off taunting and slurs by simply expressing that if a black man is willing to fight and possibly die beside him in war, the least he could do is treat him with due respect and a warm handshake. The words seemed to fall on deaf ears, but who really knows where seeds are planted? If nothing else strong roots were growing inside Albert, and I was so thankful for that. His father's unsavory ideas were losing power over him by the day.

RECENTLY, I HAD GOTTEN VERY FAMILIAR WITH COLUMbus, the large, nearby city. I'd been shopping with Mabel and Esther a few times and was starting to know my way around, a bit better. Vivian and the other girls really didn't have anything to do with me now. I tried on several occasions to start up a chat with them, but they would have nothing of it. They snubbed me and left me standing in the PX feeling awkward and quite silly. Like Albert now, but to a much lesser extent, my beliefs of what was right were being challenged. My pappy always told me there is the easy way and the right way, and usually they aren't the same. Right at that moment, more than anytime previously in my life, I was finding out how true those words of his really were.

———•—•—

ONE MORNING, MABEL CALLED ME UP AND ASKED IF I wanted to join her and Esther on another shopping spree in the city. As usual, I was free, so I accepted. We shopped for shoes all over town. We found that all three of us had a passion for the subject. It was a wonderful day. The sun was out. The skies were blue like something from a painting, with wispy white clouds that looked like God had sprayed whipped cream from the heavens. Mabel drove us in her husband's car while he was working on base. When we were all done and shopped out, we got back in Mabel's car for the trip back home. She turned the key several times, but the engine wouldn't start. Being ladies of the time, none of us knew the first thing about automobiles, so popping the hood as they say in America, was out of the question. I suggested we call for a tow truck. Mabel said her husband wasn't really much of a mechanic himself, but I told her not to worry that Albert certainly was. Having grown up on a farm there wasn't much of anything

Albert couldn't fix that had an engine and wheels. "We'll have it towed to the base and have Albert take a look at it," I told her.

She happily agreed. Mabel then came up with her own suggestion. She thought it might be wise if I was the one who called for the tow truck. She would give me the money for it gladly. Mabel next suggested that we would get better service here in Columbus if I was the one who orchestrated the enterprise. I instantly knew what she was getting at. We had spent the day ignoring ugly stares and looks from people who showed little humanity for others. A few of the businesses we passed by outright refused to allow blacks in their stores. One's that did, treated us like I was the plantation owner and Mabel and Esther were my servants. They sadly were accustomed to such treatment, but for me, it was a first, and I despised it.

It was more of the same rubbish when the tow truck driver finally showed up. He did take a look at the engine of the car between stares at me. I could read his bigoted thoughts with wee effort. He told me, largely ignoring Mabel and Esther's presence, that the starter was shot. He would tow the vehicle to my home on base as long as I had it ok'd by base security. I assured him I would. Now, how would we get home? He told us that city buses had routes that went to and from the base if we didn't want to pay for a cab. He had only room for one of us in his tow truck, and he made it quite clear that I would be the only one to occupy that seat. So, the girls and I talked it over and decided that the buses were our best alternative. We watched together as Mabel's car was towed away. Right after that, we began our walk to the bus station a few blocks away.

At Mabel and Esther's bequest, I went to the ticket counter and purchased the three tickets for us. We sat and waited for about thirty minutes for the next bus heading to the base to be ready. We ignored more stares and head shaking by fellow riders sitting in the station, who apparently had not seen a white woman sitting with two black women often in their life.

When our bus was finally ready to depart, the three of us boarded it and I without thinking followed Mabel and Esther's lead. They went straight to the back of the bus to find their seats. I followed suit and sat down next to them. The bus was relatively empty, although there were a few other white passengers aboard who I assumed lived or worked at the Army base. The doors of the bus closed, making that loud sweeping sound that I was so familiar with from growing up riding city buses in my hometown of Northampton, England. We all waited for the bus to begin to take off, but it wasn't for some reason. The bus driver hollered from his seat. "Lady, what do you think you are doing?"

At first, I didn't know who he was speaking to. Moments later, Mabel and Esther told me they were hoping they were wrong, but they assumed he was talking to me. He said it a second time and this time it was loud and clear and certainly directed toward me.

"Are you addressing me, Sir?" I called out from the back of the bus.

He made it obvious he was. "You can't sit back there."

"Why the devil not?" I responded.

This seemed to annoy him greatly, judging by the exaggerated rolling of his head and neck. He soon turned to the

Andrew Scott Bassett

back of the bus and stated his complaint directly. "That's the Negro section of the bus. You need to sit up toward the front, ma'am."

I asked him what difference it makes? The bus was mostly empty I proclaimed, so why did it matter where I sat? He barked at me that rules were the rules, and the back section was for Negro's only.

"That's rubbish!" I pronounced loudly for all to hear.

Mabel and Esther began to try to get me to do what he was so rudely asking. They said it was fine to them for me to sit up in the white section while they sat in the back. I would have none of that nonsense. "I'll sit up front, good man, as long as my lady friends here can sit with me."

The driver refused my compromise. "That doesn't work either, lady. Just follow the rules already! I'm going to be getting behind schedule if we don't get going soon!"

The situation didn't get any better when I told him that some rules should be broken. I went on about the greater rules of nature and God that carry more weight. Those comments seemed to go straight over his head and everyone else's on the bus. By now, Mabel and Esther were pleading for me to just do as he said. I saw the fear in their eyes when the driver announced he would call the police if I didn't either move to the front or leave the bus entirely. My entire body shook in disgust at his ultimatum. "Fine then!" I said in a huff, as I moved to the front of the bus.

The few other passengers seated on the bus greeted me with looks that could kill as I moved past them on the way to the very front. I sat down directly behind the driver. I hoped he could feel my disgust by sitting so close to him. I immediately glanced back toward Mabel and Esther who offered me reassuring smiles. They seemed relieved by my decision. Now the driver, without spitting out another word, began to pull the bus out of the station. I made sure to get his attention one more time. "You ought to be ashamed of yourself," I told him defiantly.

He turned his attention to me for only a second, gave me a dirty look, and then kept on driving.

"What happened?" Albert asked me in a soft but demanding manner.

I had a feeling I knew what he was speaking about, but I pretended to be in the dark.

"The bus in Columbus, now does it ring a bell?"

"Oh…," I replied. "That."

"Yes, that! Do you want to tell me what happened, Rosey, because it's all over the base?!" Albert proclaimed with frustration.

I carefully explained the sequence of events to Albert to the best of my remembrance. He was upset, with me I assumed. He bit his lip the whole time I was speaking. Then he shared with me that his commanding officer at the base brought him into his office to discuss the matter. I didn't know what to say. I apologized to Albert the best that I could, but I could see that he was very shaken up from the whole episode.

"What did he say to you?" I wished to know.

Albert rubbing his eyes as if tired out by it all recollected the best that he could. "Well, first he made it clear that our conversation was off the books. Then the colonel told me that I needed to get you under control."

"Under control, what does that bloody well mean?!" I stated, feeling insulted.

Andrew Scott Bassett

Albert explained what it bloody well meant, and I was aghast.

"No more fraternizing with the 'coloreds' in social settings," Albert shared. "The colonel made it clear that such relationships between whites and blacks caused too much turmoil on the base for everyone involved." I felt when hearing Albert's report of his meeting with his c.o. that I was back living one hundred years ago.

"Maybe I should go and speak with your commanding officer," I offered as help.

Albert was quick to shoot that thought down. "Don't you dare!"

Rarely in our new marriage had Albert spoken to me in such a way, and it caught me quite off-balance, indeed. I tried to justify why it might be a splendid idea for me to have such a chat with the colonel, but again Albert squashed the discussion with rare forcefulness. "I forbid it Rosey?! And I mean it! Sorry to be so angry about it, but I'm already in hot water with the colonel over this stuff, and if you talk to him, who knows what would happen."

Normally, I wasn't one to be ordered around like a chambermaid, but in this case, I could see Albert was truly worried about his position in the Army. But deep down I knew that if I could speak with the colonel, I could make things better for everyone. I wasn't about to be bullied by this colonel or anyone else for that matter. How could anyone tell someone else who they could associate with in a social setting? Even for me, a hard-boiled Brit, I knew this was un-American in so many ways, at least I hoped it was.

When Albert subsequently pointed his finger at me, ordered me to stay away from the colonel, and told me to do the same with Mabel and Esther, I said nothing. I smiled and fluttered my eyelashes at him. Albert believed that Mabel and Esther would understand the situation and why we couldn't see them personally right now. "They know how things are. That's why their husbands didn't come over that first night. That's why both of them looked like scared puppies the first time they came into our home."

I smiled some more and fluttered my eyes some more. Albert went on and on about the differences between how things should be and really are. I didn't listen to a word. I was too busy in my mind drafting the speech I was going to give to the colonel of the base when I saw him. Oh… yes, I was definitely going to see him and see him very soon. No matter what Albert believed, I knew in my heart of hearts that I could make things better, fix all of this. Well, at least I was determined to try.

With Albert off to work on base, I put myself together the best that I could and marched directly to the camp commander's office, a Colonel Dykstra. He had his own civilian secretary, a pretty redhead, working for him. She greeted me with a toothy smile that seemed to go from one ear to the other. When I asked to see the colonel, she immediately told me that I would have to make an appointment and that she would have to know what this was in regards to. I told her it was a personal matter involving myself and my husband, Sergeant Albert Adams. She glanced at the appointment book on her desk and started offering me some times, the next week, or the week after that, to meet with the colonel.

"No, No, No," I said. "I wish to speak with the colonel today."

"I'm afraid that's impossible," she retorted.

"Nothing is impossible," I fired back. "Is the dear colonel not on base today, or is he in a top-secret meeting with other military brass, or possibly President Eisenhower?"

"Ha, ha, no," she laughed.

"Then, I shall wait right here," I said as I made myself comfortable on the colonel's settee.

"Right, here?" the secretary said with surprise.

"Yes," I informed her. "I'll wait all day if I have to, dear."

There was no smile traipsing her face now as she picked up her phone and deliberately turned her back to me. I could hear her whispering, speaking with the colonel in the other room. When she hung up and faced me again, her fake smile had returned. "The colonel will squeeze you in for a few minutes, ma'am," she told me.

"Thank you so much," I replied, as she led me to the colonel's office door and then opened it for me to enter.

The colonel was waiting for me, and in a gentlemanly way took my hand and welcomed me into his office. "Mrs. Adams, it's a pleasure to meet you. I have heard much about you."

"I bet you have, Sir," I quickly replied.

He next offered me a chair in front of his desk, which I gladly accepted.

"Now, what is such an urgent matter, Mrs. Adams, that you were willing to spend the entire day in my lobby to speak with me about?"

Even though he was a colonel and I was just a base wife, I knew not to show any fear or subservient attitude to him. Men like him respected strength and feasted on weakness. My best path forward was to look him straight in the eye and speak my business without wavering. "I think we both know why I'm here, Colonel," I began.

Surprisingly, the colonel didn't play coy. He agreed with me. "I suppose we do," he said.

"I'm not here to rehash the discussion that you had with

Albert, my husband. You have every right to talk with him on any subject that you wish, as his commanding officer."

"Do I?" the colonel responded. "Well, thank you for that, ma'am."

Not knowing the man personally, I couldn't decipher if he was being sarcastic or civil with me, so I plodded on. "I am instead here to say that Albert has nothing to do with whom I choose to befriend in my personal life, nor does Fort Benning or even yourself, Colonel, Sir."

This statement brought a knowing grin to the colonel's face. "You are a British spitfire, aren't you, Mrs. Adams?" he declared out of nowhere. "I admire your guts to come in here like this, knowing what negative consequences your speaking with me could mean to your husband."

I didn't know if he was attempting to intimidate me or not, and frankly, I didn't care. Now was not the time for weakness. "I believe, from what I have been told that you are a fair and just man, and that is where I put my confidence, Sir."

He smiled and shook his head. I think I was amusing him with flattery.

"You really are something, madam," he responded. "This is fun, whatever this is about. Sadly, I'm a very busy man. If you could make your main point now, directly, I would appreciate it."

He waited in his chair for me to get with it, still wearing that silly grin.

"Well, Colonel, it boils down to this. I will be friends and associate personally with whomever and whatever I choose. And unless my personal relationship is with someone who is an enemy of the state or a threat to our democracy, I don't see it as being of any business at all for you or for Fort Benning for that matter. And furthermore, my dear husband has no say over this matter, and he is not required to partake in my personal friendships, be it with white people or any other persons of any other color. And in conclusion, if you or the Army threatens him in any way over this matter, I will be forced to make a real stink of it with officials greater than you. You see, I would think national media outlets would have some interest in the Army harassing their soldiers and their wives over such matters."

The colonel looked stone-faced in response to my diatribe. A sigh came out of his mouth before he could form his words in response. Then he composed himself and began to fashion his remarks. "You are a spitfire, and personally I like that. I am not one who is threatened very often, veiled or not. Strangely enough, I kind of enjoyed that. Still, there is a problem."

I interrupted at that point to ask what that might be.

He cheerfully explained. "I am responsible for many things on this base. One of the most important is the morale of my men. Anything that hurts that, well, it must be dealt with and eradicated immediately, madam."

I interrupted again. "And my befriending black ladies, as they like to be called, not colored or negros, ladies who are like me, married to soldiers under your command, is a morale issue, you say?"

"Yes," the colonel was fast to answer. "I'm afraid it is."

"Sorry, but I thought that your President Truman already integrated the military and put matters of these to bed, so to speak," I challenged him.

The colonel searched for the right words to further his point. He found them after a few moments of silent consideration. He went on, "Mrs. Adams...there is what is right in the world, and then there is what is reality. What is right is easy to get behind, but it doesn't change that we have to live every day with the reality of the situation."

I shrugged my shoulders. I had heard all this malarky before.

"The military by law and declaration is integrated, but in spirit and in reality, it isn't truly yet. Presidents can change the rules that men must abide by, but they can't change the hearts of men. Your husband, and for that matter your personal time spent with blacks, as you say, instead of people of your own race, is causing friction between both sides of the racial equation that I have to manage at this base. Now, to tell you the honest truth, I have no problem with what you're doing, and I honestly believe in a few decades from now most people won't. But, Mrs. Adams, sadly as I just stated, I have to manage the reality of the situation, not just what is fair and probably right."

"So then, you are calling my bluff, are ya'?" I answered back passionately, my blood beginning to boil in my veins.

The colonel surprised me with his response. "No, I think maybe a third alternative is needed here."

"A third, what do you mean?" I demanded.

The colonel explained. "I have been giving this some thought since this matter came to my attention. Now, with you coming here and speaking with me, my mind has been made up."

"Whatever do you mean?" I replied, still confused.

"I am going to be sending your husband to Germany to be stationed there, the western side of Germany of course." The colonel continued. "I think this will be a great opportunity for your husband and will help diffuse the problems we've discussed today."

I told him that it sounded more like he was just sweeping things under the rug to me. I wondered why he thought I wouldn't just go over his head and run to the newspapers.

He found such talk humorous. "Ma'am, because you love your husband and you want what's best for him, you are not going to do that."

I didn't follow his point and told him as much.

It was the colonel's time to show that he had the upper hand and to threaten. He didn't hesitate. "This is an equitable compromise, Mrs. Adams. It takes away any dissension and morale issues I have while being an outstanding opportunity for Albert. I think you should take it. If you don't, then I can't say that Albert won't suffer grave consequences to his military career long before your threats of going to the press ever see the light of day."

The colonel had played his hand. As much as I hated it, I knew he was probably right about the consequences that Albert would have to withstand. I couldn't do that to my husband, and I could sense that the colonel understood that. The Army would likely bury my story for as long as possible, and by then Albert's military career would be finished.

"You're a European. I'm sure you'll love West Germany, Mrs. Adams," the colonel told me with a combination of disdain and cockiness.

He then escorted me from his office, wishing me a lovely day. I felt like the colonel had called my bluff and had won. I could see that he felt the same way.

———◆———

DANNY SPITS GRASS FROM HIS MOUTH, DOING HIS BEST to pick out with his fingers what he can. He's attempting to help around Lori's house by mowing her front lawn. When his sister steps out from the front door, Danny yells to her that she needs to get a new grass bag for her mower. Lori, with Danny's cell phone in her hand, yells something back to him. He can't hear her over the noise of the lawnmower. "What did you say?!" Danny asks after shutting down the machine.

"You have a call!" Lori tells him.

His first instinct is to assume that it's his ex-girlfriend, Julia. He's pretty sure at this point that's not a call he even wants to receive. "Who is it?" he asks.

Lori relays the question to the person on the phone. "It's your agent, Danny."

This call might not be one he wants either, he considers to himself before trudging over to his sister and grabbing his phone. "Kimberly, how are you?"

Kimberly immediately tells him how sorry she is for his loss. She says all the right things that a person is supposed to say in a situation like this. Danny knows that her condolences are not the reason for the call. It doesn't take her long to get to her real reason. "How's the manuscript coming? I know it must be hard to concentrate on right now with everything but… Danny, I am really getting pressured by the publisher to show them something…soon."

There is a long pause of silence as Danny contemplates his response. He can't tell her the truth. That's out the window. This is a must-lie situation, he tells himself. "It's getting there, you know. I should have the first few chapters for you in no time," he explains, while keeping a straight face for his sister who is watching his little act.

His agent is thrilled to hear what he has to say. "Great, almost finished I can tell everybody?"

"Yes…that would be accurate," he replies, not believing he's saying it.

"Okay then, that's just wonderful news, Danny. I'll let the publisher know and I can't wait to read it myself," Kimberly shares with enthusiasm.

Danny ends the call after promising chapters to her soon, if not a complete manuscript. He then hands his phone back to his sister.

"Maybe you should keep it in your pocket in case you get another call that's important," Lori suggests. She's starting to wonder where this woman he's supposed to be getting married to is.

"No, that's alright, just toss it in my room," he answers.

Lori promises to do so before stating how happy it is to hear that he has his manuscript nearly done. She also tells him she can't wait to read it as she walks back into the house. Danny smiles and heads back to the lawnmower to finish the lawn. He mumbles under his breath, "Everybody can't wait to read my manuscript. Me, I can't wait to actually write it."

CHAPTER 9

Albert's transfer to Germany didn't happen for nearly a year. It was just like the Army to take so long. My friendship with Mabel and Esther only grew as we waited for Albert's new deployment. Unfortunately, the ostracizing by most of the white wives on base grew as well. By the time Albert finally got his orders for West Germany, I was more than ready for the move. As much as I would miss the "girls" and the friendships I had created, I was worn and withered by the drama on base and in town.

As I packed up our things and prepared to meet Albert in Germany, I gave true consideration to how much I had learned since coming here to Georgia. I was naïve about so much when we first arrived at Fort Benning. In retrospect, looking back over my time since then, I saw that I would never be quite the same. For one thing, from that moment forward, sensitivity to the suffering of others was now clearly bred into me. Just standing by and doing nothing while watching the less powerful be pushed around and treated with such indignity by the more powerful, was no longer an option for me. I simply, for the rest of my life, would speak out for those who couldn't or weren't allowed to.

Finally, I packed my favorite dresses carefully away in my suitcase, I couldn't help but wonder how Albert was faring on his new assignment in Germany. I hoped and dreamed that he thought of me often. He was always on my mind, no matter what I was doing or where I happened to be.

———————•———•—•—————

THE PLANE RIDE OVER WAS ONCE AGAIN DREADFUL, BUT still, I managed to finally make it to Germany. I stayed in a small building made up of flats just outside of the base with some other Army wives. There were no living quarters for the families on base as of yet. Yet, being back with Albert made everything better for me, and he was clearly thrilled to have me in Germany as well. From the first moment I arrived, Albert was beside himself with something that happened to him on his first train ride to his base. He couldn't wait to share with me his "'train encounter,'" as he liked calling it. At first, Albert didn't think it was "him," but was told by other soldiers that it most certainly was. By the end of Albert's train trip, many of his fellow soldiers had already disembarked on their way to other American bases in the country, leaving only Albert and two other soldiers left in the compartment. One soldier was sitting next to Albert and the other was right across from him. The soldier next to Albert nudged him with his elbow. "Should we say anything to him?"

"Like what?" Albert whispered back.

"I don't know, but something. I've never met a celebrity before, you know," The other soldier remarked to Albert.

Before the whispered discussion could go any further, the "'him'" they were talking about, made the first move, according to Albert.

"Can I help you fellas?" he said.

The soldier next to Albert froze. Suddenly he couldn't

think of a word to say. Albert was embarrassed by that and offered an apology for their whispering and generally acting like little kids.

"Not necessary," the other soldier across from him answered. "May I ask your name, Sir?"

"Albert Adams, Sergeant Adams," Albert stuttered back.

The young man then reached his hand out from across the aisle to shake Albert's as he repaid the introduction. "Private Presley, Elvis Presley, Sir."

Albert chuckled at his declaration. He wondered if any American in the world didn't know who he was, and yet he introduced himself like Albert wouldn't. Albert gladly shook his hand and so did the other soldier seated next to Albert. They spent the next forty-five minutes just chatting, with Albert and the other soldier asking Elvis all sorts of questions about his life. Albert shared with me how humble and awe-shucks Elvis was and how respectful he was of Albert being his superior officer. When they got to their stop, they all realized they were going to be stationed at the same base.

Elvis disclosed to both of them that the Army brass for PR reasons wanted him to do some concerts on bases in Germany while he was stationed there. He invited them both to come to see one. "Sergeant, Corporal, if either of you make it, I'll make sure that you get a seat or table down front. I promise both of you that, Sergeant, Corporal."

Albert and the other soldier thanked Elvis for his kind offer. Albert wasn't much for his music but couldn't help but be impressed with his fine "Southern manners".

Albert told him he would surely see him again on base and then matched Elvis's salute with his own as they went off in different directions.

THE COLONEL AT THE BASE BACK IN GEORGIA HAD MADE me believe that I would be stationed with my husband in West Germany, but it was all a lie to appease me. Albert didn't know either. He had been duped as well by the colonel. There were no living quarters on base for wives or family, so I was told to make other arrangements while Albert was deployed in Germany. I would have to be satisfied with a wee little visit with my husband.

Albert got two days of r-and-r to spend with me, which I must say was at least something to cheer about. Albert took me to Berlin, at least the west side of course. My overwhelming impression of the city was blandness. Everything about the place was grey, the buildings, the sky, the poor people themselves. All of it, to my recollection, was grey and depressing. It was as if the city itself knew the pain and suffering it was going through, as the two most powerful countries in the world played a 'game of chicken' with it. Albert took me to the new wall separating East Berlin from the west. The wall was a monument to the despicable nature of communism and all its failures. It was chilling to think how many brave souls were trapped on the other side of that goliath, dreaming, wishing, praying for someone to help them. I told Albert I would love to do something for those trapped families and hoped with all my might that I would live to see the day when that bleeding wall would come crashing to the ground. Albert shared the same sentiments that I did when it came to the monstrosity. We strolled through Berlin as storm clouds, appropriately grey, formed above our heads.

Before long, our conversation changed to other things as we walked further on. With both of us waiting to be drenched at any moment, we began to discuss the subject of children. He wanted to start popping out 'little ones' as soon as it made sense for us. His difficulties with his own father, I believe, motivated him to have such desires. I wasn't so sure about the idea myself. A woman who became a mother at that time, as I had witnessed, saw their world change dramatically. Freedom and the brilliant joys that come with it mostly disappeared when a woman became a mother. I still wanted to have my fun unencumbered by the needs of little ones tugging at my stockings. I saw many of the men in my family have their views of their wives change when they brought their little babies into the world. Oh yes, they still loved their women, but through the lens of their wife now being a mother first. All too often, the excitement and the romance was no longer the same. I wasn't ready for such a change with Albert, not yet anyway. I wanted to selfishly have him all to myself for a bit longer.

Suddenly, Albert out of nowhere surprised me with some news. "I'm seeing a base doctor in the morning. It's a special request being answered by the Army for me."

"What sort of doctor, then?" I quickly replied as drops of rain began to come down.

"Just a regular doctor, Rosey. He's going to check me out down there."

I know what he meant by down there, but I didn't understand why. Albert could see that and continued with his explanation. "You know he's going to check and see if I'm shooting blanks, or whatever."

I nodded my understanding, wearing an uncomfortable smile on my face. I couldn't help but wonder why he

Andrew Scott Bassett

was worried about such things. "Do you have concerns?" I asked him bluntly.

It was a silly question. He wouldn't be seeing a doctor if he didn't have at least some concerns.

He told me that he just wanted to make sure that everything was working properly as it should be. I, being cheeky, laughed and said his equipment seemed to be in good working condition to me. He pecked me on the cheek for that. We kept walking for a few more minutes before finally giving in to the increasing downpour coming from those bloody grey clouds.

Back at the motel room he paid for us to share, our little love nest I called it, Albert asked me if I would go to the appointment with him. Of course, I said. We were in this together, and although I didn't understand his concerns, this appointment of his made me realize even more than before just how important having children really was to him.

———•—•—•———

THE APPOINTMENT CAME AND WENT. WE WOULD HAVE to wait for the tests to come back in a week or so. I told Albert not to worry. I poked and prodded him, teasing him and acting like a real wanker. I promised him he had nothing to be concerned with. He was a young chap, a strong and virile bloke, I teased. He finally chuckled, and his sour mood began to lift. He started teasing me back and tickling my feet. Albert knew I hated to have anyone touch my feet. Then he flipped me over on our motel room bed and spanked my bum like I was in trouble. We both laughed and fell into each other's arms. "I'm going to miss you so much," he said softly to me, as he nuzzled my neck, his breath driving me crazy as it always did.

"I'm going to miss you too," I replied, relishing his embrace.

The room got very quiet after that. We continued to just lie there, holding each other and watching the steady rain, drip down the side of our motel room's windows.

―――――――•――•――――――――

It was very strange to be back home. I hadn't been gone that long, a little over a year, but somehow it seemed like an eternity. I was back sharing a bed with my not-so-little sister, Sheila, and I could see that Pappy and Mum were thrilled to have me home. The first morning there, Mum made me my favorite breakfast, bangers, and soft-boiled eggs. Mum even cut up the toast into "'soldiers'" like she did when I was a child. I dunked them into my egg with exuberance and Sheila did the same. Pappy came in late for breakfast; he had the day off but had been out taking care of his land, watering his vegetables and the like.

"Well, this is lovely, Mum, having the whole gang together," he bellowed before gulping down some tea.

Mum smiled her agreement as she glanced over at me. I could tell that even Sheila, my bossyboots little sister, was happy to have me back.

Later that same day, I followed Pap back over to his land. He was planting some new tomatoes in his garden.

"Is it everything you thought, love?" he asked me.

I wasn't sure what he was getting on about, so I questioned him.

"Marriage, America, the whole shooting match, duck," he explained.

I didn't feel completely comfortable speaking about my marriage with him, so I avoided any specifics about it. I just told him that I was still getting used to the idea of sharing my life the way you have to with your husband to be married.

"Ah…yes, ducky, that is the hardest part, the sharing," Pap agreed.

"Was it hard for you, you know with Mum?" I inquired.

Pap stood up from his planting position and gave my question some consideration, he cackled a little as he did. Then he began to pontificate on the subject. "I think it's much harder for the men now than in my time, really."

"How so, Pappy?" I asked, full of curiosity.

"Now don't get your knickers in a twist, but back then, in the good old days as people my age like to say, men ruled the roost." He answered. "Women, ducky, were seen and heard a wee bit, but not heard much. They didn't have the voice they have today. I bet in the future, you won't be able to get women to pipe down," Pappy howled with laughter.

I told him I hoped so, which made him laugh even harder.

He rubbed his chin as he thought about what I said. A knowing expression graced his face. "Trousers," he spits out with conviction.

"What?" I responded.

"Trousers, my old duck, my mother and her mother before her wouldn't have dreamed of wearing trousers. Only men wore trousers in those days. Now, the women are actually wearing trousers in the family. Someday, Rosey, I wouldn't be surprised that men will be wearing the skirts and doing all the cooking and taking care of the home, and the ladies will be the only ones wearing trousers and going out to work every morning," my pappy expressed, with a cheeky grin.

I told him I wasn't sure about all that, especially the men wearing skirts part. But I did tell him to put me down for the husbands helping their wives with the cooking and the home. That brilliant sight I would love to see.

Pappy then pretended to take out both an imaginary pad of paper, and a pen. He wrote my name as one in favor of a woman wearing the trousers in the family. After that, he out of the blue asked me about what Albert and I had decided about having kids. He wanted to know if he could start practicing the boring grandfather stories that he would tell the children. You know, he said, where he would exaggerate everything about himself when he was young. I giggled at his joke and told him that Albert and I were still discussing such things, but that there was no timetable, so to speak.

"All in good time, I'm sure, duck," Pappy remarked.

He then turned his thoughts to the States, and how different they must be from England. I shared how huge America was and because of the size of it, one part of it could be so different from another part in just about every way imaginable. Pappy asked me what I was getting at.

"Some parts are like England, green with hills, beautiful. Other parts of America are brown and sandy like a desert. One part can be flat with little rainfall, while another part will have large, impressive mountains, with lots of snow," I explained.

"And the people, Rosey, are they much different, one part to another?"

Now, it was my turn to consider my words before answering. Finally, after enough consideration, I continued. "Blimey yes, Pappy, the American people are very different from one place to another."

He wanted to know how, was it just the different accents like the Brits have, depending on what part of the United Kingdom you're from? There was, some of that, I confessed, but much greater differences than that. "They think very differently about many things, even rather important things," I offered.

"Such as duck?" Pappy wished to know.

Now my pappy didn't have a prejudice bone in his body, so I thought it would be safe to share with him what I encountered in Georgia. I told him the whole sordid tale as he sat silently with a serious look on his face. I finally just asked him what he thought about such things. He arched one eyebrow, which told me he was about to make an important point. "You know, love," he began, "since the beginning, the Garden of Eden and all that, every person on this bloody planet has to choose what's going to inspire their words and actions. So, is it going to be love or hate? It's really that simple. Hate is the easy one. Anybody can find a reason to hate someone or something, but finding a way to love someone who isn't too peachy, now that's a trick now, isn't it."

As usual Pappy could melt things down into a simple and understandable way. He had a gift for that.

"And for those who choose the easy way…well, I just say bugger off to those silly sods, right, ducky," he stated with humor. "We better get home then. Your mum doesn't want me to have you all to myself now, does she."

"No, I suppose not, Pap," I replied before thanking him for our little talk. I had forgotten how much I missed chatting with my old pap.

———◆·◆———

A FORTNIGHT HAD PASSED SINCE ARRIVING BACK IN

England. Albert had called twice. He'd been especially busy, learning his way around the new base. I could hear the loneliness in his voice, so I made sure to not let him hear it in mine. He mentioned several times that he hadn't heard back from the base doctor. I tried to downplay his worry, best I could, but it was difficult to do. I wondered if he knew something I didn't and wasn't telling me.

One afternoon, as I was coming back from the market with my mum, we were greeted as we entered the house by the phone ringing. I quickly put down the bags of groceries and picked up the call. It was Albert, and I was so happy to hear from him. On the other side of the phone, there was no happiness at all. I just knew he was calling to tell me his fears were right. It was truly dreadful to hear him try to share with me the test results from the doctor. I had no words to comfort him. I was lost in my own thoughts as he began to sob on the phone.

"All I ever wanted was to have some kids of my own and bring them up to be happy, not like me," he forced out between his sobs.

"I know," I told him. "I love you so much."

He offered the love back to me the best he could. I wanted to come see him, right that moment. However, he said the base commander was halting all leaves and passes for the foreseeable future. The American Army had new concerns about possible threats coming from the Russians from the east side of Berlin. It wasn't fair that Albert would have to go through this alone. The pain he was feeling, I wanted more than anything in the world to make it go away. He needed my comfort, he needed my arms wrapped around him, my lips on his. There was nothing I could do for him except tell him from the other side of a phone call how much I loved him.

Andrew Scott Bassett

"I love you too, Rosey," he said. "I will be in touch as soon as I can, and I'll see you when I see you."

Then he hung up. I had never felt so helpless in my life. I could do nothing but wait for his next call and pray for the opportunity to be with him soon. In the meantime, I would have to put on a happy face for Pap and Mum. They were so excited to have me home and I didn't want to spoil their happiness. They didn't need to know about Albert and his test results, not now at least.

———◆·———

THE NEXT FOUR MONTHS PASSED IN THE BLINK OF AN eye. I often found myself at night sitting home with Pap and Mum, discussing Sheila and her latest boyfriend and what they thought of him. Sheila would be out painting the town when this was all happening. I suddenly realized what it must have been like for them when I was doing the same thing. However, I have to say that they were much easier on my little sister than they ever were with me. Maybe they'd softened over time, or maybe they saw Sheila, now in her early twenties, as being more responsible and right-thinking than I ever was. I'm not quite sure why, but they certainly didn't seem to like her latest beau.

As for me, I waited patiently each week for that short and unfulfilling phone call from Albert. He hadn't sounded like himself since the test results were known. He was moping and miserable, and I'm sure our being apart for so long was the major reason for it, at least I hoped so. After his last call, I had just hung up the phone when there was a knock on the front door. I yelled upstairs to Mum who was putting away laundry, and asked if I should get it. "Please!" she yelled down.

When I opened the door, I was thrilled to see my old best mate, Sheila Saunders, standing in the doorway. Her surname now was Letts, but to me, she would always be Sheila Saunders. We hugged the stuffing out of each other. "When did you get back?" I asked, with tears of joy trickling down my cheeks.

"Yesterday love, my mum's been telling me that you've been back in Northampton for months now. I wish I could have come to see you earlier, but Ralph and I have just been so busy over in Liverpool," Sheila shared with me.

"Well, love, you're here now, and that's all that matters," I told her, so tickled to see her smiling face.

"How about a night on the town? We can get caught up on everything you know. You can tell me about America and what it's like being married to a Yank. I will give you the ins and outs of running a fishing business. It's all my old man Ralph likes to talk about," Sheila said with a chortle.

It did sound like a jolly good time, and I could use some of that right now. Mum then came downstairs to see who was at the door. She was almost as happy to see Sheila Saunders as I was. We told her about our plans for the evening, and she responded that it sounded lovely but wanted us to be careful.

"About what," I questioned mum with.

"Northampton isn't what it used to be, girls. It isn't even like when you were just out of school."

"Why is that Mrs. Blackwell?" Sheila Saunders-Letts asked.

"The teddy boys, dear," Mum answered.

"We've seen them and talked with them, Mum. They've been around for a while now," I remarked.

"I know, deary, but they've become much more of a problem with their wobbly ways in Northampton, lately," Mum warned.

Sheila and I looked at each other and shared a wicked grin. We grew up with soldiers pinching our bums and drunks trying to get us into wrestling matches. The teddy boys didn't scare us much. We had crossed paths before with their sort at pubs and clubs and just giggled at their greasy hair and toughie manner.

Sheila would pick me up in her car at six. I looked forward to going to a pub with her again, and this time without my pap and mum tagging along. Mum told me to look for my sister when I was out. That brought up a good point of contention for me. "You never say a word about teddy boys when Sheila is going out, why only when I am?"

"Oh, Rosey, that's because, well your pappy and I didn't tell ya', but your sister Sheila's boyfriend is frankly a teddy boy or former one at least," Mum confided.

That's why I hadn't met him, I thought to myself as I watched my friend Sheila drive away. Still pondering that idea, I marched upstairs to figure out my outfit for the evening, I couldn't wait.

———— •—•• ————

"So, what's it like?" Sheila Saunders began our conversation, as she asked about being married to an American. I answered that I was happy and that I loved Albert very much. Tonight was a joyful occasion, and I didn't want to ruin the mood by sharing the news that I might never be a mother.

"Is Albert different from the Englishmen you've been with?" she followed up.

"Not particularly," I said. "I guess men are men no matter where there from."

With that, Sheila made a toast. She celebrated our marriages, wishing for long happy wedded bliss and gorgeous, brilliant children. I clanked my glass to hers. I wished for the same thing.

The pub was full, and I saw many familiar faces lounging about it. One I didn't expect to see came marching through the front door at that very moment. It was Sheila, the other Sheila in my life, my sister. She was holding hands with her boyfriend, the supposed ex-teddy boy. They spotted us and came over to our table immediately.

"Well, look who's here then, Trevor," my sister said greeting us. "This is my sister, Rosey, the one I told you about, the one back home from living in America."

A big grin took over her boyfriend's face. "Ah... America, I've always wanted to go there. I love the music, the rock and roll, and the telly."

"Yes," I responded, "I like the music and telly there as well."

"Trevor's big on American music. He plays guitar," Sheila added.

"Really?" Sheila Saunders joined in. "Who's your favorite rock and roller, Trevor?"

His grin was now replaced with a big toothy smile. He loved the question. "I guess if I had to say, I'd go with Buddy Holly. I've read he's producing, writing, and controlling the recording of all his music. Elvis is great, but he doesn't do all that. He pretty much just sings the songs they give him to sing."

"But he's much better looking...than Buddy Holly, I mean..." Sheila Saunders had to throw in.

"Well, I suppose, but that doesn't matter much to me of course," Trevor replied. "Now, let me get you ladies and my lovely Sheila here some drinks, what are you having?"

Sheila Saunders tells my sister that she really likes this guy as he takes down our order and walks over to the barkeep, to give it to him.

"He used to be a teddy boy," I whispered to Sheila Saunders.

"What, you don't say, that explains the hair." She replies back. "Well, he seems quite nice to me, teddy boy or not."

My sister assured us both that he is, in fact, a real dreamboat.

"Look who's here!" a voice calls out in my direction and disrupts our conversation. "It really is Rosey Blackwell, or whatever you call yourself these days."

My two Sheila's and I look up to see Ian Whitman coming our way. He was a boy I grew up with and once accompanied on a pity date. He'd always been crazy about me since we were wee high kids, but I never had any such feelings for him.

"How are you then, Rosey?" he started with.

I told him fine and that it was nice to see him again. It didn't take long to tell he was already half-pissed off his feet. His mate with him seemed just as stewed.

"Looks like you have been having a good time tonight there, Ian," Sheila Saunders interjected.

Ian admits he's a bit squiffy or tipsy as you would say in America, as he introduces his mate Mitch to all of us.

"This is Rosey, Mitch, I grew up with her. I always kind of had a thing for her you know," Ian tells his friend for all to hear.

"You're already pretty plastered, Ian. Time to go find a place to fall down, love," my sister attempts to advise him.

Ian gave my sister Sheila a dirty look before answering her request. "Little Sheila's all grown up, aye. I hope your taste in blokes is better than your sister here."

"Sheila's right, Ian, go home and sleep whatever this is off. You're embarrassing yourself mate," Sheila Saunders added.

Ian then staggered for a second before turning to his friend Mitch and sharing how I always thought I was too good for him. He said with his voice slurring from the booze, that Yanks and even German prisoners of war were more my fancy, or so he had been told. Mitch laughed whole-heartedly at that tidbit of information. When my sister and Sheila Saunders stepped in to defend my honor, Ian quipped that his favorite bird was a quiet one. "I despise birds that chirp too much, don't you, mate?" he said to Mitch.

"I think we're done here, Ian," I told him at that moment, in no uncertain terms.

"Oh, really, love," Ian responded sarcastically.

Trevor took that moment to stroll over with our drinks. My sister shared an eye roll and a wink with him and some-how from that, he picked up that these two blokes were bothering us. "Can I help you, mates?" Trevor offered to Ian and his pal.

"And who might you be then?" Ian asked Trevor, in a disrespectful tone.

"I'm Sheila here's boyfriend, and I don't recall you two gents being invited to our little soiree," Trevor fired back.

Trevor then gave Ian a look that clearly told him to beat it. Ian told Mitch that they have a real bruiser here. Mitch just smiled and said nothing.

"I've left a lot of bruises in the past on blokes a lot rougher than you two, aye. I was a teddy boy leader until recently.

Sheila here has refined me and made me a proper, gentleman. I still have plenty of teddy boy in me, though. You two chaps what to see for yourself?"

Ian and his mate became quiet at that moment as Trevor stood his ground. I looked over at my little sister and she couldn't have been more proud or titillated.

"What are you waiting for then? Time to beat it." Trevor instructed them both, quite clearly.

Ian smiled in my direction and gestured that it was time to go. "Good night, Rosey, nice to see you again," he says as he and Mitch slipped out of the pub with their tails between their legs.

"That was brilliant, Trevor," Sheila Saunders told him.

"It was nothing really," Trevor humbly answered.

I still told him how much I appreciated him making those two leave.

"This guy is a good one to have around, what," Sheila Saunders then said to my sister.

My sister Sheila agreed and squeezed Trevor's arm.

"Now, what were we chatting about?" I asked the girls.

"Maybe… about how lucky the three of us are to have good fella's to be with and not blokes like Ian and his mate, that's a good start," Sheila Saunders offered up in a toast.

"Cheers to that," I agreed. "Cheers to that."

CHAPTER 10

Once Albert finally got more r-and-r time, he sent for me to come to Germany. We would stay again in our little "'love nest,'" a dingy motel room, off base. He had a few days off and I couldn't wait to see him. I expected that my visit would perk him up after he had been sounding so out of sorts during our phone conversations. He'd been that way since we found out that he couldn't have children. Albert was definitely happy to see me. Yet, he was still not his old self, not his warm, caring self, certainly. I knew why, we both knew why. Still, I wanted to get him to open up to me about his feelings, his pain. Unfortunately, it was not considered the thing to do for a man in those days. No matter how much I offered him a shoulder to cry on, was willing to listen to his every word, he would mumble and stammer and go back into his solitary shell of misery. His disappointment about being unable to father children was eating him up inside, and there wasn't anything I could do about it. Even worse, instead of opening up and sharing his suffering with me, he was instead burying his pain in bottles of booze. I tried my best to not be angry with him. It hurt that he didn't seem to have any concern or thought about how much his news also affected me. He wasn't the only one who was now going to be childless. Mind you, I really had no desire to be a mother yet but I certainly always thought I would one day. All my attempts to bring

Andrew Scott Bassett

up child adoption only seemed to stoke the fires of anger in him more. He would snipe at me about how he wanted his own child, a child from his blood, not someone else's. I valiantly shared how I had heard stories my whole life about how adopted little ones would often grow up to even look like their parents, but the message fell on deaf ears. I was at my wit's end, and it was only day two of our time together. I had waited with great anticipation for this time, with just the two of us. Now, I was already wondering what good would come of it.

Later that second afternoon together, after coming back from shopping for a few items at the PX, I found Albert slumped over a small coffee table in our motel room. He was the drunkest I had ever seen him. Any pity I might have had for him was replaced by frustration and disgust. I shouted at him for letting himself get this way when this time was supposed to be for us. He grunted his retort. I had no bloody idea what he said. "You're not the only one hurting over this, you know!" I screamed at him.

He attempted to reach for me with his hand, why I didn't know, but I was completely fed up. I took the groceries into the kitchen and slammed them down on the counter, and then marched out of our motel room like a soldier in a parade. After that, I took a trip to Berlin. I wandered the West Berlin streets for over an hour still going over in my mind what had just taken place between us. I was argy-bargy with myself I have to say, that is arguing with my own thoughts. Part of me was making excuses for Albert's behavior, justifying everything because of his disappointment in not being able to become a father. Another part of me would have none of that. That part was telling my nicer angels to sod off about being reasonable and not flying off of the handle. It argued that I had every right to feel bloody teed off. I was too young to become the wife of a flipping souse. I had aunts that married men with such a problem. The men spent more time in pubs than at home. My uncles would stumble in at all hours of the night, drunk off their feet, waking the children from slumber. My mum shared many stories about them, and always told me how lucky she was to have married a man like my old pap, who only touched the devilish drink a wee bit. I always told myself I would never end up like my aunts. I would never spend the better part of my life cleaning up after a drunkard husband. How ironic I thought that there was the possibility of Albert becoming like those men, even with me as his wife. If he did, what would I do? What if this wasn't just a weak lapse in his judgment but instead a new lapse of character coming to fruition? These thoughts were more than I could tolerate or consider at the moment. I came to a small café. I assumed they would offer some strong black tea inside, and I could really use a cup of tea right about now, so I entered the establishment. What I found inside the café, or should I say who I found inside the café, sent shivers down my backside. I never was much for believing in fate and the like, but looking back now, how could it have been anything else.

I saw him first. Frozen in my tracks, I wondered if I should turn and immediately leave or maybe pretend that I didn't see him. What if he didn't really want to see me? There was a chance, my mind now racing told me, that he might have put all that happened during those terrible years of the war behind him, including me. Then it happened, almost like in the movies, he looked up from where he was seated in front of me, and our eyes met. The surprise of my appearance made his eyeballs seem to double in size.

"Rosey?" he greeted me, still acting like he was amazed to see me.

"Max..." I suddenly had nothing more original that I could come up with.

"I cannot believe you are here in Berlin, standing in front of me. How is this possible?" he inquired.

I asked if I could sit down at his table, if that would be all right. He quickly pulled out a chair and guided me into it. I can't deny that my heart was beating a little faster at the sight of him. Nearly eleven years later, and he still looked as good as I remembered. His sandy blond hair and piercing blue eyes still did something to me, just as they had all those years ago in England. It was at that moment I realized an uncomfortable truth. This idea changed my thinking about many things. I realized though I loved Albert as much as any wife could, I still at the same time had feelings for Maximilian. I always assumed that when you fell in love with someone your whole heart belonged to that person, that there was no room for anyone else. Only at this moment, seated next to Max, my ideas about such things were being challenged and confused.

"Why are you here in Germany?" he asked.

I told him about Albert and his being stationed here. Without warning, I turned the tables on him and reeled off questions of my own. First, I wanted to know what happened after he went back to Germany and left me behind. Truthfully, I wanted to know why he didn't stay in touch. Why he left and never came back? I didn't say those exact words mind you, but I believe Max understood that's what I was asking him. He took a minute to choose his next sentences carefully. He could see the hurt in my face.

"It is hard to explain, Rosey."

I interrupted and told him to do it nonetheless. He smirked at my forwardness. He laughed as he said he had forgotten how blunt I could be. Then he shared, "My family is very important to me, as I believe I told you when we were in England."

"Yes," I answered.

"As the oldest son in the family, there was much pressure, or you might say expectations for me to do certain things, to be responsible," he stated.

I could see that he was struggling to tell me something, beating around the bush as they say in America. I asked him directly why he didn't come back to me. I questioned if it was something I did or didn't do. I thought maybe it was my fault. I had often considered that possibility.

"Nein or no," he responded. "You did nothing wrong, Rosey. You were always on my mind, for many years in my thoughts."

"Then why did you not come back?" I asked again.

"My family wanted me to get married and to marry a German girl. I was reluctant to do so because of you, but my family had been through so much because of the war," he explained.

"Then you did, I mean you did get married?" I questioned, hoping for some reason that I wasn't really sure about, that I was wrong in my assumption.

"Yes…" he said, dashing all my hopes. "It made my family very happy. After the loss of my younger brother Boris, I felt obligated to do such a thing. I don't know what to say Rosey except that I never really stopped thinking about you, even after all these years."

His words lit me up inside. For a few precious moments, we were back in England, gazing happily into each other's adoring eyes, without a care in the world. But I quickly realized, like cold water being dumped over my head, that we weren't still in England, and we did have cares. Mine was named Albert and it sounded like Max had his own here in Germany, a wife. I looked at him sheepishly, as if I had done something wrong and was now caught. He slyly smiled back at me. A waiter then interrupted our little reunion and asked if we would like to order something. I said tea, hot and black. Max asked for the same.

"Obviously you made it out of East Berlin then," I declared, changing the subject quickly.

"Fortunately, yes. My wife and her family made it out as well, but sadly my family is still there, on the communist side," he shared as his voice became softer. "I work with the newly formed West German government as a diplomat. I am doing all I can to free my family and get them out of the eastern side. Things are very bad on the other side of the wall, Rosey. Germany is no longer Germany, at least not the Germany of my youth, the Germany that I loved. The people are in despair. Even the ones who have made it out like myself, are not whole because of their family members trapped on the other side of the awful wall. First, we had to suffer the reign of Hitler, and now this. It is sometimes, too much to bear."

I told him how sorry I was for all that he and his family had been through. I wished there was something I could do, but of course, there wasn't.

"Any children then?" I just had to know.

"No, not as of yet," he replied.

"But you're happy at least?" I followed with. Why I asked, I didn't know.

Max again took his time to answer. His words were guarded and almost secretive in nature. He acted like he wanted no one else in the world to hear him. "My wife is a good person and would one day be a wonderful mother."

"And of course, you love her?" I had to add.

"Such questions," Max countered. "I know no other woman who speaks so directly and without fear. That was one of your most endearing traits to me."

I quickly cut him off and told him he hadn't answered my question.

He said to me it wasn't something a gentleman or respectful husband could answer. I think I understood what he meant by that.

"What about you?"

"What about me…" I stuttered back.

"Is this Albert, I believe you said, is he the great love of your life?" Max suddenly put me on the spot.

I knew how he felt a few seconds ago, as the tables were certainly now turned on me. And I could see in Max's eyes that he was hoping for a particular answer from me. I wondered if I was hoping for the same when I questioned him.

"I believe he is," I managed to voice.

Max nodded as if he was accepting an outcome that he had already perceived was coming. He then smiled and said, "I am very happy for you, Rosey. You deserve to have found the great love of your life. This Albert, your husband, is a very fortunate man indeed, more fortunate than he will probably ever know."

Now, it was my turn to appreciate and offer kind words. I did my best in that manner, but my heart wasn't really in it. I think we were both feeling the same thing at that moment. Max and I were both dreaming about what could have been.

I glanced at my watch and realized it was probably time to get back to that drunken love of my life. Before I could leave, Max asked if we could somehow stay in touch. He asked if it would be improper to offer his phone number and address to me. I considered his request and almost took the small serviette he wrote them out on from his hand. I couldn't though, and I knew Max understood why. We both still had feelings for each other that were much stronger than either of us would have thought. No, it wouldn't be the proper thing or the right thing to do. Max's wife and my Albert deserved better, so I handed it back to him. I didn't have to tell him why, he knew. We said our goodbyes, and it was even more painful than all those years before. This time, neither of us expected or had much hope that we would ever see each other again. I walked out of that cafe and made sure not to look back. I realized then, that sometimes you can't look back.

———— • — • ————

My mind was overflowing with thoughts by the time I got back to the motel. When I unlocked the front door and entered, I found the place engulfed in darkness. At first look, I didn't see Albert anywhere. Then a small movement occurred, buried and hidden by strewed covers and pillows on our bed. As I got closer, I could both make out his shape from under the covers and pillows and the smell of alcohol that seemed to emit from his every pore. With a stiff upper lip, a very British trait you know, I managed to sit down on the side of the bed next to him. What a silly sod to have done this to himself, I thought.

"Rosey, you're home?" he somehow managed to say through garbled enunciation.

"Yes…I'm home now," I answered with sternness in my tone.

He struggled to extricate himself from the mess he made of our bed. "Sweetie, I'm so sorry. I'm just so sorry."

Albert then reached for me as he pulled himself up. He sat up in bed with his back against the wall.

"Rosey…I don't want to hurt you," he confessed to me. "I'm just so angry about the father thing, but I can't bear losing you too."

"You haven't lost me, Albert. You're never going to lose me, you bleeding idiot. I'm not that easy to get rid of," I promised.

My words made him chuckle a bit and lighten the mood. It was the first time I'd heard him laugh since I got to Germany.

He suddenly lunged into my arms. He squeezed me like he was afraid he would never get another chance. I told him not to get any other ideas in his present state.

"Are you sure, honey? I think I'm finally sobering up."

"You're going to have to do more than sober up," I fired back. "You're going to have to do some bathing up, and some brushing and gargling up too, my love."

With those orders in place, Albert slowly pulled himself out of bed and headed for the loo. It had a large old-fashioned tub in it. I could hear him singing as he diligently worked to scrape the layers of objectionable substances from his body.

"Most people sound much better when singing in the tub, but not you, darling." I teased him through the loo's door.

"You don't think so, huh?" Albert responded.

"No, I sincerely don't," I laughed.

"So then, you didn't marry me for my singing voice, I guess?" he joked.

Andrew Scott Bassett

"Oh love, no!" I assured him. "Although, I'm no Doris Day myself, but don't you dare agree!"

Albert laughed harder. "Ha! This makes me think I need to share with you my plans for tomorrow night."

"Oh really…and what pray tell might they be?" I had to ask.

Albert said it was a surprise and refused to tell me. I begged and pleaded to know, but he didn't relent in keeping it a mystery. He just said that I would never forget tomorrow night and that he hoped it would make up for all the misery he had put me through, so far this week.

"We'll see, duck," I told him. "But it better be pretty special then, do you hear me?"

Without notice, my strapping young husband slung open the loo's door. His grin went from one ear to the other. He was wearing a much too small white towel that was only precariously staying on. "Is there anything else, I mean before tomorrow night, that I could do that might help to speed up the forgiveness process?" he asked slyly.

I knew where he was going with all this, and I thought it was about bloody time. "It can't hurt your chances," I shared, as I let him chase me back to our bed.

Finally, for the first time since I arrived, our little 'love nest' was living up to its name.

———— • ————

THE NEXT NIGHT, I WAS INTRODUCED TO THE ARMY base's nightclub. It has been set up for the men to let off some steam. It appeared to be like any other club with a bar in the corner and a small stage in the front where the band would play. I sneaked a peek at myself in the large mirror in the foyer as we were entering the club. Albert and I were a dapper duo, he in his grey tweed sports jacket with grey matching slacks and myself in my little black dress that any fine woman of the day had to have at least one of, hanging in her closet. I pointed out our reflection to Albert, who had his arm sweetly wrapped around mine. "Don't we look lovely then?" I gushed.

"You're the lovely one, honey. I'm just the lucking galoot who gets to hang on your arm," He answered in an endearing way.

For that brilliant comeback, I gave him a quick kiss. His face went red in an instant as he told me for about the hundredth time since yesterday's drunken fiasco how much he loved me. Then he announced that we better hurry and get a good seat, so we did down by the stage. I still had no idea who we were going to see perform or what kind of music it would be. Albert had been very hush-hush about the whole thing. I guessed it would be a country-western performer since Albert so loved that style of music. He especially loved a new chap by the name of Johnny Cash. I thought he was just okay. I still loved the big bands that I had grown up with, but I found myself often listening on my radio to a new style of music that had been around for the last few years, called rock and roll. It was the music that my sister Sheila's boyfriend, Trevor, loved so much. The music was supposed to be meant for teenagers, but I loved the beat and the ease with which someone could dance to it. No matter, whatever the performance tonight, I would remember how Albert was looking at me and how handsome he was.

"I think the shows about to start, Rosey."

He was right. The emcee for the evening came out on stage and addressed the room. I was struck by not only how full the club was, but also by how many of the military brass were in attendance. I remarked to Albert that it looked like the whole base was here. Albert shared that anyone who wasn't on duty wanted to be at the show. He promised me I would like the show, probably much more than he would. Now my curiosity was at a fever pitch. "Oh, bloody hell!" I ranted at Albert. "Just tell me then. It isn't 'him,' is it!"

"You'll see soon enough," he replied in my ear.

The emcee interrupted our banter and began his introduction. "Gentlemen and ladies present, and of course military personnel and officers, we can't forget officers. I am happy to present to all of you one of the United States Army's very own tonight. This young man and his manager have agreed to allow us the opportunity to enjoy his musical talents while he's still serving the country he loves. So, without further ado, I, the United States Army, and all of Western Germany are proud to introduce Private Elvis Presley!"

My mouth fell open and hit the table. I had hoped it would be him performing tonight, although I didn't want to take from Albert's surprise. He knew how much I loved this young man's music, not to mention how handsome and sexy I found him.

"After meeting Elvis on the train to the base, I told him I would go see him sing if and when he performed for the troops," Albert whispered into my ear, as the band on stage that would back up Elvis began to play loudly.

"And you did! That's bloody amazing!" I whispered back.

Finally, he walked out onto the stage. It wasn't in a thunderous hip-swiveling tornado of movement as I expected, but more humble, almost shy. The music was still playing behind him.

Everyone in attendance was waiting for him to become the Elvis we had all heard about and seen on numerous shows and on telly and in motion pictures. He politely asked the band to pause for a second. He smiled, he almost seemed nervous, but how could that be? He then addressed everyone in the audience. "I just wanted to say how honored I am to perform tonight. While I am serving my country over here, I want to make one thing clear to everyone, and that is that I am just a regular soldier, just like everyone else."

Albert and I looked at each other with dismay, neither of us were expecting the show to start like this. Elvis continued. "I wasn't planning on performing at all during my service, but the colonel, my manager, and the military brass got together over the phone and thought it might be a good excuse for all of us to have a night out, so I agreed to it. I guess we'll be doing a few more of these in the future, here in Germany, and again I hope this takes your mind off of being so far away from home and your families, at least for a short time. Thank you very much."

And with that, the show began in earnest, as the band backing him up started again. Elvis began by ripping into *"Hound Dog"* with all his might. Half the men in the place were up and dancing. The ones with dates had to, their ladies wouldn't let them sit down. The other half of the men sat and watched, some tapping and clapping along, some looking bored. Many men in those days were jealous of Elvis Presley and just didn't 'get him'. But most women did, and no matter what they said in polite circles, with his hips gyrating and his pelvic area thrusting around, he could get most red-blooded women's pulses to flutter. Oh, and the music was quite brilliant as well. Albert and I danced, and danced, and danced some more. We had the time of our lives that night bopping and gyrating to the future king of rock and roll. Elvis was terrific, although I certainly had no idea what was about to happen next. He sort of slid across the stage. He actually seemed to glide, now that I think about it. He then scooted quickly down the steps at the side of the stage, almost skipping down them without losing his rhythm. All of us on the dancefloor, well at least the ones wearing dresses, couldn't help but keep one eye on him as he made his way toward us. It was a stiff challenge indeed to keep up with the beat and watch Elvis at the same time. Then, without warning, he strolled over to Albert and me. I thought I was just bloody lucky until Elvis gave Albert a knowing pat on the back. We both realized right then and there that he remembered Albert from the train and that there was a purpose to his standing right next to us. The last few *"Hound Dog"* lyrics roared from his magnificent voice and then the song came to an end. Elvis caught his breath as the room full of people yelled, whistled, and clapped, showing their approval. He thanked everyone for their kindness and appreciation before announcing that the next song would be of a much slower variety. And then the words I'll never forget. "This next song really isn't the same without a beautiful young lady to sing it to," he told the crowd. "So, if you fine gentlemen don't mind too much, I think I will pick out one of these lovely ladies here tonight to be my victim," he said with a chuckle.

Next, in a moment in time chiseled in my memory, Elvis looked my direction and smiled at me. I couldn't help but ask Albert if he had this planned out the whole time. Albert promised me he was innocent and had no idea. Elvis asked Albert for his permission. Albert painfully shy in front of everyone, basically giggled his okay. He then stepped aside

THE ROSEY VIEW OF THE WORLD   157

and almost waved Elvis toward me. When Elvis came close, I felt my heart race and my knees get a bit shaky. This handsome young man with the sexiest lips I had ever seen on a man, I remember that so well, was staring right into my eyes. He slowly took one of my hands that was resting at my side and pulled it toward him. I put up no resistance at all. With a knowing smile and cheeky spark in his eyes, he asked me how I was doing tonight. I squeaked out fine, at least I think I did. The dancefloor was suddenly silent, and all the people on it seemed to disappear. I lost myself in those brilliant blue eyes of his. And then his microphone seemed to come from nowhere, as he pulled my hand higher for all to see. Elvis began to sing, and the band began to play. He sang *"Love Me Tender"* to me, and I melted before those eyes. I was lost in his gaze and in his song and was happy to be not found. The song seemed to last forever and yet still ended too soon. When it was over, he kissed me on the hand like a gentleman and then handed me back to Albert. No offense to my husband, but I didn't need to be handed back so quickly. Sadly though, he did, and then Elvis marched back onto the stage as the show must go on, I suppose. As for Albert and myself, we got back to dancing both slow and fast. For some reason, however, my rhythm for the rest of the night wasn't quite right. I felt light-headed and in a daze for the rest of the show. But believe it or not, I wouldn't have wanted to feel any other way.

<hr />

DANNY SCARES THE LIVING YOU-KNOW-WHAT OUT OF HIS sister, as he races into the room holding securely in his hand a page from his mother's story. He's like a small child who has something to tell his parents and can't wait a single moment more to show it. Lori can't help but wonder what is so damn important that he has to surprise her to death like he just did.

"Did you know about Elvis?! I certainly didn't. She never said a word to me!" he exclaims to his sister.

Lori tries to get her head around his proclamations. "What are you talking about?"

"What do you mean…what am I talking about? I'm talking about mom and freaking Elvis Presley, that's all!" Danny proclaims as he raises his voice.

His sister thinks about it for a second and then remembers the story. "Oh, the dance in Germany. Is that what we are talking about?"

Danny answers her with a sarcastic glare and a nodding head. "You know the story, but I don't?"

Lori has no idea what Danny wants her to say and tells him as much. "It is pretty cool that Elvis sang to our mother though, I have to admit."

Danny is still dumbfounded. He can't believe that a piece of information of this importance could have been hidden from him, for so long. "Elvis freaking Presley… come on now!"

Lori gives her little brother an insincere hug for consolation. She then lets him in on another secret. "If you love the story about meeting Elvis, wait till you get to the part about the Beatles. It's got to be in there too… somewhere."

Danny's jaw nearly hits the ground at the news of a possible Beatles sighting in his mother's pages. While he has fond memories of listening to old Elvis vinyl records as a child with his mom, Danny has always been a lifelong devoted Beatles fanatic. If Elvis crooning to his mother and kissing her wasn't enough, now he's supposed to believe she met the Beatles and never shared that story either.

"You know how Mom was. She liked to talk about us, what we were up to. She was always tight-lipped about her past, you know that," Lori reminds her brother.

Danny couldn't disagree with that. That was indeed how his mother was.

"I think that's the reason for her sharing her life story with you. Now she's not around to answer a million questions that we would have asked, but through those pages she left for you, she can share her past, and the things she never talked about while she was alive. I think, brother, that Mom always wanted to share her life story but for whatever reason couldn't. Now, Danny, she finally can. You are the writer in the family, not me or Greg. I know it's all a little crazy, but Mom was always a little crazy herself."

Danny cracks a self-assured chuckle at his sister's thoughtful sentiments. He believes that everything she just said is probably true, "You are a lot wiser than I remember," He remarks to his sister.

"And you are still a pain in the ass no matter how old you get." she shoots back.

They both share a laugh before Danny announces that he needs to get back to his reading.

"What about your book? It sounds like you need to get on to that and get it finished like you told your agent, you would."

Danny knows Lori is right, but what his mother left him to read has all his attention and focus at the moment. It doesn't help either that Danny's own book has led him to a writer's block, a writer's block the size of the Great Wall of China.

"Besides," he declares to his sister, "how can you expect me to concentrate on anything else when I now have to at least read to the part where Mom meets the Beatles."

Lori shakes her head. She can see that Danny is becoming obsessive with their mother's story. He then bids adieu as he walks back to the bedroom and closes the door. He props up his pillows on his bed and starts right up where he left off, still mumbling under his breath about how and why his mother wouldn't have told him about her encounters with Elvis and the Beatles, the freaking Fab Four he says to himself.

CHAPTER 11

The next five years for Albert and I seemed to pass by like we were swept up into the eye of a tornado and just taken wherever the winds of chance and fate deemed fit. His assignment in West Germany lasted fourteen months. After that, we were on the move again. Albert bounced around many different bases in those five years, and I was mostly with him as he did. We both complained about the constant change, but he would always remind me that at least there wasn't a war going on and he wasn't being deployed half a world away. Those words of his would one day come back to haunt me.

As I said, we were now five years removed from the lovely memory of that nightclub in Germany. Albert and I had gone through many of the ups and downs that often plague young couples. But, for the most part, things were well with us. He had gained control over his drinking problem, hardly a spot of it since that day in Germany, in the motel room. I was very thankful for his determination and the way he fought to change himself for me. Mind you, I can't say he didn't have a drink or two now or then. He would touch the stuff when we would go out dancing or share a dinner with friends. Still, bless his heart, he never let it get the best of him. He was still the sweet caring man that I adored.

One day Albert got a bee in his bonnet and decided he wanted to fly helicopters for the Army. This decision I guess was well-received by military brass as we were quite swiftly reassigned to Fort Rucker in Alabama. This was a base where soldiers would train to learn about such things. Here I was again, many years later, back in the deep South of America. I could still see the winds of change coming up against the walls of ignorance. Albert begged me to not stir things up as I had in Georgia when we were first married. That was when I first became aware of man's inhumanity to man. Nevertheless, his career in the military certainly seemed to be taking off, and I didn't want in any way to curtail that or cause him any anguish. He had straightened up for me from his own monkey business, the drinking and the like, and I felt it was my duty as a good wife to return the favor. These were all of course nice thoughts, even admirable aspirations, but it didn't take long for them to be challenged.

———•—•——

ONLY A MONTH AFTER WE ARRIVED IN ALABAMA, I WAS coming back from the PX on base after doing a little shopping for myself and picking up a few things for Albert. The sky, which was fairly blue when I parked my car and entered the PX, was now just a short time later, dark and ominous, with thunder booming here and there and an occasional flash of lightning for all to see. Soon to follow was the downpour as the rain came down so fast that I could barely see through my front windshield. It was at this untimely moment, I realized that my defroster wasn't working. My windows began to fog up and I responded the only way I could. I swiped at them with the palms of my hands. I did this for a few minutes until I realized that between the heavy rain and fogged windshield, I just couldn't see well enough to keep driving. I finally gave up the ghost and pulled off to the side of the road. I would wait the storm out was my grand plan. It couldn't possibly keep going like this for long, I told myself. I sat there and listened to the rain rattle and splat all over the car. It was strangely relaxing. After an hour of falling into a trance-like state, and as the rain showed no desire to let up, my attention was suddenly diverted as something, or someone passed my car. When the person walking on the side of the road got farther out in front of me, I swiped harder with my hands to make a place to see them through my fogged windshield. I could make out that it was a woman, a black woman. She was getting drenched by the rain. She was apparently only wearing what looked like a flimsy cotton sweater to cover herself. I did the only thing any decent person with a strong moral upbringing would do. I jumped out of the car and began to yell at her. With the rain still coming down in buckets as my pappy used to say, I could tell she couldn't hear me. I ran after her with my jacket flung over my head. When I caught up to her, she turned in surprise and asked me in a curt manner what I wanted. I told her I had been yelling at her since I saw her walk by my car. To my surprise, she let me know that she heard me hollering at her but thought I must be crazy or something. I explained that I just was trying to help her get out of the rain. "You can come sit with me in my car until it slows down!" I said loudly, trying to speak over the showers still thundering down.

To my dismay, the woman asked why I would want to help her. I had not expected such a question and was not really in the mood for a long, drawn-out discussion, especially since we were both being soaked to the bone.

"It's pouring down out here!" I pleaded.

"I know that!" she snapped back sarcastically.

I pointed to my car. "Can we please just go get inside and get out of this, please?!"

She looked me straight in the eye and acted as if she was measuring me for something, what, I wasn't really sure. Drenched and dripping, the woman finally relented and followed me back to the car. Once inside, I couldn't help but ask her why she had initially refused my help when I was being so gracious to offer a warm dry place to retreat to. She didn't answer at first. She just gave me that bloody, measuring look again.

"What pray tell are you looking at, Miss?" I just had to ask her.

She flashed a strange expression my way before saying, "who are you?"

"I'm Rosey," I replied.

"You are definitely not from around here, are ya'?" she figured.

"No, actually not. I'm English."

"I thought I heard an accent. I guess in England it's more normal for a white woman to come running up to a black woman and ask to help her," she offered bluntly.

I shrugged my shoulders and nodded. From what I had witnessed since living here in America, what she just surmised was probably true. She then put forth, another point. "Well, it sure ain't normal in Alabama, especially when the two women don't even know each other."

Responding to that, I reached out my hand toward her and asked her name. She studied my hand like she had never seen one before and maybe she hadn't seen a white one reaching out to her. She eventually did accept my offer and shook my hand, but only reluctantly.

"And what might be your name, huh? I told you mine dear, so it only seems fair that you share with me yours," I argued.

She told me her name was Carol. "It caught me off guard a little. I'm not used to a woman like you being so nice to me. I'm not used to that. I'm sorry for being so rude," she said apologetically.

"You mean a white woman like me, is that what you mean?" I questioned with a smile.

She nodded. Then the rain stopped coming down as hard and began to hit the window at a normal and feasible rate. I could see again once I wiped the windshield with both my hands. I then would have to roll down my side window a tad to keep the front windshield from fogging up further.

"Let me give you a lift then. Where were you heading to?" I asked Carol.

"My sister's home. She lives here on base with her husband."

"Oh, you don't live on base yourself?"

"No, I don't. I was just visiting my sister when I went to pick up a few things at the PX," Carol explained.

"Well, I'll drive you to your sister's then," I assured her.

When I did drop her off, she thanked me and for the very first time that I could recall, she smiled at me.

"You are a nice lady, Rosey. I'm sorry I was… you know, at first," Carol said humbly.

I told her not to give it a second thought, but before I could drive away Carol asked me something, namely my full name. "Rosey Adams," I replied.

"Well, thank you again, Rosey Adams, for your kindness. I won't soon forget it." Carol promised me, but I'm not sure why.

We exchanged pleasantries one more time, and then I drove away. On my way back to my house, I noticed the sun had worked its way back into the sky. It's going to be a lovely day after all I thought, quite a lovely day.

———————•———•———————

THE NEXT AFTERNOON, I HAD JUST PUT MY FEET UP AND was watching a bit of telly. The doorbell of my front door sounded, ruining my moment of relaxation. I scurried over to open it, and to my surprise, I found Carol, the woman I saved from the rain the day before, standing on my front step. I was surprised as I just said, to say the least, but happily, I invited her in.

"I hope I'm not bothering you," Carol said as she entered my home.

Of course, she wasn't, and I told her as much. "How are you doing, Carol?"

"Fine," she replied. "At least I am dry today," she offered with a snicker. "How are you, Rosey?"

"Lovely," I answered in a hoity-toity British way.

I next invited her to come in and have a seat. I quickly turned off the telly so I could put my focus on her. "Anything to drink, any refreshments, love?" I asked as any good host would. She told me no, she was quite good in that department. But then she mentioned something I will never forget. She told me that I was the first white woman to ever call her love. That's when she said she knew she had come to the right place. I, of course, had no idea what she was on about. Because of my ignorance, I inquired about what she was implying. Carol had already struck me as a serious person, someone focused on what they wanted to accomplish, whatever that was. She proved me right by wasting no time in sharing why she was sitting in my living room. "You were so nice yesterday to do what you did."

I told her thank you of course, and that anyone should have done the same thing. Carol however quickly corrected me. "No, I don't think so, Rosey. Most white women, especially in the South, wouldn't have done what you did. I know that for a fact."

"Well, that is just…" I searched for the words. "That is just downright despicable."

"Yes, it is," Carol agreed. "And I don't know if it's because you're from England or not, but no matter, you see things very differently than most."

I was very flattered by Carol's kind comments and kept listening intently.

"You're probably wondering why I'm here today," she next opined.

"To give me a big head with all this flattery?" I joked.

"Ha! Maybe so," Carol replied.

She started to grin as we paused our chit-chat. She seemed to be preparing to ask me something. I was right about her asking me something.

"You have heard of Reverend Martin Luther King Jr., I suppose?" she began.

"Of course," I answered.

"Well, with his leadership, we, or I should say black people all over this country, especially in the South, are fighting for our equal rights," Carol continued. "In just the last five years we have made important steps to bring about this equality. Now, it's actually against the law to discriminate against black people on buses and trains, thanks to Reverend King's leadership."

It was at that moment that I butted in to share with

Carol my Georgia bus stories from years before and how awful I felt about what I had seen. She told me that just confirmed to her that I was the kind of person they were looking for. That raised two big questions I had for her. First, the kind of person for what, and secondly, who exactly are "'they'"? She went on to explain to help me understand better. "The Reverend King has made it clear to all of us that we, I mean black people when I say we, can't bring change, the kind of changes we need alone. We need white people with us to show everyone what is really possible when a person's skin color doesn't really matter anymore. Whites and blacks together, arm in arm, standing up for what's right, what's justice. That's when great changes will take place in this country."

And of course, I agreed. But exactly what she hoped to receive from me, I had no idea at all.

"Our church, like many churches throughout the South, is leading the way in trying to bring equality to black men and women. My church is planning sit-ins at businesses in the area that discriminate against blacks. This is something being done across the South to try to bring attention to the blatant racism going on. But, of course, Rosey, my church like most in the South is segregated because of history, not by plan. We have a few white members who have just started to attend services over the last few years, but not nearly enough."

I suddenly knew where this was all going and what was being asked of me. With all my heart I wanted to say yes to Carol, but there was one small matter, actually a very big matter indeed, Albert. I had promised him I would avoid getting involved in things like this so as to not bring scrutiny to him by higher-ups in the Army. I knew the Army had been desegregated by Truman since 1948, but that didn't mean the brass, the officers were happy about it. My past experience showed me they weren't. I explained all this to Carol, and she understood but still couldn't help but show her disappointment.

"Albert has sacrificed many things for me, so I'm sorry, Carol, but I think I need to do what he wants in this situation."

Carol, her smile turned to a pathetic frown, told me a second time she understood my need to support my husband as a good wife. She only wished there was another way since I would have made such a wonderful example to others of what a white woman without a racist bone in her body looked like. Her kind words made me tear up a bit. When she got up to leave, I asked her to stay a little longer. Maybe I told her, there was a way I could do both. Carol asked me what I meant.

"You know, dear…help your church with what it is doing and still not bring unwanted attention to my husband from his base commanders," I replied.

"How? I don't understand," Carol questioned, unsure of where I was going with my train of thought.

Honestly, I didn't really know either, but I thought there must be a way to help without causing Albert problems with the Army brass. There just had to be, right? "Albert would never tell me not to go to church if I wanted to. He is a big believer in church for other people, including me."

"What are you saying, Rosey?" Carol wondered.

"I'm saying, my good lady, I'm just going to be going to church, that's all. Do you understand?"

Carol's smile returned. Her frown was replaced. "You are just going to church, I get it," she said.

"What kind of church did you attend in England?" Carol asked.

"Oh, Church of England, of course. Why do you ask?" I inquired in return.

With the happiest expression I had yet seen cover her face, she let out a loud belly laugh. When I asked her what was so bloody funny, Carol laughed even louder.

"I think you are going to find my church somewhat different than what you are used to, Rosey."

———— ·•· ————

At the time I wasn't exactly sure what Carol meant about the churches being so different, but I soon found out. I discovered Carol wasn't just pulling my apron strings. All churches are certainly not the same, not in the mildest of ways. I can honestly say that in all the many years I spent in church, the Church of England that is, I never remember feeling worn out like I was that night, at Carol's church. Their service was something unique, strange, and breathtaking all at the same time. It certainly wasn't what I was expecting, there's no arguing that. In the churches back in England, you only stood for short, fleeting moments during a service. You might stand to recite the words of the minister at his urging, or during some hymns. At Carol's Southern Baptist church, I was spent by the end of the service as we stood throughout the singing of hymns and even jumped up often during her minister's, or pastor as she called him, sermon. And even though there were only a handful of folks like myself at the service, that is people of white-skin persuasion, I really never felt out of place. Strangely, I have to say, everyone there made me feel comfortable and accepted. I pondered later if the reason for that was that they, the black men and women of the church, had been made to feel uncomfortable themselves in so many situations in life that they were hell-bent not to let others have that same awful experience. Whatever the reason, I had a lovely time and realized that there were people whose passion for the Lord was much more pronounced, at least on the surface, than my own. This fact about myself didn't bring resentment toward them, as you might think, but instead made me realize that my upbringing and beliefs were not the only ones living freely in the world. I actually admired how their faith strengthened them in this fight they were enduring every day of their lives against bigotry and just plain meanness.

After the service, Pastor Mitchell invited all who were interested into a back room of the church to discuss what Carol had brought me here for. I noticed all the white folks stayed after church to attend. Evidently, they were here for this meeting as much as for the church service. Pastor Mitchell spoke about the planned sit-ins as he called them, to take place throughout the area very soon. People of several racial stripes would join together to go to places where segregation was still at its worst. These hot spots for the sit-ins included restaurants, department stores, and office buildings all over the county. According to the pastor, many churches in the area were joining under a call for action, led by the distinguished Reverend King himself. These were to be peaceful and respectful defiance of immoral laws and practices, the pastor explained. The Reverend King demanded us to all act in these ways as to garner favor with those who observed the protests. The nuts and bolts of what made up these sit-ins came next and as best as I could see, they entailed going to a place and demanding nicely

Andrew Scott Bassett

the services or products the business offered, be given to anyone, regardless of their skin color. We were told to sing hymns or pray while "'sitting in'". We needed to be peaceful, respectful, and kind at all times. It all sounded very pleasant indeed, for such a terrible situation. That is, until the pastor mentioned an important caveat to our activities, that we all could end up in the hoosgow, or the slammer as the Yanks like to call it. Yes, being arrested was a real possibility as an end result of our protest. It was at this moment of the night that I first realized I might be in a pinch over my head. When it came time to fill out some paperwork and be assigned the place to go for the sit-ins, I had to speak up, and it surely wasn't easy. With Carol staring right at me, I had to say that as much as I wanted to be a part of 'this', and truly wished that I could, well…I just couldn't. Carol was disappointed, but once again she knew the reason why before I even had to say it. "It's your husband, isn't it?"

I nodded sadly. I couldn't take a chance on being arrested and the consequences that would follow for Albert with the Army. Carol was understanding. She knew from our earlier discussion on the subject where I stood. She hoped that the church service and the meeting tonight would change my mind. I told her in no uncertain terms it had made me much more supportive of civil rights for black people. Still, any direct action by me, like a protest or a sit-in, was not possible right now. Before Carol could say another word, her pastor interrupted and after overhearing me, asked if I would still be willing to come to the church and help behind the scenes. After a quick consideration of his idea, I told him I would be happy to do what I could from behind the scenes. I also said I would be delighted to continue to attend church services. He and Carol were both very pleased with my decision. She gave me a big welcoming hug, to cement our agreement, Pastor Mitchell did the same.

"Your insight, Rosey, both as a white woman and as someone coming from another country, could be valuable for our fight for civil justice in this country," he shared with me.

I didn't know if I could bring all that much to the fight, but I was happy to help in any way that I could.

He chuckled as he asked me how I liked my first Southern Baptist church service. I grinned as I shared with him that although I enjoyed the experience, it was very different from the church services I was accustomed to.

"It is a bit different from the English churches, I imagine," The pastor responded.

"Like the difference between having a president, and a queen," I told him. "They both are rulers, but they do it so very differently."

I don't believe the pastor really understood what I meant by that, but we still all shared a good laugh nonetheless, and then I said my cheerios for the night.

———— • • ————

THE SATURDAY THEY SPOKE OF FOR THE SIT-INS THAT first night at the church turned out to be three weeks away. So, during that time, I went to each mid-week church service and even a Sunday morning one. Albert was fine with me going to church as long as he didn't have to tag along. I, of course, didn't give the full amount of details, you know about the coming sit-ins protest that I was helping to organize or the fact that the church I was attending was primarily a black church. I didn't plan on allowing myself to get involved in a manner that would bring consternation to Albert from his superiors. Anyway, what I was doing was important, incredibly important actually. It was up to people like myself to stand up for what's right, to help bloody well bring changes to the country that it so desperately needed no matter if the country knew it or not. So, there you have it. I was justified in my own eyes. What I was doing was important, and Albert wouldn't be in the least bit hurt. It was all a smashing success until the last mid-week service, right before the first sit-in would take place on the weekend. I was helping Pastor Mitchell and some other ladies after service in the church offices. Carol was with me. We were working on more signs and making last-minute calls to sympathetic white folks in the area. We were asking for support and for many of them to come out and participate in the sit-ins. Suddenly, Pastor Mitchell came into our room and interrupted our work. He was looking straight at me, and unlike his normal expression, he looked very serious.

"Is everything all right, Pastor?" I asked him.

He forced a smile to his face as he told me there was someone out front to see me. I thought for a moment about who it could be. The pastor could see what was germinating between my ears and made it easy for me. "Your husband is out front, Rosey. He wants to speak with you."

It was one of those strange times in life when you leave the present for a moment and feel like you have stepped back into time. I remembered being a child and being caught by my pappy trying to steal a piece of treacle pudding from our kitchen counter. He slapped my hand before the fork entered my mouth. It's still so vivid because it was the only time I could recall my old pap laying a hand on me. I was caught then, and I was caught now, albeit this was a noble cause and not a just desire for sweets. Regardless, it was time for me to take my medicine, face the music, and all that riff-raff. Happily, Albert was smiling when he saw me come out to greet him. "I'm not as mad as you think I am," he said as I walked up.

"Why not?" I blurted back at him. It was all I could think to say.

Albert shared with me he was at first, extremely angry when he found out I had been coming to 'this church', behind his back. When I tried to interject that in truth, I did tell him I was going to church, he cut my words right off. "I know you did, but you didn't tell me it was this kind of church."

"And what does that matter then, eh?" I countered, feeling my own temperature rising in the conversation.

"Let me finish! Alright!" Albert argued in his defense. "As I said, I was mad at first, but the minister here..."

"Pastor Mitchell," I offered.

"Yeah, him. He talked to me when I got here, Rosey. He seems like a swell man, and, well, he told me what you were doing here to help with what the church and other people in the area were trying to do.

"And?" I replied.

"And...then he told me how he and others here wanted you to participate in the sit-ins, but you wouldn't because of me," Albert continued.

I stood quiet, letting my defenses down a tad.

"He said you only agreed to help with things behind the scenes because you were afraid I might get in trouble with the Army if they found out."

"That about sums it up," I added.

Next the unexpected happened, Albert came over and

took me in his arms. He kissed me on the lips the way he did when he shared with me how lucky he was to have found me.

"You're not, as you Yanks like to say, pissed then?"

Albert burst out in laughter before saying. "Not anymore, I know how much you care about people and want to help, but what I really realized after speaking with the minister here is how much you care about me."

I have to admit a small tear rolled down my cheek when Albert said those words to me. I was in love with him at that moment, as great as I had ever been.

"You keep doing whatever it is you're doing here. And even though I don't need to tell you this, yeah, if you could keep it under wraps so the Army doesn't find out and put my butt in a sling, that would be nice."

I nodded I would, as I now returned the loving embrace. Albert then shared that he had something he needed to talk to me about soon. I asked him what it might be, but he said it could wait till another time, nothing urgent he said. With that, he told me to get back to work, that he would see me when I got back home. He left as Carol came out to see if everything was all right. I told her I just learned a valuable lesson.

"What's that?" she asked.

"I didn't realize how good I had it," I told her.

"He's okay with this?" she questioned.

"Surprisingly so," I answered. "I really underestimated him. I hope I don't do that again."

"Shall we get back to work, huh? There are still calls to make and a few other things to finish up," Carol reminded me.

"Let's indeed," I said with a laugh, hardly able to contain how brilliantly happy I felt at this moment.

It wasn't until the next night that Albert and I finally had a chance to talk. I could tell that he had something important to speak to me about. However, when he made me take a seat on our sofa for some chit-chat, I really became concerned. He started with how lucky we had been since he joined the Army since there had been no wars that the United States had been involved in. I have to say I wasn't thrilled with the beginning of our conversation. Then, after several more minutes of beating around the bush, he made it to his real point. He asked me what I knew about

Vietnam. In a silly fashion, even for me, I asked if he was talking about the country. This lightened the mood in the room for a moment as it was much too solemn for my liking. He gathered his serious self quite quickly and continued. "The Army feels that we are on the edge possibly, and I only mean possibly, of a conflict beginning in Vietnam."

"You don't mean another bleeding war? Oh, my sweet lord, you must be joking!" I responded with disbelief.

Albert attempted as best as he could to calm my fears, but sadly he failed.

"Not again, Albert! You just missed out on going to Korea, and now this rubbish!"

I was fit to be tied. I had already experienced more war in my lifetime than I ever dreamed of, and I certainly didn't want to go back to living like that again. As I watched Albert try to explain what he was being ordered to do, all I could think of was my Uncle George kissing me on the cheek one minute and then leaving for war to never be heard from again. I knew I could not go on if the same fate were to happen to my husband. "Why do you have to go?"

Andrew Scott Bassett

"I've become such an accomplished helicopter pilot Rosey that they want me to train and lead other pilots over there. You see, there are a lot of jungles in Vietnam, and we need to be prepared for military operations if need be. I will teach other pilots how we operate in such conditions," Albert explained.

I was still not understanding. "You've only been flying for a short time. How can you be training others?" I questioned.

"Well, I'm going to be preparing for flying in those conditions as well. You see, they, my commanders, feel I'll be a real asset helping the younger soldiers not only with the flying in the jungle but also the stress of the situation, you know being so far from home and all."

I pleaded with him to ask if he could just not go, but Albert would hear none of that. "It's my duty, Rosey. I'm a soldier. Just preparing for military action doesn't mean that it has to happen. You know, I think that President Kennedy is a pretty smart fella. He understands war, and I'm sure he learned from what happened in Korea," Albert added, attempting to ease my concerns.

He didn't. "I hate bloody war! Why does this country have to be over in Vietnam anyways?" I demanded to know, my voice rising with frustration.

"It's about stopping the spread of communism. You know, first they took over half of Europe, and you saw what they did in Germany. The next thing you know they're here in the States," Albert proclaimed, trying to justify all he was telling me.

I understood all of that of course. I was old enough to have heard the same arguments about the Korean War. I reminded Albert how that war ended. It ended with nothing really being accomplished, as far as I could tell. There were, of course, in the Korean War, the usual results of such endeavors, many young men dead and many young widows created.

"What about World War II? Should we have not waged war against Germany, should we have just let Hitler take over the world?" Albert countered suddenly.

I told him as my temper began to get the best of me that he didn't need to remind me of that war. I already knew more about it than I ever could have wanted to.

"My point, Rosey, is that some wars are worth fighting. Stopping the Nazis was one. I think stopping the spread of communism is another. If we had kids someday, would you want them to live in a communist country?" he challenged me with.

I thought it strange he would bring up children when we weren't able to have any of our own, and he had no desire to look into adoption. And though I conceded that he was right that there were times when the awful thing called war was a necessary evil, I also pointed out that like what happened in Korea only a decade earlier, that some wars didn't make any bloody sense. For me, this Vietnam situation sounded too much like Korea all over again.

"When do you have to leave?" I asked, not really wanting to hear his reply.

"Next week I'm afraid."

I was stunned it was so soon. "How long will you be gone?"

He didn't know.

"What about me then? Will I be staying here in Alabama on base, or what?" I inquired, as my emotions began to get the best of me, and the tears began to roll.

"You'll stay here on base. Nothing will change for you, Rosey," Albert replied as he reached out and wiped away my tears.

"Except… that I will wonder every moment of the day and night if my husband is still alive. That will be my big change, Albert," I said, now wiping away my own tears.

He scooched closer to me and pulled me close. He promised me that nothing would happen to him, that he would come home safe. I heard his words, but all I could see in my thoughts were my Uncle George's face.

"Saturday's your thingy with the colored church, right?" Albert threw in, as he tried to take my mind off of his leaving.

I mumbled as I snotted and swallowed, and eventually said yes, but reminded him that they want to be called black, not colored.

"Right, sorry about that, well…that's something to think about, you know, get your mind off of me leaving and all," he stated, hoping it really might help me.

Between gulps of air and more swallowing snot and sniffling, I told him fine. I guess he had his orders, and there was really nothing I could do. Unfortunately, a new grim reality was about to overtake me. My mind was captured with the idea that this might be the last week of my life, with my husband. All the going on about an unjust world and complaining and moaning to Albert wasn't going to change a damn thing. After a few hours of suffering and soul searching, I came to my senses and made up my mind. If this was possibly the last week of my life with Albert, I was going to make it one to remember for him. I was determined to give him a reason to make it back to me, a reason to come home from the bloody jungles of Vietnam.

THE DINER CHOSEN FOR OUR SIT-IN, THE ONE PICKED BY the church I had been attending with Carol, was packed with people both inside the building and out. Ten people from our congregation, all black, grabbed seats at the diner's front counter and waited to be served. I watched from a nearby booth with several other white folks who also attended our church. This place was chosen for its awful racist policies toward black people. It did not take long for the drama to begin to unfold, as the waitresses working in the diner refused to even give menus to their black customers. When our team demanded service, the workers got more heated and finally, the cook came out of the kitchen and demanded that the blacks leave at once. We knew this would happen, we planned for it. The church had photographers on hand with tape recorders and legal help at the ready, with a civil rights attorney able and willing to help. When the cameras started snapping photos, the cook went off the deep end and grabbed a telephone to call the police. For the next fifteen minutes, we all waited for the police to show up. During that time, I and many others in the restaurant pleaded with the staff of the place to do the right thing. We demanded that they serve and treat their black customers just as they would their white. Others, however, in the restaurant, told us to be quiet, before stringing together racist profanities directed right at us. The cook and the waitresses did the same to our team of ten, who bravely only smiled and promised to pray for them and for the diner. Then our guys and gals began to sing church hymns as they demonstrated in perfect illustration, Reverend King's ideas of peaceful resistance.

Andrew Scott Bassett

Finally, the police showed up. The cook and waitresses had lost their minds with anger when they saw our cameras snapping away at them. They tried to take the cameras away and so did some of the other customers in the diner, not sympathetic to our cause. The mob successfully grabbed all but Carol's camera. When they grabbed for hers, Carol didn't react peacefully, she pushed back. She even shoved one larger white man onto his backside, and this made me fear for her safety as the mob came to his aid. Fortunately, by now law enforcement was pushing the sides apart and beginning to regain order. When the police figured out what was going on without really listening to our side of things, they began to haul away our team of protesters and anyone they believed supported them. The man who fell after being pushed by Carol pointed her out to the police, as one of the main protesters. When she saw this, she quickly handed it to me from behind, out of the sight of the mob, her camera, and tape recorder. The civil rights attorney instantly came to her aid and demanded to know what she had done, or anyone for that matter who was being arrested. Law enforcement yelled for him to shut up. They didn't care who he was or that he was a civil rights attorney. They next snatched up Carol and pulled her outside. By this time, the local television news reporter was onto the story and waiting outside for everyone as they were being escorted to police vehicles. There weren't enough seats for everyone in the back of the police cars, but local law enforcement didn't care in the least. With no concern for safety or respect for the people they were hauling away, the cops just threw all of them into the backseat, piled up in any manner they pleased. Our members, and others being taken away, were scrunched together, sitting on each other's laps or worse.

It was a disgusting display of a lack of respect for human beings, and I told the officers as much. They told me to be quiet or I would join the others on their trip to the jail. At that moment I thought of Albert and all I had promised him, so I backed away. I did yell to Carol as the police car with her jammed in the backseat, pulled away. "You'll be out in no time, dear!" I hollered.

She couldn't wave with her hands cuffed behind her back, but she smiled and nodded her head, letting me know she heard what I said. The attorney now standing next to me assured me they would all make bail shortly, that his organization would make sure of it. I couldn't help but wonder if all this today had really made a difference at all. I asked him his thoughts.

"Peaceful resistance is more powerful than you would ever believe," he retorted. "Gandhi showed its power years before in India, and that is where the Reverend King learned these lessons."

"Being peaceful didn't work with Hitler," I quickly reminded him, throwing in my own two cents.

For some strange reason, he found my comment humorous. He chuckled at it.

I wondered what was so bloody funny.

"Nothing would have worked with Hitler, except killing him," the attorney remarked. "But we will prevail in this battle against injustice and bigotry."

"How can you be so sure?" I questioned.

"Because, my fair lady," he said, "just as with Hitler, we have to win."

I said no more. I just chewed on his words for a bit. I knew he was right.

Andrew Scott Bassett

THE NEXT WEEK WAS A BLUR OF ACTIVITY FOR ME. Happily, Carol was released from jail as a civil rights organization sent the money to Pastor Mitchell for her bail. I was still worried for her as the authorities still had not dropped the charges against her. The pastor said that he was confident that Carol would get off with only a warning after he spoke with the same attorney I had spoken to. I certainly prayed they were both right. Then, without an emotional break, the day was upon me that I most feared. Albert was leaving for Vietnam. His leaving had stirred up so many terrible things in me, god-awful memories. I had hoped that war would never be a part of my life again. Now, the United States wasn't in a war at this point, so maybe I was being irrational, but something told me it was coming. This whole bloody thing in Vietnam reminded me of the news-reels we watched in regard to Korea. America at first started by sending in advisors and small units to support the side fighting the communists, and then the next thing you know they're caught with their trousers down, and they're knee-deep in a full-fledged war. I mentioned none of this on our last night together. The last thing Albert needed right now was to have all my fears thrust upon him. I'm certain he was afraid, but he didn't let me in on it. We sat on our little sofa and shared cocktails that he made for us. We snuggled and acted like two silly teenagers, fooling around when the parents weren't present. If he had significant fears of the deployment he was beginning tomorrow, he wasn't behaving like it. When I tried to get him to open up about such things, he only offered that he was fine. He promised me everything would be okay, that his training all these years had prepared him for all this. His words again reminded me of my Uncle George. This again, I did not share with Albert. I saw no point in it.

Later that evening, we made love. It was tender and sweet. And though I enjoyed it as I always did with Albert, part of my mind kept telling me that this could be the last time, we were, you know, "'together.'" Afterward, as I lay in his arms, I listened to his breathing as he fell fast asleep. My thoughts raced with so many dreadful considerations that sleep was not even an option for me. I listened to Albert breathe all night. If I was about to lose him, I was going to cherish every second I had with him on potentially our last night together.

<hr />

I DIDN'T GET TO SEE HIM OFF AT THE AIRPORT. I JUST watched as he climbed into the front seat of an Army truck. Before he left that morning, I asked him if it would be okay for me to go back to England. He said it was probably a good idea and that I should go visit my family. We both knew it was necessary for me to have my family with me to help support me, as I feared night and day that something terrible was about to happen to Albert. He didn't give this as the reason he thought it would be a good idea for me to go home, but we both knew it was the proverbial elephant in the room. I put on a brave front and received happily the kisses he blew me as he disappeared into the truck. I clutched and stored them somewhere inside of me, determined to not lose them until he could replace them again with the real thing.

CHAPTER 12

Danny hears a knock at the front door. It disrupts him from hunting for a snack in his sister's kitchen. He's not sure where Lori's at, so he yells out to no one in particular that he will see who it is. He finds his sister's ex-boyfriend, Bobby, lurching on the front porch with a huge sheepdog beside him.

"Hey, yo', Danny boy, how's it hanging?"

Danny invites him in, dog and all. Lori finally comes strolling from the back of the house and immediately heads over and grabs the dog by the leash and takes it away from Bobby.

"Your dog?" Danny inquires.

"Oh yeah, you haven't met before, have ya'? This is Yoko, you know like Yoko Ono, John Lennon's wife," Bobby explains.

Danny is quick to assure Bobby that he figured the dog was named after Yoko Ono since there aren't many other famous Yoko's, he's aware of. Bobby doesn't get the sarcasm.

"We're going to be dog-sitting her for the next few days. Bobby's going out of town," Lori shares with her brother.

"Really, hmm," Danny responds, not sure what else to say. "She must eat like a small elephant's portion of kibble every day, I'm guessing."

"Ha! Almost," Bobby replies with a laugh.

Lori crouches down eye to eye with the mighty beast, rubbing it under the chin. "How's my sweet baby girl today?"

For Lori, who never managed to have children, her pets have always been like her kids and treated better than most children are by their parents.

"Hey…also good news on the veteran's cemetery," Bobby pops off with.

"Oh, they're going to meet with us?" Lori asks him, being surprisingly nice suddenly to her ex.

"Yep, I pulled some strings and talked to my buddy over there. You've got an appointment in two days. You just have to call them up, and here's the number," Bobby relates as he hands her a piece of folded-up paper. "My buddy whose name's on the paper, he's expecting your call."

"Wow! You really came thru, Bobby," Lori tells him, acting surprised.

Bobby returns her half-hearted compliment by boasting, "That is just how I roll."

Lori does some rolling herself. She rolls her eyes at his not-so-humble declaration. Still, Lori is thankful for what Bobby did in getting them this appointment. This is the first that Danny has heard about all this. "What's going on?"

Lori lets him know that they are going to get to talk to the officials from the most prestigious veteran's cemetery in the whole area. It's where their mom wanted to be buried. Danny is taken aback by the news. "Veteran's cemetery? Why did she want to be buried there?"

"Because she wanted to be buried there," Lori answers curtly.

Danny finds that puzzling after reading so much of his mother's story and remembering her words, both in the pages she left for him, and in real life. The burial doesn't seem to jive with his mother's feelings about war and the military. He can't help but ask again if Lori is sure that this is what Mom wanted. "She said those words, I want to be buried in a military veteran's cemetery?"

"Yes. The military played a big part in her life, Danny. She was married to a soldier for a long time," Lori answers, defending her statement. "What's your problem with that?"

Bobby then adds how beautiful a place it is and that Danny should go out and see it for himself.

"I'm sure it is," Danny answers. "Just after what she always said about war, and from what I've read so far in her biography or whatever you want to call it that she left me, it seems like a strange decision for Mom."

"Well, that's what she wanted, Danny. She spent most of her life living and dealing with the military. It played a big part in her life. I pledged to Mom that I was going to make sure that her wishes were granted."

Danny said no more. He could see that his sister had made up her mind and there was no changing it. Bobby looked at his watch and announced it was time for him to get going. He wished them both good luck with the meeting at the cemetery. Bobby couldn't promise if they, the cemetery officials, would approve of her burial or not, but at least they were meeting with them. Danny wasn't aware it was so difficult to get in.

"It's a process, and there's a lot of people trying to get loved ones buried there, so, yeah, it's not a slam dunk or anything," Bobby explains to him.

Bobby then gives his hairy canine a smooch and squeeze before escaping out the front door. Lori takes Yoko, the sheepdog, out to the backyard, to give her a tour of the place. Now, with the house quiet, Danny goes back to his bedroom to work on his second book. He finishes another chapter. It is excruciatingly painful and when he rereads it, he is anything but impressed by his own words. Danny is so frustrated he slams his laptop down onto the small desk in the room. His agent and his publisher will be calling soon. They will be expecting something good, and good is not something he has for them, and he knows it.

———— •—•—• ————

I MADE MY WAY BACK HOME TO ENGLAND BY SHIP ONLY weeks after Albert left. I never really liked to fly, and thanks to being a frugal person, I had saved enough to make the trip. It would take fourteen days to cross the Atlantic Ocean by luxury liner, and I enjoyed every day of it. The food alone made the trip worth every shilling I had spent. Being a woman on my own I, of course, received the attention of every single man aboard the ship. Some ladies might not appreciate the attention, but I rather liked it. Not, mind you, because I would ever be tempted by another man's charms, but because it reaffirmed that I still had it. There are times when an old, young married woman like myself, still needed to know that there was still a little sizzle in the pan. As gentlemen after gentlemen attempted, but failed, to sweep me off my feet for the rest of our trip, I found out that without a doubt there was still a small bit of heat coming from my fire. It was a fun adventure, and for at least some of the time, my thoughts of worry for Albert were not controlling my every moment. And please don't take me the wrong way, I never once showed any of the young brood of men flashing their pearly whites in my direction the slightest amount of flirtation. I was polite to them not cruel, but never flirtatious. My heart as always only belonged to Albert.

We pulled into the docks of London at night. I would see my family in the morning. I was so excited to spend time with them, and I hoped that they could take my mind off of Albert and the danger he was likely in. I knew in my heart that if there was anyone in the world who could help me keep things in the right perspective about my husband and all the worry that I carried around with me like a big sack of bricks, it was my old pap. I missed his wise words, his understanding of the world that somehow always made me see things in a better and clearer way. That night, I slept poorly. My dreams were taken prisoner, and after weeks of mostly not going barmy with thoughts of my husband's demise, I was this last night bombarded with them. I woke up the next morning in my cabin on the ship in a cold sweat. Thank God, I'll see my family today, I thought as I sipped a nice cup of coffee. It wasn't English tea, but it would have to do. It was now time to get ready for the big day. I dressed and put on my face. I packed my bags, and then I was ready to go. My family was out there somewhere waiting for me, and I couldn't wait to see them. It certainly had been too long since I had been home, and England would always be home.

———— •—•—• ————

MY EYES SCANNED BACK AND FORTH ACROSS THE LONDON docks searching for my family. It didn't take long for my old pap's grinning face to make itself known amongst the crowds of people who were there to greet their loved ones. He saw me at the same time, and I could see him give a wee nudge to my mum to let her know that I was spotted. I was surprised to see my sister, Sheila, and her boyfriend, Trevor following behind them. "Rosey!" Sheila screamed out toward me.

I waved to let her know I heard her. In a few moments we were all together, and the tears began to flow.

"Oh, my dearest ducky!" my mum cried out when she saw me up close for the first time in what seemed like donkey years.

Mum started balling as she grabbed me and wrapped her arms tightly around me.

"Mum's a tiny bit happy to see you I guess," my sister said with a sarcastic giggle.

Then it was Pappy's turn. He almost lifted me off the ground, but I wasn't a child anymore and he wasn't as young as he once was. "Be careful then, Pap, you'll hurt yourself." I nagged him.

"I don't care, my old duck, I'm just so bloody happy to see ya,'" he shot back.

Next, it was Sheila and Trevor. Their smiling faces were a wonderful surprise because I had no idea that they would be here to pick me up with Pap and Mum. A few minutes later, we were all packed like sardines into Pap's van and on our way back to Northampton. I was in the backseat sitting with my sister and her boyfriend. Those two kept making faces at each other and acting like silly sods. I felt like there was a joke going on, and I was the only one who didn't know what it was all about. I finally, quite rudely, asked them if they were getting a rise out of me or something.

"Making fun? I'm quite sure I don't know what you're on about, Rosey dear," Sheila argued in her defense.

I then turned my attention to Trevor. I put him on the spot. "Tell me truthfully then, Trevor old dear, are you taking a mick out of me?"

A grin filled his face from ear to ear. "A mick out of you? A mick out of you, Rosey? God forbid, I would never do that to you, haha!"

"Blimey then, why are you both acting so barmy, you

and Sheila?" I demanded to know.

"Oh, Sheila dear, you better tell her now," my Mum chimed in from the front seat.

Pappy agreed. "Yes, you two better just let her in on your big secret already."

"Secret, what's this secret business all about then?" I wanted to know.

Sheila and Trevor looked at each other trying to decide who would spill the beans first. "She's your sister," Trevor whispered, which seemed to sway the decision.

I, at that point had, had enough and demanded that somebody tell me something.

"We're getting married!" Sheila at last blurted out.

"Oh, my goodness! That is wonderful news!" I hollered back. Sheila and I suddenly embraced. It was the second time that morning.

"I know it is. It's been such a long time with us, but we finally thought the time was right," Sheila shared enthusiastically.

"It is about bloody time for you two, enough with your living in sin," my Pappy spouted off from the front seat, as he took his eyes off the road for a moment to give Trevor a dirty look.

Mum elbowed him and told him to keep his mouth closed and his mind on his driving.

"How could we be living in sin, Pappy, when we never even lived together?" Sheila argued.

"You know what I mean, duck. I wasn't born yesterday." Pappy answered.

"Be quiet then, Fred. They're finally getting married and that's what's important now, isn't it?" Mum said to Pap, scolding him, using her stern voice.

Pappy grunted his agreement and stopped butting in on the conversation.

"So then, tell me, when is the big day?" I asked with excitement.

"In ten days. We've been waiting for you to come home first," Sheila replied.

"You've been waiting for me? All this time waiting for me to come back to England so you could get married?"

"Yes," Sheila responded. "I wanted you here, of course, for the wedding. I want you to be my matron of honor."

Now I was feeling more than a tad emotional. I reached out and held my little sister's hand. I was truly touched by the news.

"Trevor and I knew you'd come home to visit eventually, and we decided when you did that we would get married while you were here," my sister explained.

"And I'm glad you finally decided to visit, Rosey dear, because I couldn't have held out much longer," Trevor suddenly interjected, with a chuckle.

"And what is that supposed to mean then?" Sheila asked him, accompanying her question with a menacing look.

Trevor laughed some more as he told me that this is what he was talking about. His response didn't please my sister, and she told him so. I pleaded with them to not start something when I just got here and was feeling so jolly good from the big news.

"It's nothing, darling. I just love you so much and couldn't stand to wait any longer to make you my bride." Trevor told Sheila, in a sincere but cheeky way.

When he tried to give her a little snuggle, she pushed him away. "Oh, shove off then! You are so full of beans," my sister fired at him.

"Now you too behave yourselves. This is very unbecoming to talk to each other in such a way right before your wedding," my Mum said, lecturing both of them for their behavior.

When Mum asked Pap to back her up, he told her that he was minding his own business just as she had ordered him to.

"Do you two always go on like this, then?" I asked both my sister and Trevor.

Trevor nodded, trying not to laugh. Sheila sighed and did the same. "He's a royal pain in my arse, Rosey, but I still love him."

With that, Trevor grabbed at her again and this time she let him.

"Are you two going to make it for the next ten days?" Pappy chirped in, his words dripping sarcasm.

Mum elbowed him again. "Keep your eyes on the road, Fred, eyes on the road."

———————◆———————

SHEILA TWIRLED BEFORE ME LIKE A CROSS BETWEEN A ballroom dancer and a princess. She sparkled and stunned in her gorgeous white wedding gown. I had been back home only a few days when she invited me over to her flat to see her wedding dress and to try on the matron of honor one she had picked out for me. It seemed almost frumpy compared to her lovely design. I wouldn't dare tell her that, mind you. This event wasn't about me. It was about her, and, boy, did she know it. Sheila and I had always been very different, even as children. Now, we were both prone to speak our minds for certain, but Sheila was always more flamboyant and dramatic than me. I could give and take a little more of what life wanted to throw at me. My little sister, however, demanded her way or the highway. In truth, I always admired that about her. She didn't put up with anyone's bullocks. Trevor was cheeky and a bit of a wild lad, but he still knew who wore the trousers in their relationship, and it wasn't him. It sounds terrible, but I often thought that Pappy and Mum were a bit afraid of Sheila. She did tower over them in height and stature and also by force of personality. She had a Jane Russell figure, full-figured and ready to intimidate the opposite sex. I on the other hand, literally and figuratively couldn't hold her brassiere if I wished to. That body and that personality made many a man melt before her wry smile and wicked laugh. I knew that she and Trevor had had many ups and downs over the years and more than a few break-ups. Mum wrote me letters keeping me up to date on such things. But at last, Sheila seemed ready to settle down and tame her wild ways, and I was happy for her.

"Well then…how do I look? You're being awfully quiet over there," Sheila declared, as she studied herself in the full-sized standing mirror she had in her bedroom.

My sister loved compliments, no actually, she insisted on them. I happily acquiesced and told her how beautiful she looked, even though she already knew.

"Try yours on then, Rosey," she ordered me.

I did as she asked, and I looked frumpy and plain as I thought I would.

"You look so lovely in that dress, Rosey," she told me.

I thanked her for her kind words even though we both knew I didn't.

"I can't believe I am finally getting married, can you?" Sheila exclaimed. "I wasn't sure at times if it was meant to be with Trev."

"Really?" I responded, surprised by her comment.

"No, I really at times had my doubts that we would ever get to this place, but I guess that's only natural, aye?"

"Of course," I agreed.

"Oh, and listen to me blather on then. I'm sure you have similar thoughts with everything going on with Albert," Sheila added.

I had no idea what she was on about and asked her to clarify.

"Oh, you know with all the uncertainty, the terrible uncertainty about Albert and his safe return," she went on.

Now, I understood what she was getting at. "Are you asking if I worry about what happens… if Albert doesn't come home safe?"

Sheila for a moment stopped her primping and posing to look me in the eyes. She sensed that she had hit a nerve with me. "All I'm saying, love, is it would be unnatural if you didn't think about such things."

"You mean life without Albert, meeting new men, and all that malarky?" I retorted.

She shrugged and sighed. That was exactly what she was getting at. I didn't want to even give those kinds of thoughts any foothold in my mind. Surely, I did think those things at times for a brief moment, but I would quickly squash them with all my might. "I don't ever think or believe or let myself believe, that Albert is not coming back to me. You know it's not even war over there yet."

"Of course not, you're right, dear. One shouldn't even give consideration to such ideas. I'm sorry I even broached the subject, love," Sheila said, as she realized her words had stirred things up in me.

I made her believe it was fine, nothing to worry about, but of course, there really was. In an attempt to lighten the mood, she let me in on a trip that she and I and the other three bridesmaids would be making to Hamburg Germany, only two days before the wedding. It would be the last blast of jolly good fun for Sheila before the 'big' day.

"Why Hamburg?" I questioned. "Isn't there someplace in London we could go?"

Sheila laughed at me as if the idea was silly about London. "Hamburg is the place to go right now for fun. It's a bit like your Las Vegas in America, only for Europeans," she said.

"Lots of shows and things to do then?" I questioned.

"Nightclubs, dancing, music, naughty things, the whole bleeding shooting match, dear," Sheila promised.

"What do you mean by naughty?" I wondered, both nervous and curious.

"Oh, I don't know, Rosey…lots of fun, some nudity, but mostly lots of fun and music. I understand that American rock and roll music is very popular there, almost like being in America."

The music aspect sounded fine, but I wondered about the naked part. I was no prude, but still just a few days before her marriage to Trevor. I wondered if it was wise to partake in such things.

Sheila assured me there was nothing to worry about, that we would all have a lovely time right before she settled down with her new husband and her new married life. "We'll take a look around and enjoy the sights and have a bit of fun, Rosey. That's all, love. I'm sure Trevor and his mates will be doing the same thing, right here in Northampton or Kettering, where some of his mates live."

Andrew Scott Bassett

At that moment, a funny thought came into my head. What if we bumped into Trevor and his mates in Hamburg doing the same thing we were doing? When I shared this crazy idea with Sheila, it stopped her in her tracks. "That bloody sod better not be in Hamburg. I'd castrate him right on the spot," she said with an evil laugh.

That got me to join in on the humor. And before we knew it, we were both lying on her bed laughing at the very idea of both the groom's gang and the bridal party bumping into each other while celebrating in Hamburg. "He would be a dead man, Rosey!" Sheila shouted at me, before beginning to laugh deliriously once again.

<hr />

A FEW DAYS LATER, BUT STILL CHEWING ON THE IDEAS that Sheila brought to the surface, I had some time to myself with my mum shopping in town. I decided to walk over and see my old pap on his land. He was about two blocks from the family home. I knew he was off work that day from his shoe factory job and would be spending his time tending to his garden. I could hear Pappy singing as I made my way past his greenhouse and to one of his work sheds. I wasn't sure which one he was in, so I followed his voice. He didn't have a good voice, but that never stopped him from singing his heart out. On this day he was attempting to sing *"Walk the Line"* by Johnny Cash, the American country-western singer. My pap loved country music for some reason that I never understood. His favorite was Hank Williams. How often did I hear him butchering '*Hey, Good Lookin'*'? I couldn't even count. I did finally find him in his work shed, his "'garden office,'" as he liked to call it. He was attempting to find something that was missing, probably a garden tool.

He immediately stopped his crooning as soon as he heard me walk up. "Hello, ducky, what brings you here?"

I really didn't know the answer to the question, but something told me, an inner voice possibly, that for some reason one of my old pap's talks was just what I needed. Sheila's questioning me about Albert's return, or the possibility he wouldn't, God forbid, had my insides swirling like a washing machine. I had tried so hard not to think about the what-ifs, to tell myself that there was presently no war going on in Vietnam and that President Kennedy wasn't going to let such a thing start, but…

"You and your sister got all the bridal trip details ironed out, then?" Pappy inquired.

I told him we did, and that I was very surprised that he was going to drive us to the ports of London, from where we would catch a ferry across the pond that would eventually lead us to Germany.

"Well, with you with her, ducky, I feel much better about the whole business," he confided.

I thanked him for his confidence in me. "You must be happy, Pap, that Sheila and Trevor are going to finally tie the knot," I stated.

"It was about time," he answered with a snicker.

"You and Mum like Trevor it seems?"

Pappy hesitated to answer me at first. I realized at that moment that I never had really asked him or Mum, in all this time, what they thought of the bloke.

"You know, Rosey…" he started with. "At first, I didn't care for the young man, but now all these years later, I've seen him mature into a fine and stable young chap. You know, duck, Trevor isn't flummoxed easily. That character trait will be extremely useful being married to your sister."

Sometimes I couldn't distinguish between Pap being serious, or just him showing his witty dry humor. This was one of those times. "How about you then?" he turned the tables on me and asked.

I didn't know what he was asking, and I told him so.

"Sheila said you got upset when she brought up Albert the other day at her flat."

Oh, now I knew what he was on about. I denied the upset part because I certainly did not feel like I got upset in any way, shape, or manner.

Pap finally discovered what tool he was looking for and let out a loud hoot, showing his joy at his discovery. "Well, ducky, if you did get upset or are worried about Albert, one couldn't blame you."

I stoically agreed with him.

"I know I'm worried for him, even as his father-in-law."

"You are?" I responded, having not given my pap's fears about Albert being in danger much thought until this very moment.

"Certainly, dear. What's happening in Vietnam reminds me too much of what I've already seen. History does sometimes repeat itself, duck. I only hope and pray that it doesn't this time," he expressed.

Pappy's words had me churning inside even more. My old pap, as he always could, could see it too. He came over to me and wrapped his strong right arm around me, from the side. He looked at my face with that knowing expression that I could never hide from. I began to weep and crumble into his arms.

"There, there, my old duck. It's all going to be all right, you'll see," he promised me, as he held me in a way that made me feel so safe. With his large and well-worn left hand, scraped and scarred from years of work in the shoe factory and on his land, he stroked my hair like he so often did when I was a child.

"I'm just so afraid of Albert not coming back to me, of never seeing him again!" I bellowed out.

"I know, love, I know," Pap whispered to me softly. "And you must not let those thoughts take charge of you, no matter how real they might feel right now."

I asked him how I could do that, how anyone could do such a thing.

He cupped my face with both hands and slowly but surely helped me to get control of my emotions. When I finally did, Pappy told me to look down. I asked him why, but he just told me to do it. So, I did as he said, but still had no idea why he was asking me to look to the ground.

"What do you see?" he whispered softly.

I still wasn't sure what he was on about. I told him I saw the floor.

"No, duck…what do you see of yourself when you look down?"

I looked again. "My shoes, or I mean my feet," I answered.

He grinned. "That's right, my Rosey, your feet. Now those feet of yours are the most important thing right now. Do you hear me?"

I nodded my understanding. In truth, I still wasn't sure what Pap's point was.

"It's those two feet of yours, love, that's the key, duck. You have to keep moving, taking one step at a time. That's all the good Lord asks us to do, and that's hard enough sometimes, isn't it?"

I turned to face Pap and ask him the one awful question terrifying my thoughts. "What if he doesn't come back to me? What if he dies over there in the jungle, Pap?"

Pappy gave me one of his looks that I had seen so many times before. It was the look that had comforted me in the toughest times of my life.

"That's maybe a dozen steps ahead of where you are right now, love. You need to just take the next step, the one right in front of you, duck. That's enough for you right now. I want you to promise me to not consider those other steps that may or may not ever present themselves. We will take those steps together if they ever come, and I promise you one thing, Rosey. You won't take those steps alone."

As always, I felt better after baring my heart with my old pap. I kissed him on his forehead and thanked him for always being there for me.

"It's my main purpose, you know, you and Sheila and, of course, your mum."

"What would I ever do without you?" I unashamedly asked him.

He didn't hesitate to tell me. "You'd take one step, and then you would take another, and then the next step. That's what you would do. You know, duck, it's like when you are about to climb a large flight of stairs. You don't worry about the top step of the stairs now, do ya'? You only worry about taking that next step. You'll make it up to the final step of those stairs soon enough."

I knew he was right. He always was.

"Now, before you're too busy having your fun in Germany and flitting around with all this wedding stuff, you want to give me a hand in the garden. I could really use it, Rosey," he said.

"Definitely, Pap, I'm all yours," I answered, and it was true. Part of me would always be all his, my good old pap.

CHAPTER 13

Hamburg Germany was wild. I had never been to any place like it, in my whole life. Sheila, myself, and the three other bridesmaids all walked through the city at night with our mouths wide open, gaping open, really. The place wasn't much to look at in the daytime, a bit scruffy truth be told, but it came to life at night. Sheila had said it was much like Las Vegas in America, and that might be true, but I had never been to Las Vegas and certainly had never seen a city like Hamburg before. Prostitutes were out in the open, selling their wares. The city was located by the sea, and many sailors prowled around. We were all going to spend two days here, which seemed like a short stay since it took numerous hours in my pappy's van and ferry boat to get here. But Sheila wanted to take in the sights and sounds and experience the wild vibe of the place, as she liked to call it. She said this trip was important to her before she settled into domestic life. The first night we were all exhausted from the trip, but at Sheila's insistence, we still managed to go out on the town, although yawning all night. We danced a tad, drank a lot, and listened to some of the musical acts. One bartender, a very nice bloke, gave us a tip on some young Brits who were playing several shows a night down the street at a dingy nightclub, his words, called the Star Club. The bloke told us that these young Brits played American rock and roll and were quite the entertainers on stage. One of the reasons for the trip here to Hamburg was to hear American music, so all of us girls decided that we would make our way to this club to check out the British boys on our second night. For now, we would go back to our cheap hotel, just off the main drag, and collapse in our two beds, one for me and Sheila to share, and the other for the remaining girls.

The next morning, I was one of the first to wake up. I had always been an early riser, probably because I wanted to see my pappy before I went to school. He would often head to his factory job before my day even began. So quietly, I got dressed and strolled down the street to grab a newspaper. I couldn't read the German newsprint, but I scanned all the photos in the paper. Next, I found a quaint little coffee shop, the sort of place you would more likely expect to find in Paris, than here. I had a cup of strong tea, not coffee, and tried my best to understand the stories in the paper by the photos surrounding them. It didn't really work. I had no idea what I was reading. It was then that I had a vision or a daydream, whatever one calls such a thing. It was Maximillian, my old German flame, strolling down the street right in front of me. He smiled and waved like the Queen does when she passes by. Max acted as if he knew me, the way you know the folks who were your neighbors. He didn't act like I meant anything special to him. I had to snap myself out of my strange vision. It seemed so real, but of course wasn't. Why am I fantasizing about Max when Albert is putting his life in danger right this very second in Vietnam, I asked myself. I suddenly felt guilt and shame because of it. Sheila's loud voice pulled me back into reality. "You're the early bird, aren't ya'?"

I agreeably smiled between sips of my tea.

"The air is crisp today, don't you think, love?" she asked me as she took a deep breath.

"It's a nice morning," I offered.

Then, the waiter came over to our table and took Sheila's order. For the next few minutes, we conversed in blasé' meaningless dribble like sisters often do. Since I was feeling so comfortable with her, I let her in on my strange daydream. I asked her what she thought it meant.

"No bloody idea. But why don't you try giving this fella you used to know a call? How do you know this German chap anyways?" Sheila asked.

I wasn't about to tell her my big secret, the one I had kept from her and Pap and Mum all these years. My pappy would still to this day and after all these years, probably keel over if he knew I had ever dated a German prisoner of war. "He was an old friend I met years ago after the war. He was working in finance in London at the time and had a girlfriend in Northampton," I told Sheila for cover.

"Was his girlfriend anyone I would know?" Sheila inquired.

"I don't believe so," I answered.

"Well, I would try calling him. How often are you in Germany Rosey?"

My sister was right, how often was I in Germany? For all I knew this could be the last time. Unfortunately for me, those old feelings of guilt and shame reappeared just as I had gotten the gumption to phone Max. I asked myself why exactly I was calling him. I was married, and happily at that. What if Max's wife picked up the phone? I couldn't be sure of my motives and that bothered me immensely. I knew deep down I still had feelings for Max, and hearing his voice was only going to exasperate such ideas. I loved

Andrew Scott Bassett

Albert now, and I decided that my peculiar vision was the only contact I was going to allow myself with Maximillian. This whole conversation I just had was going on in my head, as Sheila sipped coffee across from me, completely unaware.

"Earth to, Rosey, you in there, love?" Sheila interrupted, trying to rescue me from my own thoughts.

I quickly apologized for being so ill-mannered and for ignoring her.

"You should be," she responded with a chuckle. "Now, let's get the others up and going so we can take in the sights around here, maybe do a bit of shopping, aye."

I told my sister whatever she wanted, this trip to Hamburg was all for her benefit.

"Well, lovely then. Tonight, let's check out that club the bartender spoke about, you know with the British boys playing American rock and roll. What do you say, Rosey?" Sheila threw out there for my consideration.

"Whatever you like," I replied.

Later that night, we all made it to the club. It was smokey and much smaller than we thought it would be from the outside. You could certainly see that the word was out about this place, or at least about the musicians who were about to perform. A large curtain opened after we had waited for more than ten minutes for the show to start. Five young lads, already in position to play, loudly and I mean loudly, began their set immediately. They performed for almost two hours and mostly played songs I'd heard before. Some of the songs were rock and roll tunes, but many were more traditional popular songs from the last decade or so. The lads were quite good, even if as I said, a bit loud for me. They joked and were quite cheeky with the audience. They certainly had charm, and their Liverpool accents only added to it. Sheila and I danced to most of their songs, especially the faster ones like *"Roll Over Beethoven"* and *"Twist and Shout"*. We even danced slowly to a tune called *"Till There Was You"*, sung by one of the particularly cute members of the group. Oh, and Sheila and I only danced together, not with men at the club. She was getting married in a few days, and I was in no mood for misunderstandings and wrestling matches. Men were not part of our plan in Hamburg for good reason. The other girls had no such qualms and danced with as many men as they liked. But by the end of the night, I could see that they were fighting off some of those blokes' advances. The audience was made up of Hamburg citizens as well as foreigners from all over Europe. After the show, we were all soaked with perspiration. The club was so jammed-packed and poorly ventilated that we couldn't help but be wet by the end of the evening. Afterward, Sheila demanded that we go to a pub across the street to cool down from all the excitement, take the edge off the night, before heading to bed. This trip was for her, so we all did what she wanted and followed her lead. After about an hour of sipping cocktails and eating pub food, not like the delicious pub food in England, mind ya', I and the other three bridesmaids were ready to go back to our hotel room and call it a night. Sheila wasn't and let us know she was staying longer. She asked me if I would stay and keep her company. How could I tell her no when this whole adventure was for her benefit, so I stayed while the other girls went back to our room. I already had enough booze in me for the evening, so I requested a cup of coffee from the barkeep. Through the front entrance, the boys from the band we had just watched came waltzing in. There were only four of them, one of them was missing. They sat down at the table next to us. I quickly realized they were almost as loud in person as on the stage. Their cheeky laughter filled the now sleepy pub. The boys were quite charming in person, even if it was in a childish, juvenile sort of way. They were still wearing their matching outfits, which consisted of black trousers and grey long-sleeve dress shirts. I was quick to notice that the top button was no longer fastened as it had been when they were on stage. All four boys ordered pints of beer. A couple of the lads barely look old enough to be drinking alcoholic spirits in public. The loudest and cheekiest of the quartet spotted Sheila and me watching them. He raised his glass toward us. "Good evening, ladies!" he said with a booming voice.

Sheila and I responded to him by flashing a polite smile in his direction. He seemed to need no more invitation as he came over and sat down at our table. "Are we having a lovely evening?"

"Quite," Sheila responded.

"Glad to hear it. How about you, Miss?" the same lad asked, as he turned his attention to me.

I told him I was, and I shared with him that we had just watched him and the other boys play. He seemed tickled by my revelation. "Hey, lads! We've got some fans over here. Come greet and meet."

Quickly responding to his command, the other young lads followed, grabbed chairs, and plopped themselves down at our table.

"May we buy you ladies some drinks?" the one who first came over asked Sheila and me.

"No, I think I'm okay with my spot of coffee, but thank you," I replied.

Sheila, however, was happy to accept his request.

"What are you drinking, love?" he asked her.

"How about something different? I'll have a rum and Coke, darling." Sheila told him.

The four lads all started to hoot with delight at her request. Sheila wondered if they were taking a mick out of her and asked them as much.

"No, No, love! It's because that's our favorite drink, you know, the group's favorite poison so to speak. You obviously have wonderful taste, mum. First, you come to see us play and then order a drink we all love. It seems that fate has brought us all together tonight."

Sheila blurted out a laugh at his bold declaration. I stayed quiet. He was amusing, but also cheeky, and I was never drawn to that type.

"So, tell us your names, anyway," my sister questioned the forward one with.

He quickly apologized to us both for his lack of manners. "Oh yes, of course, my name is John. This is Paul, George, and the serious one here with the face that makes birds swoon is Pete."

"And where is the other lad from your group, he played guitar and piano?" Sheila asked.

"Oh, that's Stu. He's off somewhere with his new girl. She's a local, you know German," John quipped.

"How about the rest of you? Do you speak or does John here do all your talking for you?" Sheila then spit out, unabashedly.

The lads all started to laugh at her accusation. John pretended to be the puppet master for two of the other boys, Paul and George. The one they called Pete smirked but didn't laugh or joke like the other three. He stuck out like an old penny.

"We do talk, Miss. John just speaks the loudest," The one named Paul shared with a mischievous grin.

Another lad, George, clearly the youngest of the four, asked us how we liked their show tonight.

We told them the truth. We thought they were brilliant, albeit a bit loud.

"Really? Loud then. Well, the audience gets loud, so we have to play louder than them, you see?" Paul attempted to justify.

"You are obviously Brits like us. Where do you hail from in England if I may ask such a personal question?" John asked away, changing the topic.

"We're from Northampton. How about you lads?" I responded.

"We're all from Liverpool. Can't you tell by our accents or has playing in Germany really mucked them up?" John stated with a chuckle.

Sheila was quick to assure him it hadn't. She told them that we guessed by their accents that they came from that part of England. She then asked them how long they had been playing here in Hamburg. We were surprised by their answer.

"Almost two years now," Paul offered.

"Two years, that's a bloody long time!" Sheila exclaimed.

The boys shrugged and smiled at her declaration.

"How much longer do you intend to be playing here?" I interrupted.

"I guess until something you know breaks for us," Paul chipped in.

"Yeah…we're going to be big one day, bigger than Elvis," John proudly proclaimed to our amazement. I nodded politely at his bold statement, but Sheila couldn't help herself. "Bigger than Elvis, you must be barmy!"

"You just said you thought we were brilliant tonight," Paul countered.

"Yeah, but bigger than Elvis...really?" Sheila fired back.

"What about you, ma'am? What do you think?" the younger lad named George asked me politely.

Before I could answer, Sheila butted in. She told them that I was the perfect one to ask such a question because I had seen Elvis perform in person, and even met him. This revelation stunned the boys, and they then hung on to every word I spoke.

"Elvis was wonderful and of course is a brilliant performer. He also was quite the gentleman. But you boys are very good in your own way," I suggested.

"We love Elvis too, and we're not trying to disrespect him in any way, but I know in my own heart and in my own mind, we're going to be just as big, if not bigger," John said in a quiet, determined way.

He also shared how they were going to be the first British group to succeed in America. "No one's been able to do it yet, not even Cliff Richard, but we will."

"And you call yourselves...what again, the Ants?" Sheila chimed in.

"The Beatles," John answered with a swagger as if he knew the world would one day know that name.

Sheila and I assumed it was spelled like the insect, but John explained it was spelled differently.

"I hate to tell you, lad, but you misspelled the word," Sheila remarked with a hearty laugh.

Paul then jumped in to explain their reason for the spelling. It was beat as in musical beat. That's the reason for the way it was spelled.

"Why the name Beatles?" I questioned.

He thought for a moment before sharing. "We love American rock and roll obviously, and one of our favorites was Buddy Holly. His band was the Crickets, so we wanted to emulate him, and then after his death, it became kind of a tribute, you know."

Sheila and I both shared that we too loved Buddy Holly and his music. Then from nowhere, an unexpected and impolite yawn escaped my mouth. I told everyone that I was ready for bed. John, in his cheeky way, said that sounded like a wonderful idea and wondered if I wanted any company. I without hesitation told him no, I was a married woman. I pointed to the wedding ring on my finger, which they of course all noticed. Sheila, likewise, shared her news of getting married in only a few days. John wondered why she wanted to do that. Sheila forcefully told him because she loved the man she was marrying.

"Maybe it's time you and Cynthia get hitched then, John," Paul said with a chortle.

John told his mate to bugger off. He said it wasn't funny because she wanted as much. John asked us, more like pleaded with us, to stay a little longer. He and Paul wanted to hear all about my meeting with Elvis. George and the other lad named Pete also joined in and wanted to hear the same story. These four young English lads, so cocky and full of mischief, suddenly seemed like four innocent children begging for their mother to tell them a bedtime story. I couldn't resist. First off, I demanded a cup of something hot, tea or coffee. John yelled across the now mostly empty pub to the barkeep to bring me whatever I wanted. He said it was on him, and I thanked him for his kindness. Sheila told me to get on with it since she was also now starting to get sleepy. We ended up spending another two hours with the lads, much too long, but they were such wonderful company, a sheer delight to talk to. They loved my story about Elvis and then got me to blather on about what America was like, the good and the bad I had seen. Finally, Sheila and I had, had enough and were dying to get to bed. The boys told us how much they enjoyed our company and appreciated the time we spent with them. They shared that we had brought a little bit of home, England, Liverpool, something, with us that they dearly missed. I realized then that behind the cheekiness, the constant mucking around, that there was something more to these lads. There was something deeper and much more serious about them below the surface. Sheila and I said our cheerios. As I waved goodbye to them that night and exited the pub to go back to our hotel, I had a strange premonition that John's words were going to come true and that I would hear the name the Beatles again. I was, of course, right.

⸺ • ⸺

THE WEDDING DAY ARRIVED, AND SHEILA LOOKED STUNNING. Trevor, pressed and cleaned, wasn't bad himself. The All Saints Church was filled with every relative you could imagine from both sides of the aisle. My old pap and mum gleamed with joy and probably some relief that they were finally marrying off their youngest. Sheila Saunders, my dear old best mate who had been on holiday in Spain the whole time since I got back home, made it back to England. She was in attendance. It was so lovely to see her again after all this time. We made a vow to get together before I went back to the states.

The ceremony went off without a sniff of a hitch. We had a big reception afterward in a banquet hall owned by the church. I saw and spoke with family I hadn't seen in years, some many years. We danced, we toasted, and we all stuffed ourselves on the tables of fine British cuisine that took up the back of the banquet hall. Later, we threw rice and cheered the newlyweds as they drove away in Trevor's dark blue MG coupe, with streamers of red, white, and blue attached to its bumper. I asked Pappy how it felt to see his youngest married off after all these years of waiting. His answer surprised me. "Like I just died a little bit, Rosey."

I couldn't help but ask him what he meant by such a strange statement.

He shook his head before saying, "You know, duck, there's only so many magical moments in a lifetime. Seeing your children get married is one of the big ones. You can't help but question how many more you're going to get."

I told him that this was too happy an occasion to be talking about such somber subjects. He immediately flashed his wonderful smile at me and agreed. "Let's go get your mum and go home aye. I'll make us a lovely cup of tea, what'd ya' say, Rosey dear?"

I hugged him and told him the only thing I could. "That sounds like a brilliant end to a wonderful day, Pap."

After that, we rounded up Mum and headed home, my home, the house where I grew up and had so many wonderful memories of, the middle red brick house on Franklin Street, Northampton England.

───────◆•─────

I STAYED FOUR MORE MONTHS IN ENGLAND. ALBERT wrote letters whenever he could. He said that everything was fine and dandy in Vietnam, and he hoped to be in the States for a visit soon. I knew in my heart that he wasn't telling me the whole story. Things were beginning to escalate in that area of the world. The same ideas that brought about the Korean War a decade earlier were beginning to rear their ugly head in Vietnam. All I wanted was my Albert home with me, in my arms again, sleeping next to me. When I prayed, I asked the good Lord for just those things and not much more. When I went to board my ship in London, I still had no news of Albert coming back to the States. This time, Pap and Mum saw me off alone. Sheila and Trevor were both busy working and couldn't get the time off. For some reason, that I did not understand at the time, I felt much more alone boarding that ship for America than I did boarding the one that brought me back to England. Years later, I came to realize why. Heading to England I would at least have my family to greet me. I would have my family to be with, laugh with, and spend time with. On the voyage back to the States there would be no family waiting for me, A few friends like Carol, I hoped, but no family. Those eleven days crossing the Atlantic were so sad. Unlike the trip over, this time I spent most of the time in my cabin. I didn't socialize much or take part in any of the activities. I just wanted to get back to the base, and to mine and Albert's home. I only wished that my husband would be waiting for me when I arrived.

———— • ————

"DANNY, COULD YOU DO ME A FAVOR AND TAKE THE DOG outside? She needs to pee!" Lori yelled from the back of the house.

Danny isn't sure why Lori can't take care of the dog but yells back that he will, just the same. "Front yard, back yard, does it matter?"

Andrew Scott Bassett

"I don't care!" Lori replies.

"Come on, Yoko, let's go pee. Come on, girl," Danny says as he opens the front door and directs the dog outside.

The Arizona heat meets him straight on as he walks outside with the dog. The front yard has a fence around it, although the large English sheepdog could probably jump right over it if it saw fit to. While Danny is remembering why he doesn't miss the weather in Arizona while living in New York, a car pulls up in front of the house. He watches as a familiar face exits the vehicle. He can't help but smile at the sight, why he's not sure. Julia his ex, comes walking up the driveway. She greets him with a wave. Danny rushes to open up the gate for her.

"Hello, Danny. I hope it's okay that I've come here?"

"Okay," Danny thinks to himself. He's just happy that she has forgiven him enough to make it all the way out to Arizona.

"I thought I would surprise you. I hope it's a good surprise," Julia states as she comes into the yard.

"Of course it is," Danny responds. "But I am definitely surprised to see you here after, you know everything in New York."

Julia lets off a large sigh as she recalls all that 'stuff' back in the Big Apple. She then shares why she made the long trip to see him. "I may not know where we are at, you know as far as our relationship, but I still care about you a great deal, Danny. And I wanted to be here for you as you deal with all this, your mother dying, and all of this."

Her words bring a smile to Danny. He can't help but be happy to see her, especially considering he was wondering if he would ever see her again.

Julia chuckles at Danny for not really responding to her initial inquiry. "You haven't told me yet."

"Told you what?" He asks.

Julia at that point questions if Danny was even listening to her, so she says it again. "Is it all right for me to be here?"

Danny shakes his head. He can't believe she would even ask such a thing. "What are you talking about? I'm really happy you came."

That was enough for her to move toward him and give him an uncomfortable embrace. Now that she knew she was wanted, she had a second question for Danny.

"What's that?" he wonders.

"Do you think we could go inside the house or go somewhere else where there's air conditioning? It's crazy hot out here!" Julia exclaims.

Danny laughs at her honesty. He certainly can't disagree with her. "Let me get the dog back in the house, put on some fresh clothes, and then I'll take you to a coffee place a couple of blocks away."

Sounds great, Julia thinks. Danny does all those things, as well as introduces Julia to his sister. In no time, the two of them are off to a more private, and just as importantly, cooler place.

Over two icy cold, blended lattes, Danny gets her up to speed on everything that has happened to him since getting back to Phoenix. Julia thinks that he is holding up well considering his mother's passing and the pressures of the deadline for his second book coming so fast. They both keep the topic of their own relationship issues off the table. They behave as if they are just old friends catching up, which maybe they are right now, Danny fears.

"Right, so, on the subject of your book, how's the new manuscript coming?" Julia out of nowhere brings up.

Danny, for a split second lost in his own thoughts, considers lying. He, however, remembers that Julia can always tell when he does. He decides right then and there to unburden himself of all he is carrying around and just have the pleasure of sharing with someone the truth. "I've got nothing."

Julia isn't sure what he means exactly.

"I mean my manuscript, my book. It's a large load of crap right now," he continues.

She is shocked by all this, but still wants details.

"What I'm saying is I don't have anything good for the next book, and I have a deadline coming up. I'm going to be one of those one-hit author wonders. I guess I only had one good book in me," Danny proclaims, his words echoing disdain for himself.

Julia for one isn't buying his pity party and tells him so. "I don't know what's going on with your new book, Danny, but I do know you are an excellent writer. I think you're forgetting all the other things you've written in the last ten to fifteen years that I've had the good fortune to read. You're a great storyteller, Danny. You always have been. I think maybe you're still searching for the right story, the one you really want to tell."

"What are you getting at?" Danny challenges.

"I don't know. It's just that with your first book and so many other things I've seen you write, published or not, you were really passionate about your story. I just wonder if this second book is more about duplicating the success of the first book than really telling a story you are excited about, passionate about," she declares.

Danny considers Julia's words. He knows she's right. He also knows that he has a literary agent and a large publishing company expecting him to have a brilliant manuscript for them in only a few days. "What am I going to do?"

Julia takes his hand in hers. "I guess if you don't have a story you're excited about ready to write, you just have to be honest with them."

Danny knows Julia is right again, but it still doesn't make it any easier. "I wish I had a story like my mom's life. I can tell you, Jules, my mother lived a pretty amazing life."

Julia questions him about his mom's story. Danny explains how his mom left it for him to read. He shares how he has been reading through it to get away from the frustration of his mental block. Julia finds it all very interesting. "Why did she leave it for you, and not your brother or sister? Did your mother want you to turn her story into a book?"

Danny hasn't really given it that much thought. He's been too preoccupied with his own problems, like planning a funeral and watching his reputation as a bestselling author go down the drain. Julia quickly points out the obvious. "Why not?"

"What? You mean turn my mother's life story into a book?" Danny shoots back, as he considers the idea.

"Yeah, if you think there's enough there," Julia adds.

Danny takes a few more sips of his latte' as he ponders the possibility before grim reality takes over and enters his thoughts. "My agent and my publisher would never go for it. They're expecting a book just like my first one."

Julia nods. She gets his point but then brings up another important fact. "Since you don't have anything good to give them like your first book, maybe if you make your mom's story into something great, they'll be happy with that?"

Danny has no better ideas, and he knows it. Still, he tells Julia it probably won't work. Not to mention it will probably be the end of his writing career, but what the hell he figures. Beggars can't be choosers, as his mother liked to say.

"Can you turn your mother's writings into a manuscript in time, you know before your deadline?" Julia asks, concerned that there might not be enough time to get it finished.

"That is the question…isn't it?" he answers with a deadpan delivery. "I guess I better first finish reading it. I'll have to work night and day to make it by the deadline."

"You can do it. I'll help you if you let me," Julia is kind enough to offer. She squeezes Danny's hand, again.

He then cups his other hand over hers. She can feel things heating up in a hurry and wants to bring everything back down to a place where they are on firm footing. "I'm here for you, Danny, like I said."

Danny thanks her once more for that as he strokes her hand.

"But I'm not saying everything is fine between us or anything like that. I'm still upset with you and how you have been treating me the last year," she says with gusto.

"I know, I know," Danny answers.

"I don't know what our future is. I just know that I need to be here right now with you," Julia tells him.

Danny nods. He thanks her a third time and then asks if she wants to stay at his sister's house with him, in a separate bedroom of course.

"Your sister would be okay with that?"

"Okay, after meeting you she would probably think I'm an idiot for letting you walk out on me," he confesses with a laugh.

Julia loves his honesty and accepts his invitation.

Danny still has to admit though, that he's not sure he can put together his mom's story effectively in such a short time. When Julia hears this confession, she has to remind him of something he told her many years ago.

"Remember when you told me that it's as much about how good the story is as it is about the storyteller?"

Danny nods. He remembers that.

"Well, you're a great storyteller, Danny. If your mom's story is good, you can't fail," Julia promises him.

Danny hopes Julia's right, as he pauses in response before confidently saying, "It's a great story, a really great story."

CHAPTER 14

Nineteen sixty-three, what a year it was. The British lads that Sheila and I had met that night in Hamburg were now taking over England with their music. I hadn't heard anything about them over here in the States, but I was still tickled to hear they were becoming quite famous back home. As for me, I was settled back in at Fort Rucker, Alabama. Albert was still over in Vietnam. The storm clouds of war still seemed to be forming in that part of the world, and I hadn't seen my husband in what seemed like an eternity. Now, firmly in my thirties, I couldn't help but be melancholy about life and what I hoped it would be. I felt so alone. I guess this is the life of someone married to a soldier who has risen up the ranks and is too brilliant at his job for his own good. I also could not help but feel my maternal clock spinning faster and faster. Blimey, it felt so unfair. Now that I was finally ready to be a mother, I had a husband a half a bleeding world away.

And of course, not to mention, my husband was only able to shoot blanks from his gun if you know what I mean.

Thankfully, I still had my friend Carol to help keep me sane. I was still attending her church in town. It was primarily a "'black'" church, although with me included, there were now many more white people in the congregation. The world was changing slowly but surely. Many folks didn't even take notice of the changes, but I did. My work with Carol and the other ladies at the church, fighting for equal rights for blacks, helped me cope with my worry and loneliness. I was thankful to be a part of this wonderful group of people working for something this important. The church had joined forces with a civil rights organization in Alabama called the Alabama Christian Movement for Human Rights. The group was led by a man named Fred Shuttlesworth. His organization had fought against the awful, segregated busing practices in the South and for the integration of black students in schools. The organization also demanded that people of color be able to have equal access to railroad stations. Mr. Shuttlesworth was one of the first to use sit-ins as I witnessed in Montgomery with Carol in the diner. He championed such practices on college campuses to bring awareness to civil rights. The organization's 'Freedom Rides', that is black folks riding on buses where they weren't wanted by racist bus companies, even brought enough pressure to bear that President Kennedy pushed through legislation that put a ban on such unholy practices. Now, Mr. Shuttlesworth and his group were going to be joining forces with the Reverend King and his own organization, the Southern Christian Leadership Conference, in order to protest racist activities in Birmingham Alabama. All our church members were going to Birmingham for Easter week to put the screws on businesses that were discriminating. We would picket, do sit-ins, and march throughout the city protesting the way the area treated minorities. I had already packed my bags and was ready to go. I knew my involvement was risky business and all, but I no longer cared what the military thought. If Albert wasn't valuable to them now after all his sacrifice, well, they could just bugger off, pardon my French.

Andrew Scott Bassett

As I was preparing a small meal for myself on the stove, I heard a jingle at my front door. I went to check it out. There standing in my doorway to my utter shock and dismay was Albert. He yelled, "Surprise!"

I didn't know what to do for a moment. I was frozen in place at seeing him. Fortunately, he knew the correct actions to take. He ran up and grabbed me as if I weighed no more than a cocker spaniel. He looked at me like he hadn't seen me in years, which wasn't far off.

"Oh! You are such a sight to behold, Rosey!" he told me with a joyful expression that I had missed so much.

"What are you doing here?!" was all I could muster back.

"I finally got some extended leave to come home. You don't have any idea how much I have missed you," I was happy to hear him say.

In my normally cheeky way, I argued that I absolutely had an idea about how much he missed me because I missed him much more than that.

He was amused at my feistiness. Then he planted a kiss on me. It literally took my breath away. When I finally gathered myself, it seemed as if all the other stuff, the worry, the loneliness, everything else had vanished. I asked him if he was hungry, and if I could make him something to eat. I remembered only then that I needed to turn down my stove. He followed right after me into the kitchen.

"I'm hungry, but not for food," he said to me bluntly, with that whisper in his voice and twinkle in his eyes that made my knees weak.

I certainly was not about to argue with him. I ran toward him and jumped into his arms. The rest of the day and the night, in my memory, is just a fuzzy blur. What I do remember is that by the time we finally got to sleep, sometime in the middle of the night, we were both entirely spent and completely at peace with the world.

The next morning, still glowing from the events of the previous night, I cooked Albert and myself some breakfast. It was nothing fancy, mind you, just some eggs and chips as we like to call French fries in England. I still couldn't believe he was home and seated across from me.

"The Army finally had mercy on me and let me come home for Easter to see my beautiful wife," he spoke between bites.

When he reminded me about this being the week before Easter, alarms went off in my head. The protest trip to Birmingham would be leaving this weekend. Suddenly, all my flush of wonderful and tingling feelings subsided, and I felt stress. What was I to do? Carol was counting on me, so was Pastor Mitchell from the church. All the ladies were. But my husband was home, after nearly a year of being gone. I couldn't leave now. Without disclosing anything to Albert, I phoned Carol. I spoke almost in code when I got a hold of her. It was one of the worst calls I had ever had to make, and I could hear Carol's disappointment from the other side of the line. Albert was sitting at the kitchen table and didn't appear to decipher what I was talking about. In the end, though, Carol understood. She congratulated me on having my husband home, safe and sound. I wished her all the luck in the world with everything that would be happening in Birmingham this next week. I also asked her to please keep safe. We all knew that the South was becoming a giant powder keg, ready to blow at the touch of any small spark.

After I hung up, I turned to Albert and asked him if he wanted to do anything special today. A mischievous expression suddenly took control of his face. "What's that for then?" I couldn't help but question.

He motioned for me to come over and sit on his lap, so I did. As he touched my lips with his finger, he said, "How about we do what we did last night, again… then maybe, I don't know, I take you shopping, huh?"

He made me giggle like a schoolgirl at his idea. I asked if he had the energy for another round like last night. He joked that he certainly did. He said with a chuckle, "Rosey sweety, I've been saving up all my energy for almost a year for you."

"Brilliant answer," I told him, as I covered his mouth with mine.

<hr />

ALBERT'S LEAVE WAS ONLY FOR TWO WEEKS. IT WAS simply not long enough for either of us, but as he told me, even getting that much time off was like pulling teeth. Still, it was at least for us, the best fortnight since our honeymoon. Whenever I brought up anything in regard to Vietnam, Albert quickly stopped me and asked if we could discuss something else. He wished for nothing to exist except us right now. Albert said the world and all its problems could wait till our time together was done. It sounded very romantic, and I understood completely. The only problem was the world did not care if we were having a second honeymoon or not. It kept spinning out of control. When I could sneak a second, I would turn the news on the telly to see how things were going for everyone in Birmingham. The news, of course, was on the side of the authorities and therefore was slanted against the protestors. I hadn't heard a word from Carol and couldn't help but be concerned for her safety. The news clips showed the police were showing little restraint, and you could see that they wanted oh, so badly to come down hard on the protestors and stamp out all future events like this from happening. I assumed that Carol would under only the worst of circumstances place a call to me. She didn't want to disturb my time with Albert or maybe just as importantly, let him know how involved I had become in the cause for civil rights. Whatever the reason, I hadn't heard from her since the day I called to tell her I couldn't make it to Birmingham.

Back to Albert and me. We thoroughly enjoyed every moment we had together. We went to the movies almost every day. I think we saw every new movie that was playing at the time. He also insisted on taking me shopping several times. When I told him I really didn't need anything, he scoffed.

I would then offer to him, "Albert dear, you're all I need right now, this time together."

He still wouldn't have any of it. Albert said I deserved whatever my heart desired and certainly only the best things in life. When I said I already had everything I needed, he would buy me things he thought I could use. He splurged ridiculously on me. He bought me jewelry, clothes, hats, shoes, even a fur coat, though it was obviously too hot outside to wear. I really felt a bit embarrassed by the whole thing, but I couldn't tell him that. He was having such a wonderful time showering me with gifts. I shared about my trip back home to England and Sheila's wedding. I even told him about the British band we met in Germany who were now going like gangbusters back home. When I told him the name of the band, The Beatles, he just howled. "Well, nobody with a silly name like that is ever going to make it over here, you know in the States."

Hearing that, I reminded him about Buddy Holly and the Crickets.

Andrew Scott Bassett

Albert had a swift answer for that. He said that it didn't take long for Buddy Holly to realize that he needed to get rid of the bug name, and so he did. I wasn't about to argue with him over such trivial things.

Then on Good Friday, with him leaving in only a few days, I was preparing a dinner of ham and potatoes for us. I wanted to attend a church service to celebrate the special day. I always loved the music that churches played during the holiday seasons, be it Christmas or Easter. But there would be no service tonight, with most of the church congregation still in Birmingham supporting Reverend King and Mr. Shuttlesworth. So, while I prepared the dinner, Albert was at the PX picking up a few things he would need when he went back overseas. Suddenly, in the middle of cooking, I was interrupted by my phone ringing for one of the few times it had in over a week. It was Carol. I was so relieved to hear her voice, to know that she was okay. But I could tell that everything wasn't as it should be.

"What's going on, love?" I asked.

She first apologized profusely for calling me and interfering with my time with Albert. I let her know it was fine, and I still wanted to know why she was calling. I knew it had to be important because otherwise, she wouldn't want to call and risk interrupting us. Then I considered, that maybe she was just calling to wish me a Good Friday or a happy Easter. But there was something in her voice that my intuition told me wasn't right.

"The Reverend King has been arrested in Birmingham," she finally let out of the bag.

I was surprised, but not completely shocked. We all knew that being arrested came with the territory when protesting authority that was backed forcefully by law enforcement.

"Are they going to bail him out right away?" I inquired.

Carol said that the organizations behind the protest had run out of bail money and that the reverend knew this when he peacefully allowed himself to be arrested. "We're all wondering what comes next. I was pushed, spat at, and cussed out by white people and police in Birmingham. I knew that some white people could be horrible, but this has really shook me to the bone. You know It's like I have lost my confidence in people doing the right thing," Carol shared passionately.

I pleaded with her not to lose faith in all people of my race. "There are so many of us out here, all believing in the same things that you and Reverend King believe in. I know that more people are coming to our cause all the time, and when I say that, I mean people of all races."

Carol told me she hoped and prayed that I was right. I promised her I was. She said she would keep me informed on Reverend King's plight in jail, and I thanked her for that. I shared that I would keep him in my thoughts and prayers as well, and then I hung up. Only moments later, Albert came home. He could see that my mind was pre-occupied, somewhere else at that moment. "Everything okey-dokey?"

His question snapped me out of my funk. I smiled and said everything was lovely. We only had a few more days left together, and I wanted nothing to take away from them. "Dinners about ready. Do you have much of an appetite this time?" I asked him.

"I could eat a whole cow right now, I'm so hungry," he replied.

"Sorry, we're having ham for our Good Friday dinner," I let him know.

"Well then, I could eat a whole pig, how's that?" he responded, with tongue firmly in cheek.

We then both shared a hearty laugh because with as much food as I made, way too much for two people, he might have to.

———— ◆ ————

IT HAD BEEN FOUR MONTHS SINCE I SAID MY GOODBYES to Albert and watched like a powerless twit as he headed back to Vietnam. The Reverend King's stay in jail was short-lived, thank God. Carol and I and most of our church family had taken a long bus trip to Washington D.C. to see the Reverend King and many other influential civil rights leaders speak. The trip itself was not a particularly enjoyable endeavor. We only had two buses to fit everybody who wanted to make the trip from our small congregation. The air conditioner on the bus worked rather poorly and being it was summer, it made things quite unpleasant indeed. Squeezed in together and sweating like hogs on a farm would lead anyone to have a bit of a sour disposition, but bless their souls, not our group. We all somehow knew that this trip, this gathering at our nation's capital, was going to be a special event, maybe a turning point in American history. I believed at the time that it could be. The sentiment of the country seemed to be moving toward the Reverend King and those of us who were fighting for equal rights. There were even positive signs coming from the president and his brother, the attorney general.

The motel we checked into the night before was a sight for sore eyes for everyone. My bum was basically numb from the bus trip, so Carol and I walked around the outside of the motel and around the parking lot just to stretch out our poor legs and get some blood flowing once again. Carol was amazed by the idea of a motel that had no problem with a white and black woman sharing a room. I reminded her that the whole country was not like the South. She chuckled at such truths. "No matter what lovely words I hear tomorrow when Reverend King and the other speakers make their speeches, I think this motel and the freedom it afforded me, will carry just as powerful a memory for me," she opined.

I was profoundly touched by her words. Sometimes in life, it's the little, somewhat insignificant bits and bobs that carry the most weight.

———•———

THE NEXT MORNING, WE ALL GOT BACK ON THE BUSES and went to the capital. It was like nothing I had ever seen before. There was a sea of people wherever your eye wandered. The speakers would appear, fittingly, before the Lincoln Memorial. Our group was somewhere stuck in the middle of a mass of people. As a person of no unique color, as Carol likes to tease me, I was the most at home I had ever felt during any of the civil rights demonstrations I had attended. The brutality of what had happened in the spring in Birmingham had forced many whites like myself to finally stand up and say, enough is bloody enough. I saw white faces throughout the crowd that day. The biggest smiles and the warmest looks came from the black men and women, however. They especially knew the importance of this day, and they appreciated people like me, white folks, who were willing to be brave and stand shoulder to shoulder with them.

We couldn't really see the speakers very well. We were too far away. We made up for it by listening intently. Even on this uncomfortably, hot summer day, we hung on every word. There were many who spoke and though they discussed different parts of the racial problems, together all things were covered in this crusade entitled the jobs and freedom march. There were white speakers, female speakers, and even entertainers like Ossie Davis and Ruby Dee. Bob Dylan and Joan Baez both inspired with words and music. Reverend King made the last true speech of the day. I have to admit by the time he came to the microphone, I was spent. I had been touched, moved, angered, and inspired by all that I had heard before him. I wondered if he could top all of that. Somehow, he did. His *"I Have a Dream"* speech both mesmerized and captured me. There were parts of me that would never think or act the same again. His call for unity based on the content of one's character and not the color of your skin, summed up for all of us what this long and bitter struggle had been all about. All people deserve respect, the same treatment, not special treatment, but equal treatment. We all wanted a level playing field that didn't tilt in the favor of the majority at the expense of the minority. His wish at the end to see children of all colors and religious faiths sitting together as one, brought tears to my eyes. The reverend's words made everything I had been doing for this cause, whatever little it was to that point, worthwhile.

After it was over, we milled around for a while taking in the gravity of what we had just witnessed. None of us felt we would ever be quite the same after that day, and even more importantly, we believed the country would never be the same either. We, of course, were right on both counts. The trip back to Alabama was just as hot and sweaty. The ride was just as long and tiring. But you know what, on the way back home, no one cared a teensy bit.

THE MONTHS THAT FOLLOWED THAT MAJESTIC DAY IN Washington D.C. were challenging for me, with only a few sparse letters here and there coming from Albert. I did write him back every time and then waited anxiously for his reply. The waiting for his response was god-awful. I did my best to stay busy at the church and with whatever I could do to help with the civil rights cause. Carol and I, by now, were the closest of friends. She was the only one I really had to talk to about all I was going through, missing Albert and the like. She pressed me to get him to telephone me instead of just sending letters. Carol knew that words written on paper were not enough. I needed to hear Albert's voice. Therefore, I started to ask him in every letter that I sent to please let me know if he could place a call to me. At first, he said it would be extremely difficult where he was at to make a call home. That continued for several letters until finally, thank heavens, he got permission to place a call right around the American holiday of Thanksgiving. I was on cloud nine and couldn't wait to hear his voice again. It seemed to take forever for the day to arrive, but happily, it finally did. I waited patiently, glued next to my phone on November twenty-second. I had the telly on as I sat on our sofa and tried to not stuff too many sweets into my mouth. I just knew that even on the telephone, Albert would be able to tell I had put on a few stones, or pounds as you Yanks measure it.

I was watching the coverage of President Kennedy on his trip to Dallas. The city gave him a gift of cowboy boots for visiting and the amused look on his face was so endearing. He was the first American politician that I really paid attention to. He was young, handsome, and had a lovely dry, witty sense of humor. Most importantly, against much backlash, he had really shown a willingness to fight for black Americans and stand up to both his own party and the other side, when they fought to keep the status quo. His youthful energy and vitality seemed to be rubbing off on the entire country, and I loved it. I was making myself a bit of lunch while still listening to the telly in the background. The president and his wife Jackie were about to get a tour of Dallas with the Texas governor. "Ring! Ring!"

I raced to my phone. My heart leaped with joy when I heard Albert's voice on the other side.

"Honey, how are you?" he greeted me.

"Lovely, darling, it's so wonderful to hear your voice," I responded.

I had to push back the emotions that were welling up inside me. I had no desire to waste this opportunity to speak with Albert by letting my sobs get in the way. "How late is it there?"

"Very," he answered.

I told him I missed him so much and needed to know if he had any idea when he would be able to come home. "It's been since April, Albert. I don't understand. It's not like the U.S. is at war or the like."

I knew he could hear the pleading in my voice as he sighed several times from the other side of the phone. He asked me to be patient, but I already had and was now missing him so much that I could hardly stand myself.

"What about for Christmas?" I challenged him.

He was silent in responding for too long, and that gave me my answer. He only promised he would do his best. As I pressed into the sofa and listened to Albert share how much he missed me, sweetly as always, my eyes were also on the telly. I watched as the president, the first lady, and the governor and his wife all got into a motorcade and began driving through the streets of Dallas. Albert and I went on blathering for quite a few minutes, about half an hour or so, sharing our hearts with one another. It all came to a halt in a flash of the impossible. At first, no one was sure what had just happened. My attention was diverted from Albert to the telly as I had this sickening feeling that the worst thing imaginable had just occurred. Albert asked me if everything was okay. I wasn't sure as I watched the events unfold on the telly. I only offered in response to Albert's inquiry the one thing I felt I knew. Something terrible has happened in Dallas. Then I heard a voice, not Albert's, coming from the other side of the phone. He was suddenly distracted by the other voice. I couldn't hear what was being said. It was muffled. Finally, he got back on the telephone with me. "I've got to go, Rosey."

I recognized the fear in his tone. "Is it because of what's happening in Dallas?"

"Yes…you were right. It is terrible what we are being told," Albert shared, as he again said he had to get off the line.

Quickly as possible, and as painful as could be, we said our goodbyes. Tears rolled down my face. Then without mercy, the news quickly confirmed what I hoped and prayed wasn't true. President Kennedy had been shot. He was being rushed to the hospital with severe wounds. My tears no longer trickled. Now they flowed down my face. I fell to my knees and prayed for him, the governor who was also shot, and their wives.

I was numb for the next hour. I waited to hear if our beloved young president would live or die. When the

Andrew Scott Bassett

news broke that he had officially been pronounced dead, I strangely didn't cry anymore. I guess by now I was in shock maybe even numb to the idea that such an awful thing as this had happened. Later that day, I sipped some sherry while sitting in the dark of my little base home in Alabama. My house was silent, the telly was turned off. I just couldn't watch anymore. I sipped my drink and did my best to cope with idea that had come over me, the idea that this was a watershed moment in the world. I had lived through this sort of thing as a child. When Germany declared war on England, I had this same feeling of dread. I knew then that things were about to change dramatically, and dramatically for the worse.

<hr />

Nineteen sixty-three ended not with a bang but with a whimper. After President Kennedy's assassination, a gloom, an air of depression hung over America. Pappy and Mum called me up and shared that a similar thing was going on back home in England. We were all trying to understand how this dashing young president with so much still left to do could have been taken from us like this. The war drums began to be ratcheted up in Vietnam, at least that was the sense Albert was getting from the Army. By February of nineteen sixty-four, my only correspondence with my husband was by mail. It had now been officially ten months since I'd last seen him. I was going crazy and was so lonely. Only my volunteer duties at the church kept me sane. I made a big decision, at least it was for me at that time. I decided to get a job. This would be my first job since coming to America. Albert didn't want me to work. He was old-fashioned that way. He believed his Army pay was enough and there was no need for me to find a job. He didn't understand that money wasn't the issue. Keeping myself busy and feeling challenged and important in the world was. To my surprise, I was hired after only applying to a handful of places. I started working in an insurance office in town. Mr. Denton was the insurance agent in charge of the office and my supervisor. He was a snake-oil salesman in the disguise of an insurance representative. Two other ladies worked with me in the office. One, a Mrs. Carpenter, was about as old as Moses. She also quoted the Bible about the same amount as the Jewish leader. The other woman was a lady about my age, Nancy Sue Lee. She was reportedly, well in her words, related to the confederate General Robert E. Lee. Thankfully, her views on the rights of black Americans were more in line with my own, and not those of the general. Nancy and I became good friends almost instantly. She was only a few years younger than me, and surprisingly, because she was gorgeous, had never been married. When Mr. Denton, our boss, wasn't watching, we would often discuss our lives and troubles, mostly man troubles. Nancy's problem was finding the right man, while mine was that I never got to see my Mr. Right. When Mrs. Carpenter overheard our woes, she would just tell us to pray about it, that God would bring the answer. I certainly believed in strong prayer as much as the next protestant, but not being honest about how Nancy or I felt, not talking about it, certainly wasn't helpful. I hoped that the good Lord would step in, but I also believed in free will, which is God-given.

———————— • · · ————————

THERE WAS STILL NO OFFICIAL WAR DECLARED AGAINST North Vietnam, at least not yet. Albert had shared only recently in some of his latest letters that the Army was gearing up in Vietnam like there was going to be one. Albert told me that was the main reason he had not made it home for so long. He had become even more of a big wig as an Army helicopter pilot. His commanders wanted him ready if the fighting began. My worry over Albert was overwhelming at times, I shared it with Nancy. She was a good listener and had taken me under her wing in the office. She also surprisingly warned me about Mr. Denton. She told me how he could get quite fresh with the ladies who work for him. Not, of course, Mrs. Carpenter. She was too past her prime for such shenanigans. Since Nancy had been working there, three different women had quit because of Mr. Denton's advances. I had only been working there a month, but I had yet to see any such nonsense directed at me. I joked with Nancy that I wasn't sure if it was a bit of an insult that he hadn't acted so randy toward me. She assured me it would probably still take place. "He waits usually, honey, until you're comfortable in the office and comfortable with him. Then he will become very forward and handsy," she declared to me.

I couldn't help but wonder why Nancy was still working here with such shameful things going on.

"Not to be vain, Rosey, but I'm used to it. I know they like my red hair and my freckled face and skin. Most of these men you work for these days are just like Mr. Denton. What I mean, dear is if they can get you to hanky-panky at work, well they surely will do just that," Nancy explained.

"Well, that doesn't make it right, love," I argued.

Nancy didn't disagree. She just reminded me that it was the nineteen sixties and that's just how things were for working women.

"Well," I proclaimed defiantly, "it shouldn't be that way at all, not at all."

Nancy loved my spirit. We promised to look out for each other whenever Mr. Denton was around. Then, out of the blue, she asked me if I had heard about the big bug infestation coming to the States. Nancy said she has been hearing all over the radio that beetles are coming to America in a few weeks. I knew instantly what she meant. I took the next hour to explain who those "'Beatles'" were and how I had even seen them in person once. Nancy was red-faced at the revelation. I thought the only decent thing to do would be to invite her to my home the night of the Ed Sullivan television show. Carol would be coming over too, although she didn't seem very interested. No matter, I as a proud Brit, would again have something to remind me of my home, and something to help me at least temporarily forget how much I missed my husband.

———◆··———

THE NEXT SIX MONTHS WENT BY LIKE A WHIRLWIND. I received a few letters from Albert, but not nearly enough for my taste. I buried myself in my job at the insurance office while still helping in any way I could with the church and the civil rights battles it was engaging in. The new president, Lyndon Johnson, seemed determined to pass a historic civil-rights bill in nineteen sixty-four. You could feel it in the air that change was coming for blacks in America, at last. All the hard work of little churches like the one I was attending and their support of Reverend King and other civil rights leaders in the country seemed to be finally reaping a harvest.

My boss, Mr. Denton, was training me on many differ-ent lines of insurance coverage. He believed with my charm and lovely accent that I could do a whiz-bang job in selling new policies for his office. At first, I was concerned that all this interest in me was just a ploy to get me alone, and for him to show his randy side to me. Now, after being alone with him many times and not having him make any attempt to even flirt with me, I was oddly a bit disappointed. I wondered if I wasn't attractive enough to the other sex for them to even bother. I know this sounds barmy, but such thoughts do occur to a woman who has only had the company of her man a handful of times in the last few years.

Mr. Denton asked me on one Friday in particular, if I could work over my scheduled time and go over some sales charts with him. He felt that it would be invaluable for me to see how some of these numbers work in dictating who, and where, we put our most aggressive sales campaigns for the rest of the year. He told me he was ready to unleash me on the people of Alabama and that I was a born salesperson. I was flattered to death, of course, so I stayed after. Mr. Denton brought out a cardboard box full of sheets with graphs on them. He scanned around the office lobby and made a bit of a stinky face before announcing we would be better off working on all this in the employee lounge, in the back of the office building. I thought nothing of the idea and followed him to the back room. Once there, he placed the box on a coffee table in front of an old sofa he had for us girls to take comfortable breaks on. He mentioned how warm it was getting lately as he took off his sports jacket and sat down next to me on the sofa. Our eyes made contact as he sat down. He flashed a sort of crooked smile toward me as I noticed him slowly nudge closer. His leg was now right up against mine, and I was for the first time since going to work there, uncomfortable with him. Nothing else took place for the next hour as we went over the stack of worksheets in the box. Suddenly, however, without warning, Mr. Denton let out a large yawn and stretched his arms widely. "This stuff isn't the most exciting thing in the world, you know," he bellowed.

I laughed at his attempt at humor, but before I even noticed, his demeanor changed quickly and he got a more somber expression on his face. "It must be so difficult for you, Rosey dear, so lonely with your husband so far away." He blurted out of nowhere, and for no good reason.

I did my best to answer, but I was no rube to be played like a fool. I feared that everything Nancy had warned me about was now materializing. I just wondered why it took him so long to reveal his true colors.

"How long has it been dear?" he asked next.

"How long has what been?" I countered.

He squirmed in his seat as he tried to explain his inquiry, without really doing it. "You know…since you have been alone with…you know."

With those words, he had crossed a line, and I let him know it. "That's a personal matter. My private life, Mr. Denton, is really none of your concern," I argued.

He apologized at the same time that he rested his left hand, on the top of my leg. You talk about bloody mixed messages. He was apologizing to me for being rude with his mouth while being completely rude and disrespectful with his hand. I stared down at that hand of his as he continued to babble on. He didn't move it, and I didn't take my eyes off of it. Finally, I had enough of his games and told him to remove his hand from my leg, immediately. He did as if he was shocked that it was even resting where it was, like it had a bleeding mind of its own. He apologized a second time, and then it got quite strange. He admitted to me about being in an unhappy marriage, that he was lonely like me. He dreamed of being intimate with a woman like myself, a woman he respected and thought was going through the same struggles. I…quickly told him with a look that could melt icicles that I was nothing like what he described. I loved my husband and would never be unfaithful to him.

"I thought you wanted to make a career here. I guess I was wrong about you," he abruptly said.

His countenance and attitude quickly changed. He seemed miffed at me for not playing along with him. He told me next that maybe I really wasn't ready to go back to work. My blood boiled at his words. "How dare you say that to me! Your bloody hand on my leg or your schoolboy fantasies about getting me out of my knickers has nothing to do with how I do my job, Mr. Denton!"

"It's a man's world, Rosey. The Sooner you figure that out dear, the better things are going to go for you," he offered in his pathetic defense.

I told him no thank you in its most forceful way. "If this is indeed what a man's world looks like, Mr. Denton, then maybe it's time that the women take over being in charge!" I exclaimed, my voice rising almost to a feverish pitch.

He mumbled some more rubbish as I grabbed my handbag and stormed out of there. I didn't need to formally resign. I think we both knew I would no longer be working there.

———— • ————

IN THE NEXT FEW MONTHS, I STARTED WORKING FOR A temp agency. I worked at numerous firms around the area and found that Mr. Denton's pronouncements about male behavior on the job weren't far off, sadly. I was pinched on the bum, cuddled from behind, made the punchline of too many sexist funny quips to keep track of, and propositioned more times than I can remember. When I went to the next job, I felt like I was getting into the ring like a professional wrestler. The battles, however, were both physical and emotional, and all the rules of fighting seemed to be on the side of the men. I quickly could see that my declaration to Mr. Denton that last night in his office was more truthful than I had ever thought. It was time for women to take charge in the business world, maybe the world in general, not so much at the expense of men, but at least to help make men better. Absolute power is never a good thing, and that is what men had at the time. Women needed to take some of that away for the betterment of other women and even for the betterment of men. If men could see women more as their peers than just some toy or plaything, maybe just maybe, the better angels of men would begin to surface again. One could only hope and dream of such possibilities at the time, but it's through hopes and dreams that such new realities are made.

CHAPTER 15

After much difficulty, I finally found a job where the threat of being groped or leered at by men was unlikely. My new position was as a teacher's aide at a grammar school in town, outside of the base. With the salary I made and money from Albert, I was able to leave base housing and get my own one-bedroom flat in the city. I didn't tell Albert of my decision to move off base. Maybe because I felt justified by how much time in the last few years I had lived alone. If I was basically living as a single woman, although of course married, why shouldn't I live in a place of my own choosing? Now that I was working, and with some help from my dear old pap and mum, I could afford the new place. I certainly was not getting rich from working at the school, but spending time with the little tykes did seem to somehow make up for the fact that I had no little ones of my own to lavish attention on. One day, a letter arrived from Albert shortly after I moved into my flat. It had been forwarded from the base to my new address. The letter said in a glorious fashion that Albert would soon be coming home for a whole month. I had hoped he would be coming home permanently, but apparently, I wouldn't be that lucky. Sometime in June, he would finally arrive. I, at lightning-fast speed, sent him back a letter letting him know of my decision to move off base. I assumed he would be quite unhappy with my choice and felt the more time before he arrived back here, the better for him to come to grips with my change of residence.

I wondered if I would receive another letter before Albert got back. I hoped I would, but no letter came.

The next few months went by so unbelievably fast, as I fixed up my quaint new home. Most of the time I spent outside of work was with my two close friends, Nancy and Carol. I was always with one or the other, but never were the three of us together. I must admit I felt some shame for not spending more time with both of them, in the same company. I did not want to believe it was because Nancy, though a dear lady and certainly not a bigot in any way, didn't share the same passion for social change and especially civil rights issues that I did. I couldn't see her and Carol having much to speak about, so I kept them apart purposely. I had to consider if I was protecting my friends from feeling uncomfortable or myself. It was a question I was hiding from and wasn't sure I would like the answer to. Even After all my time spent in a black church in Alabama, working diligently for civil rights, there were still hidden areas in me that were more concerned with fitting in than doing what was right. I prayed for the strength to be able to openly discuss such things with Nancy. I knew at some point the subject would come up and I would find out if I was a coward or not.

———— • ————

BEFORE I KNEW WHAT HAPPENED, IT WAS THE END OF June. My pastor and a few other ladies including Carol and myself were all celebrating the idea that a new, historic civil rights law was about to be passed by the United States Congress and then signed into law by President Johnson.

Andrew Scott Bassett

This was something that President Kennedy had put together before his death. Now in his memory, and with the entire country still mourning for him, it looked like the new bill had a good chance to pass. Because of this, our church decided to throw a huge shindig if it did indeed make it into law. We would fittingly time the party with the church's Fourth of July celebration. I promised to whip up some English foods for everyone as part of our get-together. As I was trying to decide in my mind what would be the best choice to serve for the event, I was suddenly distracted by the sight of Albert standing on the front step of my flat. With all the things I could be thinking of at that moment, the first thing that came to mind was if I was wearing enough makeup and if my clothes were too wrinkled. I wet my lips and checked my breath for good measure before I ran outside to meet him.

"Boy oh boy, have I missed you," he greeted me as I surrendered into his arms.

We squeezed each other tight, holding on like our lives depended on it. I don't know how long we were standing on the front step, but I'm quite sure we put on a lovely show for the neighbors. When we made it into the flat, I assumed he would want to head straight for the bedroom. I would have no problem with that for it had been such a long time, but he didn't. Albert instead wanted to just sit and talk. He said he wanted to just be sitting on a sofa again with me, a "'normal thing,'" he called it. He sat close to me and held my hand in the sweetest way possible. I could feel my heart race with each squeeze of his fingers.

"So, this is the new place?" he remarked.

I told him I hoped he wasn't too upset by my leaving the base. I shared with him how separated I now felt from military life, with him not around. He surprisingly seemed to understand. He confessed that he was angry at first when he read my letter disclosing the big move, but after considering my point of view and how difficult things have been for me, his anger slipped away. I interrupted to ask if things would change soon. I wanted my husband back with me, and I wanted to know if he knew when or how that might happen. His answer crippled my emotions. "I wish I could give you good news, Rosey darling, but I can't."

"What do you mean?" I replied, not sure I really wanted to hear what came next.

Albert did his best to explain himself and not make me upset. "Nothing is official mind you, but what we're hearing in my platoon is we are gearing up for the real thing in Vietnam."

"The real thing?" I asked.

"Yeah…the real thing, war," Albert answered to my heartache.

"Why, why bloody war in another country halfway around the world!" I yelled, unable to control my emotions.

"It's just like Korea all over again. You've got the communists in the north supported by China, and the would-be democracy in the south, supported by us, the U.S.," Albert explained further.

"Well, it hasn't bloody well started yet, they still have time to stop it!" I shouted in anger.

Albert seeing my distress pulled me into his arms again. He promised that no matter what, we would make it through this.

"You always said to me that at least we weren't at war, but now you're saying we're going to be. It's not right, Albert," I argued forcefully, while still attempting to keep my emotions from getting the best of me.

Albert agreed with me about the unfairness of all of it as he held me close. He begged me to not tell others about this "'war business'", as he called it. "The military brass doesn't want anyone to know what's going on, honey, so as hard as it might be, keep this conversation between us. You know maybe it'll go another way and calmer heads will prevail. You never know."

"When?" I did want to know.

Albert shook his head. At this point, he didn't even want to talk about it anymore, but for my benefit and sanity, he did. "We're hearing later this year, or possibly next year. It all depends on what China and North Vietnam do next."

"Who cares!" I said with my anger at full boil and my chin buried in his shoulder.

"I don't know. I don't understand all this either, but as I said, whatever happens, we will get through this," Albert assured me a second time.

For the rest of the evening, we just held each other close, and then when the time was right, we finally discussed other things. When I asked him about what he was doing in Vietnam, he wanted nothing of it. Instead, he changed the subject in a blink of an eye and asked me all about what I had been up to. I went along with him and shared about my new job, my new friend Nancy, and even about what was going on at the church. I let him know about the excitement in the air over the proposed civil rights bill.

"Well, if they do pass the new law for blacks, I would love to go to the party with you at the church, if that's okay with you," Albert surprisingly mentioned.

My silly goose of a smile certainly answered his request. Because of his inquiry, I was on cloud nine. Albert's showing interest in something so incredibly important to me made me feel even closer to him than I already did if that was possible. I took him by the hand and told him it was time for bed, enough chatting. He laughed and said he wasn't very sleepy yet. As I led him to the bedroom, wearing a devious look on my face, I asked him, "Who said anything about sleep?"

Mrs. Wallace from the church invited everyone over to her home for the combined Fourth of July and civil rights law passing celebration. Her husband owned several businesses in the area that serviced many black people in Alabama. He was a black man himself who had become quite successful, not an easy task in this state. Albert and I were only a few of the many white folks to attend the gathering. We were all family, regardless of the color of our skin, all joined by the desire for justice and to celebrate this historic occasion. We had all worked so hard to see this day come. If you studied Albert, however, you might have thought we were the only pale faces to show. He was a nervous wreck. I guess he had never been around so many people of a different race than his own, before. He was sweating, which is common of course in Alabama in the summertime, but I knew him well enough to see how uncomfortable he was in the situation. Almost everyone in attendance there was laughing, hugging, and clanging glasses together. We thanked God almighty for President Johnson's signing of the new law. We all knew it would bring unprecedented new freedoms and equality for black Americans everywhere.

I thought my best plan would be to break the ice for Albert as quickly as I could. I took him around and introduced him to everyone there. Being he was with me and seeing how beloved I had become at the little Baptist church, all the folks there welcomed him with open arms and hearty smiles. I think the kindness and warmth they showed Albert took him by surprise. Knowing that he was in the Army and serving in Vietnam, the men at the party wanted to hear all his stories about what was going on over there, while the ladies wanted to wish him their best regards and pray for his safety. Albert was thankful either way. After an hour of laughing, singing, and just plain chin-wagging with each other, our church pastor settled us all down. He made us all sit and break bread together and sip the grape juice that represented the blood of Christ. He led us all in a long and thankful prayer. He reminded everyone there how lucky and blessed they were to see this day when real change had come to America. "Numerous ancestors and even family that have only been departed from us for a short time would have loved to have seen this day. I hope and pray that they too can partake of this victory. At least, I like to believe that from their perch in the heavenly realm, they can see the seeds they tilled have finally brought forth fruit. Now, we know that the movement for equality for black Americans is far from over, and this is much more of a great beginning than an end of anything. Still, brothers and sisters, this has been a magnificent last few days. We should all celebrate the great victory that we have achieved," Pastor Mitchell proclaimed, before pausing to search the faces of all of us there. He then continued. "For those of you here today, and I am specifically speaking to our white brothers and sisters of the Lord, I say to you this is a great day for you as well."

Several amens sprang out from the gathering to interrupt the pastor's thoughts for a second, but he went on. "This is a great day for you, our white family members, and that's exactly what you are, and don't ever think we don't know how important you have been to making this day come to pass. As the Reverend King, one of our true spiritual leaders has often said, if one of us lives without justice, none of us have justice, if any of us lack freedom, we all lack freedom. God bless everyone here, and God bless this country."

Albert turned to me after the pastor stopped speaking to tell me he thought that was an inspiring speech that he just heard. I took the opportunity to ask him if he was having a good time.

"Yes, yes, I really am," he whispered back to me.

All I could manage to do was grin at him. I was so happy at that moment. I was happy that my husband was sitting here with me after so much time apart. I was happy about the incredible achievements we were all witnessing in the country. And I was happy that I could share such an important part of me with Albert and have him accept it. That afternoon and evening was a high point in my somewhat young life, as I cuddled up close to my Albert, my dear Albert. I didn't know then that it would be one of the few wonderful moments I would have the opportunity to take part in, for a long time.

———————◆————————

YOU KNOW HOW YOU HAVE SOMETHING LURKING, ALMOST hiding away inside of you for what seems an eternity. You dread that it ever comes to fruition, but something deep down in the pit of your soul tells you it will. That's what happened to me next. Since World War II ended, and to my relief, I survived it, I have felt the shadow of war in all its awful glory and misery chasing me. I cannot say why I always felt this way, but I did. It's as if me and bloody war had unfinished business to take care of, and it was inevitable we would meet again. The next year, nineteen sixty-five, it all came to pass. The war in Vietnam began in earnest as our worst fears, mine and Albert's I should say, became our terrible new life. On the outside looking in, my life didn't seem any different. I was working at the school doing my best to calm the fears of the children there who had fathers in the armed forces. I still had my cute little flat and still went to my cute little Baptist church with Carol, my dearest friend, who was the rock of my life. Yes, on the outside things weren't seemingly much different, but on the inside, I was terrified every day. Always in fear that two Army officers would knock on my door to tell me that Albert was dead, gone from me forever. I would have these 'spells', we didn't call them panic attacks at that time, where I couldn't breathe correctly. Sometimes they would only last for a few minutes. Sometimes these attacks on my system would last much longer. I spoke with Pastor Mitchell about them, and he thought they were likely brought on by stress and anxiety. He recommended a doctor in town if the Army didn't offer one, someone who could get me some medicine to help. Often when these 'spells' hit, my mind was blank. I wasn't really thinking about Albert and what kind of danger he might be in. Others, including Pastor Mitchell and Carol, said they thought the stress was probably on a subconscious level. They thought maybe I wasn't willing to deal with it on a conscious level. Carol wondered if the mere thought of losing Albert was too much for me to even consider after all I had been through and seen as a child in England during the war. I couldn't say if she was right, but I sure couldn't say she was wrong either.

Therefore, I buried myself as I had done before when Albert was gone, in my own work and the causes that mattered to me. Somehow, I was like a person cut in half, a half-person you might say. My husband was away, and I was alone. I would go to the market or shop in town and see women many times younger than I pushing a pram or holding the hands of their little ones. In stores, I would personally eavesdrop on mums and their children as the boys argued for a new baseball glove or the girls begged for a new doll. As a young wife, I didn't want the responsibility or loss of freedom that children bring. Now, however, my biological clock was ticking faster than ever, and I ached for motherhood. None of these thoughts, of course, were of much help, so I pushed them down deep inside of me. I felt trapped and saw no escape in sight.

———————•————————

THE NEXT THREE YEARS WERE DREADFUL. THE WAR IN Vietnam raged on. It took all my stiff upper lip and hearty Brit makeup to see me through it. Albert came home on leave only twice in all that time. He told me he was now considered an essential officer for commanding helicopter raids and attacks throughout Vietnam. The military powers that be were reluctant to give Albert any time off and kept adding more tours of duty. Each time he thought he might be heading back stateside for good; we would be devastated by the news they were sending him back over. Because of all this, Albert was becoming more distant, more disillusioned about the war, and more heartbroken from the suffering and horrors he had witnessed. And as one might expect, sadly, he was drinking heavily again. It was difficult for me to say anything about it really. I knew that he was hurting in so many ways, ways I did not even understand. The last thing I wanted to do was add to his pain by coming down hard on him about his drinking. I looked the other way. I turned the other cheek; I bloody well didn't utter a word. When he got leave and came home for a short break, I always hoped there would be a moment when we were together when we could discuss our future, you know, what we would do after the war was finally over. I so badly wanted to broach the subject of adoption with him again. He wanted only his own children when we were first married, his own bloodlines. I respected his feelings at that time. He was going through so much. Now, I wanted him to respect mine. But in Albert's state, I could never really have that conversation. I never found the right moment when he was ready to discuss such things.

By nineteen sixty-eight, I like most of the country was fed up with a war that seemed like it had no end. It felt as if the president and the military brass had lied to us all. This was supposed to have been an easy war for the U.S. to have won. Sadly, just as in the war in Korea, their predictions were wrong. Stateside, with a new election year upon us, we were all ready for a change.

I was excited to be taking on a new cause close to my heart. I had become even more of a fan of the late President Kennedy and now despised Lyndon Johnson. I believed with all my heart that Kennedy would have never let Vietnam become what it now was. He would have put a stop to the war, one way or another. Now his brother Bobby was running for president to replace Johnson. I couldn't have been more excited by the prospects of a new President Kennedy in the White House. I joined his political campaign in Alabama, and even though it cut down much of my time for civil rights work, I felt it was worth it. After all, it was really President John Kennedy's desires that helped to push the civil rights law of nineteen sixty-four. Just think what another Kennedy in charge could do, I told myself. Things were going smoothly as we moved into the spring, all of us involved in the campaign, and many church members who joined me, including Carol, felt that Bobby Kennedy was destined to win the nomination. Even with the war raging on and protests against it breaking out all over the country, I was hopeful again that things were going to get better. A new shining knight was coming to the rescue, it seemed to so many of us.

Then, it all started to unravel and slowly the hope for change began to slip away. Reverend King was shot and killed while speaking in Memphis. It was crazy that in only four years after the new civil rights law was passed, so much good had been wasted and forgotten. At the news, Carol and I just fell into each other's arms and wept uncontrollably. We knew that this would bring new divisions between the blacks and whites in America, the one thing we had been fighting against for all these years. Martin Luther King was our leader, and now I felt like we had no such person of his stature to follow. We all believed that Bobby Kennedy was now our best hope to bring the races together. He was the one person with the legacy of his brother to fall back upon who could unite blacks and whites. After the tragic day in April, he was trying to do his best as he crisscrossed the country, reaching out to poor folks and minorities.

———— • —— • ————

ONE NIGHT, I INVITED ALL MY FRIENDS OVER TO CEL-ebrate what I hoped would be glorious victories for Senator

Kennedy in the South Dakota and California primaries. My small flat was full to the brim. I made several trifles and treacle puddings for the sweet tooths that I knew would be coming over to share the big night with me. Carol came over first, and not long after my friend Nancy showed up. I had always kept them apart for some reason that I always justified. I was surprised Nancy even came to our shindig. She was a staunch Republican and a supporter of Richard Nixon. Still, she did come, and I was delighted. The more the merrier I felt. Before we knew it, everyone else showed up with bells and whistles on.

We got the results late at night, being three hours ahead of California time. Bobby Kennedy, the Massachusetts senator, had just won both primaries and now seemed a shoo-in for the Democratic nomination for president. All of us, stuffed into my itsy-bitsy flat, also stuffed our faces with crisps, finger foods, and my British afters. We were now all glued to the telly as Senator Kennedy made his speech from his headquarters at some hotel in Los Angeles. His looks and, of course, his voice brought back the memory of his older brother, and now it seemed he was going to finish what his brother had started…it seemed. After his speech was over, some of the folks at my place began to pack up and leave, while others, like Carol and Nancy, joined me in continuing to watch the festivities. Nancy even complimented Bobby Kennedy on his speech. "As a Southern girl it might sound silly to say, but there is something very attractive about that Boston accent that the Kennedys all have."

"That's what you take from his speech tonight and his wonderful victories today?" Carol asked Nancy point-blank.

Nancy, surprised by Carol's poking at her, responded by saying, "No, no…his speech, nothing to write home about, darling. But he did win today, so good for him, although I am still a supporter of Vice President Nixon. I do understand how important the Kennedys have been to your people, but it was Republicans who really made that civil rights law get passed, you have to know."

"Oh, really now?" Carol sniped at her.

"Yes, it's certainly true, darling," Nancy fired back.

I suddenly realized why I didn't get these two together for social occasions. I loved Carol and I liked Nancy very much, but they were from two different worlds and had ideas that the other would have a hard time swallowing. I offered more trifle to try and divert their thoughts and distract their arguments. I was only partially successful in my attempt, thankfully, Nancy decided it was probably about time to call it a night. But then, in the next few minutes, the unthinkable, which had now become almost common in this last decade, reared its ugly head again. Shots rang out from the hotel where Bobby Kennedy had just spoken. Mass confusion followed as we were left watching in stunned silence. We knew it wasn't a good thing, but surely this time, the man the country trusted and believed in would survive. When we found out Bobby had been shot, we all started to pray as hard as we could. Our sadness and sorrow made it difficult to pray or keep our composure. After a few hours of this, and with the senator at the hospital fighting for his life, one by one the ladies still left at my home, began to solemnly march out. Carol and Nancy were the last two to go. I hugged Carol one more time as she went for my front door. "When will this all end?" she said to me, shaking her head.

Right at that moment, Nancy butted in. "It will end when people like us, who are still different in many ways, realize we have more in common than we think. When we can love each other as the good book says, even if we don't agree on everything."

Carol smiled in response to Nancy's words. She knew it was Nancy's way of sort of apologizing and saying she was sorry for the events of the night. I will always remember what happened next as these two very different women embraced. One had white skin, and one had black. They had different political beliefs in many ways. However, they shared one important thing: They believed in loving others, even others you don't necessarily like or agree with. I couldn't help but tell them both how much they meant to me and how much I admired them. They then each embraced me after hugging on each other. Nancy again told me how sorry she was about everything and how she hoped and prayed that Bobby Kennedy would pull through. I thanked her again and watched from my front porch as she and Carol drove away. Bobby Kennedy died twenty-six hours later, and the world went to hell in a handbasket.

———— ◆ • ————

DANNY IS HAPPY TO HAVE JULIA, HIS EX-GIRLFRIEND, and one-time future love of his life, sitting next to him. He and his sister Lori are meeting with one of the heads of the local veteran's cemetery just outside the Phoenix area. Danny still finds it odd that their mother requested to be buried in such a place after what he has read about her struggles as a military wife. But, with only six days to the funeral, they need to nail down exactly where their mother's body will be laid to rest. he lets off a loud yawn. The three of them are still waiting patiently for the lady they are meeting to arrive. Danny is visibly tired from spending last night and most of yesterday working to turn his mother's story into a manuscript.

"You awake there?" Lori asks her kid brother sarcastically.

He grunts that he's fine. But he does let it be known that he wishes they had stopped at a Starbucks on the way over.

"It's two o'clock in the afternoon?" Lori jabs at him.

"He's barely slept since yesterday, Lori. He's been working on his book non-stop," Julia interjects in Danny's defense.

"Is it just the book that's been keeping him up, or are you having something to do with that, haha!" Lori replies in jest.

Julia, not exactly seeing the humor in the situation, strenuously restates that she is just here to support Danny and that's all she was doing last night. Julia reminds Lori that she is in a separate bedroom in the home, not that Lori cares one way or another. "None of us are kids anymore, so… you know, like whatever." Lori's comments, brim-full with innuendo, only serve to irritate Julia more.

"I stayed up with Danny for as long as I could last night, for moral support. He's working so hard to get this book finished by next week," Julia explains, defending herself to Danny's sister.

"By the by, what's the new one about?" Lori asks her brother, oblivious to how she's made Julia feel. "I'm assuming it's another thriller like the first one."

Danny is stoneface in response to her inquiry. He's not really sure if he wants to share the fact that he is now turning their mother's life story, into a novel.

"Cat got your tongue, Danny?" Lori adds when her question gets no response.

"Oh…yeah it's a little different, more of a melodrama of sorts," he finally answers.

Lori is excited to hear that. She is more a fan of family drama-type stories than thrillers. "I can't wait to read it, little brother. I only wish Mom was here to see the second book. I'm sure she would have loved the story."

Danny agrees while Julia for her part holds back any expression. She feels guilty for knowing about the true source of the new book when Danny's own sister doesn't.

"I have to say that I think Mom would have really related to the story and enjoyed the main character immensely," Danny suggests, having some fun with the situation.

Julia gives him a little elbow in the side for being so sneaking with his sister.

Lori out of the blue stands up and announces she can't wait anymore. She needs to relieve herself of all that tea she had earlier. Still waiting for the woman to show up for the meeting, Lori leaves to find the nearest bathroom in the building. Danny and Julia are left alone in the office waiting for the meeting to begin. Danny tells Julia he hopes his constant work on the book isn't too boring for her to be around. She laughs at the suggestion. "I'm here as a friend, to help you any way I can," she says in support.

"Just as a friend, huh?" He lets slip.

"Yes, are you surprised?" She challenges him.

Danny realizes he needs to speak carefully and not say the wrong thing. He has never had much of a knack for doing that in the past, so this is a 'real' stretch for him. "No, I mean, I don't know."

Julia is interested to know what he's really trying to say. Danny claims to mean nothing, as per usual. His anxiety rises because he's not sure what she wants to hear.

"After New York, do you really think I would just come down here and act like nothing happened?" she tells him sternly.

Danny shakes his head. "Of course not. I guess I hoped maybe you coming down here was a sign that maybe you…"

"That I what? I'm here because I care about you. I wanted more out of our former relationship, of course, but you didn't, so that's that," Julia explains, as Danny recognizes the tension and frustration in her tone. "Now we are good friends, or does my being here now somehow offend you?"

Danny considers his next words, wisely, he can tell she's about to explode on him like a human grenade, and he wants to defuse her if he can. "No, no, Julia, I'm really thankful you are here."

"Would it be easier if I just went back to New York? Oh, don't you worry about it as soon as the funeral services are over, I'll be heading back," she tells him angrily.

Danny tries to get her to understand that's not what he wants at all, but now she's replaying in her head all of his past transgressions against her and not listening to a word he says.

"I'll get a motel room after this, that way I won't be in the way," she snipes in his direction.

Danny explains again that she won't be in the way and that she doesn't need to get a motel room. Unfortunately, she's already mad at him, and all the reasoning in the world isn't going to make a bit of difference.

Finally, the lady they have been waiting for all this time arrives. She apologizes for being so tardy, and boy does Danny wish she had been on time. Maybe, he calculates, if this gal hadn't left them waiting for so long Julia wouldn't have had the chance to churn up all those past hurts up and then hurl them back at him. He feels, emotionally speaking, like someone is throwing a snowball at his head. Then Lori makes it back to the office after using the bathroom. It's now time for the matter at hand: Is their mother eligible to be buried at the V.A. cemetery or not. Melanie, the woman they're meeting with, studies their application. She hems and haws as she reads and audits every word. At last, she looks up with a crooked smile and states that she doesn't find in the paperwork where their mother was in the military. Lori is quick to explain that there is a simple reason for that. Mother wasn't.

"Does she have a husband still alive who was a veteran?"

"No, not for quite a few years now," Lori answers.

"Oh my," Melanie says. "I'm afraid then your mother isn't eligible for burial at our facility. I'm truly sorry."

Lori doesn't understand and lets it be known with strong indignation.

"It is just the policy here that the person for burial must either be currently married to a veteran at the time of their death or be a military veteran themselves. I am afraid there is no way around these policies," the lady declares, showing no signs of relenting from the rules.

Lori by now, sitting across from her, is fuming. She lets the lady know in no uncertain words how strongly she disagrees with their regulations. "This is bullshit! My mother wants to be buried here and sacrificed half of her life for the military. She deserves to be buried here just as much as anybody else!"

Danny and Julia tried to calm the situation, but Lori isn't listening. She gets up and storms out. Danny knows his sister well enough to know he is going to have to give her a few hours just to calm down. He somewhat apologizes for his sister's actions as he and Julia get up to leave themselves. When they walk back to Lori's car, they find her waiting for them. Danny chuckles to himself as he realizes at that moment just how much the women in his life can get fired up in an instant, first Julia and then his sister. When they get into the car, Lori is talking to herself and still fuming. "What are we going to do Danny?! Mom's funeral is this weekend! We need to have a place to bury her, and this was supposed to be it!"

Julia sighs from the back seat. She doesn't dare say a word. Danny does his best to encourage Lori. "We'll figure something out, Sis, it'll be okay. We'll start making calls to other veteran cemeteries in the state."

"I wanted Mom buried here, in Phoenix. I don't want her far away from where I can't even hardly go visit her," Lori says with disdain.

Danny reaches out and puts his arm around her. "Don't worry. We'll figure out something."

Lori still huffs and puffs, Danny's words only quenching her fire for a second. She eventually starts the car and they drive away. All the way home, back to her house, Danny and Julia do their best to calm Lori down and keep her from speeding. They are only somewhat successful on both fronts.

———•——•——

DANNY JUMPS RIGHT BACK INTO HIS MOTHER'S STORY when he gets back to his sister's house. He wants to call Julia on her cell and try to smooth things over, but in his gut, he knows it's too soon for that. He resists the male impulse to try and 'fix the problem', and instead decides to let everything simmer down for a while. Julia's busy getting a rental car and booking a motel room, so Danny at least gets a chance to get back to the manuscript. It will not be the manuscript his publisher or literary agent are expecting, and it might be the end of his bestseller days, but it is the best story he has. So, he plants himself at the desk in the spare room and feverishly turns his mother's story into his own. The clock is ticking as his agent and publisher are expecting the first-draft manuscript by next week, and not just a few chapters at that. Fortunately for him, his mother was a brilliant author in her own right, and it took little effort to take her pages and make them his. "Now, where was I?" Danny whispers to himself. "That's right, the end of the sixties, and now a trip to Washington D.C."

CHAPTER 16

Albert had been home for a short time, less than two weeks, before being rushed back to the other side of the world by the Army. The fight against the North Vietnamese and China was still raging on. It was one of the first times that part of me was happy to see him leave, and I felt awful about it. I knew the kind of danger he was in, believe me, I did, and I prayed every day for his safety. The dreadful, truth, however, was that we fought when he was here, more than we ever had before. He spent a large portion of his time meant for us, drinking, both at home and in nearby pubs. He knew how much I hated to see him drink, so he would leave the flat and shove off the first time he saw an unapproving look come his way. I think maybe both of us having lived apart because of the damn wars and rumors of wars for so long, had become almost accustomed to such a lifestyle. Now, when we would finally be allowed to see each other by the military powers that be, even if it was only for a short time, we seemed to not be able to compromise our independence. We were now more like two single people, trying to be married and live together. When I tried to get Albert to open up about his drinking, he would stonewall me completely. He would tell me he didn't even want to have to think about the reasons for it. I could see clearly that Albert didn't want to relive the horrible things he'd seen in Vietnam by having to share them with me. Like any wife, I wanted to be there for him. I wanted him to be able to open up to me and be comforted. I wished he could unburden himself to me. When he left for duty, once more, I wondered with much trepidation and concern what the Army would leave me for a husband when all this damn fighting business of theirs was finally finished. My heart's desire was to discuss adopting a child together, but even a silly Britt lass like me could see that now was not the time or place.

----•----

IT WAS THE THIRTY-YEAR ANNIVERSARY OF THE BEGIN-ning of World War II. There was a big exhibit opening in Washington D.C. with many speakers coming from around the world. I decided to save my pennies and go to it. I was, of course, especially interested in the exhibits that had to do with the 'Battle of Britain' and 'Dunkirk'. My only problem was I didn't want to make the trip alone. I asked both my girlfriends if either would tag along with me. To my surprise, both Nancy and Carol said yes. I expected only one of them to be able to make the trip at best, never both. The two of them hadn't been in the same room in over a year. The last time was the night Bobby Kennedy was shot, and though that night ended well between them, even on that occasion they had few words between each other. Now, I would have to break the news to them that the other one was coming. I really had no other choice. Again, to my surprise, both of them told me that they were still coming. Carol said she wanted to support me and get to know my history the way I had for her. Nancy wished to see the capital for the first time and thought it would be quite a hoot. Fortunately, we were all able to get time off from our jobs. We flew together, which helped me greatly since I still despised flying, or at least crashing.

The exhibits in Washington were spread out over several venues around the city. On the first day there we made an effort to see as much as we could. Both of the girls were in awe of much of what they saw. They, of course, knew many things about the war but not the details that were now being shown to them in such a vivid manner. For me, the exhibits showing London being bombed by the German Air Force and the tank battles in North Africa were the most moving. I couldn't help but think of my dear old pap fighting the fires in London and my Uncle George who never returned from the fighting in North Africa. I never would have believed that photos of tanks in battle would have brought tears to my eyes. Yet, because of my uncle, they most certainly did.

Near the end of the first day, the girls and I decided to make it to one more exhibit. This one fascinated me, I have to admit. It was photos and speakers from the German side of the war. Carol and Nancy weren't as interested as I was but played along with me, nonetheless. After walking through a huge gallery of photos depicting Germany just before and all the way to the conclusion of the war, the three of us found seats so we could listen to the German speakers at the event. The speakers were all spread out, sitting on folded chairs around a small stage. The American diplomat who was MC for the event pointed behind himself to the people seated to his back left. He told us that they were the German men and women that we could look forward to hearing from today. I took a moment to study their faces. My eyes fixated on the man sitting in the back corner. It was Maximillian. I wanted to ask Nancy or Carol to pinch me, to make sure if I was really seeing what I thought I was. I didn't though. I knew they would think I was bloody bonkers or something. I wondered if he noticed me. I know it's silly. If I spotted him, he must have spotted me, likewise. My heart skipped a beat as it was finally his turn to speak. I did not let on to the girls that I knew him. It was far too long of a story to explain in such a venue. Then he started, and as I expected, he was brilliant, just wonderful. He shared the horrors of growing up in Germany during Hitler's rule. He spoke powerfully about not wanting to fight for the fascist government but really having no choice in the matter. Many childhood friends of his were brainwashed into becoming part of 'Hitler's Youth', but not him. He ended his speech with an inspiring story of how surprisingly happy he was the day he was taken prisoner by the English military. At that moment he had survived the war and was confident the English Army would treat him much better than the Germans treated their prisoners of war.

At the end of everything, the audience began to slowly move toward the stage platform and the array of speakers standing upon it. People were thanking them for coming all this way to share their perspectives on the war, a unique German perspective, at that. Carol and Nancy followed me as I made my way toward the stage. I couldn't take my eyes off of Max. I could tell he hadn't noticed me yet. I wondered how close I could get before he did. The answer was no closer. His eyes now met mine. A look of delirious disbelief captured his expression. He pushed past the people in front of him and then down the steps to the stage to greet me.

"Rosey, is it really you?"

I could hardly speak as Carol and Nancy standing beside me inquired how I knew this man.

"I can't believe you are here," he continued.

"I'm having a hard time believing this myself," I replied.

"It is so good to see you," Max then said in a flattering tone.

Carol and Nancy exchanged sly glances. They could tell there was more here than meets the eye. They figured we were more than just two old friends who hadn't seen each other in a long time. Feeling their stares, I quickly introduced them to Max, who barely acknowledged their existence. His mouth said nice to meet you too, but his eyes never left mine.

"I am done for the day here. I would love it if you could have dinner with me tonight?" he asked.

I motioned toward Carol and Nancy standing next to me. It was my attempt to show Max that I wasn't alone at this affair, poor choice of words, but that I was with my girlfriends. I remarked how nice dinner sounded, but at last, I was here with the girls, so…

"It's really not a problem, Rosey, is it, Nancy dear?" Carol suddenly interrupted.

"Not at all, Carol. In fact, Rosey, we were just saying how nice it would be for us to spend some time together without you, you know, get to know each other a little better," Nancy said with her tongue firmly planted in her cheek.

I knew what the girls were up to. For whatever reason, they were both doing their best to make this dinner with Max take place.

I directed a dirty look at both of them. I knew they didn't really want to spend time with each other without me as a buffer. No, they were sacrificing their own possible good times for me.

"You two run along now and have a lovely dinner. Rosey, Carol and I will have a fine time without you. We'll go shopping and buy some shoes, right Carol dear?" Nancy promised as she and Carol made it virtually impossible for me to turn Max's invitation down.

I knew I should turn down the offer, but for some reason, I wanted to accept it, so I did. Max was thrilled. Carol and Nancy scooted off together as they locked arms and giggled at my situation. They found something other than my friendship that they had in common. They both equally enjoyed mucking with my life.

"It is a little bit early for dinner, but we could still go and have some tea or coffee together before the meal if you would like. I know there is so much I want to tell you and ask you as well," Max told me as he motioned for us to go.

I smiled and happily agreed and then graciously followed him. Only once did I look back toward the girls. They saw me and waved before laughing hilariously together at my expense. I was extremely happy that my dinner date of sorts with Max could bring them such pleasure. I'm only being bloody sarcastic, of course.

———— ◆ ————

WE HAD NOT EVEN CONSIDERED DINNER, AND I WAS already full to the brim with cups of tea and coffee cakes. The quaint little café Max had taken me to was quite lovely in every way, and we spent the next two hours just chatting about, well everything. He shared with me the loss of his young wife in a car accident about five years earlier in West Germany. He hadn't remarried.

Instead, he just buried himself in his work as a diplomat for his country. Like Albert and I, they weren't able to have any children, except in their case it was because of Max's wife being sadly infertile. He had taught some at several universities in West Germany, mostly political science and German history. His position as a diplomat and his history as a German prisoner of war, led to others, like the organizations behind these exhibits commemorating World War II, to reach out to him as a speaker. He told me he was honored and even excited to have the opportunity to bring a better understanding to the West of what really happened in Germany before the war and during the time of Hitler's reign. "So many people in the world, especially in America, think all Germans during that time were Nazis and followers of Hitler. Events like this held here in Washington D.C., give me the chance to show them that is not true. In many ways, Germans were just as much victims of Hitler's evil plans as other Europeans and Americans were. I am proud, Rosey, to open eyes to these truths."

I told him he should be and that it was wonderful what he was doing to bring better understanding between countries. I commented on how lonely a widower he must be, having to travel by himself so much.

"I try to do not think about it," he confessed. "But it can be very difficult and gives one much time to remember his past."

I could not help but ask him what he thought about when he dwelled on this past of his. I was curious if I was in those memories, at least somewhere. He started to share these memories with me. His story of growing up in Germany before the war and being raised by a well-to-do family and all the trappings and privilege that came with such a life. He eventually got to recalling his time in battle, subsequently being captured by the English, and then finally getting around to meeting me. Now, at last, we were on the part that truly piqued my interest. But, as I waited with bated breath on what came next, Max volleyed the conversation back onto my lap. "I've been talking too much. I hope I am not boring you."

"Of course not," I quickly replied. "Why would you even say such a thing?"

"Good," Max said with a sense of relief. "Enough of me now, tell me more about your husband and what he is doing in Vietnam."

When he asked me that, I felt odd. I didn't know why I did or why such a normal type of inquiry would bother me so much, but somehow it did. I skipped through my answer to his question as fast as I could and with almost no detail. Max I could tell, realized I felt uncomfortable discussing Albert with him.

"It must be very difficult being married, yet apart so much?" he asked next.

I confessed that it was. Yet I still felt wrong about discussing my husband and my marriage with a man I knew I still had some sort of feelings for. All those years ago when we bumped into each other in West Germany, I was at that time a young wife, completely and unequivocally in love with her husband. Now, all these many years later, I still loved Albert, but not with the same intensity as I did then, and that worried me very much at this moment.

Max asked if I knew when Albert might be home for good.

I shared I did not but prayed it was soon.

"I suppose that I am not the only prisoner of war at this table," Max proclaimed, out of the blue.

I wasn't sure what he meant, so I asked him to explain his words.

"It only seems to me that you and Albert and your marriage are also prisoners of war," he went on to say.

After that, we sat quietly for a few minutes as if sizing up all of what we had just said to each other. A waitress came over and asked if we wanted to order anything more. We both responded with, "What are your soups today?" We laughed at our shared thoughts and how we both knew we had stuffed ourselves too much with tea and sweets.

Afterward, we took a walk. We strolled over to the Lincoln Memorial. I shared my story of being here in the crowd as Martin Luther King changed the world with his '*I Have a Dream*' speech. Max was impressed with my stories of working with civil rights groups in Alabama. It then donned on me that even now as he commended me on such activities, I really wasn't sure how Max, being a German, felt about these things. I considered that he was only being agreeable to civil rights for blacks because he could see how important it was to me. Right, snap dab in front of the giant statue of Abraham Lincoln, I nudged him a tad. I wanted to know. Max immediately knew what I was asking. "You question me about this because I am German. Isn't that true?"

I now felt put on the spot, a bit embarrassed. I could tell he was surprised that I had my doubts about him.

"Let me just say when I was still a youth in Germany before I was a man, I watched American sprinter Jesse Owens, a black man, defeat my fellow countrymen in the Olympics. Jessie Owens destroyed Hitler and the Nazi Third Reich's ideas of one race being superior to another. I never understood even as a young boy how the color of one's skin could make one person better or worse than another. When Jessie Owens stood on the medal platform and received his gold medals, I could say nothing out loud for fear of reprisal from others. However, Rosey, inside I cheered his triumph and Hitler's failure."

"I'm so sorry, Max," I interrupted. "I guess I was assuming the worst as so many others do, that I disagree with."

"It's not problem," he uttered back in his somewhat broken dialect. "Do you know that football is my favorite sport?"

"No?" I answered.

"Not the football they play in America, but real football as we play in Germany and your England," he continued.

"Of course?" I said, not sure what the point he was making was.

"And do you know who my favorite footballer is or as they call them here, soccer player?"

I answered that I would assume it was one of West Germany's best players.

He was quick to point out to me I was wrong. "No, my favorite footballer is 'Pele'. He is from Brazil and is black."

Now, I understood the point too all this. He was proving to me he wasn't a bigot as if his story about Jessie Owens wasn't enough.

I told him I should have never doubted him. A smile of satisfaction suddenly covered his face as we continued on our way walking, side by side.

Max escorted me back to my hotel an hour later. In the lobby, he started to speak about how strange this world could be. I asked him what he meant. He brought up how it seemed that fate kept bringing us together. First in the English pub when he was a prisoner, then a few years after the war in West Germany, and now. Max called it fate tempting us both. What the temptation was, he didn't say. For me, it was more like fate was teasing us with what could have been if past choices in our lives had been different. Either way, it seemed a bloody waste of time to dwell on what might have been but never was.

Before we knew it, it was quiet between us for the first time in hours. I don't think either one of us wanted to say goodnight because that probably meant cheerio and good-bye forever. The odds of another fateful meeting were not favorable, and we both knew it.

"I would ask you to breakfast in the morning, but I'm afraid my plane leaves early for home," Max shared.

"It's alright, really," I replied. But I was only being halfway truthful. In reality, part of me didn't want him to go. But another part of me, the more rational part of me, knew he had to leave.

"Since we don't know when, or even if we will make acquaintance with each other again, will you consider one request from me?" Max asked shyly, like a schoolboy asking a girl to dance for the first time.

"What is that?" I inquired, somewhat worried about what his request might be.

"As I asked, many years before, would you be willing to stay in correspondence with me?" he said almost with a stutter.

I didn't actually answer him at first. I was too busy considering the ramifications of such a correspondence.

"Not by phone of course. I am sure your husband Albert might not approve. I was just thinking of letters, Rosey. I was thinking letters sent occasionally between two old friends, nothing more," he added.

In my heart of hearts, I thought Albert would probably not approve of letters either, but for some reason, I still told Max yes. The trickle of guilt dripping down my spine, I ignored, as I wrote down my address back in Alabama for him.

"Max," I said. "Please keep the letters as a friend would send to another, please. I wouldn't want to tell you I couldn't correspond with you anymore because I felt like I was betraying my husband. Do you have an inkling of what I'm getting at?"

Max said he understood. "I promise you letters that you could share with Albert if you wished."

I told him that was lovely, even though I had no intention to share Max's letters with Albert, no matter how innocent the correspondence might be.

We then said our goodbyes. Max embraced me for a quick moment. My heart skipped a beat at being so close to him again. We took one long look at each other, shared a warm and knowing gaze between us, and he was gone. I went back to my hotel room, the one I was sharing with the girls. They were waiting for me like an army ready to ambush. They both had a million questions for me. They wanted to know what went on tonight, how I knew Max, and if I would see him again. I told them both enough, to shut their chatting chins up. I certainly didn't tell them everything. I wasn't sure at this point if even I understood all of it when it came to Maximillian, my long-lost German love.

———◆·———

THE NEXT DAY, THE GIRLS AND I WENT TO A FEW MORE exhibits in the morning and then spent the rest of the afternoon shopping at the luxurious stores nearby. I needed something to get my mind off of Max's departure. The girls and I were having a most delightful time together and it was nice to see that this experience, the trip together, had created a budding friendship between Carol and Nancy. It's funny how shopping and spending money with someone can bring you closer together even if you have distinctly different backgrounds. Later, at the end of the day, as we were walking back to our hotel quite exhausted from all our fun, we crossed paths with a Vietnam War protest march. The young longhairs, as Albert liked to call them, were yelling and chanting, often their words laced with obscenities. They were protesting not only the war but also the talk of a military draft lottery, to be starting soon.

"I love their passion, and I agree with their cause, but they should clean up their act and stop with the filthy mouths, already," Carol remarked as the mob walked past us.

Nancy agreed. "We should call their mothers on them and put some soap in those filthy pie-holes of theirs."

I didn't appreciate the profanities either but certainly understood the anger. People today were freer than former generations and were going to speak out much more boldly than they had in the past. Like, the mostly young people in the protest, I also hated war. I had already donated a bit of my time to helping the cause back in Alabama. I was even considering at the present to get more involved with the issue in the future. Indeed, as in civil rights and women's rights, fighting the evils of war was close to my heart.

As the three of us watched, our hands completely full, clutching the store bags from our shopping spree, we saw a young soldier in uniform walking across the street. He was holding hands with a young woman, an attractive little blonde. When the protesters took notice of the uniform, they stopped in their tracks and then rushed toward the unsuspecting couple. The protesters started by hurling slanderous names at the young soldier and his companion. The girls and I were stunned, frozen in place by the chain of events happening right before our eyes. The young soldier attempted to shield his gal as the mob encircled then and began to shout disparaging names at him. They called him many awful things with "'baby killer'" being at the top of the list. Then, they wouldn't let the soldier or his gal pass through and walk down the sidewalk. They blocked their path. When the mob began to spit at the couple, I had seen enough. "This is bloody rubbish!" I yelled from across the street.

"What are you doing?" Carol asked me in a whisper.

"Leave them alone, you bloody bullies!" I hollered a second time.

Nancy quickly grabbed my arm and recommended that we go to our hotel right away. I could see the fear in her eyes. But I told her that one thing I could not stand were bullies, no matter what their motivations.

"There's nothing we can do except notify the authorities, the cops," Carol chimed in as she was now working with Nancy to try and get me to head back to our hotel.

I was, however, not going to do anything of the sort. I yelled out once more as I broke free of Nancy's grip and ran across the street and toward the protesters. The girls hesitated for a second before deciding to follow.

"Leave them alone!" I screamed at the top of my lungs to get the mob's attention.

I pushed my way through the crowd without even giving it a second thought so I could stand by the soldier and his girlfriend. Carol and Nancy reluctantly did the same thing.

"Get the hell out of the way, lady!" one of the protesters screamed right at me.

"Why are you sticking up for this pig bastard, this baby-killing son-of-a-bitch!" another yelled, from the crowd.

"She's a warmonger probably!" still another let loose.

By now, I was angry enough that my Brit juices overcame any fear in me or common sense, I suppose. I challenged the mob of protesters' shouts and insults with my own passionate words. "I'm not a warmonger! I hate bloody war as much as the rest of you!"

"Then why are you defending this piece of shit!" someone else from the mob screamed out.

Carol and Nancy by this point were scooched in close to me. They were as afraid for my safety as they were their own. But I was defiant for some reason or reasons that I wasn't quite sure of at the time. "Because he's just doing what he's been told to do! He's as much a victim of this dreadful war as the rest of us!"

The protesters didn't agree with my sentiment and slandered my good name and the young man's some more. They were still very agitated and dangerous, but I was unrelenting. "He was lied to, just as all of you feel lied to! He was sent around the world with no way home! He was forced to do as he was ordered! Protest the orders! Protest the government and military that gave him those orders! But don't protest a young man just doing what he was ordered to do and who had little choice in the matter!"

"Oh! She's full of shit too, with her swanky English accent!" I heard someone slander me.

"She's not even an American! She needs to shut her mouth and get the hell out of the way!" came next.

The young soldier now with fire in his eyes had said little. But fearlessly he pushed himself in front of me and the girls. His gal crumbled to the ground and began to cry she was so frightened. As the mob threatened us more, finally and thankfully, the local D.C. police showed up. Several people watching the unfolding events called them. There were several cars and many police officers who showed up to break up the protest. They brandished batons and showed little mercy to the protesters, which only seemed to reinforce the group's notions about their country and authority in general. In the melee that followed, people were running and screaming, doing their best to escape arrest. The police brought more, for no better word, paddy wagons and started hauling people away. With no idea who we were, they snatched us up as well. The next thing we know, we are all sharing a large cell with numerous dirty-haired and somewhat atrociously dressed female protesters. The girls and I carved out our own spot in one of the corners of the cell. The cell itself was full to capacity, but for some reason, which we were quite happy about, the other young ladies there left us alone.

Carol chuckled at the irony of the situation, and that completely upset old Nancy entirely.

"Now, I know how it feels to be on the other side," Carol declared with a laugh.

"What's that supposed to mean?" Nancy questioned, with irritation in her voice.

"Only dear that I spent most of this last decade being a protester, and now I was in jail, again, for standing up against protesters. It's darn ironic, that's all," Carol clarified.

Nancy still did not see any humor in the situation.

Fortunately for us, our plight did not last that long. A police officer called us out from the cell and took us with him. He told us we were being released without any charges at all. The girls and I were of course grateful but didn't understand why.

"Did they come to the conclusion, officer, that we were only defending the soldier and not with the protesters?" Nancy asked him.

"In a way, yes," the officer answered. "I guess the young soldier was a nephew to a senator. He called the senator, and the senator called us. Now boom, bam, and you ladies are free to go."

"Well…thank you Jesus, and let's get out here," Carol said as we left to make it back to our hotel. Fortunately for us, our gift bags from shopping all day were given back to us on leaving the police station, therefore making not the entire day a large waste of time.

———◆———

I ORDERED A BOTTLE OF WHITE WINE FROM OUR HOTEL'S restaurant to be delivered to our room. When it arrived, we wasted no time enjoying it thoroughly. As the girls and I collapsed in our two-bedroom suite and attempted to let a little alcohol take the edge off of what had turned into a quite distressing day, a knock on our front door disturbed our plans.

"What else did you order up, darling?" Nancy turned to me and asked.

I shrugged, "Nothing."

"Did you order dinner to be delivered by room service?" Carol wondered.

I shrugged again. I was considering doing that, that is ordering dinner for the three of us, but I hadn't got that far yet and would have certainly asked the girls for their preference for meals. A second knock, and this time I answered it. A man in a blue suit with a matching tie of the same color was waiting for me on the other side of the door.

"Are you the British lady?" he asked me immediately.

I told him I was from England and then asked as politely as possible who he was.

"I should probably introduce myself," he answered. "I am Senator Bainbridge from the state of Colorado. The police department was kind enough to tell me which hotel you were staying at. I got your room number from the front desk. I hope you don't mind."

Senator, I thought, this must have been the man who bailed us out of jail. When I asked him about that directly, he admitted he was the one who helped us.

Carol and Nancy overhearing his confession, came over to thank the senator for what he did.

"You're welcome, ladies, I'm sure. But I'm here to thank you for what you did, especially you, ma'am," the senator responded.

"What do you mean?" I asked.

"I'm talking about how you came to the aid of my young nephew and his fiancé. He told me all about it, Miss."

"Yes... I see, your nephew was the soldier that was being picked on by the protesters," I assumed.

"Precisely, Miss. That was a very brave thing that you and the other ladies here did. Are you living here in the states, Miss, or just visiting our fair country?" he then asked me.

I happily told him that I was married to an American soldier fighting in Vietnam and was currently living in Alabama, not far from my husband's base. The senator shared with us that he was once in the Army himself. "When I was a younger man, more than a few years back."

It couldn't have been too long ago, I thought, since the senator was still a relatively young man, probably about my age, or even possibly a spot younger than me.

"It was right after high school, and I only served for four years. I got out before the Vietnam War, started," he explained.

THE ROSEY VIEW OF THE WORLD

At that moment, it dawned on me that the senator was still standing in our entryway. I was quite embarrassed that we hadn't yet invited him in. "Please come in, sir. I'm so sorry for having forgotten my manners."

I offered him some of our wine, but he said no thank you. He was quick to make sure that the three of us were all right after the events of earlier in the day. The girls and I all assured him that we were quite fine and in good spirits.

"I'm glad to hear that," he told us as he smiled broadly. "You certainly helped protect one of my family members, and for that, I am very grateful. In my family, ladies, we never forget when someone does something like you three did today."

"I owe you ladies a favor, and as I said, in my family, we never forget to repay those who have helped us out in the past."

"Can you bring my husband home from Vietnam? Would that be asking too much then?" I popped off out of nowhere.

He laughed in response to my request.

I told him that I was serious because I was.

"How long has he been over there?" the senator inquired.

"Too long," I remarked.

His warm smile left his face all of a sudden, as he seemed to consider my request a bit more seriously. Next, out of nowhere, he did the one thing I wasn't expecting, he gave me hope. "I'll make some phone calls, see what I can do."

I didn't know what to say. Although nothing had changed, Albert was still in Vietnam. But, for at least a second, I had hope for something better. The girls came over to me and embraced me from each side. They knew what this meant too.

"I can't promise you anything, Miss...what is your name, anyway?" he asked, realizing he didn't actually know it.

"Rosey, Rosey Adams, Senator. My husband is Albert Adams, and he is a helicopter pilot over there."

The senator seemed to take a minute to digest the new information. "As I said, Rosey, I'll make some phone calls and see what I can do."

I thanked him for that. I thanked him for the smallest bit of hope he had just given me.

The next day we all returned to Alabama. I had the senator's business card with his contact information, and he had my home phone number. I would now just have to wait and see if my chance meeting with the senator made any difference at all. I had hope still that it did, but I also had doubts, doubts born in the realities of the world that people rarely keep their promises to strangers.

IT WAS ONLY A FEW WEEKS LATER, TO MY SURPRISE, THAT I received a phone call from Albert. He was ecstatic I could hear it in his voice. "I'm being reassigned, Rosey, back to the States."

I couldn't believe his words. I listened in stunned silence.

"My commanding officer just told me. I'll be heading back to Alabama in a few days!"

I was utterly speechless as he shared his wonderful news.

"Are you there, honey, did you hear me?"

"I am and I did, sweetheart. I'm so thrilled," I somehow managed to say.

"Great! My commander said someone pulled some strings for me in the Pentagon. He didn't know who or why, but it's getting me out of here a lot sooner than I was supposed to get out of here. I can't figure it out, but I'm so thrilled to be coming home," Albert shared enthusiastically.

I said again, in a weepy voice, how happy the news had made me. He told me he would see me at the base in about three or four days. After hanging up the phone I grabbed the nearest box of tissues I could find. I then looked for and found Senator Bainbridge's card. I sat down with my flowered stationery and in my best handwriting, I wrote him the most sincere thank you letter I could come up with. I wasn't completely sure if he truly was responsible for this wonderful news about Albert, but I certainly thought he was. I also committed to myself that Senator Bainbridge would be receiving a lovely Christmas card from me every year going forward. The Christmas card was one promise on that day that I was determined to keep. I would, every single year after that.

CHAPTER 17

Danny grins from ear to ear as he saves the last few words he wrote on his laptop. He hops up from his desk chair and races out of the bedroom. "I think I've got an idea!"

His sister, Lori, comes stumbling out of her bedroom reacting to all the racket her brother is making. "What is up? It's six o'clock in the morning and because of Mom's funeral and everything, I don't have to go to work. You know this," she says, as she comes down the hallway desperately wiping the sleep from her eyes.

Danny apologizes for disturbing her. He thinks he might have a way of getting Mom into the veteran's cemetery after all. Lori still struggling to become coherent, wants to know what he's talking about. He doesn't answer. He opens up the laptop he carried with him from his room and begins an internet search. Lori has no idea what he's up to.

"There he is!" he shouts. "Now, is he still alive and kicking, that is the question?"

"Who?" Lori asks. "Who are you talking about? You know, Danny, that I have to iron out exactly where mom is going to be buried, and I have to figure it out right away. The funeral home insists on knowing immediately. I need more sleep."

"I got it!" Danny says with excitement, completely ignoring his sister's words.

"You've got what?" Lori inquires.

Danny again ignores her. "Just don't do anything about Mom's burial until I get back."

"Where are you going this early in the morning?" Lori wonders, as her brother darts back to his room to get dressed and to leave for somewhere.

She asks him the same question a second time as he flashes by her in a hurry and heads out of the house.

After Danny leaves, Lori crawls back under her covers and drifts back to sleep. Danny races to his destination in Lori's Beetle. He hopes his sister doesn't need her car today. His trip is going to be an important one, and a very long one, and time is not on his side.

———————◆———————

WHEN DANNY ARRIVES, HE'S GREETED BY A HUGE STONE fence and a rock-solid metal security gate. He's been driving for over six hours to get here and has no intention to be stopped by any obstacle now. Danny spots an intercom button on the gate and pushes it. A few moments later a voice comes from the other side, a woman's voice. "Yes, may I help you?"

Danny is tongue-tied for a moment, as he attempts to come up with his explanation for being there.

"Can I help you with something?"

He eventually comes up with a response to the question. "I was hoping to speak with Senator Bainbridge."

"I take it you don't have an appointment with the senator," the woman asks.

Danny admits he doesn't as he scrambles for the best reason he can come up with for being at the senator's home. He goes with the only thing that he can think of and hopes

Andrew Scott Bassett

that the senator still has a good memory. "My mother is Rosey Adams, at least that's probably the name he would remember her by. I need to talk to the senator about something in regards to her, if I may."

There is no response from the lady on the other side of the speaker for what feels like an eternity, just dead silence. Danny wonders if she has walked away and is hoping he will do the same thing.

"The name again?" the woman's voice breaks through and asks.

"Rosey Adams, that's the name the senator would most likely remember," Danny restates.

A couple more minutes of silence, and then the lady comes back on with instructions. "When entering the compound, please park your vehicle to the left of the big garage and wait for security to come out to meet you."

Danny says sure. What else can he say? After parking, as instructed, two big fellas in suits come out to escort him. They ask him in a serious tone that is a little unnerving if he has any weapons on his person. Danny assures them that he doesn't. They frisk him anyhow to make sure. "Alright then, follow after us please," one of the men instructs.

Danny doesn't hesitate, as he follows right behind the two well-proportioned security guards. They lead him into an office at the back of the mansion. The huge office has its own beautiful brick fireplace, not something you see every day. Sitting behind the desk is an elderly man, with only a wisp of silver hair left on his head and, large, black-rimmed glasses adorning his face. He smiles as he motions for Danny to take a seat in front of his large oak desk.

"What's this about Rosey Adams?" the old man begins with.

"Rosey was my mother," Danny starts to explain.

The senator can't help but hear the word "'was'" in Danny's sentence.

"I'm afraid she passed away a few days ago," Danny shares with him.

The senator's fixed smile disappears at the news. "I am very, very sorry to hear that."

Danny could tell by the glint in the senator's eyes at the news that he still remembered his mother.

"She was a wonderful woman. We go way back," he shares with Danny. "I only met her twice in person, but always looked forward to her Christmas card each year and the lovely long note that accompanied it."

Danny finds the opening he was looking for and shares how he had read about what happened in Washington D.C. with the senator's nephew all those years ago. The senator wonders how he read about it.

"My mother left me a biography of sorts to read after she passed."

The senator nods. Now he understands. A grim expression suddenly overtakes the old man's face. "My nephew, the one your mom defended that day, sadly he died about a year later in a combat mission in Vietnam."

Danny is quick to tell the senator how sorry he is to hear that.

"The fortunes of war, I'm afraid," the senator replies. "But I am quite certain you didn't come all this way to listen to me wane on about the past. What can I do for you?"

Danny takes the opportunity to explain his reason for making the trip to meet with the senator. Senator Bainbridge is instantly receptive to Danny's special request. "I would be glad to make some calls on Rosey's behalf. It wouldn't be the first time I've done that for her. For what your mom did that day back in Washington D.C. for my nephew, and for the kindness she always showed me in those notes and cards she sent every year, Son, I would be glad to do my best to make sure your mother is properly buried. I've got a few prominent retired generals who still have a lot of pull that I can contact. I'll get on it right away."

Danny reaches out his hand toward the senator to shake his. He is thrilled and relieved that his long drive here was not in vain.

———————•————————

THE NEXT MORNING, DANNY SLEEPS IN LATE. HE IS STILL worn out from all the driving he did the day before. When he finally forces himself out of bed, he finds his sister Lori sitting at her kitchen table with Julia sitting beside her. Julia is holding her hand and trying to comfort her. It doesn't take long for Danny to see that his sister has been crying. "What's going on?" he asks them both with concern.

Struggling to gain her composure, Lori tells him about the phone call she received about an hour ago from the funeral parlor. "They told me I have to come to pick up Mom and take her to another place," Lori says between sniffles.

Julia rubs her shoulder in a sweet way. She whispers to her that everything is going to be okay and that she will help her find a new place for their mother's funeral. Danny is touched by the kindness Julia is showing to his sister. But right now, he's not sure if he should make a phone call to Senator Bainbridge or not. He was confident this would all be taken care of, the issues with the military cemetery and all, but now he's not so sure. It's only been a day, so maybe they just need more time for the senator to make his calls.

"How long till we have to make other arrangements?" Danny questions.

"Apparently, they're not happy with you guys not having a burial place all set up, so they want your mother's body picked up today," Julia chimes in.

Between sobs, Lori says that they will just have to bury Mom in the closest public cemetery they can find, against her wishes.

Julia butts in again to ask Danny about where he went yesterday for so many hours. "Lori tells me that you were going to try and fix this with the military cemetery so that your mother could be buried there. What happened?"

Danny shakes his head in response. He thought he had fixed it. Now it isn't looking so good.

Lori abruptly scrambles to her feet and moans about having to get ready to go out and find another facility for their mother's funeral and another place to bury her. She slams her bedroom door behind her as she goes to get dressed and cleaned up.

"I guess whatever you were doing yesterday, didn't work, huh?" Julia snidely chides Danny.

Lori's cell phone with the old-fashion telephone tone goes off while sitting on the kitchen table. It breaks through the gloomy atmosphere in the room that you can cut with a machete.

Danny snaps up the phone, even as Julia scolds him for taking a call that is meant for his sister. The funeral parlor is calling, so says Lori's cell phone. After the funeral parlor asks to speak to Lori, Danny lets them know that she is indisposed at the moment but that he is her brother. The man from the funeral parlor informs Danny why he is calling.

"You mean we can keep the funeral there?" Danny responds to the man's words.

"Yes," the man answers. "We just got a call from one of the main directors from the veteran's cemetery where you wanted to have your mother buried, and well, she's now been accepted there for full burial services."

"Yes!" Danny can't help but yell out with delight.

Julia can tell it's good news and demands to know what he was just told.

Danny motions with his hand for her to wait for a second until he's finished with the call, as the man from the funeral facility is still disclosing things to him. When he finally ends the conversation, a huge sense of relief takes over Danny.

"They changed their mind about your mom?" Julia guesses.

"In a manner of speaking, yes," Danny replies.

"That's fantastic Danny, but why the about-face?" Julia wonders.

"The veteran's cemetery changed their minds and contacted the funeral parlor. They're letting Mom in after all," Danny tells her, matter-of-factly.

Julia doesn't buy such a simplistic answer. "More like, someone changed their minds for them. Why do I have this feeling this has to do with you disappearing yesterday?"

Danny shrugs. He doesn't need credit for anything. Knowing that his mother's wishes in her final years are going to be fulfilled, is good enough for him.

"You better tell your sister. She's going to be beside herself, at the news Danny."

"Yeah…" he mumbles.

Danny, with Julia right behind him, knocks on Lori's bedroom door. When she opens it, she wonders why the happy faces. "What? What is it?"

When they share the good news, she shrieks with delight. She wants the who's, how's, and why's of the situation, but Danny plays dumb. "Whatever the reason, all that matters, Sis, is Mom's going to get buried alongside all those soldiers and military personnel, as she wanted."

"You made this happen somehow?" Lori gushes at her brother.

He just chuckles. Julia chips in that she thinks the same thing. Then Lori squeezes the stuffing out of her brother. "Thank you, Danny, for this. Mom would have been very proud of you for fighting for her."

Danny grins. Yeah, I guess I did fight for her, he whispers to himself.

———————◆———————

THE FIRST FEW MONTHS THAT ALBERT WAS HOME WERE pure bliss. He didn't touch even a sip of alcohol or disappear from me for a second. It was like the old days when we were first married. Both of us of course would have to adjust to life together, after so much time living apart. For me, the most frustrating aspect was that I still couldn't get Albert to talk to me about what had happened during the war. He still attempted to openly share some things about his experience in Vietnam, and God knows he was sweet to me and all that muck. I guess he was just so thankful to have made it out of the bloody war alive.

After Albert came home, I found myself a new job. I was back working in insurance, but this time for a wonderful, older gentleman. It was a small office near our flat in town.

I was hired as a secretary. My new boss, Mr. Harold Roberts, was a kind and gentle soul. He was retired Navy and loved to hear about my childhood in England, and especially my stories about World War II. Occasionally, Albert would make it to the office and Mr. Roberts would take the opportunity to ask him about all sorts of things relating to Vietnam. For some reason I couldn't understand, Albert seemed more comfortable opening up to Mr. Roberts than he did to me. Still, I was happy to see Albert talking about such matters, regardless of who it was he spoke to. Yes, things were looking better for the first time in a long time. Now, with a new decade only just beginning, a new job, and what felt like a new marriage, things were finally coming together, except for that one nagging desire of mine.

———— ◆ · ————

I CAN REMEMBER THAT SUNDAY MORNING LIKE IT WAS yesterday. We were all wrapped up in our bedspread, naked to the bone. I had stopped attending church services on Sundays and had instead begun to go on Wednesday nights only. Albert loved to sleep in on Sundays and usually fool around a tiny bit. Not to mention I had a much better chance of getting him to go with me to a service on a Wednesday night than on a Sunday morning. He had already gone several times with me to the mid-week service, which thrilled me indeed. This particular morning, we had spent most of the time in bed enjoying each other and our new found happiness. When I was able to finally wrestle myself out of his grasp and that of the bed covers, Albert pleaded for me to get back into bed. He slapped my poor defenseless bare bum as I attempted my get-away. "Ahh! It doesn't get much better than this, Rosey, now does it?"

I interrupted my getting dressed just long enough to look back at him. He was stretched out on our bed, on top of the covers, naked as a jailbird. He had the biggest smile on his face as he stared at the ceiling.

"Well, you do look quite content, I must say," I tossed back to him.

"And why not," he replied happily. "I'm still alive, back in the good old U.S. of A., and married to the most beautiful woman in the world."

This time I didn't respond, just kept getting dressed. He picked up from my silence that maybe I wasn't feeling exactly the same way. "Aren't you happy, you sure were a few minutes ago," he said with a chuckle.

I was of course, and told him that, but...

"There's something you're not saying, I know you too well," Albert suddenly challenged.

He was right, you know, but I didn't want to bring it up at this moment. So, I lied and said everything was perfect, though it certainly wasn't. Albert, however, was content with my ploy of deception and moved on to other subjects. Whatever he conversed after that, I really didn't listen to. I could only hear my own thoughts, the ones I wouldn't share with him.

THE NEXT DAY AT LUNCHTIME, I MET UP WITH CAROL for a bite at our favorite sandwich shop. She was going on about how only a few years earlier she wouldn't have been allowed to sit in here at this table, and certainly not with a white woman like myself. I was so preoccupied with my own thoughts that I heard only about half of what she said. Carol finally took notice and asked me what was wrong. I wasn't sure at that moment if I wanted to discuss it, but she pushed me to spill the beans. She always had a knack for getting me to open up to her.

"I feel like I'm living a lie," I began with.

That got Carol's attention immediately. "How so?"

"It's the motherhood thing you know," I let out.

Carol understood. She was a bit younger than me, but she too felt her biological clock spinning faster and faster. And like me, she hadn't been much interested in becoming a mother in her younger years, but with the possibility of such an endeavor beginning to slip away like sand slipping down an hourglass, it was a burden she carried, just as I did.

"Rosey, you have to be honest with Albert," Carol said pointedly.

I couldn't, I told her. I knew how he felt about adoption, and I was so afraid I was going to damage the relationship between us, right when things were going so well.

"But you're not happy, Rosey. You can't just pretend for Albert's benefit because eventually, your unhappiness is going to affect him too."

She was right. I couldn't just pretend away this huge void in my heart forever. I wondered if I would begin to resent him as Carol believed for not allowing me to be honest with my feelings.

"What about Maximillian?" Carol then dropped into the conversation without warning.

"What do you mean?" I questioned.

"You know, the letters, is he still sending letters to you from all over the world?" Carol was curious.

Right then and there, I wished I hadn't shared with Carol how much Max and I were corresponding through the mail since seeing each other in Washington D.C. It's just that she was my closest friend and unlike my other girlfriend, Nancy, Carol would keep matters to herself if told to do so. Now, however, I must say that it seemed as if Carol was using that trust against me.

"You know if I recall from what you shared with me, Maximillian has no kids because his deceased wife was barren, isn't that right?"

"Yes…and what does that have to do with the price of tea in China?" I answered in an irritated way.

Carol laughed as she suggested that maybe if things didn't get better with Albert, there was a second option. I was aghast at her line of thinking, humorous or not, and told her as much.

"Look, I'm kidding, mostly," she responded, still giggling too much for my liking.

"I stopped sending and receiving letters from Max," I then confessed, out of the blue.

Carol was surprised by my disclosure. She asked me why I did that.

"I started to feel guilty about the letters, like I was cheating on Albert or something. Why? Do you think I'm being silly?" I asked Carol.

"No. Only you can work all that out, honey," Carol told me as she held my hand in hers. "I only know that you have to be true to yourself and to your own heart. If you're not, Rosey, you'll never really be happy, and ultimately, those feelings will rear their ugly head in your marriage too."

I knew she was right, and I knew how trapped I felt between what I wanted in life and what I had. If only I could be satisfied with things the way they were right now, forever. Unfortunately, I knew I probably would never be able to do that.

Carol shared one last thing with me that ripped out my heart. She told me that she was considering moving to Arizona. I was beyond stunned by her revelation. It was for a career-type job. She would be working with a civil rights non-profit organization that had national outreach. As much as it was terrifying for her to consider leaving the only home she'd ever had, Carol thought it might be time to make changes in her life. "It's an unbelievable opportunity, Rosey. I don't know if I can pass it up. What's really hard, though, is how much I would miss all my family and friends. And how much I would really miss you too."

Now, it was my turn to hold her hand. "We'll always be like sisters the two of us," I confessed. "Wherever you go, we will always share our lives, our loves, maybe not in person, but we'll always share our lives, sweety."

Carol reacted to my words by flashing that brilliant smile of hers. A tough nut indeed, but I still noticed a tear roll down her cheek at my proclamation to her. She would go on to accept the new job and only three weeks later she would leave for Arizona. Part of me went with her when she left, the best part of me.

———◆·—

FOR THE NEXT SEVERAL MONTHS, I TRIED MY HARDEST to put my thoughts of being a mother behind me. Albert was busy working on base, training helicopter pilots. I was still working at the insurance office, which Albert wasn't wild about, and then coming home to our little flat and doing my best to be the happy homemaker. This routine went on for several months until one evening when I was tired and in the female way, I let my guard down for a moment. Albert was intently watching American football on the telly, his favorite thing to do these days. I don't exactly know why, but I got a bee in my bonnet and decided to be honest with him. "Could we discuss something, love?"

"Right now?" he answered, not at all happy with my timing.

"If we, could darling, it's important to me," I stated.

He sighed, clearly not wanting to take his eyes off his game. I knew I was tap-dancing on quicksand and would have to be very careful.

"What's so important, huh?" he asked me, with his eyes still glued to the telly.

I started slowly explaining myself. I was having a difficult time finding my footing in the conversation. But, before I even got to the real heart of the matter, Albert figured out where I was going with all this. He attempted to shut me down before I could go any further. "We've been through this before, Rosey. I know, I know. You're over forty years old now and you wish you had kids. I get it. I really do. I wish we did too."

"Well, if you feel that way, then why can't we adopt. I know you'd be a wonderful father, Albert," I argued in as nice a way as possible.

My kind words sadly had no effect.

"Damn! Rosey! You know I am not interested in adopting kids! I wanted my own children, my own flesh and blood, not someone else's. It wasn't meant to be! Why is that so hard for you to understand?! Not to mention you are not the only one getting older around here. I'm over forty now too. I don't want to be a father now. I want to relax and enjoy life. I have earned that after going through the hell I went through overseas!"

I let him rant on for several more minutes until the steam came out of his engine. Then as calmly and as nice as a feisty Brit lady could be expected to act, I let him know my equally important unhappiness. I explained in vivid detail the emptiness in my soul. I shared the sadness I felt about the idea of never having children in my life, to never be called a mother. When I was finally done, my words were met by nothing but cold, unmoving silence. Albert only sighed again and shrugged his shoulders in response. After a few minutes of realizing how silence could be even more hurtful than angry words, Albert grabbed his car keys and left. Where he went, I had no idea. I just sat down on our sofa and contemplated many difficult things. My best friend, Carol, who I leaned on so often, was now in Arizona. My old pap and his wise words were back in England. Finally, my only other real friend, Nancy, who was still around, was just not one to chat with about these sorts of things, you know feelings and the like. I realized then that I would have to face all this by myself. My stiff upper lip was about to be tested.

———— • • ————

AFTER OUR CONVERSATION ABOUT ADOPTING CHILDREN, our marriage went from good to worse, too miserable. We were now like an old married couple. We were living together, but in truth, we were far apart. Albert began his drinking again. At first, it would only be a beer after work to settle his nerves after a long day. Next, it would be several, actually too many, and if I said a single word about the whole business, he would walk out on me in an angry march back to a nightclub on base or some pub here in town. He was finding more and more reasons all the time for scampering out of our flat and heading to the nearest 'watering hole'. All this trouble came to a head one night when Albert shared with me an idea he had. "I'm about ready to get my twenty years in and retire."

I looked at him with a quizzical expression. I had no idea where he was going with all this.

"I'm thinking it's time to start considering our future. You know, Rosey, where we want to live, what kind of bigger house we want to get."

I didn't know how to answer him. As bad as things had gotten between us, I really had no interest at the time to discuss our future. I presently was too concerned with our now. My real blunder, however, was when I told him that. Albert with a can of beer in his hand as usual lately, slung it across the room as hard as he could. He cursed and yelled and stomped his way out of the house. And this time it was different. I felt bad, bad I guess for being so bloody honest with him, at probably the wrong time. Before I could apologize, I heard his car start and then slowly drive away. I ran outside following after him. Quickly as I could, I jumped into my car to pursue him, to tell him I was dreadfully sorry. I thought he would be heading back to the base club for more drinks with his Army mates, but he turned and went a different way. I stayed in pursuit as he was driving away from both the base and the city, and I had no idea where he might be going. There were no pubs out here on the outskirts of town that I was aware of, but maybe I was mistaken. I made sure to stay back, and it was clear he had not spotted my car. Then, after almost twenty minutes of driving, he abruptly pulled into the driveway of a small cottage-style home. I pulled off to the side of the road and parked. I was down the road a bit but still could see the front door of the home as Albert approached it. Nothing in life before had prepared me for what happened next. As I sat there like a lump on a log, I watched a young, pretty woman, open her front door to greet my husband. She greeted him with hugs and kisses and then invited him in. I just sat in my car in shocked dismay. I had heard all my life of these sorts of things happening to other people, but certainly, I thought it would never happen to me. I had married a good one after all. Now, the words of my dear friend Carol, who I already missed so much, were playing like a recording in my head. She said no man could be trusted when it came to sex. All men were wolves in sheep's clothing when it came to such matters. I never believed that, and with all my resolve I still refused to believe that. But sitting quietly in my car, down the street from a house where the love of my life, my husband, was doing God knows what to God knows who, suddenly, Carol's words sounded more plausible than ever. An hour passed as I still just sat there, debating to myself my two choices. I could catch him in the act and humiliate him and his, whatever. Or secondly, I could quietly go back home and pack my things and prepare for a new life as a divorced woman. The first choice would have been very satisfying, but I chose the second. I was emotionally wrecked and not looking to create a scene or another row. Without uttering a word, I started up my car and I drove back home to pack.

———————•—•———————

I waited for a long time that night, but Albert didn't come home. So I wrote a letter and pasted it to our refrigerator door where I knew he would see it. To get his beloved booze to drink, he would have to gaze upon my words. The rest of the night I spent at my girlfriend Nancy's home. She was kind enough to let me sleep on her sofa and store some of my things in her tiny little garage. I shared what happened, but we didn't talk much. Nancy made me a cocktail and cuddled up with me on that sofa of hers. She told me I was welcome to stay with her as long as I needed to. I was so thankful to her for her kindness. We then turned on some late-night movies and fell asleep sometime before they ended. Somehow that night I got a few winks in me, how I'll never know.

———◆———

THE NEXT MORNING, I GOT READY FOR WORK LIKE NOTHing had happened. I still hadn't spoken to Albert. At this point, I really didn't want to see him. The shock to my system and everything I believed was still too new. The fact he hadn't made more of an effort to find out where I was, just added to my pain.

I felt obligated to let my kind boss, Mr. Roberts, know what had happened. I would need to take some time off and possibly get away. Where I would go, I had no idea, but anywhere else sounded quite lovely right now. Mr. Roberts asked me directly where I thought might go to regroup. Being put on the spot, only two places really came to mind. I could go back home to England and see my family, or I go to Arizona and visit Carol and see how she was doing with her new job and life. I wasn't sure about much of anything at this point, I shared with my boss. As I expected, he was completely sweet and willing to give me the time off I needed. I thanked him profusely for his understanding. Suddenly, before either of us could say another word, he cleared his throat in a strange way. It was the way someone does when they are trying to tell you something. And that is exactly what Mr. Roberts was trying to do. He had just spotted Albert getting out of his car right in front of the building. I turned to face Albert as he walked into our office. He wore an uncomfortable expression on his face as he walked up to me. Mr. Roberts pretended to be busy in his back office, though I'm sure he was listening to every word.

"I'm sorry about last night," Albert started with. "Where did you go?"

I couldn't help but look at him with disgust. He didn't know that I knew, and he still had the nerve to stand here, lying to my face.

"I think the better question might be, where did you go last night?" I said with venom coming from my tongue.

Albert went pale when he heard my question. He now realized that I knew. "You know where I went don't you?" He said in a whisper, clearly afraid of my next words.

I nodded.

For the second time in the last twenty-four hours, I was shocked by Albert's behavior. He didn't try to lie to me or cover up anything. He knew the jig was up.

"I never thought I'd be that guy."

"What are you talking about?" I wanted to know.

"You know, the kind of guy who cheats on his wife," he answered slowly and without emotion.

"So why did you do it then?" I wanted so desperately to know.

Albert had no real answer for me. He shook his head, and his eyes began to suddenly well up. "Now what? I suppose a divorce, something I said I would never do."

I asked him if that's what he wanted. I was stunned for a third time when he said he did. I guess I expected he would fight for me, fight for us, but I was terribly wrong.

"I think I'm in love with this other woman. I'm so sorry, Rosey," Albert said to me, so without emotion that it all seemed surreal.

How could my husband for all these years be so comfortable breaking the news to me that he was in love with another woman?

"Are you sure she's in love with you when she finds out that you are committing bleeding adultery on your wife?"

Albert couldn't or wouldn't answer. I could hear poor Mr. Roberts in his office pretending to be making a phone call, so we wouldn't think he could hear us.

"I did not mean for things to turn out like this. You've got to believe me," Albert pleaded for some strange reason.

"No man ever does," I remarked back snidely.

I told Albert that I would expect the divorce papers to be signed as soon as he got them. He could have the flat we lived in if he so desired. I no longer wished for anything in my life that reminded me of him, as harsh as that sounds. We ended our 'conversation' like a business meeting. We would split up and go our separate ways and treat each other with as much respect as we could. Except there was one last thing, well actually, several last things I had to share with Albert. "I just want you to know that I could have done the same thing that you did to me, many times."

Albert's eyebrows raised at the consideration of my pronouncement. He suddenly seemed almost jealous, as if he had any right at all.

"The point is, husband of mine, I never cheated on you, even though you and the Army left me all alone for all those years. I spent more than half of our marriage being more married to an idea than a man. I think you should say to me, thank you for your service. Isn't that what some people say to you who respect what you went through in Vietnam? Well, I went through a lot here at home, and I think I deserve the same consideration."

Albert gazed at me after I said all that. He looked like he didn't know what to quite make of my request. But finally, he shrugged and said, "You're right. Thank you, Rosey, for always being there for me."

He offered me one last smile of appreciation, and then he left. It seemed impossible to believe at the time, but I would never see him again. We both kept our word, and the divorce went as smoothly as those things can. I now had to prepare for a new and different future, a future I never

dreamed would come to pass. With no husband, no children, and my dearest friend living half a country away from me, I felt alone again, even more than when Albert was in Vietnam for all those years.

CHAPTER 18

I was dumbfounded at how little had changed at my old family home, back in Northampton. I decided a trip home would be the best medicine for what ails me. While sitting in my pap and mum's living room, and feasting on her homemade pastries and British tea, I knew I had made the right choice. There were some changes, however, that were apparent. Pap's hair was greyer and there was much less of it. Mum's figure was fuller, and her face had lines on it I had never seen before. But the biggest change of all was the sounds of silly children running around the place and being perfectly adorable. In my absence of almost ten years, my sister, Sheila, and her husband Trevor had gotten busy. They now had two little munchkins to care for. A son named David had been born six years ago and then a daughter, Tracey, a few years after that. Sheila announced on my first day back that another one would be added to the brood. She was pregnant again and carrying another girl. This one they would name Michelle. "Like the Beatles' French song?" I remarked at the news.

"Exactly! Yes," Sheila gleefully agreed.

By this time, David and Tracey had discovered that I was a new person in the room and their aunt to boot. The two of them begged me to play with them so what could I do? I chased and roughhoused them until my forty-something joints ached. I have to admit, hearing myself called auntie for the first time in person was a special moment indeed. Trevor eventually showed me mercy and took over playing with the children. He chased them outside to the backyard leaving Pap, Mum, and Sheila, alone with me to enjoy the delicious banquet before us.

"These tarts with the lemon curd, are to die for Mum," I exclaimed between bites.

"Do you miss the good old teatime, dearie?" Mum replied to my excitement.

Trying to answer with my mouth full and with moans of pleasure coming from my taste buds, I somehow uttered, "Uh-huh."

Sheila giggled at the sight of my engorged cheeks. "You act like you're starving or something, like you haven't eaten in years, Rosey."

"Sorry," I struggled to answer while swallowing at the same time. "I forgot how amazing English pastries can be."

"Oh yes, love, I bet you have then." Pappy chimed in.

This being my first day back home in England, I was bracing for the eventual conversation that I dreaded. I hadn't told my pap and mum, or Sheila for that matter, about my divorce from Albert. I didn't want them to worry as I knew they would. That was another reason for coming home so quickly after the divorce became final. I didn't want to see another letter or card from them asking how Albert was doing. Worse yet, have a phone conversation where I had to pretend that Albert and I were still together. I knew it was now time to break the news and be done with it. "There's something I have to tell you all."

I got all their attention with that.

"I'm afraid…well…"

"What is it, love?" Mum was the first to interrupt me.

Pappy then followed. "Yes, ducky, just spit it out then, you're with family now."

Sheila said nothing but looked very intrigued by what was going to come next.

I took a deep breath and as my pap said, then, I spit it all out.

The room got very quiet, very quickly. My mum put her hand over her mouth. She was the most surprised by the news.

"Well bloody hell." Sheila let out.

Pappy told her to watch her language as he himself said nothing in response to the news.

"What did he do then?" Sheila asked me, with a tone of voice that seemed to be too joyful for the occasion.

Mum chastised her for asking such a question at a time like this. But Pappy agreed. He wanted to know as well.

Looking down at my feet, almost too ashamed to make eye contact with anyone, I stuttered out the difficult words. "He was unfaithful."

"Well bloody hell!" my pap let slip out.

This time Sheila got to warn Pap about his language, and his hypocrisy.

"You both need to button it up then, climb out of the sewer as my dear old mum used to say," Mum was quick to warn them both.

It got quiet again as no one knew what to say next. Even Sheila, never one to be afraid to say what was on her mind, kept her thoughts to herself so as not to upset me more. They all could sense by looking at me that my wounds were still raw and needed to heal. I prayed that the next three weeks back home in jolly old Northampton would help the healing.

Andrew Scott Bassett

As what always seemed to be the case, I found myself asking Mum where Pappy was. Now that he was retired, I should have already known the answer: He was out on his land. He lived for his bit of "'heaven on earth,'" as he called it.

I walked over to the property and found him working on his knees as usual. "Hello, ducky, what brings you over here?" he greeted me.

I asked him what he was working on today.

"Oh, duck, just planting new seeds," he responded.

"Ahh…need any help then?" I offered.

He shook his head no. "This is actually the last one right here that I'm planting for now."

"Cucumbers I see?" I guessed, remembering that this was usually the part of the garden where he grew them.

"You are a sharp one, aren't ya'?" Pappy replied with a laugh.

"You've had this land since I was born," I remarked, as I thought about how it had always been here, at least as long as I could remember.

"Purchased it right before you were born with some pounds I won from betting on the fights.

Don't tell your mum that. She thinks I saved up the money from working extra hours at the shoe factory. She always despised gambling you know?"

I promised him his secret was safe with me.

"So then, now what? How long before you see some real growth from these seeds?" I inquired.

"All in the right bit of time, dear. Everything in life, duck, is set to a certain time. Everything ends, but then everything begins again if you let it," Pappy shared with me, trying to make a point.

"And of course, Pap, you're speaking about yours truly and my life."

Pap laughed as he was caught, and he knew it. "I keep forgetting you're old and wise now, and I'm only old."

"Ah…I think you're still pretty wise, even if you are getting older," I let him know.

He chuckled some more at my words. "Anyways, duck, what's next?"

I shook my head. I didn't have a single clue.

"It must be trying for your soul, waiting all those months and years for him only for this," Pappy remarked as he washed the dirt from his hands with his garden hose.

"Yes," I answered. I couldn't come up with anything better.

Pap finally stood up, dusted off his trousers, and seemed mostly satisfied with his seed planting.

"Well, you know, duck, we will pick these cucumbers in a wee bit of time, and they will be lovely for our supper and on sandwiches. And then we will have so many of them will get tired of them and not want to eat them anymore. And after a bit, we will miss them again and start all over just like I did today. I'll plant them. I'll water them, make sure the bugs don't get at them. And eventually, they'll grow back as good as ever to be enjoyed all over again."

I smirked after he was done with his little gardening story, comparing my life to cucumbers. "I'm not barmy, Pap. I understand what you're gettin' at."

"I honestly, love, don't know what you are you talking about? I was just telling you about cucumbers and how they grow," Pap offered slyly, in his defense.

Andrew Scott Bassett

"Nonetheless, I've never worried about you. You're a lucky one, always have been," he added.

My old pap had always told me that same thing since I could remember. Luck and fate were popular topics with him. He was quite the superstitious man. If he spilled salt, he would toss it over both shoulders. You could never cross your utensils on your plate. That was considered bad luck. He almost never went anywhere without a lucky rabbit's foot in his pocket. And if he saw a penny lying on the street, he would always pick it up. It was good luck all day long for the person who did. At this moment in my life, I didn't feel the least bit lucky about anything, but I loved that my father was, as always, in my corner. He was, and would always be, the one man I could count on.

A week later I said my cheerios to Pap, Mum, and Sheila at Heathrow. One by one, they told me to keep a stiff upper lip and not to worry. Things would all turn out for the best. I would eventually see, they promised. Mum begged me to stay in England to not go back to America.

She had been telling me that the entire time I was home. I really couldn't say why I was heading back to the states, actually. I could have easily just stayed in England. Something, however, inside of me told me I needed to go back. It felt like I had unfinished business there. What, I had no idea. I had already phoned Carol, and she would meet me at the airport in Phoenix, Arizona. She said her new husband could get me a job with American Express. The company's headquarters were in the Phoenix area. I missed Carol terribly and was tickled pink to have the chance to see a new part of America. It was time for me to plant new seeds, as my dear old pap would say. It was time to grow new roots somewhere. As I said my cheerios that day, my only wish looking back would be that my dear old pap would have lived long enough to see those new roots bloom into something good. He was the rock of my life, and sadly only a few months after I left, he was gone. From what Sheila told me, like always, he was walking to his property one morning and crossing the same street that he always did. As he crossed the road, Pap spotted a shiny penny just laying there in the middle. "This is good luck," I'm sure he muttered to himself.

He stopped and bent over to pick it up. And that's when my dear old pap didn't see the bus rolling his way. Neither, I suppose, did the bus driver see him standing in the middle of the road.

A COUPLE OF YEARS HAD PASSED SINCE MY DIVORCE became final. Now living and working in Phoenix, I was finally getting used to the idea of not having a man in my life. I found my own flat or apartment, as Yanks call it, not far from where Carol and her husband Len lived. The job at American Express was going swimmingly. Quite naturally, all the married women at work had been trying desperately to fix me up since I got here. It seems that each of them knows at least one eligible bachelor that would be "'perfect for me.'" I granted their requests and went out on several dates with some of these blokes, but none of them to that point had really done anything for me. In fact, I found more enjoyment in remembering the men from my past, my father who I still missed dearly, Max, who I recently started writing letters to again, and even Albert. I know, I know, why would I miss him after all that went on and after he so quickly tossed me aside. Well, life is strange that way.

It's very difficult to just turn off the feelings you have for someone completely. My old pap used to tell me that there is a fine line between love and hate. The greater the love, the stronger the hate will be for the same person if they hurt you badly. I never really put much stock in how that worked until Albert broke my heart. One minute I would hate him and what he did, but the next minute I would remember a lovely time together and it would bring a smile to my face. As for Max, I hadn't yet disclosed in our correspondence that I was now divorced from Albert. I'm not really quite sure, why? Maybe it was the fear that it wouldn't really matter to him, that he wouldn't come running here for me. Not of course, that he should do anything of the sort, but I couldn't deny that deep down I wish he would. No, I decided to keep my marital status my own business. Besides, Max probably had remarried by now and had numerous children, even though he never mentioned anything of the sort in his letters. This was all really rubbish to ponder and a waste of one's energy. I had greater things to concentrate on as the country's two-hundredth birthday was upon us.

Carol was about to have her first child, and I being her best friend, was put in charge of her baby shower. The whole experience was beginning to light those same old embers inside me for having a child of my own. I believed I could adopt kids, but I was old-fashioned. I believed I needed a husband to make it possible. Of course, if I adopted on my own, then maybe I could be a mother on my own terms, not a man's. After much contemplation, I decided that trying to adopt would be my best option. When I shared all this with Carol one day as we were preparing her home for the big 'baby party', she took me by surprise with her negative thinking. "I don't know, Rosey. It wouldn't be easy for you to adopt."

"I don't know why adopting a child if I decided to do so should be so bloody well difficult." I fired back, displaying a tad bit of fire and brimstone in my voice.

Carol was sympathetic to my wanting to be a mother as much anyone. She knew my history and all I had been through. She wanted it for me almost as much as I did, but she still said, "There's what we want, and there's the way the world works."

I had her that before, and as always, never cared for those words.

"It's just that most people think that the best situation for children who are adopted is with a regular family, you know one with a mom and dad," Carol continued.

I actually didn't disagree with the notion of a mother and father in the home being the best situation, but with so many children that we hear about needing to be adopted, there had to be room for loving, single-parent families as well. Carol wasn't so sure. She wondered if I was only setting myself up to get hurt some more from the real possibility of being turned down in any efforts to adopt I might entertain. She had already seen me hurt plenty, she confessed. She didn't want to see me suffer anymore.

Her sincerity moved me. I gave her a huge, sloppy hug, and even rubbed her large baby tummy. I even felt the little rascal kick me once or twice.

"This is something I have to try. For my own sanity, love. I have to give this my best shot. I hope you can understand and help me get through this, no matter the outcome," I told her in a soft voice, face to face.

Carol returned my embrace. She promised she would always be there for me. I thanked her for that. We then both laughed our heads off as we hugged. We could only get so close with that 'Buddha' belly of hers.

Carol's baby came a month early. The baby was fine, just a tad bit small. I basically lived at her home to help out until her family flew in from Alabama. At the same time, with Carol and the baby taken care of, I turned my attention once again to the idea of adoption. Holding tiny Lilly May in my arms made my desire for having a child of my own as great as it had ever been. I made appointments with several different adoption agencies. These were public ones since after exploring private agencies, I found I didn't have enough money to afford that avenue. My first appointment was the next day. I anticipated it the way a child looked forward to Christmas.

———— •—•—• ————

THE MAN BEHIND THE DESK, A MR. DILBERT, STUDIED my application and supporting documents like an IRS agent doing a tax audit. He rarely smiled at me, and when he did it was as if the whole experience of smiling was new to him, and he was still figuring it all out. He looked at me through his thick-brimmed glasses with a certain level of disdain, at least that's how it felt. He hummed and cleared his throat often as I just sat there and waited. What I was waiting for, I had no idea. When I asked him if he had any questions for me, he finally addressed me. "It all seems to be here, Ms. Adams."

"Lovely," I responded with optimism.

I was premature in my optimism as he took his glasses off for a second and wiped them, before putting them back on and sighing. "Not lovely, I'm afraid."

"I don't understand," I replied.

"Well, let me help you if I can, Ma'am. This adoption agency like most agencies that place children in homes, feels that it is best to find two-parent families for placement. There is a strong set of data that shows us it is very important for children to have both a father and a mother in the home."

I interrupted Mr. Dilbert's next sentence. I let him know that I understood such findings and ideally that it was probably the best scenario for children, that is to have a father and mother as parents, but in my experience not always. He questioned me on what I meant by my statement.

"All I mean is that, although I was blessed with a wonderful father, I've witnessed many that aren't. In fact, Mr. Dilbert, I've seen quite a lot of fathers who were more interested and spent more time with their telly than their children," I confessed.

"Be that as it may, Ms. Adams, overall it is considered to be for the best if we place children in two-parent families," he repeated.

By now, I was becoming less polite and more agitated. I could sense my dreams of motherhood were in danger, and I wasn't about to have them end without a bloody fight. I challenged his "'findings'" talk. "What about all these poor children I hear about with no homes, not enough families willing to adopt. Surely, Mr. Dilbert, it's better for even an unmarried woman like myself to adopt one of those children than to have no one adopt those children at all."

He considered my point for a moment before mentioning something that made no sense at all and was complete rubbish. "We, and I mean the government when I say that, still believe it's in the best circumstances to try and wait to place a child with a two-parent home."

"Best for whom, Mr. Dilbert? It's certainly not best for the children who are stuck in a foster home or bloody group

Andrew Scott Bassett

home or shelter. I don't understand why this should be so hard, Sir?" I commented.

Then he brought up my single status and flaunted it in my face. As you might guess by now, I wanted to just forget my manners and grab a pen from his penholder on his desk and shove it in his bleeding mouth. I was fed up with being talked down to in such a condescending way. "I did not choose to be single, Mr. Dilbert. My husband committed adultery if you must know. He left me with no choice but to divorce him."

"I am very sorry for that, but still…" he interrupted.

I demanded to know why I should be punished for my husband's indiscretions. Why my desire to have children of my own, to love and raise them, should be stopped for things that I had no control over? Mr. Dilbert wasn't done yet, however. Oh no, he seemed to have a list of things at his disposal to use to crush my hopes and dreams. "Also, Ms. Adams, I have to ask if you are a United States citizen."

"No, Sir, but since I was married to an American for many years, I have obtained legal status to be in this country," I declared forcefully.

He shook his head and then sighed again as he took another look-see over my application. It took all I had not to choke the life out of this cheeky little snot.

"Well…I am really so sorry, Ma'am, but being a single woman with no husband in the home, and not even a citizen of our fair country, not to mention your age, well… I'm afraid I won't be able to approve your adoption request."

After taking a moment to gather myself after being so thoroughly put down, it was my turn to shake my head with disgust. I was disgusted at the whole unfairness of the situation. "Mr. Dilbert, may I just say this one thing before I leave. This whole process of yours is prejudiced and lacking in intelligence. You should be looking closely at the person who is sitting in front of you. You should be examining the type of person they are, what kind of home they would provide for their adopted child. You should be investigating what type of character and morals they have. This is not how you should decide who may love and raise children, by how many parents are going to be in the home. I, as a single mother, Sir, may not be the best situation for all children to call home. But, Mr. Dilbert, I am if you would consider me fairly, at least a very good choice, certainly much better than a string of foster homes or orphanages. Good day, sir."

I grabbed my purse, raised my chin in defiance, and stormed out of his office. Mr. Dilbert spoke not a single word to stop me. When I got home, I cried over the telephone to Carol. I moped for several days after that. Then at Carol's insistence, I tried other adoption agencies in other counties in Arizona. I basically got the same treatment with them as I did with Mr. Dilbert. My dream of being a mother seemed to be an impossible hope.

A FEW MONTHS LATER AND WITH THE FOURTH OF JULY and the country's two-hundred-year birthday upon us, Carol came by to let me know that she and Len would be flying to Las Vegas, Nevada for a couple of days. It would be the first get-away for the two of them since the baby was born. Lilly May was only three months old and still breast-feeding, so I was a bit surprised by Carol's announcement. She, however, shared that she had pumped a large amount of breast milk into bottles and that they were refrigerated and ready to go. She assured me that little Lilly May was doing quite well already with being bottle-fed some of the time.

"I would be happy to take care of her while you're gone," I offered to Carol.

After the utter complete waste of time of trying to adopt as a single parent, taking care of Carol's baby was as close as I was going to get to having a little one of my own. Carol thanked me but surprisingly said no. Her no knocked the wind out of my sails. Suddenly I felt like I wasn't even good enough for being a babysitter for my dearest friend. With my feelings truly bruised, I looked away long enough that I didn't notice the large grin on her face.

"What's so funny, then?" I snapped at her when I finally took notice.

She started to howl with laughter.

"I don't understand why you are doing this to me?" I responded, holding back tears. Why was I, I thought to myself, not only not good enough for a child of my own but also not good enough to be a caregiver for my best friend?

"You're coming with us!" Carol interrupted my pity party with, still laughing as she said it.

"I'm what?" I answered, dumbfounded.

"Len and I are taking you with us to Las Vegas, Rosey! That's the reason for the trip!"

I still had no idea what she was on about. "Why would you be taking me to Las Vegas and who's going to take care of Lilly May?" I questioned.

She then took the time to sit down next to me and explained their whole scheme. They wanted to get me out of my moping state, you know the state I had been in since the final adoption failure. Carol and her husband Len decided a trip to Las Vegas on the Fourth of July during the big bicentennial celebration, would be just what the doctor ordered for me. "Len's mother is going to be staying here at the house while we're gone. She's going to take care of the baby for us."

I then unselfishly asked if it wouldn't be better if she and Len went alone, make it a romantic get-away sort of thing.

"We'll have our own room, Rosey. We'll have some time to ourselves. But both of us wanted to take you on this trip, more for your benefit than anything else. You've always been there for me. Rosey, it's time I was there for you."

I knew Carol well enough by now to see that she had made up her mind, and when she did, there was usually no changing it. I thanked her with all my might. I seemed to be doing a lot of that lately. A second ago I was upset and hurt, now I was flattered and humbled by her and Len's concern for me. I wondered how at that moment I could have ever doubted my best friend.

———— · ◆ · ————

LAS VEGAS REMINDED ME OF THE LARGEST CHRISTMAS tree in the world. Every part of the main drag or the "'strip,'" as Len, told me it was referred to, was lit up for the two-hundred-year birthday of America. I had never in all my years seen a place quite like this, even Hamburg, Germany all those years ago didn't measure up. After an evening dinner buffet directly on the 'strip', we hopped from casino to casino playing slot machines, cards, and anything else that looked marvelous. Later on, Carol playing slot machines right next to me stopped and checked her watch. "It's almost time for the fireworks show to start. We've probably got about a half-hour before they get going," she announced.

I said that sounded lovely. I was following them and having a wonderful time. Whatever they wanted was fine with me. I was just thrilled to be on this trip with them, which they by the way paid for.

Len made his way over to us. He had been playing blackjack at one of the tables around the corner. "I think that it's time, honey," he whispered to Carol.

She grabbed my hand and began to direct me out the door of the Sands and back to the strip. We walked for about two blocks and then came to our destination, they told me. I didn't understand what they were talking about. All I saw was a small Las Vegas wedding chapel, the kind you see talked about on the telly and in the tabloids. "Where are we going then?" I asked.

"Right here, Rosey," Carol informed me, as she pointed toward the chapel.

I turned to her and flashed a perplexed look. I had no idea what she was getting at. "Why are you pointing to this chapel?"

"Because, Rosey, that's what this whole trip was about. It was about getting you here tonight,"

Carol attempted to explain, though it made nothing clearer in the least.

Len attempted to interrupt to try to shed some better understanding for my benefit. "This whole trip was all a setup, Rosey. We have a big surprise for you, and we better get this show on the road because the fireworks and the big birthday party starts in a few minutes."

I still had no idea what was going on, and then from the dark of the night, he appeared, seemingly out of nowhere.

"Hello, Rosey."

My jaw flung open like a pelican scooping up fish in the

sea. I couldn't believe he was here and wondered why was he here? "Max…what are you doing in Las Vegas?" stumbled out of my mouth.

He met my question with a huge grin and pointed toward the chapel. When I looked at Carol and Len, smiling and giggling like kids fooling around on a playground, a thought crossed my mind, but it was too far-fetched.

"I am here to…," Max said before stopping himself and then falling to one knee.

"Oh, my Lord," I said to myself. "You came all the way here to ask me to marry you?"

Max's blue eyes twinkled against the Las Vegas neon lights. He had a firm grip on my hand and certainly didn't seem to want to let go.

"And you two set this all up?" I said next, as I stared at Carol and Len still behaving like silly children.

"This is what you want, Rosey, and what he wants," Carol offered, to my complete surprise.

I pulled my hand out of the vice-grip that was Max's clenched hand over mine. I took a step back for air and clarity. "I don't understand, Max. Why didn't you reach out to me yourself if you felt this way?"

Max, struggling to get back to his feet, said in his defense that he was afraid to do so. I asked him what he was afraid of.

"I was afraid you didn't feel the same way as I did," he answered, his expression more serious now.

"But you came all the way here…to Las Vegas to get your answer?" I countered, still searching for an explanation for tonight.

Carol and Len were becoming less excited. They could see things weren't going as they planned.

"Your friend Carol here, she got in touch with me. She told me about everything, your trying to adopt children of your own, everything." Max shared. "I am here because of faith, Rosey."

I shook my head. I didn't understand. I was learning fast tonight, not understanding was the normal situation for the evening.

"What faith? What are you saying, Max?"

He then stepped closer to me. He reached for my hand again, and this time it was not a vice-grip. This time his hand was gentle, sweet. His eyes seem to search mine. I remembered then how much I loved those eyes of his and how they would turn me into jelly in what at this moment seemed a lifetime ago.

"My faith was in us."

"Us?" I faintly whispered back.

"Yes, in us. Our paths had crossed so many times, but it never seemed like it was the right time for us, if you understand," Max said as he began to explain in more detail.

Now I thought I was beginning to figure things out, but I certainly wanted to hear more.

"I always believed, even when there was no evidence to support my dreams, that you and I were supposed to be together," he continued.

"Oh my!" Carol said loudly, thoroughly enjoying everything she was hearing so far. Her outburst reminded me that we still had an audience.

Max, bless his heart, didn't let it slow him down a bit. He went further. "My faith was, I was right in believing all of that. When Carol contacted me, I thanked God that I had one more chance."

I didn't know what to say. He smiled broadly at me,

and I could tell he was waiting for me to say something in return. Carol and Len were waiting for the same thing to be truthful. I struggled to get my thoughts in order. This was all so surprising, to put it nicely, in so many ways. Without warning, I blurted out the first thing that came to my mind. I asked Max why he wanted to marry me after all these years, and not when we were young, back in England.

He took a minute to consider all that. It was a lot to throw at him, but I needed to know.

He finally said that he was ready to answer like he needed permission from me. Carol and Len urged him to get on with it because the fireworks were starting soon.

"When we were in England all those years ago, I did fall in love with you."

While Max was saying this, I was thinking, that's a pretty good start.

"But, when I got back to Germany and I saw how devastated our country had become because of the war, I felt my first obligation was to my family, my friends still alive," he confessed.

I asked him to go on.

"My people were in such a poor state of affairs. My family members needed me to stay home and try to help rebuild from the rubble of what was our home city. I never forgot you, Rosey. I never before or since, even with my wife, felt the way I felt about you," Max explained beautifully. "And for the last, almost thirty years since I got to West Germany, I have been trying to free my parents and siblings from the evil grip of the East Germans. My quest to free them has taken me to places I never would have believed a boy from a small village in Germany could have gone to. It's what led me to become a diplomat for the West German government. It's what has taken me around the world, and most importantly across your path."

I was fighting the tears welling up in me and I could see that Carol was doing the same. Len was staring at his watch and becoming agitated. I was about to tell Max how I felt about him when he started up again.

"When we saw each other again in Washington D.C., I wanted so badly to tell you all these things. My wife, who I married more out of family obligation than love, was deceased. But you, Rosey, were still married to your husband. I could never have expressed my love for you and put you in such a difficult position. Because of that, I did the honorable thing and said goodbye."

"Oh Max, I'm so sorry," I shared, as tears began to stream down my face.

Max wanted to hear nothing of my being sorry. He was too happy considering what could be our future, starting tonight. "Fate has given us another chance, and that is why I am here."

Almost the same question I asked only a few moments ago, suddenly popped into my head, only a tad different this time. "Why do you want to marry me, at all?"

His huge grin reappeared. This time he did not have to think about his answer. "Because you're the only woman I have ever truly loved."

Carol started to bawl after hearing that. Len held her while imploring that we decide our fates quickly. The fireworks were now only minutes away.

I looked at Max as I wiped my eyes. I told him I loved him too. I always had. He moved to hold me in his arms, but I stopped him. "There's more to life I'm afraid than just feelings that people have for each other."

Carol hearing that, pulled away from Len, got her composure and asked me what I was talking about.

I looked at her and then at Max. I had subverted my will and often my happiness for many years for Albert and for duty. I thought it was the right thing to do, but now I wasn't so convinced. My desire now was to have children, to be a mother, to work if I wished, and to chase my dreams for a change instead of someone else's.

I wasn't willing to be a submissive wife, even to a man I knew in my heart I always had loved. It was bloody difficult, but I told Max all this in not so many words. I told him the truth. I told him what was important to me. Then for some strange reason, he laughed right in my face. When I looked toward Carol and Len, they were holding back laughter themselves.

"What's so bleeding funny about what I just said. I thought it was quite the serious point I was making." I barked with irritation.

Max grabbed my hand again. I had lost count of how many times he had. "You don't understand, Rosey. That's also why I am here," he announced with a gleam in his eyes.

Carol ordered me to just let the man speak, so I did.

"Carol told me all about all the problems you have been having with getting the adoption through the proper channels," Max said next.

"And…" I quickly spit out.

"And… I not only want to marry you and love you for the rest of your life. I also want to be a father, a parent of children, with you," he shared, his words filled with sincerity.

My irritation disappeared fast. Obviously, Carol had told him how I had failed in my adoption pursuits, how I had hit a brick wall every time, for one reason or another.

Max smiled broadly, as he explained more. "You see Rosey, it's all taken care of now. You are going to adopt a child, hopefully as many as you wish."

"What do you mean?" I said with utter awe from what he just had told me.

"Working with officials in the American government for so many years, Rosey, has afforded me special relationships with very powerful people in both West Germany and the United States. I spoke with the West German ambassador to the United States, who in turn spoke with President

Ford, who in turn spoke with your governor here in Arizona… and that's how it works in diplomacy," Max shared.

"But you're not a citizen, and neither am I. I was told specifically that I couldn't adopt a child here without being an American citizen," I challenged Max, still not convinced by what he was telling me.

He next confessed his "'big secret'" to me, how he had just become an American citizen only a week ago.

"I didn't know you wanted to become an American citizen," I replied without thinking.

"I didn't either," Max said with a chortle. "I didn't do it for me, Rosey, I did for us. Needing to be a citizen was the one thing that even President Ford couldn't make go away if I wanted to adopt children with you."

"This is all true, Max? You really do want to marry me and raise a family together?" I asked him eye to eye with the lights of Las Vegas surrounding us and making the moment seem more magical than it was, if that was even possible.

Still holding my hand, and with his eyes locked on mine, Max said, "I want this more than anything in the world, Rosey. I want to make you happy more than anything in the world. You have spent your life trying to do what's right for others, now it's time that someone does the same for you."

I bit that stubborn stiff upper lip of mine. I could no longer deny how I felt anymore. I couldn't believe how blessed I was to have this man standing in front of me, wanting to share my life, my desires with me.

"Will you marry me, Rosey?" Max said as he grunted in his attempt to get back down on one knee. I told him he didn't need to bother. Neither one of us was a spring chicken anymore, you know.

"Yes…gladly," I whispered back.

We went to seal all these wonderful plans with a kiss. Unfortunately, Len stopped us. "Not yet, you two. We've got a ceremony to get through. Now I need both of you in this chapel, right now!" He ordered.

Carol supported him and began to herd both of us into the tiny chapel. It was a simple enough place, but who cares I thought. I never in a million years believed that tonight would have turned out like this. This was simply too marvelous to have ever in my wildest imagination, even dreamed. There was, we found as went inside the chapel, one problem, namely there was no minister to perform the nuptials.

"I'll go get him. I think I heard him in the back," Len said, as he darted behind the curtain at the back of the stage.

"We spared no expense for your wedding, Rosey honey," Carol shared. "Even the king himself is here to make this all official."

"Elvis Presley, my goodness gracious, you got Elvis to be the minister at our wedding?" I yelled out with excitement.

"Well…not the real one, but I hear he is a wonderful Elvis impersonator at some of the smaller clubs off of the strip," Carol remarked with a laugh.

Then, with perfect timing, faux Elvis made his appearance on stage following Len's persuasion, his white jumpsuit, and all-too-real Elvis belly made it a wedding ceremony to never forget. Before he could get to the "do you take this person to be your whatever part," the fireworks celebrating the birthday of America began. Len let out a few curse words because they were missing the start of the show, but he was quickly reprimanded by Carol for his outburst in a "'somewhat'" place of God. A few moments later, and Max and I were married. I thought it would happen almost thirty years earlier, but the timing wasn't right. But now, as Max and I walked out arm in arm onto the strip to see the fireworks explode in the sky, I believed with all my heart the timing was finally perfect. Carol and Len soon joined us as we all gazed up in astonishment at all the beautiful colors and wondrous sounds. Later, now married and walking back to our hotel, I showed Carol the diamond ring that Max had placed on my finger.

"It's so lovely, Rosey," Carol said in a tender voice.

I told her how much I loved her and thanked her and Len for all of this. "I have so many things in life to be thankful for, Carol," I whispered to her, out of the earshot of either Max or Len. "And right now, I think I can honestly say that your friendship is what I am most thankful for."

Her expression, so emotionally sincere, so touching, told me she felt the same way. Sometimes in life, words just get in the way. This was one of those times.

CHAPTER 19

Max and I settled into a new home just outside of Phoenix. As he promised me the numerous layers of red tape and regulations that had kept me from motherhood were suddenly gone. With Max by my side, we adopted our first child, Lori, your sister. She was only a few weeks old when we brought her home. Two years later we got Gregory, your brother, and then a few more years passed, and we added you, Danny, to the family.

It is strange how things work out in life. When I was a young wife, I wanted to hold off on having children and being a mother for a long time. When I found out that my first husband was unable to have children, I wasn't that unhappy, at least not for the first few years. But over time my ideas changed on the matter. Over time I began to realize that I was missing out on a huge part of what makes life so worth living, children. The longer I went without the void in me being addressed, the greater the necessity I felt to fill it. Thankfully, I was finally blessed with the opportunity to become a mother when your father, Max, came back into my life. Raising my children, not my adopted children, but my own kids, became the greatest joy of my life. Oh…and you were all so different in so many ways. Lori, maybe because she was the oldest, was always independent and free-spirited. I guess in many ways she was much like I was at her age. That's probably why we butted heads so often.

Gregory, your brother, was always much more serious and driven. He knew what he wanted out of life, and he made sure he got it. He's one of the hardest-working people I have ever known. And then there's you, Danny, my youngest. You had bits and bobs of all of us. You were always interested in how things worked and why they did. Your imagination reminded me of my own, never-ending in scope and magnitude. All those thoughts and vivid ideas had to have a place to go, and so you became a writer. I was so proud of you and still am. I left you this, my life story, in your capable hands in case you, the brilliant author that you are, ever had any time between best sellers to do something with it. Well, that's not entirely the truth, love. I think I just wanted you to know my story. I appreciated your storytelling so much and always considered becoming an author myself. I don't know, maybe all this was to show you that I may have been a small part of your success. Either way, dear, wherever the truth lies about how much I contributed to your wonderful gift of writing, this is where my story ends, and our story begins. The rest of my life from this point you know all about. You lived it with me. If you're reading this without me, I have passed on and I am now sharing with your old grandpappy and nana, and even your Uncle Trevor and Aunt Sheila, just how proud I am of you, of all of you, my children. Remember, Danny, as your wonderful father used to say, follow your heart like a trail that leads to happiness, but allow your mind and wisdom to be the markers on that trail that help you to not make a wrong turn. We are expected to have both a soft heart and a wise mind. You should strive for both. They will bring balance to your life. All my love forever, son, your proud mother, Rosey.

DANNY TYPES IN HIS LAST FEW WORDS: THE END. HE IS finished. He wipes the weariness out of his eyes as he ponders his grand accomplishment. A knock on his bedroom door jolts him back into reality. Julia whispers from the other side, not daring to interrupt him. "Is it alright to come in?"

Danny without hesitation says yes.

"How's the manuscript coming?" she asks right away.

"As a matter of fact, I believe I just finished," He confesses, showing more a sense of relief, than excitement.

"Oh…that's fantastic, Danny! I knew you could do it!" Julia says with the kind of enthusiasm that was missing from his statement. "You should be proud of your hard work. Now you'll have something to give to your agent."

Danny agrees as he tries in vain to fight off an attack of yawning.

"You haven't slept much, mister, have you?" Julia remarks, stating the obvious.

"No, ma'am, not lately actually," Danny chuckles.

"Well, now you can. You can get some sleep knowing that you have made your mom proud by turning her story into a book," she tells him.

Danny is too tired to argue. His mother's funeral is only about six hours away. A nice nap sounds like a fine idea. His only problem is standing in front of him. "Enough about me, what about you?"

Julia flashes a knowing look toward him. She apologizes for her little meltdown at the V.A. cemetery office several days earlier. "I expect too much, you know, from you. I've been thinking a lot about that in the last few days."

At this point, Danny tries his best to interrupt and explain his feelings on the subject. She rebuffs him. She acts as if she doesn't even hear him. "It's not all your fault, Danny. I think my latent desires, you know to take our relationship to the next step…well…I think I pushed you to a place you weren't willing to go, you know."

Danny again attempts to force his way into the one-sided conversation. "You had the right to want that, I just…"

She cuts him off again. "Look, whatever, I just now see that we need to live in the real world, and not some fantasy. Hopes and dreams are all fine and dandy but, you can't base a life on them."

"But, Julia, I…" Danny tries once more.

"No, we are better friends. I think that's where we're at. And that's not such a terrible thing, Danny," Julia proclaims defiantly to him.

When he attempts to argue a new point, she shuts it down and tells him she'll see him at the funeral. Then, Julia adds, right after the funeral she will be heading back to New York. Danny asks her to stay longer.

"No, no, I have so much going on at work, you know, but you call me when you get back and, you know, we'll go grab a lunch together," she offers. "I better get going. I'll see you at the service."

Danny offers her a half-hearted wave goodbye as she takes off. Lori who heard some of the conversation, comes into the room to see how her brother is fairing. "You okay?"

"Yep, I suppose so," he answers his sister glibly.

Lori understands and is about to leave him to his own thoughts and space when Danny asks her a question about relationships, namely, why are they so damn difficult. Instead of responding, Lori begins to cackle with delight.

"I don't know, little brother, and with my history, I am certainly no expert on it!"

Her response and attitude bring a smile to his face. He wonders how their mother had such a good relationship with their father. Lori's heart is warmed as she considers the question. "Dad was such a rock for her. That's what I remember. What do you remember?"

Danny slinks back in his chair as he considers Lori's question. "He was a rock. Did you know if it wasn't for him, Mom wouldn't have been able to adopt us?"

Lori shakes her head. She had no idea that was the case. "Is that in her pages that she left you?"

"Yeah," Danny shares. "He married her and became a U.S. citizen so that Mom could adopt us."

"I never knew that," Lori replies. "I just always remember how much in love they seemed to be. When he died, a big piece of Mom went with him."

"Maybe so," Danny responds. "They spent much of their life missing each other and when they finally got together, I think they made sure to cherish every moment they had. At least that's how I see it."

Lori agrees with everything her brother just said. She goes on to express to Danny how lucky they were to have the parents they had growing up. "I never felt adopted, Danny. I know you were only, what about fifteen when Dad died. I certainly hope though, you still recall some of the things he taught you."

Definitely, Danny tells his sister. "He was such a calm, unflappable guy, Dad. I could still learn something by acting more like him."

Lori without hesitation goes over and kisses her little brother on the forehead. "You may not be unflappable, but you're a good guy too."

Danny quickly mentions how Julia might have a counterview of that thought.

"Well…like we just were discussing, relationships are hard. One thing though I can tell you, she's head over heels for you," Lori reveals confidently.

Danny isn't quite so sure. "She's talking about just being friends now, so…I don't know?"

Lori cuts him off. "She doesn't want to be your friend, Danny."

"No?" He quips back

"No," Lori retorts. "She's only saying that because that's really all you're offering her, that she can live with. She wants the whole package, the whole enchilada, and since you're not willing, she's protecting her feelings the best that she can."

"Really?" Danny says, feeling completely lost in the conversation.

"To Julia, friendship is better than the alternative you're offering," Lori articulates, summing things up rather well.

The lightbulb kind of goes on for Danny, at least a bit of light is shed. Lori leaves him to his thoughts so she can get some rest before they get ready and head to the funeral chapel. Behind the closed door of the room, Danny has many things to consider. He's relieved that the first draft of his book about his mother's life is finished. Unfortunately, this will not be the kind of book that either his agent or publisher will be looking for from him. His career as a successful author, that is one that makes "'real'" money, might be over. Then there is Julia, what to do about Julia? Is he really ready to let her go? Or is he ready to settle down and makes things right with her? He clutches a pillow close to him, as he lies down on the bed. Danny has much to figure out, to make heads or tails of. Oh…and on top of all of that, his beloved mother's funeral is today. If only she were here to tell him what to do.

———— ◆ ————

Danny's older brother, Gregory, and his family show up at Lori's home a couple of hours before the funeral. They follow Danny and Lori over to the funeral chapel where the celebration of life will be held. After arriving, Rosey's three surviving children stay in the lobby and greet all those who have decided to attend. Danny for one is overwhelmed by the sheer number of people who have come to honor his mother's life. Between shakings hands, receiving hugs, and accepting sympathy, Danny spots an elderly man just entering the building. He has a cane and slowly walks toward him. Danny recognizes him almost immediately. It is Senator Bainbridge, with two security guards, one on each side. The senator makes his way straight for Danny. "Hello, Son," he greets him with. "After you told me about your mom…well, I couldn't find it in myself not to be here."

Danny thanks the senator for coming and reaches out his hand to him. He then introduces the senator to Lori and Gregory.

With the ceremony about to begin, only a few stragglers are left to meet and greet in the lobby. Danny tells his sister and brother to go in, he will take care of the last few. Soon Julia arrives and Danny instantly feels awkward.

"I was wondering if you were going to make it?" Danny teases her as she walks up.

Julia only smirks at his attempt at being humorous before stroking his face in a kind-hearted demonstration of her feelings for him. "You know me better than that."

"Your right, I knew you would show up. I don't know why I even said that," He replies, trying his best to be cute and adorable.

Julia strokes his face a second time. "Neither do I, but I'll still see you inside just the same."

A few more folks stumble in after Julia. Bobby, Lori's ex strolls in. Lori seats him next to where she will be sitting. Then she comes out to tell her brother that the ceremony is about to start. Danny begins to follow Lori in when suddenly he hears the front door to the funeral parlor open. Lori hollers to her brother to let them seat themselves. Danny is fine with that, but still manages to turn and look back to the person, or persons, coming in. Something tells him who she is the minute he lays eyes on her. He doesn't hesitate a second more to walk toward her. The wheelchair she is being pushed in stops right in front of his feet, almost hitting him. The woman doing the pushing is surprised that he is blocking their path.

"Can I help you, young man?" the elderly lady sitting in the wheelchair, asks him.

Danny smiles from ear to ear as he makes her acquaintance. "You must be Carol," He guesses.

"Yes, I must, and you must be Danny," she answers back.

"Ha, how'd you know?" Danny wonders.

"You, first," Carol counters playfully.

They then both share a laugh. Even the woman pushing Carol's wheelchair does. She introduces herself as Lilly, Carol's daughter. Danny tells them both how thrilled he is to meet them. He talks for a moment about his mother's biography and how he feels he knows Carol very well from reading it. Carol is flattered by his words.

"How did you know I was Danny, Rosey's son?" he inquires, turning the tables on his guests.

Carol laughs loudly at such an absurd question. "Your mother was my dearest and closest friend. Even after my husband's new job forced us to move away from Phoenix and to the other side of the country when you were still only a little tyke, Rosey and I still spoke every week by phone and wrote letters every chance we got. Your mother never shut up about you three kids, and especially you Danny. Rosey's family was her world."

Danny knew that everything Carol said was true. He thanked her for all she meant to his mom and even for bringing his parents together. "You know, from what I've read, without you, I wouldn't be standing here today."

Carol is touched by his sentiment and moved by his kind words. "Your mother did so many things for me throughout my life. It was my honor to pay back her friendship in such an important way."

The sound of music starts in the church altar where the celebration of life is now beginning. Danny offers to lead Carol and her daughter into the sanctuary. Carol is happy to take him up on it. Hand in hand they enter the church. Danny requests that she park her chair just outside the front pew where he will be sitting with Lori and his brother. She is honored once more by his kindness and gladly follows Danny down front.

Rosey's minister from the local church she attended speaks first, and then so do Gregory and many of the people in attendance. A microphone is passed around through the pews, and anyone who has anything to share may if they wish. Danny spots his agent, Kimberly, sneaking into the back of the church. Late, as usual, he thinks to himself. The microphone eventually finds its way back to the front and to Lori. She can't find the words and freezes up. She passes

Andrew Scott Bassett

it over to Danny like it is on fire. He stands up from where he is sitting like everybody else has been doing. He clears his throat a couple of times and takes a deep breath. He's searching his soul for what to say. Then he glances back only for a moment. He sees Julia to his left. Somehow, she inspires Danny to consider what his mother would have him say if she were here right now. A hush falls over the entire chapel. Everyone in the building is filled with great curiosity as they wait for what Rosey's youngest son will have to say about his mother. As he studies the faces all around, Danny starts with the only thing that comes to his mind that makes any sense at all. "You know if my mother was here today, first I think she would say, wow, not bad, not bad at all. She would have been so humbled by all of you showing up today like this. Mom wasn't a wealthy person. She did okay when it came to money. She wasn't a well-known person. There aren't going to be any streets named after her. She never held public office or had an extremely important job or job title. She didn't even start a family until almost middle age. Yet, I think when looking at the size of this crowd, she would have said, wow…not bad, not bad at all."

Danny pauses. He again looks around at all the people who have filled the chapel to pay their respects. He hangs onto the microphone a little bit longer. He isn't done speaking just yet. "That's what I think my mother would have said if she was here with us."

There's a smattering of laughter and a few amens in the audience as he points to his mother's coffin in the corner. "Now, this is what I want to say… on behalf of my mother."

His next words draw everyone in. "What I really want to say is this. We all need to learn something from today. My mother didn't care much about investing her money.

She did, of course, but the subject bored her. She wasn't interested in learning about mutual funds or annuities or high-yield savings accounts. No, her interest was in investing in people. Everyone here is proof that she invested wisely. And I can see, at the risk of making a pun, that she received a ton of compounded interest on her investments. She tolerated money and its trappings, but she loved people. She made an effort to touch, inspire, or as my mum would say, as she liked to call it, bloody well straighten them out. My mother put up with many things from people but not hate. She believed in the power of love and that God put us all here as his hands and his feet. I would say you did well, Mum, certainly not bad for a middle-class girl from Northampton, England. No, Mum, I would have to say you did very well, very well indeed."

As Danny finishes, he hands the microphone to the minister of his mother's church and then sits back down. Lori embraces him and tells him that his words were fantastic. Gregory gives him a thumbs up. Finally, Danny takes the time to look over at Carol, her approval of his "'little spiel'" would mean as much to him as anyone there. She returns his glance with a warm smile. Carol then motions for him to lean down closer to her. She whispers in Danny's ear. It's something for only the two of them to share. Carol lets him know in no uncertain terms how proud his mother is of him after what he just spoke in her behalf.

"I hope so," he whispers back.

"I know so," Carol replies, confidently.

This conversation between the two of them allows Danny to thank her for everything she did for his mother and for his family.

Andrew Scott Bassett

A few more people speak from the audience, and then the minister leads everyone in prayer. Shortly after that, the ceremony is over, and people began to file out. Those who want can follow the procession that will be leaving in a few minutes and heading over to the veteran's cemetery for the burial.

Most of the people in attendance at the funeral will pass on the burial proceedings. Almost all of them still take the time to come over to Danny and heap praise on him for his words on behalf of his mother. He thanks every single one of them for their kindness and is glad they got something out of what he had to say. Kimberly, his literary agent, walks up and gives Danny a warm reception. She tells him she was very touched by the whole affair. Of course, she then interjects about his manuscript, the biggest reason she made this long trip out west from New York. Danny promises her he will get it to her by Tuesday, the day after he gets back to the East Coast.

"Terrific!" Kimberly eagerly responds. "I look so forward to reading it, Danny."

"I hope so," Danny mumbles to himself, as he tells her goodbye.

Julia follows behind her. She is sporting an expression that makes her face almost look like it's sparkling. Danny loves it when she beams like that. It's been a while since he's seen her that way.

"Every time I forget about how wonderful you are with words, you remind me again, like today," Julia confesses in a heartfelt way.

He thanks her for saying that and for staying for the funeral.

"Your little speech, what you had to say about your mother, made me feel like I knew her. I wish I had. Please call me when you get back to New York, Danny. Maybe we can at least get together for lunch, huh?" she tells him as she offers him, her goodbye.

Lori walks up, she overheard Julia. She mentions purposely how wonderful Julia appears to be.

"Yeah," is all he can articulate in response.

A few hours later, Danny, Lori, and Gregory, accompanied by his wife and kids, join a few other close friends of their mother, including Carol and Senator Bainbridge, and they all follow a van from the funeral parlor all the way over to the veteran's cemetery on the outskirts of Phoenix. It is a surprisingly windy day, and the gusts of air push around all those who quietly watch as Rosey Blackwell Baden, formerly Rosey Adams, is laid to rest. Danny finds comfort that his mother will be surrounded by people, who like herself, have sacrificed so much for country and uniform. Though military and war had cost her much in this life, he knows firsthand that his mother was a patriot. She always told him that not all wars are equal. Some battles must be fought for the greater good and some should never be fought at all. Blind faith in anything is pure foolishness, Rosey would lecture Danny when he was young. But then in the next sentence, she would say, but no faith in anything is just as foolish. How he wished she could be here right now to lecture him on something, anything, one more time. Danny with his brother and sister by his side, watch as their mother's casket disappears into the ground. There are American flags fluttering from the strong winds in every direction. Danny had asked the director of the cemetery beforehand if it would be okay to display two flags next to her grave. He was granted his wish. He drove the pointed end of the Union Jack into the ground on the opposite side of where the Stars and Stripes would guard her headstone. It was only fitting that both flags should stand at attention next to their mother's tomb, he told Lori and Gregory. They both wholeheartedly agreed.

Their mother was a woman of two countries, and in her own way, she loved them both.

CHAPTER 20

"Hmm…" Kimberly mumbles, as Danny painfully watches her go through his manuscript.

It had been a week and a half since Danny got back to New York and his agent had received his work. Now, after having all that time she needed to read, peruse, whatever, Kimberly was acting as if this was the first time she had looked at the "'thing'". Finally, after uncomfortably watching her pretend to be studying it, she looks up from her desk and makes eye contact with her client. Danny doesn't dare speak first. He waits for her.

"Wow, how about that…huh?" she starts with.

Her words don't help Danny feel any more at ease.

"This certainly isn't what I was expecting, Danny," she says next. "Not to say that it's not very good, mind you, it is. I, however, was under the impression that you were an author of mystery or thriller novels."

He does his best to interrupt her but is quickly cut off.

"I wonder why I was under that impression? Oh, that's right, because that's the kind of book you were supposed to be writing," Kimberly scolds him, her sarcasm dripping off of every syllable.

"I understand that, but…" Danny tries to explain before being cut off again.

She sighs deeply and stares at him. She is wearing a grimace like someone, or something has just died. Maybe that's true, Danny thinks to himself, maybe his career as an author has just died.

"Look, I appreciate all of what you're going through with your mother's passing, I really do," Kimberly continues. "And this is a lovely tribute of a story to her. In fact, it's a great read altogether, Danny."

"Alright, what's the problem?" He slips into their chat.

"The problem is, your publisher was expecting a book similar to your first one, you know the bestseller you wrote. How am I going to sell them on this one?"

Danny's heard all she's had to say. He understands her predicament. He offers her his best advice. "Kimberly, all I can tell you is that this is the best story I ever wrote. This is much better than my first book, even if it was already basically written for me."

Kimberly upon hearing him say that makes sure it is his own original work and not something that someone could sue them about later. Danny put her fears to rest. "It is my mother's life story, and I promise I own all the rights to it. It's my book. It's the best thing I've ever written. That's what you can tell the publisher," he says emphatically as he stands up and begins to leave.

Before he can, however, Kimberly stops him at the door. She promises him she will sell it with all her heart and soul to the publisher, with a caveat. "I can't make any guarantees, Danny."

He turns to her and declares. "One thing I've learned from my mother's life, her story, is there are no guarantees in life, there's just life, and you do the best you can with it. So, Kimberly, just do the best you can with my book. That's all I ask." On that note, Danny exits his agent's office with his head held high and his guts in the right place.

THREE DAYS LATER, DANNY IS SITTING OUTSIDE AT A café watching streams of New Yorkers walk by. The person he is waiting for has suddenly arisen from the masses of people only a few feet away from the cafe. He hasn't seen or spoken with her since the funeral, and at this moment all he can think about is how she is certainly a sight that makes his heart skip a step or two faster. More than anything else though, he is just relieved that she agreed to see him.

"Hey, Danny, how are you," Julia declares as she walks up.

He answers the standard "'fine,'" and then invites her to sit down.

"Well…come on then, tell me how's the book going?" she follows.

Danny only found out a few minutes before this 'lunch date', from his agent Kimberly, that his publisher, although disappointed with the genre change from one of its new, bestselling authors, was still willing to publish his mother's story. They, however, as his agent shared with him, were not interested in anything new from him, at least until they saw how this next book of his sells. He shares this news with Julia. There is no one he would rather share it with. She is more than a little surprised that he doesn't seem too worried about those ominous words coming from his agent. Danny only shrugs at her trepidation.

"You aren't acting like you usually do. I don't get it," Julia tells him.

Danny for a moment considers what she is saying and then offers his take on the situation. "You know while reading and then putting my mother's story into book form, I learned more than just things about her."

Julia with her hands under her chin leans in closer to the table. She's interested in what he has to say.

"I guess I realized more than ever that life is much shorter than any of us can imagine. Every day it moves faster and faster all around us, in my humble opinion," he continues. "And the funny thing, Jules, is we don't even really notice it. You know it's like how the Earth is spinning around the Sun in our part of the galaxy. We're all standing here with no idea that we are on ground that is hurdling through space at this very moment. It is, but we don't take notice."

"And… you're telling me this because? Are you saying, Danny, that you're more aware of everything now? Is that what you are trying to say?" Julia replies, attempting to make heads or tails of what he is getting at.

After ordering drinks for them both because he still knows what she likes, he continues. "Yeah, I think you could say that for sure. But it's more than just that. I've learned from my mother's story that life is about walls, and when I say walls, I mean obstacles."

"Okay then…" Julia quips, still listening.

"My mother faced so many in her life, and usually they were man-made," Danny shares. "Walls built to separate people by race or sex, walls to separate by status or position, even walls between countries that eventually tear apart love and the relationships of ordinary people. My mother faced all those walls her whole life."

"Sounds like she was a pretty strong woman, your mother," Julia is quick to add. "Again, I wish I had got to know her."

He tells Julia he wishes the same thing. Then, without warning, he changes his focus to the more…present. "I want to be more like my mother."

She interrupts. She offers the thought that such an idea might be a good thing.

Danny is quick to agree with her before he continues his diatribe. "What I mean by that is, I want to be like my mother because when she faced a wall in her life, she didn't try to go around it. Jules, she didn't try to barely scale it, even if she could. No, when my mother faced a wall in her life, she tore the wall down. She did everything she could to destroy the bloody thing... as she would have said."

The waitress then interrupts Danny's thoughts by delivering the drinks they ordered. Julia wants to know if there is more he has to say since he has her complete attention now. There is more, he promises. "The biography my mother left me ended when we, her kids, came around."

Julia isn't sure what his point is, so Danny adds more detail. "She ended her story, the one that she gave to me to read after her death, when she adopted my sister and brother and then me. I guess she figured I knew the rest of the story because I lived it with her."

"That makes sense," Julia interjects.

But Danny has one more story about his mother to offer. "When I was eight or nine, something like that, my mother and dad, who was originally from Germany, took a trip to Europe. Us three kids stayed behind. We all spent about two weeks living with our friend's families. I didn't know why they went to Europe without us, not until a few years passed, and I guess my folks thought I was old enough to understand, by then."

"What was the reason?" Julia is curious to know.

Danny stops to take a sip of his drink, and then he clears his throat. He goes on to tell the story, the way his mother told it to him. "My mother couldn't believe when they got there, my father and her, how so much chaos, so much destruction, could be such a wonderful thing. The ugliest, dirtiest, most despicable wall in the world was in tatters. People, ordinary mothers and fathers, sometimes with little ones, were flooding in from the other side. My father and my mother waited for several days to pass, but it was all worth it when my father's parents, his sisters, and brothers, and their children, all made it through to the side of freedom. There were tears everywhere when my father with my mother at his side, ran to meet his family. She didn't know those people from Adam, but she still couldn't stop herself from bawling her eyes out at the sight of them reuniting with their oldest son. My father had spent most of his life trying to get his family their freedom. In the midst of all the laughter, tears, and embraces, was a wall being ripped apart, chisel by chisel, hammer by hammer, and hand by hand. My mother at that moment knew that no fight was impossible. She told me if enough people come together and believe in fighting for what is right, anything can be achieved. She also realized as she watched my father with his family, how she had for too long allowed the obstacles in her life to keep her imprisoned from her own happiness. She made me pledge to never build walls in my own life that would separate me from my happiness, as they did hers."

"You remember all that?" Julia asks because she's impressed.

Danny nods before confessing that he had to write down the story on paper several times to capture it correctly, the way his mother told it. Julia is still totally enthralled by his retelling of it.

Sensing that now is the time, he reaches out and takes Julia's hand. Julia, a little surprised by the sudden move, pulls her hand back away from his. "Danny…look, we're not kids anymore. I know what you are looking for in a relationship, and I'm not interested in that anymore."

Danny stretches out his hand toward her again, this time with his palms up, almost begging for her hand.

"Friendship, that's safe, I think I can live with that," she tells him while ignoring his still waiting hand.

He shocks her with what comes out of his mouth next. "I don't want to be your friend Jules."

Julia doesn't know what to make of what he's just said.

Danny begs her to hear him out. "You need to listen to me, please!"

"Why?! What is there to discuss that's new?!" she says, raising her voice enough that other customers seated nearby suddenly take notice.

"I'll show you what's new," Danny answers, as he gets out from behind the table he's sitting at and moves to her side. He then falls to the ground on one knee as his father had done so many years before in Las Vegas.

"What are you doing? Are you insane?! What are you doing right now?" She exclaims, embarrassed as much as excited as people around begin to take notice.

Many of those seated around them begin to clap. This only makes Julia more uncomfortable.

"Listen to me, I've let obstacles or walls, or whatever you want to call it, get between so many things in my life. As my mother would say if she was here, it's time to tear down those walls, and be happy," Danny says, confidently.

Julia tries to digest his words, as the crowd around then claps even louder. "What are you saying? You think that marrying me is one of those hurdles or walls that you need to tear down. I've got to say, that's not the most romantic thing I have ever heard."

Danny can see he is losing her. He attempts to better explain himself. He knows it's probably now or never with Julia. If he fails with her now, after embarrassing the crap out of her, it's likely he won't get another chance. "All I'm saying is that I've been in love with you for a long, long time. And I know you feel the same way about me. I know you do. I built up all this fear about really committing to you, sharing my life with you."

A voice from the crowd of customers yells out for him to ask her already. The proclamation throws them both off for a second. But Danny suddenly gets back the control of his thoughts and where he's heading with all this. "I don't want walls between us anymore, Jules. I don't want anything to be between us. Will you please help me tear down these walls? Will you marry me and make me the happiest and luckiest, guy in the world?"

"Say yes! Say yes!" people all around them begin to holler in chorus.

Julia considers his words, even with all the noise of the folks around them. "Are you really sure you want this?"

Danny still on one knee, still reaching out for her hand, insists he does to the pleasure of all the café patrons in attendance. "I want the whole ball of wax. I want the ball, and I want all the wax, Jules," he answers with a cheeky laugh.

"Well…if you're really sure about this, and you are really sure, right?" She questions him one last time.

his loveable smirk, the one she first fell in love with, tells her all she needs to know.

"Then yes, Danny," she answers with a laugh, "I will gladly help you tear down those walls."

A guy in the crowd shouts to Danny to ask her again.

"Oh right!" He answers. "Will you, Jules, marry me?!"

"I guess I have to, now," she chuckles. "Yes…Danny, I will marry you. And you will, by the way, pay for embarrassing me like this, and I totally mean it, mister."

The new couple is immediately showered with applause and calls ring out from everyone at the cafe for Danny to kiss her and make it official. He can't argue that it's not a great idea and happily does the deed.

"I really love you, Danny," Julia whispers into his ear as they hold each other close, surrounded by the multitudes.

"I love you too, so much," he whispers back.

The next hour looks like an improv wedding reception has just broken out on the streets of New York. The café brings over five plates of appetizers, a little of this, a little of that, for the happy couple. Then the drinks flow, many of them paid for by Danny. In truth, this is a celebration fitting a new life together that probably wouldn't have been possible without the lessons from an older one.

———◆———

THAT NIGHT, AFTER AN EARLIER TRIP TO THE COURT-house made everything legal, Danny pulls up a chair next to a window inside of the plush and completely too-expensive-for-what-you-get hotel suite they rented for the night. Still, this day was a long time in getting here and Danny wanted everything to be special for his and Julia's first night as a married couple. As he watches her sleep, a sense of satisfaction takes hold of him. She is sleeping like a baby after pretty much wearing him out. A bottle of champagne with only a few sips left in it sits on a nearby table. He quietly, so as to not wake up his new bride, pours himself part of a glass. The stars are shining bright in the clear, dark sky through the window. He lifts his glass toward the spectacular view.

Then he toasts with his glass in hand, "Thanks for everything, Mum, oh and cheerio for now, only for now."

Julia stirs in bed but doesn't wake. Danny finishes his champagne and quietly sits and enjoys the night and all its glory from his hotel window view. For once in his life, Danny can't wait to see what the future holds.

THE END

Above: On May 7th 1945 Germany surrendered. The next day was designated VE-Day, Victory in Europe. Crowds of people on the Market Square look almost stunned by the happy news.

Left: The New Inn, on the Kettering Road, improvised makeshift floodlights and crowds gathered to dance and sing with the locals in the road.

Right: In St. Michaels Road the residents brought out all the old furniture that they could find and broke it up to improvise a bonfire in the middle of the road. The scars remained for many long years afterwards!

Rosey celebrating the end of World War II, she's dancing in the center of the party in her hometown of Northampton England.

Rosey at sweet sixteen.

Rosey with her little sister Sheila

Rosey's rock, her good old pappy.

Her beloved uncle George, who died in World War II.

Rosey's wedding day.

Sister Sheila with her husband Trevor to her left.

Rosey and her children, the loves of her life.

The Rosey we all miss, the life of the party.

Printed in Great Britain
by Amazon

20244015R00215